S0-BZW-443

"LOOK AT ME"

Toby raised his head. Her eyes were shiny black, and terrifying. Her features were noble, beautiful, deadly. Her smile touched only the scarlet lips and not the fatal eyes.

Evil comes to the glen, the witchwife had said, and Toby knew, somehow, it had arrived.

She wheeled her horse and spoke to one of the black-robed men. The inside of his cowl was dark, as if, as if—

Idiot! thought Toby to himself. How can a man not have a face?

"An exciting tale of fantasy and adventure from an accomplished storyteller. I thoroughly enjoyed it."
—**Terry Brooks**

"Hood's breathless tale has all the flavor of its Scottish location, a great story, and some fine new characters full of arrogance and charm. A great introduction to a new author of considerable stature and skill. Enjoy it as much as I did."
—**Anne McCaffrey**

ATTENTION: ORGANIZATIONS AND CORPORATIONS

Most HarperPaperbacks are available at special quantity discounts for bulk purchases for sales promotions, premiums, or fund-raising. For information, please call or write:
Special Markets Department, HarperCollins*Publishers***,
10 East 53rd Street, New York, N.Y. 10022.
Telephone: (212) 207-7528. Fax: (212) 207-7222.**

THE YEARS OF LONGDIRK: 1519

DEMON SWORD

◆— KEN HOOD —◆

HarperPrism
An Imprint of HarperPaperbacks

If you purchased this book without a cover, you should be aware that this book is stolen property. It was reported as "unsold and destroyed" to the publisher and neither the author nor the publisher has received any payment for this "stripped book."

This is a work of fiction. The characters, incidents, and dialogues are products of the author's imagination and are not to be construed as real. Any resemblance to actual events or persons, living or dead, is entirely coincidental.

HarperPaperbacks   *A Division of* HarperCollins*Publishers*
                    10 East 53rd Street, New York, N.Y. 10022

Copyright © 1995 by Ken Hood
All rights reserved. No part of this book may be used or reproduced in any manner whatsoever without written permission of the publisher, except in the case of brief quotations embodied in critical articles and reviews. For information address HarperCollins*Publishers*,
10 East 53rd Street, New York, N.Y. 10022.

Cover illustration by Jean François Podevin

First printing: March 1995

Printed in the United States of America

HarperPrism is an imprint of HarperPaperbacks. HarperPaperbacks, HarperPrism, and colophon are trademarks of HarperCollins*Publishers*

❖ 10 9 8 7 6 5 4 3 2 1

This is a work of fantasy. Any resemblance between the world depicted and any other world known to you is entirely imaginary.

The next morning we drove north toward Fort William, skirting the shores of Loch Lomond, where some of the world's most famous mountain scenery was hidden by a roaring downpour. . . . The weather had improved only slightly when we reached Strath Fillan. We dutifully admired the picturesque ruins of little Lochy Castle, at the mouth of Glen Lochy, but without leaving the comfort of our transportation. . . .

A one-mile digression on the old road leads to the Longdirk Monument, but the turnoff should be better posted. Many visitors must whip by it without realizing that they have thereby missed the district's sole claim to fame, the birthplace of its most famous son—its only famous son. . . . [The] museum and gift shop are open from ten to four during the tourist season.

All the calendars and postcards in the world cannot convey the bleakness and loneliness of these hills. It is hard to realize that in Longdirk's time, when great modern cities like Glasgow were little more than villages, the Highlands supported a rural population, whose fighting men were renowned all over Europe. Now only scattered heaps of stones on the hillsides show where the cottages stood. . . .

Jan Flint, *Travels in Western Scotland*

ONE

——◆——

A Day in the Life

1

"Hey, bastard!"

The voice rang out in challenge from somewhere at Toby Strangerson's back. He did not look around. A defensive reflex made his right leg twitch, but he overruled it and brought his foot down firmly on the dirt. Without breaking stride, he continued his hurried walk along the road.

"I'm talking to you, bastard!"

It sounded like Vik Tanner. Women gossiping at their doors turned to see who was shouting, men stooped in their gardens straightened. Two youths up ahead were already looking this way, already grinning, standing with their feet apart and arms folded. So there was a rumble planned and they were in on it.

Having no choice, Toby kept on walking, wondering how many of them there would be. Didn't matter—there would be enough to do whatever they wanted to do. Then he recalled the warning Granny Nan had given him at dawn and his scalp prickled. This trouble had been prophesied.

"Oh, bastard? Can't you hear me, bastard?"

No question, that was Fat Vik Tanner yelling. The pair up ahead at the potter's house were Neal Bywood and Willie Bain, which meant Bryce Burnside and Rae Butcher would be involved as well, and perhaps two or three more he could call to mind with no effort. There were few young men left in the glen now.

The early morning wind was cruel, yet he was sweating. Granny Nan had kept nattering at him and getting in his way while he was doing the morning chores. So he'd had to run all the way to the castle, then right away Steward Bryce had sent him off back to

Tyndrum. Again he had run most of the way, because he was expected to run when he was on the laird's business. Between the running and the weight of his plaid, he was sweating.

So what could a man do about it—explain? *I'm sweating because I've been running, so please don't think I'm afraid of being maimed.*

"*Bastard?* Are you deaf, bastard?"

The wind didn't mask the hateful taunts. The normal sounds of the village seemed to die away as people stopped work to listen—the click of the women's looms, metallic clinking from the smithy, the crack of a mason's hammer. Geese honked. A dog barked in the distance, shrill children chanted lessons in the schoolhouse, and a deep rumble of millstones told of flour being ground. Farther away yet, soldiers drilled outside the castle to a steady drumbeat.

"Bastard, I'm talking to you, bastard."

The voice was closer. Toby could hear stones rattle as his tormentors closed in behind him. They would time their approach to catch up with him as he reached Neal and Willie, closing the noose.

The street was part mud, part rock, part weeds—an uneven trail winding through the village. Vegetable patches were enclosed by low stone walls, and everything else was road or rock or pasture, where dogs sniffed, poultry foraged, tethered cows grazed. Tyndrum was less than a score of cottages straggled along the banks of the river: walls of rough fieldstone, roofs of sod, window slits closed by shutters. No one could tell where the village ended, for the cottages just spread out farther apart along the glen and up the hills until they blended into the scenery. There was nowhere to hide, and nowhere to run.

"Traitor! If you won't answer to bastard, *bastard,* will you answer to *traitor?*"

Vik was only a few paces back now, yelling so all Strath Fillan could hear. Toby was not afraid of Fat Vik. He was afraid of Vik plus four or five others. Granny

Nan's warning echoed round and round in his head. She often acted strange these days, but this morning she had been stranger than ever.

She had come to him while he was milking Bossie. *"Do not get into a fight!"* She had repeated it over and over. *"Evil comes to the glen. Terrible things will happen if you get into a fight today."* Even as he'd fed the chickens and fetched water and chopped wood and done all the other usual morning chores, she'd been hobbling along behind him, waving her cane and talking about evil coming to the glen and how he must stay out of fights. Whatever she thought the hob had said, it had upset her greatly. She'd still been on about it when he ran off to report for work at the castle.

He hadn't paid much heed, for the idea of a fight today had seemed absurd. Next week at the Glen Games, yes. Then he would have to defend his title, if any man wanted to contest it. He had been thinking of an honest match, of course, man to man, which was not what Vik had in mind.

"Traitor, traitor! I'm talking to you, traitor. Sassenach bastard! Turn around, bastard!"

Snappy Fan Glenlochy stood at her door, yattering to big, blowzy Olga Potter. They had turned to stare disapprovingly at the drama, and he was going to pass right by them.

Without slowing his stride, Toby doffed his bonnet to the women. "Fine morning to you, ladies!"

They turned their backs and resumed their talk. His fast-moving feet took him past them and on toward Neal and Willie like a leaf in a stream.

"Fine mornings don't have bastards in them!" Vik crowed. "They don't have traitors in them. You're a Sassenach-loving traitor!"

It was a lie, but Toby Strangerson would dearly welcome a glimpse of an English uniform right now. He was within sight of the miller's house. He could see the cart outside, already loaded. That was where he was headed. He wasn't going to make it.

Neal and Willie unfolded their arms and sauntered across to block his path. Half the population of Tyndrum must be watching.

Terrible things will happen if you get into a fight today.

Fighting—not boxing. He was bareknuckle champion of the glen, but boxing was not what was planned. *Terrible things* sounded more like gouged eyes than just broken bones. He'd thought Granny Nan was having one of her strange turns when she'd started in about fighting this morning. He'd thought the hob didn't speak to her when she was strange, but perhaps this time she'd been normal until she learned whatever it had told her. Pity the hob hadn't explained how a man could avoid a fight when others insisted on it.

The pretense was over. There was no use trying a smile and a cheery greeting to Neal and Willie—not with the expressions they wore or the way they stood across his path. Toby marched straight at them and then made a quick feint to the right. They jumped to block him and he spun around in a swirl of plaid to confront Vik Tanner. As expected, he had Bryce and Rae with him, but he'd also brought Neal's brother, Colin. That was a sickening shock.

If it was just to be fists, Toby would take on any two of them and probably enjoy himself. All together they could certainly beat him, although he would do some damage. But it would not be only fists. There would be holding, and no time out when a man went down. There would be feet. There might even be blades, although the Sassenachs hanged any Highlander they caught wearing as much as a dirk.

Trash! Fat Vik was very nearly as tall as he was. His arms were thick and furry, but the meat on them was flab, not muscle. He looked dangerous on the outside and had nothing inside. Bryce and Rae were born followers, and still just gangly kids. Today they were two of six and could afford their excited, nervy smiles.

But Crazy Colin . . . Colin was older; twenty or more. Colin was wrong in the head, the one who killed sheep at full moon. Even as a child, he'd been odd. He had gone off to the war two years ago, and when he came back from Parline Field with the other survivors, he'd had even fewer wits than before. Now he was leering at Toby, eyes and mouth twitching eerily. He had both hands behind his back. If Vik had given Crazy Colin a knife, then there was murder in the air.

Six of them in a circle, the traitor in the center.

Toby concentrated on Fat Vik, the big one, the leader. His father had more money than most, which was obvious from the fancy pin in Vik's bonnet to the shoes on his feet. Even his plaid was bright, the green and black dyes of the tartan not yet faded, and his belt buckle was metal, not horn or bone—very grand was Vik the tanner's son. He wore a very confident sneer as he stood within his private army.

Evil is coming. Terrible things will happen if you get into a fight today.

Toby Strangerson was not the only man who worked for the English, but he was the only one without family to back him. Everyone knew he had been fathered by a squad of Sassenach soldiers, so roughing him up or killing him would be a gesture of defiance, a message to the Sassenachs and all their other hirelings. Nobody would remember who'd done it. *Didn't see. Just a bunch of bairns. . . . Would've stopped them if we'd realized . . .*

He put his fists on his belt so they wouldn't shake; he swallowed the odious fear taste in his throat. Sweat raced down his ribs under his wool plaid.

"Was that you screaming, Vik?"

Vik's mouth twisted. "Oh, you can hear, can you, bastard?"

"You talk too much. I'm busy right now. You going to challenge at the games?" Toby had won his last seven fights. He could take Fat Vik in one short round.

"You won't be in the games. No traitors—"

"No? Then meet me at the ford tonight. Three rounds? Or no limit? I don't care."

Vik glanced briefly at his cronies. "And a gang of

your Sassenach friends there to help you? Oh, no! We'll settle this right here and now, traitor."

The circle was closing, moving in very slowly, enjoying the suspense.

"Settle what?"

"Traitor, traitor!" Crazy Colin was already jittery, his face twisting in an idiotic leer. Demons! Had they given Curd-brain a knife?

"Traitor, is it?" Toby hardly minded being called a bastard—he'd worn that badge all his life—but he did mind being called a traitor. "Remember when you joined up, Colin, three years ago? When the laird called on the men of Fillan to back King Fergan? Remember that day, Colin? I was there, Colin, up at the castle. I tried to enlist with Laird Dalmally, too."

The laird had laughed. Toby had been one of many fuzz-faced boys trying to join up that day, but he'd also been the tallest man there, even then. The laird had called him the longest fishing pole in the glen. But he *had* tried! He'd been refused. He might have died on Parline Field. He might have come back maimed, or crazed like Colin, but he was not a traitor. He wouldn't work for the English now if anyone else could give him a job. Every one of these six would jump at a chance to take his place on the Sassenachs' payroll.

Crazy Colin leered. "Death to traitors!" There was nothing in his head to argue with.

Toby turned his attention back to Vik. "I don't recall seeing you at the castle that day, Fatso."

"I was there!"

"You must have been kneeling, then."

That won a chuckle from Rae and Bryce. Pale with fury, Vik stepped nearer and the others closed in also, tightening the belt one more notch. Conscious of the two behind him, Toby waited for the kick in the kidneys or the first flash of blades.

"So you're on your feet now. Why're you making so much racket?"

"You stay away from my sister, traitor!"

Stay away from my sister . . . Stay away from my daughter . . . Toby knew those words well enough, too. No family in the glen would let Big Bastard Strangerson near its unmarried girls. But in this case, the charge was absurd. Meg Tanner was only a child, with a bad habit of wandering around near the castle. Toby had seen her safely home the previous evening. That would be excuse enough for Vik.

"Meg? You're the one who messes with kids, Vik, not me." Toby raised his voice to shout down whatever was coming next. "You should look after her better. Keep her away from the soldiers."

"I'm going to keep *you* away from *her!*" Vik howled.

That should have been the cue for the action to begin, but it didn't. Obviously Vik did not trust his followers to back him unless Toby hit first.

Only Granny Nan's prophecy held Toby back. His heart thundered, his fists were clenched and shaking. *Terrible things will happen . . .* "You're a coward, Tanner. Tell you what: You meet me tonight at the ford, and I'll fight you with one hand tied behind my back." He could not hope to win, but the whole village would turn out to watch, so there would be fair play.

The others exchanged surprised glances, tempted by the chance of seeing a three-fisted fight.

"He's lying!" Vik shouted. "He's the bastard son of a Sassenach! He's a traitor and a bastard."

"Hit me, then!" Toby stuck out his chin. "What's the matter? You scared, Campbell?"

Vik Tanner was really Vik Campbell, and that was the root of Toby's trouble—they were all Campbells, every one of them except Willie Bain. Just about everyone in the glen was a Campbell, which was why they all had other names as well.

Vik grew desperate. "Colin! Do him, Colin!"

Crazy Colin giggled and produced a cleaver as long as Toby's forearm.

Rae shouted, "Wait! Hold it!" He grabbed the madman's wrist. Bryce rallied to his aid.

Toby became aware of jingling and clumping and a squeaking of axles behind him. The miller's cart was bearing down on the group, with Iain himself cracking the whip. The mob scattered out of the way—Colin gibbering and frothing and fighting against the others' efforts to control him.

Salvation!

"Oh, Miller, sir!" Toby said, forcing his throat not to shout. "I've got a message from the steward!"

"Whoa, there! Whoa, I say!" The fat man hauled briefly on the reins, slowing the rig. "Up here with you, lad! What's the old scoundrel wanting now?"

Neal made a grab for Toby, but Toby slipped by him and jumped for the cart. The miller's whip cracked in the air behind him, making his pursuers dodge back. He snatched hold of the boards and swung a leg up; was almost thrown off as Iain lashed the horse and the ramshackle outfit lunged forward, rocking and rattling over the uneven road, creaking mightily under its load of meal sacks. The gang yelled taunts as the miller bore their victim away to safety, and a moment later the horse was splashing across the ford.

2

For several minutes, Toby could only cling to the bench and sweat through a flurry of cramps as his stomach tried to empty. His whole body shivered, his heart thundered. There was a taste of acid in his mouth. He enjoyed a fight if it was honest and sporting and no hard feelings after; what he couldn't face was the thought of a rat pack—being held, knives, kicking, down on the ground, unable to fight back . . .

It hadn't happened. He was still whole. He had avoided the fight, so Granny Nan's prophecy did not matter anymore. He hoped the hob would tell her so and she wouldn't have to keep worrying until he got home tonight. It usually tattled to her about what was happening in the glen. Folk used to say if a child sneezed twice, Granny Nan would appear with one of her simples before it sneezed a third time. Women going into labor had always known that the midwife would arrive when she was needed. She couldn't get around much now, but when he came home in the evenings, she usually knew more of the news than he did.

"Thank you, sir," he mumbled eventually. Already the little cart had left the river behind and was climbing the gentle slope to Lochy Castle.

The miller had not said a word since his passenger embarked. In Toby's mind Iain Campbell was always linked with childhood memories of leading the donkey around and around the millstones, one of the chief joys of village youngsters. He saw now that the donkey probably enjoyed the company but would certainly manage equally well on its own.

The miller was the fattest man in the glen and bragged of it in a croaky, wheezy voice that never seemed to have enough air to function. He was not only short of breath, he was also insufferably long-winded, which hardly helped. His hair and beard were naturally sandy, but a permanent coating of flour made him a pale buff shade all over—under his nails and in his ears; even his plaid had faded to that same drab shade. He was a human meal sack. His eyes seemed tiny, but only because they were encased in folds of fat like a pig's; they were as sharp as a pig's, too.

"Well, now. And what did old Bryce have to say?"

"He wants another six loads of flour before you bring any more oats."

"Six loads, is it? Does that sound like a siege he's expecting? And it is far from a hint that the Sassenachs'll be taking their leave of us soon, I'm feeling. Well, it's oats I've got, so it's oats he'll get this time." The miller chortled a wheezy laugh. "Or do you want me to turn back?"

"If you do, I'll get off! I'm grateful for the rescue, sir."

The old man stole a narrow, inquiring glance at him. "They meant real mischief?"

"Just wind, I think, but I was glad to get away. Thanks."

"Was no more than a man should do for his kin."

Toby straightened up so fast he almost fell off the bench. There was not much room left with the miller there too. "Sir?"

Iain seemed amused. "Didn't know that? Your grandfather was my mother's cousin. I think that's right. You'd have to ask my sister—she can rattle off families like a chattering magpie."

His sister was a shrew.

"No, I didn't know. Granny Nan always told me I had no family."

The miller's laugh became a wheeze. "None close." He shot another glance under his snowy brows. "But maybe closer than you suspect."

Toby was already hanging on tightly; now his fists clenched on the cart hard enough to hurt. "You're talking about my mother, sir?"

The miller shrugged his bulky shoulders. "About both your parents, I suppose."

"I know what my name means, sir."

"It means your grandfather wasn't rich."

"Huh? I mean . . . What?"

The miller wheezed an oath at the horse, which ignored him, plodding doggedly up the long slope.

"Nineteen years ago, son, the cream of the hills fell at Leethoul."

The old man was embarking on one of his rigmaroles. Toby said, "Yes, sir," and prepared to be patient.

"The Battle of the Century, they called it, and the century won't likely see another like it."

What Toby recalled was that Leethoul wore that name because it had been fought in the year 1500. And the century had already seen at least two more like it— almost as bad anyway.

"A fine company we were!" The miller sighed. "Nigh two hundred of us marched off with the laird at our head—Kenneth Campbell, that was, the last of the real lairds of Fillan. His family had held Lochy Castle for hundreds of years. Not like these traitor puppets they put over us now." His porcine eyes turned to study the effects of this treason.

"No, sir."

"There's never been fighters to match the Campbells of Fillan. King Malcolm himself said so, when he inspected us on the eve of the battle. We tend to be small, he said, but we make up for that in enthusiasm. True that was! The best of the Highlander array, we were. Volley after volley the English fired, and our charge never wavered. Not forty of us came back to the glen, you know, lad. 'Twas a sad day for Scotland. King Malcolm himself fell, and two of his sons, and the laird of Fillan and both his sons, and the manhood of the Highlands was scythed like corn. The Sassenachs slaughtered us."

"Yes, sir." Leethoul had not been the first disaster, nor the last. It had been bloodier than most because King Edwin had grown tired of putting down rebellions every few years and had resolved to teach his Scottish subjects true obedience. Leethoul had been only the first lesson.

History was a very depressing subject. As taught in the Tyndrum schoolhouse, it comprised long lists of battles where Highlanders wielding spears or claymores faced Lowlanders or English—or sometimes both—armed with muskets and cannon. Result: massacre. In Toby's own lifetime there had been Norford Bridge and Parline, and Leethoul the year before he was born. There must be a limit beyond which raw courage became sheer folly. A boy learned not to say so in Strath Fillan.

Iain Miller bunched his thick white brows. "They put a garrison in the castle that winter. Soldiers need women —but you know this."

Toby knew only too well. "They rounded up six girls from the village."

"Aye, they did. Was shameful. And six women between so many men was more shameful yet. In the spring, when they marched away, they let the girls loose, every one of them with child. One of them was Meg Inishail. She wanted to call you Toby Campbell of Inishail, but your grandfather swore he wouldn't have his name hung on a . . . on an Englishman's bastard."

"I didn't know that! Inishail?" Family gossip was a new experience.

"Rae Campbell of Inishail. Och, lad, he was a bitter man even before, was Inishail. Two wives he'd had, and both dying young. He never found a third. Meg was all he had, and he couldn't forgive. Not that it was her fault, but he couldn't see that. He wouldn't let her under his roof again. He didn't have much to spare, nothing to offer anyone to care for her, too proud to accept help."

"My grandfather was a Campbell from Inishail?"

"Oh no, he was born here in the glen. I think it was his father came from Inishail, or his grandfather."

Granny Nan had always been evasive about Toby's mother. Now he could see why—unexpected answers brought more questions. A man's clan and kin were determined only by his father, of course, but he did have Campbell blood in him, which he'd never known before. Where had Iain Miller been while his kinswoman was being rejected by her own father? Why had she been forced to bear her babe in the witchwife's cottage, with no company but Granny Nan herself?

"She named me Tobias."

The miller shrugged and looked uncomfortable, as if he wished he had not brought up the subject. "Doesn't mean anything, does it? She couldn't know which of the Sassenachs had scored. Granny Nan took her in; Meg bore you, and she died. That broke old Rae's heart, if it wasn't broken already. He died two days after you were born. He never saw you."

His daughter had named her baby Toby with her dying breath—so Granny Nan said, and no one else could know. Tobias was not a Scottish name. Perhaps the Sassenach Tobias had been the one she liked best, or just hated least. Had he been a little kinder than the others? Didn't mean a thing about fatherhood, though.

Just wishful thinking. Tobias Strangerson—Toby the bastard. Nobody could ever know who had been his father.

The cart was already high enough now that the village lay spread out below it. The sod roofs blended with the grass, but roads and walls showed like a cobweb. Farther away, halfway to Crianlarich, stood Lightning Rock, with Granny Nan's little hovel by its base—birthplace and home. Bossie would be grazing on her tether, but he couldn't see her at this distance. He could barely see the house. There was fresh snow on the summit of Ben More.

The miller jiggled the reins. The horse ignored his impatience.

"Are you knowing what happened to the other five, lad?"

Not much. "I always heard that they left the glen."

Who would speak of such things anywhere near Toby Strangerson? All Granny Nan would ever say was that they'd been sent off to visit kin over the hills and bear their bastards out of sight and mind. She had never admitted that any of them had come back later. She had never admitted that there might have been refugees come to Strath Fillan in exchange, although the English behavior had been just as barbarous elsewhere in the aftermath of Leethoul. The Taming, they had called King Edwin's revenge. It had kept Scotland quiet for ten whole years, even the Highlands.

"Some went," said the miller. "Dougal Red lost his sons at Leethoul."

Dougal Who? Toby felt as if he'd dropped something and should turn around and look for it. "Sir?"

"Dougal wasn't like Rae. He welcomed his Elly back. Young Kenneth lost a leg at Leethoul, of course. Ploughman with one foot'd go in circles all the time, wouldn't he?"

Oh, so that's where the conversation was heading!

Kenneth the tanner was a gloomy man, heavy in body, dark in spirit. Being a cripple, he rarely left his house, and he drank too much. Toby didn't care for him, and could not imagine him as having ever been young. Being married to screechy Elly might excuse a lot, and having a no-good son like Fat Vik a lot more.

"A house and a trade—that's what Dougal paid to buy a husband for Elly and a name for her babe. We chaffed young Kenneth a lot about what he must be selling. That Vik of theirs was born just a few months after the wedding—'bout the same time as you."

"He's a week older than me, sir."

Iain nodded. "Well you're the biggest man in the glen now. He's but half a hand shorter. The two of you do stand out! I'm saying he'd no right to be calling you what he did, and I think maybe you have kin closer than me. You not know this?" he added skeptically.

"No, sir. I never guessed."

Did the miller really think he was *that* stupid? Of course he'd known. It was obvious. They were the same age and almost the same size. Fat Vik had straight black hair, Toby's was brown and curly, but at school their height had marked them out in their age row. They'd always been foes. The other boys had taunted them by calling them the Twins, until they'd learned better, for that had been the one way to unite them. No one could ever prove it, but it was a reasonable guess that they'd been sired by the same anonymous English soldier. Toby Strangerson had a half-brother who had just tried to get him killed.

Forget him. Vik Tanner was a liar, a lazy do-nothing, a bully who pestered young girls and already drank more than his stepfather. He wouldn't even make good pike bait.

Much more interesting was why Iain the miller was confessing his own kinship—now, after all these years. From what Toby could recall of the glen's complex lineages, if he was related to Iain, then he was related somehow to at least a quarter of Fillan, quite apart from the general Campbell connection. They could have said, couldn't they? So he wasn't a Campbell and never could be, would it have been so terrible to acknowledge a motherless, fatherless boy being raised by the local witchwife, who was older than anyone and out of her mind half the time? It wouldn't have needed much effort. Couldn't any of them have broken the wall of silence?

And why had one of them done so now? It was too late for a woman to play auntie and hug a toddler who had fallen and hurt his knee. It was too late for a man to take another boy along when he took his own sons to dangle worms in the loch or poach the laird's deer—which everyone tried, but few ever managed. None of them had ever said. Or done.

The miller had been kind enough. He had let little Toby lead the donkey around, but he let all the kids do that. He still dropped off a sack of meal to Granny Nan once in a while—but a lot of the villagers brought her gifts. They did that because she was the witchwife and kept the hob happy, not because she'd taken in a rejected, abused girl and saved her baby and managed to rear it without even the help of a wet nurse.

So why had Iain the miller let out the secret now? Was he testing Toby's loyalties? He took English silver, too. He probably made more money out of the garrison than anyone else did. He had just rescued Toby from a very nasty confrontation.

The old man was waiting for a response, and the cart was under the black walls of the castle already. On the open turf, the Sassenachs were at their drill, marching to the beat of a drummer. A brief moment of sunshine made their helmets and muskets gleam, then they were hidden as the track detoured around a spur of rock.

"You're telling me that Vik Tanner may be my brother, sir?"

"It's possible. I wouldn't say it to anyone else."

"Neither would I." Fat Vik wasn't worth the horse dung to turn him green.

Iain turned the cart into the archway. "You'll have to decide soon, Toby Strangerson. You've got no inheritance in the glen. Will you be going off to seek your fortune elsewhere, do you think, one of these days?"

Toby would like nothing better than to wipe the glen

off his feet and begone forever, but he couldn't go yet, and what the miller seemed to be hinting was that the village was no longer safe for him.

"Granny Nan needs me."

The cart clattered through the gate and into the echoing yard. The old man reined in and the horse lumbered to a halt. He turned his clever piggy eyes to study his passenger. Now he was going to get to the point.

"You're a strapping lad, Toby," he wheezed. "Whose man are you to be? You won't have much time. Better to make a free choice than swear an oath with a blade under your chin. Both sides are recruiting that way now."

Meaning which side would the strapping lad choose? More than two years had passed since the rout of Parline Field, and Fergan was still at large—the fugitive king of Scotland was said to be hiding somewhere in the hills. The English king's puppet governor ruled in Edinburgh and, although the Lowlands were relatively quiet, rebellion still flickered in the Highlands.

Iain Miller had fought at Leethoul, the Battle of the Century; he had lost a son at Norford Bridge. He had proved his loyalty, surely? But he took the Sassenachs' money. He had just rescued their hireling, reminded him of his English parentage, and tried to turn him against the villagers with tales that might or might not be true.

If Toby gave the wrong answer it would get back to the wrong ears, and he did not know which was the right answer.

"Yes, sir. I know the problem. But my first loyalty is to Granny Nan. As long as she needs me, I'll stay in the glen."

Rescue or not, he would never trust his throat to a Campbell.

3

As a child, Toby had been taught that Lochy Castle was a great and fabled stronghold. The English soldiers had corrected him on that. It was just a tall stone house with a high wall around it, they said. It looked impressive enough in the glen, where there were no other buildings with more than two rooms. It had withstood sieges in olden times because it had a good spring, but modern cannon would knock holes through its battlements in minutes.

Bringing cannon to the glen in the first place would be another matter, but Toby knew better than to mention that.

Another odd thing he'd learned from the Sassenachs was that, man for man, they weren't all that bad. Take an English soldier out of his uniform, and a Highlander out of his plaid, and you wouldn't be able to tell them apart. The Sassenachs had funny names, like Drake and Hopgood, or Miller and Mason, although they were soldiers, not millers or masons, and certainly not drakes. They griped in drawly voices about their food and So-and-so Sergeant Drake's unending drill and this bleak mountain wasteland they had been stuck in. They were unhappy and homesick. More than anything they yearned for female company. Perhaps the Taming of eighteen years ago had been a failure, or King Nevil preferred different techniques from his father's, or perhaps King Fergan's long-festering rebellion made a difference, but this time the garrison had been forbidden to touch the local women. As a result, all the men were screamingly horny, except presumably Captain Tailor, who had his wife here with him.

The drill squad came marching in through the archway with Sergeant Drake barking like a dog. The drummer's beat echoed back and forth between the walls. Captain Tailor lurked on the sidelines, watching. If Toby Strangerson had notions of joining the Sassenachs' Royal Fusiliers, it would not be because he wanted to spend his days doing musket drill.

He sprang down from the cart. Steward Bryce was approaching, but there was no need to wait for orders. The load must be moved to the granary, and it would travel on Toby Strangerson's back.

Bryce of Crief had been steward in Lochy Castle since history began. He had served Kenneth Campbell, the laird of Fillan, before he went off to die at Leethoul, and probably his father before him. Lairds had come and gone, but Master Crief had remained like the battlements themselves. He was easily the oldest man in the glen, as ancient as Granny Nan. Although he must have been tall in his youth, now he was stooped and leaned heavily on a cane. Most the flesh and all of the hair had gone from his head, so it looked like a skull in a leather bag. Even in summer, he went around swathed in a fox fur robe, and his skeletal hands trembled all the time. Yet he still had eyes like dirks.

He had been here during the Taming. Once in a while Toby would feel a mad impulse to accost the dread old man and ask him if he recalled any of the garrison of those days. Did he remember an exceptionally big one— a virile young man, who had fathered two of the six children conceived that winter? Had there been a gentle, kindly one named Tobias?

He had never asked and never would.

He hauled a sack of oats from the cart, settled it on his shoulder, and turned to find the old man barring his path.

"You carry the sacks into the granary, Strangerson."

"Yes, sir." Did he think Toby had put one on his shoulder to run off with?

The disconcertingly sharp eyes stared up at him. "And come and see me right after."

"Yes, sir."

Toby headed for the granary. As he departed, he heard the old man's querulous complaint that he had ordered flour first, followed by the start of the miller's whining excuses. It sounded as if he would blame Toby for loitering on the way, and that would mean half a day's pay lost, at the least.

The sun never penetrated the courtyard. The main house formed one end, stables and guardroom flanked the arched gate opposite; high walls along each side connected them. Apart from a water trough and a couple of small sheds, that was all there was to Lochy Castle. Sentries paced the battlements, but it had no moat, no drawbridge, no cannons.

The granary was on the ground floor of the house, and the door opened as Toby reached it. "Over there!" said Helga Burnside.

He pulled a face at the heap she indicated, for it was shoulder-high already. "We've got a whole cartload, you know." He swung the sack into place with a great gasp of effort.

She laughed scoffingly. "Ah, and you just a puny slip of a boy! It'll put some muscle on you."

"Double helpings at lunch, then!" he said, hurrying off to get another.

"That'll be a change from the triples you usually eat!" she shouted after him.

Everyone liked Helga, a big, cheerful woman from the village. Yet she took English money, too. Was there a difference between men and women working for the enemy? Of course there was—women were not expected to kill them. Men were.

He reached the cart and took up another sack. The miller had disappeared, probably into the kitchens. No one else had appeared to help the odd-job boy with the unloading—not that he cared. If he wasn't doing this, he'd be cleaning out the stable or the latrines, chopping brush, hunting rats, running errands. He might even be sent back down to the village for something or other, and he would rather not go there again in the immediate future—certainly not today, with the hob's prophecy still in effect. He would much rather heave meal sacks around.

The fusiliers were into musket drill, with Sergeant Drake barking as loud as ever and the drum beating:

"Shorten your scouring stick!"

Rat-a-tat-tat!

"Try your match!"

Tat-tatta-tat!

The lad with the meal sack was hardly more burdened than those poor sucker fusiliers. The guns alone were so heavy that the men must also carry rests to set them on when they fired. Each man was festooned with a sword, dagger, shot purse, smoldering match, powderhorn, scouring stick, and probably other things Toby had forgotten. Some had pistols tucked in their belts, as well. They wore spurred boots and white—*white!*—stockings. Their russet doublets and breeches were so padded and puffed that they weighed more than his plaid, and on top of it all went a spherical steel helmet with a brim that came to a point in front. They spent half the day drilling with muskets and the other half just cleaning and polishing their gear. He would rather be the odd-job boy any day.

Joking apart, hard work built muscles on the glen's bareknuckle champion, with a good chance to take the weight-lifting title from the smith this year. Maybe the caber tossing, too. If the previous laird of Fillan could come back from the grave, he wouldn't call Toby Strangerson a fishing pole now.

Would he call him a traitor? A dozen villagers toiled in the castle most days. There was no shame in wanting to eat, and precious few ways to earn a living in the glen. They worked for the steward, and the steward worked for the current laird, Ross Campbell of Gareloch.

That was another problem in loyalties. The ancient line of the Campbells of Strath Fillan had ended when Kenneth and his sons died at Leethoul, almost twenty years ago. The earl of Argyll, chief of Clan Campbell, had declared the estate in escheat and appointed a replacement, a Campbell from Dalmally. He had never won the loyalty of the glen.

His son and successor had done better. When Fergan had escaped from captivity in England in 1516 and raised his second rebellion, the Campbell of Argyll had supported him, at least for a while. So the laird of Fillan, his vassal, had switched sides also. The glen had answered his call enthusiastically and marched off to die for King Fergan at Parline—leaving one sad fishing pole boy behind.

Now there was yet another laird in Lochy Castle, Ross Campbell of Gareloch. Toby Strangerson worked for Steward Bryce. Steward Bryce served Laird Ross. Laird Ross was loyal to the earl of Argyll, who was back on the side of the English.

Were they all traitors? Two more sacks completed the layer on the pile. The next one would have to go higher.

If Fergan was rightful king of Scotland, then yes, they were all traitors: earl, laird, steward, odd-job boy. That was what the likes of Fat Vik thought—the English killed our fathers and brothers and so we must kill them.

On the other hand, Captain Tailor and his men had no doubt that it was Fergan who was the traitor, or that soon they would catch the rebel and hang him. Then the Highlands would be at peace again. So they said. In spare moments they lectured the odd-job boy on how the kings of Scotland had been sworn vassals of the kings of England for centuries—between all the suicidal rebellions, that was. You couldn't trust a Scotsman's word after the echoes stopped, they said.

Another layer of sacks in place, and Toby was enjoying himself—heart thumping strongly, sweat running, arms and back tingling pleasantly.

The miller's question drummed in his mind: Whose man was he to be? As long as he stayed in Strath Fillan, of course, he was the laird's man. The laird determined his men's loyalties, and the earl determined his. But when Granny Nan died, then Toby Strangerson would be gone over the hills like an eagle. Whose man would he be then?

And consider King Nevil himself, self-proclaimed king of England, Scotland, Wales, and now numerous other places also. Technically he was a vassal of the Khan, but he certainly had not been behaving like one. He had defeated the three previous suzerains in battle and seized their kingdoms and their allies', until he now controlled most of Northern Europe. Each time the Khan had appointed a successor suzerain, Nevil had immediately made war on him, and he made no secret of his intention of conquering the continent and then marching against the Golden Horde itself. He was reputed to have sworn he would clear every last Tartar out of Europe.

In other words, treason depended on how good you were at it.

Another layer. Now he was having to throw the bags up above head height. The exercise became an interesting challenge in itself, leaving little energy for worrying about loyalties. He did not solve the loyalty problem before he had emptied the cart and laid every sack tidily where it should be.

He emerged into the gray daylight of the yard and wiped his forehead with a corner of his plaid. The clouds were racing across the sky, but he could see a pair of eagles soaring. There were always eagles over Castle Lochy.

He headed off to the kitchens. It was too early for lunch, but Helga could usually find a snack for a growing boy. Still wolfing down a freshly baked bap liberally spread with goose fat, he located the steward crouched in his little office. The old man was poring over accounts, a litter of papers covering the table. He looked up with a familiar sour expression on his dried-apple face.

"Need another job, Master Crief," Toby said with his mouth full.

"What's this I hear about you getting into a fight?"

Toby swallowed. "I didn't, sir. Just got baited about . . . about a girl, sir. It was nothing. No fisticuffs."

The dirk-sharp eyes studied him for a moment. They did not reveal what their owner thought of that version of events. Iain had been blabbing, obviously.

"One of them was Crazy Colin?"

"Er, yes sir. He was there." Had the miller noticed the addlehead's knife?

Fortunately the steward did not ask about knives. He twisted his bony mouth in a grimace. "I wouldn't feed that one to pigs." For a man who never left the castle, Bryce of Crief was always uncannily well informed about events in the glen.

Bryce of Crief—Bryce Campbell had probably lived in Fillan for twice a normal lifetime, but he was still Bryce of Crief. A man was identified by his clan, of course, but then by his birthplace. When he was in his birthplace he was identified by his residence, or his occupation, or his father. If he had no clan, if his father wasn't known, he was called something like Strangerson.

"How is Granny Nan?"

Old Bryce was remarkably chatty today.

"She has good days and bad days, sir." *She spends hours collecting pretty stones.*

Crief nodded, but his expression still gave away nothing. "Look after her well, lad. Has she ever mentioned . . . a successor?"

"No, sir."

"I don't know who we'll get to keep the hob happy when she's gone."

Toby took another bite of greasy bap and mumbled, "No, sir."

"An unhappy hob could make lots of trouble in the glen."

"Yes, sir."

The old man leaned forward and bared a few yellow pegs of teeth in a sly and withered smile. "Who's going to take you on at the games, mm? Anyone crazy enough?"

He meant boxing, of course. Boxing had more glamour than weight lifting or caber tossing. Moreover, there was money to be made on boxing, bets to be laid, and that probably explained why the steward was wasting valuable time chattering with the odd-job boy.

"Dougal Peat's promised to go a few rounds with me, sir, if nobody else will. We'll put on a show for the crowd is all."

What the smith's son had said was, "We'll just bleed a little for 'em, right?" but what he had meant was, "You won't make me suffer too long, will you?" Dougal was enough of his father's son that he was incapable of faking; he would fight till he was fairly dropped.

"No chance of his father coming out of retirement?"

Toby shook his head sadly. "He could still beat me if he did." He had watched the blacksmith box—and win— at every games as far back as he could remember, but the year he had turned fourteen and been allowed to fight with the men, he had failed to make the finals. That had been the year Eric retired, so they'd never met in the ring. Somehow, Toby could not feel he was really champion, when he had never fought the smith.

"The Sassenach . . ." Toby corrected himself quickly. "Some of the soldiers, sir. Some of the captain's men, were talking about a challenge match in wrestling, Castle versus Glen, sir."

The steward scowled. "The laird forbade it! It might lead to trouble."

"Yes, sir."

"Besides, our lads know nothing about wrestling." The sharp eyes stabbed at him. "You tried wrestling with any of *them?*"

"No, sir."

"Those English have all kinds of sneaky holds and throws. Now, if they were to offer a challenge in boxing, I might be able to talk the laird into it—but they won't!" The steward shrugged, dismissing such frivolous topics. He leaned back and regarded Toby with a snaky intensity. "Just between the two of us?"

The odd-job boy blinked in astonishment. "Yes, sir?"

"If you lose in the boxing, I've got five shillings for you." The old man pulled back his lips in a skull-like leer.

Five shillings? That must be about a year's wages! But *cheat?* Toby could not do that! Half the glen would put a farthing or two on the boxing, and they would all come to watch the sport. They would expect a display of courage, not dishonesty. It was unthinkable. Never!

Yet for a man of his lowly station to refuse an order from the steward was equally unthinkable. He would be out on his neck in a minute, and lucky if he weren't beaten first. Faced with this impossible dilemma, Toby just stared at the old man. His throat, as it so often did, closed up completely and made not a sound.

The smile faded like a sunset into dark. "Think about it," the steward said coldly. "Come and see me later. Meanwhile, Himself wants the dungeon cleaned out. He thinks the rats are coming from there. I'll send someone to help you after lunch."

"Er?" Toby dragged his wits back to business. "I don't know where the dungeon is, sir."

"Off the guardroom. You'll need a lantern. Just one, mind, because there's no air down there. Move all the old straw outside the walls and burn it. And take a dog or two with you." The steward dismissed him by looking down at his papers.

Toby said, "Yes, sir," and hurried away. *Cheat?* Cheat so that the old bag of bones could clean up on the betting?

4

He borrowed a lantern from the cooks, found a shovel, rounded up Spots and Nipper, and headed to the guardroom by the gate. He had never been inside it before, and the first thing he saw when he entered the gloomy place was a wall rack full of muskets. There were benches and a table, a couple of chests, a few cluttered shelves, but no guards. That seemed excessively careless, considering how much King Fergan's rebels would like to get their hands on those guns. They were chained, but Toby thought he could break them loose if he wanted to—besides, there were dozens of keys hanging near the window.

He walked forward and jumped as a big man appeared in a shadowed doorway—except it was a mirror. A full-length mirror! He had never seen such a thing in his life before. It must be there so the Sassenachs could inspect themselves before going out on parade. He glanced around the room again to make sure he was alone, then took a hard look at his reflection. His face was too boyish to be so far from the floor. He rubbed his chin, wondering yet again if he should let his beard grow in. He adjusted the hang of his plaid. He was certainly more man than Fat Vik. He took yet another glance around, moved back so he could not be observed through the door, then crooked an arm to see the muscle. His reflection grinned at the result and he scowled at its vanity.

At the far side of the room, a gate of thick iron bars led to darkness. It was unlocked and creaked loudly. Nipper rushed ahead down the stairs, with Spots following more circumspectly, nose busy, tail wagging. Narrow and treacherous, the staircase curved sharply into the ground, so the dungeon must underlie the guardroom. He pulled the gate shut behind him in case the dogs tried to defect. Then he started down. After about a dozen steps, he set a foot into something soft and squashy.

He waited there until his eyes adjusted. He was in a long narrow cellar, cold and creepy, stinking of rot. Most of it seemed to be carved out of the rock of the mountain. The ceiling was masonry—arched and short on headroom even in the center. There were no windows or air vents. What a nightmarish place! His skin crawled at the sight of the rusty chains and the staples set in the walls. The floor was deep in rotted straw, which the dogs were exploring with much interest. This job promised to be much less fun than heaving meal sacks, but the sooner he began, the sooner it would be done, so he hung the lantern on a staple and began.

He began by banging his head on the roof.

Cursing Bryce for not choosing a shorter man, he proceeded to the far end and set to work with the shovel. The dogs squirmed around underfoot, growling with excitement, lunging at the mice that came pouring out in all directions. The place was alive with them. The stench of decay became sickening.

Horrible, horrible place! How many wretches had been chained up here in ages past? He wouldn't keep pigs in such a hutch, let alone people. How long would a man stay sane shackled to the rock in a cell like this? He wondered uneasily about torture. He wondered how many of the victims had been innocent of whatever crimes they had been accused of. . . . He wondered what he was going to do with the litter. Already he had raised two big heaps, and obviously he couldn't bring a wheelbarrow down those stairs. He should go and find some sacks—or a basket, perhaps.

Something flashed on the shovel. He peered at it, poked it . . . picked it up with finger and thumb. He took it over to the lantern. It was a comb of the sort a woman might wear in her hair, decorated with two or three glass spangles to make it pretty. The metal was corroded black, but the glass had stayed. Not a man's comb, certainly.

They had imprisoned *women* in this diabolical midden? Nineteen years ago, six girls from the village?

He dropped the relic with a shudder and cracked his bonnet on the ceiling hard enough to make the darkness blaze with lights. Holding his scalp and moaning, he backed away until he slammed into a cold, damp wall. He had never really wondered where in the castle those women had been kept—in the house itself, he had assumed. He had never been higher than the ground floor, so he did not know what there was upstairs in the main house. The soldiers were not allowed upstairs either, so far as he knew, and if that was true now, it might have been true then.

Had those abused girls been kept *here?* Could this cesspool have been the castle brothel? No, no! Surely no men ever born would treat women like that?

Had he been conceived in this hellish dungeon? His guts churned. He felt sick. He needed fresh air. Dropping the shovel, he hurried around the heaps of filth he had gathered and began to feel his way up the stairs, to daylight and sanity and air.

"Women! They need women!"

The voice stopped him cold. Someone was speaking English in the guardroom. Another man replied. The gate was closed and they would not know Toby was there.

He dropped to his hands and knees and crept a little

higher, just enough to peer around the curve of the stair. The guardroom, which he had thought so dim when he came through it, now seemed bright. The man standing by the window was the laird of Strath Fillan, Ross Campbell himself.

"You know that's impossible!" said the other, and Toby recognized the voice of Captain Tailor. He was addressing the laird in a way no one spoke to a laird. "I have few enough men here to hold the road. I can't be sending them off to Dumbarton to carouse."

Laird Ross waited a moment, then turned from the window. Toby had never been so close to him before. He was a small man, careworn and white-haired, his face lined and weather-beaten. He wore a belted plaid, like any Highlander, but he had a tartan shirt under it, and the pin holding the shoulder flap bore a shiny cairngorm. He had a chief's badge in his bonnet; he had shoes, woollen hose, a fur sporran, a long dirk with a silver handle at his belt. Old or not, he was a fine sight.

"Wet dreams never killed any man yet," he said wryly, as if trying to divert a conversation veering too close to argument.

Tailor ignored the remark totally. "So I can't grant furloughs. But if my men don't get access to women soon, they're going to mutiny, or start deserting. I know it! You can't keep healthy men cooped up like this without women. It isn't natural."

"Dunk them in the horse trough every night. If they desert, they're dead. Not a man of them would reach the Lowlands alive."

"Is that a threat, my lord?"

"Of course not! But make sure they know that."

"We can pay. Just pass the word that there's good money to be made. In a place this size, there's bound to be a few wives desperate enough for easy cash. Demons, by their standards, they'll be rich in a week!"

Campbell let out an exasperated snort. "You don't know the Scots! No woman here would lie with a Sassenach if you offered her a silver mark and her brats were starving. If any one of them did, the whole glen would know by morning. They'd brand the sign on her forehead and drive her out. The glen would rise, just like Queensferry did last month. Don't you know you're sitting on a powder keg, Captain?"

Boots thumped on the flags. Captain Tailor strode into view, garbed in his uniform doublet and breeches, festooned with sword, wheel lock pistol, bandolier, and powder horn. Below the brim of his helmet, his angular face was flushed scarlet. "I am responsible for the road, and I can't hold it with crazy men. You are to provide board for my men, and a woman is a necessary part of a soldier's board. If you can't find them locally, send to Glasgow for a few whores—else I'll loose my lads to courting. There's no shortage of spinsters hereabouts."

The laird raised a clenched fist, then lowered it reluctantly. "I understand your problem, Captain. See you understand mine. When I came here, I told them it would be a Sassenach garrison again, but I swore you'd leave their women alone this time. They swore allegiance—and I gave them my protection! They've kept their side of the bargain so far, but all it needs is one spark. You can't hold the glen against them if they rise. By the time help arrived, you'd be dead, all of you. Me, too, likely, but that's not important. They'll cut off the food. They'll shoot you down from cover. *Be quiet and listen!* I told the Campbell I would keep the glen quiet, and I—"

"Never mind what Argyll says!" Tailor roared. "This is the road to the northwest, and the rebels' gold and munitions—"

"They're my people, Captain, and I care for them! If one of your men lays a hand on a single woman, I'll hang you both on the same gallows!"

For a moment the two men glared at each other, but even the odd-job boy knew that the threat was wind. The soldiers held the laird's castle. Three major battles in twenty years had decimated his warband. Now it had been disarmed and the young men were drifting away to other lands and other lords.

Then the Englishman spoke—quietly, but biting off every word. "I remind you, *my lord,* that I take my orders from Edinburgh, *my lord,* not from you, *my lord.* This area is under martial law. I am in charge here, not you—*my lord.*"

Toby shrank back down the stairs an inch at a time. He should not have overheard this! If they discovered him listening, they would lock him in and leave him there, at the very least.

Now his own loyalty problems seemed almost trivial. He had never thought to wonder how loyalty looked from the top down.

5

Most of the other dayworkers were clearing broom from around the castle, making what the fusiliers called dead ground. The women had taken lunch out to them, but Toby intercepted Helga on her way back and she took pity on a starving lad. He carried the resulting hamper outside and sat on the grass by himself to gorge and ponder his problem.

When the hob said he must not get into a fight, it must have meant a real fight, not a squabble with the steward. That would be no more of a fight than an ant arguing with a descending boot.

Whose man will you be? the miller had asked him. Never mind the future—whose man was he now? In Strath Fillan, he was the laird's man, beyond question. But if Bryce Campbell of Crief, the laird's agent, gave him immoral orders, what was he supposed to do about that? The laird might approve or not approve; he would certainly side with his steward against the odd-job boy. He might even be in on the fraud himself. If the smith did not come out of retirement, if Dougal was the only challenger, then the odds on the witchwife's bastard lad would be five to one at least. He was bigger now than he'd been when he took Dougal in three rounds last year.

Ironically, the Highlanders had far less to gamble with than the Sassenach soldiers, who were paid their pittance every week and had nothing to spend it on. That did not make wrong right, though. Would it be more ethical to cheat the crowd or cheat the steward, who was trying to cheat?

Could he throw a fight? Once he got going, would his fists stop if he told them to? Not likely. If Dougal couldn't take a dive, why should he expect himself to? Once the two of them started pounding each other, they would both just keep on pounding until one of them couldn't stand up any longer. That was what real men were like. So Toby must give the steward his promise, keep his job for another week, and then see what happened.

His head ached. He gave up worrying. He leaned back against a rock and watched the geese settling on Lochan na Bi and the eagles drifting in the sky. Lochy Castle stood at the foot of Beinn Bheag, facing south down Strath Fillan. Tyndrum lay just across the river and Crianlarich down at the far end, where the strath joined Glen Dochart. The villages were merely denser clumps of dwellings. Cottages were scattered all over the flats, summer shielings high on the hillsides. The fields were mostly rocks. The living was in the cattle.

The road ran south, too, but instead of turning east to follow Glen Dochart, it headed west, over the pass into Glen Falloch, and then down to Ardlui, on Loch Lomond . . . to Dumbarton on the Clyde, and thus the Lowlands, Glasgow, Edinburgh, England, Europe.

He'd been as far as Loch Lomond a couple of times. It was only fifteen or sixteen miles away, a half day's walk, there and back.

Tiny Lochan na Bi, beyond the castle, drained west into Glen Lochy. There was a local trail there, but the main road headed north, through the cleft between Beinn Bheag and Beinn Odhar, then on down to Bridge of

Orchy and eventually to Fort William. Pondering what he had overheard in the guardroom, he remembered something from his long-ago schooldays. Neal Teacher had stressed that Lochy Castle was a strongpoint on the only real road to the northwest. That explained Captain Tailor and his men. There were few roads in the Highlands, and very, very few that were passable for wheels. Cannon traveled on wheels.

There was nothing left to eat; it was time to get back to work.

6

He had hardly returned to the dungeon before he gained a human assistant as well as the dogs. Between the gloom and the scraping of his shovel, he did not notice until a high-pitched voice exclaimed, "Zits!" in tones of deepest disgust.

Hamish Campbell was Neal Teacher's youngest and a recent addition to the dayworkers. He was dark, slight of build, currently growing a few inches every day. His arms hung at his sides like ropes and his ribs stuck out. He surveyed the cell and the filth around his toes with extreme disapproval.

"Uncivilized! What'd they catch you doing?"

Toby leaned on his shovel for a breather. "What'd you mean?"

"Old Bryce found me reading a book when I was supposed to be counting meal sacks." His teeth flashed in a grin.

Toby grunted, belatedly realizing that it wasn't anything he'd done that had landed him here, it was something he hadn't done: promise to cheat. Why hadn't he seen that sooner?

He could do worse for company. Hamish was bearable. He was clever, well-read, cheerful, and at times he would display a deadly sense of humor. Now he took hold of one of the sacks Toby had filled and lifted it. He put it down again quickly.

"Whew! Zitty heavy! Why don't I shovel and you carry out? Sooner we get it done, the sooner we'll be pardoned. Or do you think they'll lock us in here for years?"

"No, they'll hang us at dawn." Toby handed over the shovel, heaved a bag onto his shoulder, and left.

The shoveling took longer than the carrying out, and while the two of them were together, a boyish treble kept up a steady musket-fire of chatter.

"Can you lift two of those bags at arm's length?"

" 'Spect so." Yes, he could.

"How 'bout *one* of them?"

That was harder, of course. . . .

"Wow! You shave every day now, Toby?"

"Yes."

"Why not grow a beard?" He was implying that real Highlanders had beards, most of them. Only pansy Sassenachs shaved, and not all of them, even.

"Because it's too curly. I'd look like a sheep."

Hamish sniggered. "Biggest ram in the glen!" Quieter: "How far have you gone with *girls?*"

Toby dared not even smile at a girl in the glen or he would get her in trouble—but why ruin the boy's dreams by saying so? "None of your business."

Hamish was undeterred. "You going to beat Dougal Peat? . . . Think the smith'll make a comeback? . . . Can you carry *two* sacks? How many rounds to knock out Dougal? . . ."

The chatter was all right; the hero worship soon began to grate as much as the shovels. Toby had met it before. His size and fighting skill had made him the paragon of manhood for all the youngsters in the glen. There was nothing wrong with Hamish that another three or four months' growing wouldn't cure; he was just going through the stage when boys discovered they were turning into something different and worried what it would be.

Nonetheless, Toby found the adulation so unsettling

that he was tempted to linger on his trips through the guardroom, gabbing with the soldiers. He didn't—it would have been unfair to the kid shoveling his heart out downstairs—but when they ribbed him about the stench that came with him now, he bantered right back at them. Often he found the Sassenachs easier to talk with than the folk of the glen, who had known him all his life. That might be because he was half Sassenach himself.

With two on the job, the work went faster. In an hour or so the dungeon floor had been scraped bare to bedrock and swept, the final load of refuse had been thrown on the bonfire outside the gate, the last rodent hunted down. Nothing remained except the repellent chains and shackles.

"Well, they didn't lock us in after all," Hamish remarked, inspecting himself in the guardroom mirror on the way out. "You look zitty uncivilized!"

"You're not too smart yourself," Toby said. His nose and mouth were choked with rank dust, his head had acquired more bruises. "Let's report to old Bryce."

"Um. Why don't just you go?" Either Hamish was worried that he had not yet done enough penance, or he had thoughts of hiding out with his book again.

"No," Toby said firmly. "You come with me."

"Looking like this?"

"Why not? It's his fault if we stink up his office."

Hamish found that idea amusing and grinned again.

The steward was still busy at his accounts. He looked up, tightening the wrinkles around his nose in disgust. Doubtless his cramped little office had taken on unpleasant airs all of a sudden, but he might be more annoyed that his pugilist had brought a witness to the meeting.

"All done, is it?"

Toby wanted to ask how often people were shut up in that underground kennel. He wanted to ask if that was where his mother had been confined when she was a prisoner of the English, being systematically raped, night after night. He wanted to ask if that was why he had been sent there today. He dared not ask such impertinent questions; he feared what the answers might be. So all he said was:

"Yes, sir. You want to come and see?"

Bryce Campbell of Crief shook his head. He leaned back, displaying his few remaining teeth in a surprising parody of a smile. "If you say it's done, Strangerson, then I know it's done and well done. There's few I would trust like that, but I trust you. You've never failed me yet."

Toby squirmed and mumbled thanks for the compliment, wondering if the words meant more than they said.

The steward's bony fingers twitched like dying spiders amid the clutter on his desk. "Now, what else . . . Aye. Take a donkey. They need a sack of oats at Bridge of Orchy. Mind you have a wash in the burn on the way, too!"

Toby and Hamish exchanged astonished glances and made themselves scarce before the old man changed his mind.

7

At the granary door, Hamish asked doubtfully, "You think he meant both of us?"

"Yes, but stay and read your book if you want."

That won a guilty start. "No. I'll get the donkey."

"Phooey! Just one sack? We don't need a donkey for that."

"What? You can't carry a meal sack all the way to Bridge of Orchy!"

Toby snapped, "Watch me!" before he had seriously considered what he was letting himself in for. Then it was too late to back out, of course. He must be getting caught up in the hero role.

"Don't expect me to help!" Hamish said, wide-eyed.

"It's not much more than the soldiers hump around all day."

"Demons it isn't!"

"You can carry me back, then." Toby hauled down one of the sacks he had placed there before lunch and strode off across the courtyard with it slung over his shoulder. He set off up the road, his companion scurrying along at his side and muttering that it must be seven miles or more, and he was crazy.

"Beats shovelling zitty manure, though!" he added, cheering up. "Why do you suppose he gave us a nice jaunt like this to do?"

Toby had worked that out. He was being shown how much power the steward had to make his life pleasant or miserable. Vinegar and honey—cooperate or else. He didn't explain.

His companion's butterfly mind flitted to other topics. "Why do they need a post at Bridge of Orchy anyway?"

"You're the scholar. You tell me."

After a moment, the youngster said, "The castle looks south. . . . Advance warning of enemies coming from the north?"

"That's my guess." It was something to ask the soldiers.

"That's possible isn't it? MacGregor's *History of the West* lists eight times armies have attacked Lochy and four times they came by way of Bridge of Orchy. When evil comes to the glen, it often comes by that road."

Evil comes to the glen! Toby shivered, recalling the hob's prophecy. Suppose he found rebels in control of the post? That wasn't very likely, though, because couriers brought Captain Tailor reports twice a day.

Hamish prattled on about history.

The cottages were few up here, and there was no one else in sight. A few dogs barked from a distance; shaggy, long-horned cattle watched the travelers suspiciously. A flock of ravens had found a feast beside a dry-stone wall and were quarreling noisily over it.

The road headed upward, stony and steep, and the hills closed in on either hand. Soon torrents of sweat were washing the dirt from Toby's pores. The sack of oats grew steadily heavier on his shoulder. He wasn't doing this just to impress the kid. He hoped he wasn't. He was doing it because it was good for him.

"Wish I had your muscles," Hamish gasped. His shorter legs were having trouble keeping up.

"This is how you get them. This is real work, man's work!" No one would call Toby Strangerson a fishing pole now.

"It's mule's work, you mean!"

"There are worse things to be than a mule. Mules are tough and strong and they know their own minds." They were also low on romance, of course, and perhaps that was another point of resemblance. Toby wondered if girls saw him as a mule.

"You be a mule if you want. I'm going to be an owl."

Toby laughed aloud. The kid beamed.

At the top of the saddle, Toby stopped and lowered the sack to a flat-topped boulder, gasping like a stag turning to face the hounds.

"Spirits!" Hamish said, flopping to the turf. "Thought you'd never take a break!"

Toby wiped his face with the shoulder of his plaid. He stood within a tunnel, flanked by walls of Beinn Bheag on one side and Beinn Odhar on the other, roofed by low cloud. He peered out at Strath Fillan as if from a window. There was hardly a tree to be seen anywhere. Grass and scrub coated the slopes, interspersed with patches of bare rock, or heather, and bright green broom here and there, and even brighter specks of bog. The little copse around Lightning Rock was too far off to see, even the rock itself hard to make out. The castle was hidden, Tyndrum's shaggy cottages invisible unless one knew exactly where to look.

"Home!" Hamish sighed.

"Love it, do you?"

The boy flinched. "I know it's not much of a place in itself, of course," he said hastily. "Pa says it's not rich. Other glens can raise more men for war and drive more cattle to the sales, he says. But it's our home, so we love it. The Campbells of Fillan are the bravest fighters in the Highlands and that means the whole world."

"Yes," Toby said, and pulled the sack onto his shoulders again. He strode off along the road. The glen was his birthplace, but he did not love it. He had no family here and nothing to inherit—no land or trade or herds, not even a sixteenth share of an ox. He had only one asset, a powerful body, and he must make the most of that. As others might seek to nurture flocks or perfect a talent, so he would work to build strength. What he would do with it remained to be seen.

Hamish came scrambling after him. "What's the matter?" He was staring up at his hero with a very worried expression.

"When does courage become sheer stupidity?"

About thirty paces later: "You're very cynical, Toby."

"Am I?"

"I remember my pa telling you that."

"Just before he birched me, I expect. I think courage is good, but it can be overdone. If you're going to risk your life, then you ought to gamble it for something worthwhile. Just throwing it away to show you're brave doesn't make sense." He was probably ruining the boy's faith in everything he'd ever believed in.

"We have other virtues, too! We're honest and we work hard and we take care of our own."

Toby did not comment.

After another hundred paces or so, Hamish said, "But no one works harder than you do, and I suppose you haven't seen much love or care, have you?"

Toby felt thoroughly guilty now. "We mules never complain."

"You don't think Strath Fillan's worth much?"

"I think it's worth a lot."

Hamish brightened. "Really?"

"Really." Strategically it might be. The people weren't much.

As the trail descended the northern slope, it began skirting puddles of brown, peaty water. In another fifteen minutes, it was accompanied by a chattering burn, splashing over rocks and plunging into pools. Toby headed for one he knew.

Leaving the sack on a rock, he dropped his plaid and plunged in, with Hamish shadowing every move. The cold mountain water was agony and yet thrilling. They clowned a little and splashed. Hamish chattered all the while like a flock of starlings.

"How long have you had hairs on your chest, Toby?"

"This one or those two?"

His questions became more impertinent and finally he called Toby "Longdirk." That was a common enough nickname for growing lads, one that had been thrown at Toby often in the past, and one that Hamish himself must be starting to hear now. Addressed to a grown man, though, it could have more personal implications, especially in certain circumstances. As these were such circumstances and that was the way Hamish meant it, Toby roared and went for him. Hamish scrambled ashore and scampered off over the moor, squealing with glee; Toby caught him, carried him back to the pool by his ankles and dunked him head downward until he could stop laughing and choking long enough to beg for mercy.

Honor satisfied, they scrambled from the pool.

"You going to wash your plaid? Ma says August is the only month to wash plaids."

"No. Let's just give them a good shake."

Both shivering now, they shook out each plaid in turn and prepared to dress. A belted plaid was a simple length of woolen cloth—usually checkered in black and green in these parts—and up to nine feet long. Toby's was more than six and a half feet wide. He laid out his belt and spread the plaid over it. With the sureness of a man doing something he has done every day of his life, he pleated it across its width, leaving unpleated flaps at either side. He lay down on the pleats, the hem behind his knees, folded the right flap over to his left hip, the left side over that to make a double thickness in front. He buckled his belt, took hold of the corner beyond his left arm, and stood up. He pulled the left edge over his shoulder to support the weight and fastened it to itself with his pin, thus covering most of his back and half his chest. He tucked the long right end into the front of his belt and arranged all the folds to his satisfaction. With his bonnet on his head and his sporran on his belt, he was ready to go.

So was Hamish. Toby swung the meal sack onto his shoulder and set off.

"You do love the glen, don't you, Toby? Really, I mean?"

Toby sighed. The world must have more to offer than this barren gorge. It would be his home as long as Granny Nan needed him, but he felt no fondness for it. "How can I tell? I haven't seen the rest of the world yet."

"You going to?" Hamish asked wistfully. "Going off to seek your fortune?"

Again the same question: *Whose man will you be?* "Maybe. Heard any more from Eric?"

"Just what you know—he's working for a printer in Glasgow."

Hamish's brother was Toby's age, and the closest he had ever had to a friend. Like him, Eric had been too young to fight at Parline. He'd gone off to seek work, a few months ago, as so many others did nowadays—dispossessed young Highlanders whose laird had no more land to offer and no need of fighting men. Eric had been lucky, for most seemed to end up as coal miners or mercenary soldiers. None could be more landless than Toby, but he could not imagine himself as a miner. He would jam in the tunnels. As for soldiering, he would certainly offer a tempting target.

He had other ambitions. The soldiers said there was good money to be made in the prize ring in England. He was going to find a wealthy sponsor and be a prizefighter—but he couldn't leave while Granny Nan needed him, and he wasn't about to tell Hamish anyway.

"Toby?"

"Mm?"

"If you do go . . . would you take me with you?"

Startled, Toby laughed. "Why? Where?"

"Anywhere. I want to see the world, too." Hamish scrunched up his sharp features in a scowl. His father was in poor health. Everyone knew that Hamish would be the glen's next schoolteacher. Fighting men did not read books, and he already had more learning than he would ever have need to teach.

What use would a prizefighter have for a skinny bookworm companion? None. To say so would be unkind. This was the worst case of hero worship he'd met yet—complicated by too much reading of romantic books, likely. "Sure you can come! I need someone reliable to hold down the horses while I hold up the stage. We'll hang together, on the same gibbet." No matter what happened to Granny Nan, he would not likely be leaving before spring at the earliest, and by then the lad would have more confidence in himself. Toby thumped his shoulder. "That's a promise."

Hamish's eyes widened before he decided this was a man-to-man joke and required a smile. "Long as I get half the loot!"

On they went.

Strictly speaking, they had come down into Glen Orchy now, with cottages scattered around the flats and Loch Tulla a couple of miles ahead. The main length of Glen Orchy, though, stretched off to the southwest, between Beinn Bhreac-liath and Beinn Inverveigh. No one lived there. It was too marshy, for one thing.

Hamish twisted his head around to study the glen. "You ever seen the bogy?"

"Never went to look for it."

"My grandfather's uncle went hunting in Glen Orchy and never came back!"

"He probably sank in the bog."

"If Strath Fillan has a hob, then Glen Orchy can have a bogy."

True, but Toby was not interested in the bogy of Glen Orchy. The sack weighed much more than it had when he set out. He plodded grimly. His feet hurt.

Tomorrow he would ache as if he'd been beaten all over, but it would be worth it—more muscle! He felt proud of himself and at the same time ashamed of his pride. He'd made it. The hamlet and the guard post weren't far now.

"Who can they be?" Hamish gasped.

Toby looked up. A line of riders approached at a trot. He made out six of them. Who could they be?

When evil came to the glen, it often came this way.

His skin shivered. He told himself not to be a superstitious idiot.

Soon he could see that these were not soldiers, then that their mounts were of far better stock than the shaggy ponies of the glens. That meant English, almost certainly. The leader was a woman, riding sidesaddle on a truly magnificent black. Another woman followed her, and then four . . . four people muffled in dark robes with hoods hiding their faces. They bore swords, so they must be men, and either Sassenachs or rebels.

Toby had no idea who these intruders might be. He cursed himself for a craven fool, but the hob's prophecy ran around in his mind like a cat after a rat and he felt a foolish urge to run away and hide somewhere. He stepped well clear of the trail, slid his burden to the ground, and just panted.

"Hexers!" Hamish said hoarsely. "The ones with cowls? Adepts!"

He was the teacher's bairn. He read books. Didn't mean he didn't talk stable-washings sometimes, though.

"And the lady?"

Hamish shook his head, eyes wide. "A lady!"

Now he made sense. Only wealthy gentry could afford a horse like that, or the tack studded with shiny metal, perhaps even gems. The lady herself wore a robe of deep purple and a matching high-crowned hat with a black plume. Her collar was black fur, and the trim on her robe, too. When she drew nearer, Toby saw the aristocratic pallor of her complexion, her dark eyes and black arched brows. She was tall, she rode with grace; a haughty beauty, a great lady.

As she went by, he pulled off his bonnet and bent his head respectfully.

She did not go by. She turned her horse aside and rode over to him, while her followers came to a halt and waited. She reined in and looked down at him and Hamish. No, she was just looking at him. Heart hammering, he bowed and awaited her pleasure, staring at the jeweled buckles on her tiny boots, the sable trim on the rich fabric of her robe. He had never seen a real *lady* before.

"Look at me."

He raised his head. Her eyes were shiny black, and terrifying. Her features were noble, beautiful, deadly, framed by the lappets of her hat and the ruff under her chin, so he could only guess that her hair would be black and beautiful, too. Her smile touched only the scarlet lips and not the fatal eyes. She was appraising him like meat in a market. No one had ever looked at him quite like that before. *Evil comes to the glen.* It had arrived. He was certain that it had arrived, and told himself not to be a fool.

"Do you speak English?"

"A little, my lady." Actually, he spoke it better than most, because he practiced with the soldiers, even though they laughed at his accent.

"Your name?"

"Tobias Strangerson, my lady."

Again her lips smiled, but they smiled at him, not to him. They indicated satisfaction, not humor. "Are there many more like you around?"

He stammered. "M-my lady?"

"Your size? Highlanders are notoriously big."

"I'm bigger than some, my lady."

Her chuckle made the hair on his neck stir.

"Well, you are certainly adequate." She wheeled her horse and rode back to the trail. She spoke to one of the black-robed men, who turned his head in Toby's direction. The inside of the cowl was dark, as if there were no face there. . . .

Idiot! How can a man not have a face?

Then the lady rode on. Her entourage clattered after her—the nondescript woman who must be her serving maid, the four men in the spooky robes. They trotted off up the hill to the pass.

8

The fusiliers at Bridge of Orchy were just as bewil-dered as Toby, for they did not know who the lady was either. They had rushed out to present arms for her and she had ridden past without even looking at them. They had certainly not dared challenge her—she was gentry at the least, probably nobility. This sudden intrusion of excitement into their monotonous vigil did not stop them noting that Toby had carried their bag of oats all the way on his back. That now seemed like a very foolish feat of showing off.

"Couple of the men bet me I couldn't," he said. "They sent Hamish along as a witness—didn't they Hamish?"

Hamish blinked and then agreed, but an impish gleam in his eye hinted that the story was now certain to be put about.

About a mile back along the homeward road, Toby realized that his companion was being unnaturally silent.

"Tired?"

"No."

There was certainly something wrong when Hamish Campbell kept his mouth shut for more than five minutes. Bubonic plague?

"What did you mean about hexers and adepts?"

"Nothing," Hamish muttered. "We go to the sanctuary in Dumbarton every summer, and last year Pa took me to Glasgow, too. The acolytes wear robes. That reminded me. That's all."

It was not all, obviously. After a moment, he added, "Saw a picture in a book once of an adept conjuring a demon, and he was wearing a robe like that."

Toby scoffed. "Proves nothing! You're saying all I have to do is put on a flouncy robe with a cowl and you'll believe I can conjure demons."

Hamish told him he was a cynic and fell silent again.

The light was failing, cut off by cloud and mountain. They would not be home until after dark. Poor Bossie would be howling to be milked. There would be water to fetch, more wood to chop. Toby would sleep well tonight. They would be too late getting back for him to have any more nasty interviews with the steward. If Granny Nan was in her wits, he could ask her advice—although he was pretty certain she would tell him to stay honest. It was what she'd taught him all his life. Easy for her to say, but an old woman who could survive on half a bap a day might not understand a young lad's interest in regular wages.

Almost as if Hamish were listening to his thoughts . . .

"Toby?"

"Mm?"

"Don't go back to the castle tonight."

Toby took a hard look at the kid. Was this what he had been building up to? Hamish had sense when he chose to use it, more learning than Toby the bastard would ever have, and lots more brains.

"Out with it!"

"The lady. Did you see the emblem on her horse-cloth?"

"No." Toby vaguely recalled the horse's gear, but he had been much more intent on the rider.

"It wasn't obvious. A black crescent. It was on the back of her glove, too."

"You're an expert in heraldry?"

"Of course not." Hamish stalked on in silence.

"Sorry. Tell me, please. Whose arms?"

The boy shot him an anxious look. "Pa borrows books from the castle sometimes. There's hundreds there. Old Bryce lets him borrow them and Pa lets me look at them too if I'm careful."

Toby had absolutely no interest in books, but he suspected that Hamish worshiped them so dearly that he probably couldn't ever lie about them. "And?"

"About a year ago, I suppose it was . . . I was reading one and I found a poster in it. Somebody had folded it up as a bookmark. It was a *Wanted Dead or Alive* poster. It didn't have a picture, but it described a woman just like her, and it mentioned a black crescent."

"Who is she, then?"

"Lady Valda."

"Who's Lady Valda?"

"I asked Pa. She was a lady at King Nevil's court. His, er, consort. They weren't married, but she was sort of first lady, even so."

She had certainly looked like the sort of lady who would grace a court. "And she was wanted dead or alive? For what?" Nobility did not indulge in crimes like theft, and murder they usually got away with. "Treason?"

Hamish frowned in thought. "It didn't say what for. The reward was ten thousand marks!"

"What? You're joking! That's more than they've got on Fergan's head. It must have been some sort of a joke!" There wasn't that much money in the world.

"Maybe. I'll ask Pa tonight." Hamish did not seem convinced. "But it was nine years ago. . . . The poster was dated 1510. She must have been pardoned since then, or she wouldn't be riding around with her black crescent showing, would she?"

Toby tried to estimate how old the lady was and realized that he did not have the flimsiest notion. She could be any age. She was very beautiful, that was all he knew—beautiful in a sinister sort of way. Why would a former royal courtesan from London be roaming the cold Highlands of Scotland? Women might see romance in this: the exiled beauty now forgiven and making her way back home.

Hamish was talking again. "She'll certainly be staying in the castle tonight, Toby. Let me fetch your money from the steward. You wait outside."

"I appreciate the offer, but why you and not me?"

Hamish mumbled inaudibly. Then he said, "I didn't like the squirmy way she looked at you!"

A man could make a funny response to that, but the kid was obviously serious. "It was like she was thinking of buying you!"

That was the exact impression Toby had. "Perhaps she has some heavy boxes to move."

Hamish pouted at the mockery. "Do you think she'll take no for an answer?"

"I doubt she would." The lady looked as if she had never been denied anything in her life.

"Don't go into the castle tonight, Toby. Please?"

"I have to see Steward Bryce."

"Then let's go slow, so we get there too late to get in!"

"We will anyway."

By the time they arrived, the sky was almost dark, and the moon hung over the shoulder of Ben Challum. As they started down the final slope, they heard the drum tattoo that meant the gates were being closed. No Highlander would be admitted before tomorrow's dawn. The last of the day workers were already disappearing down the road in twos and threes. A lantern glinted in the shadows, revealing the two sentries at the gate.

Toby carried on along the road, heading for the bend through the rocks.

"The postern's still open!" Hamish said. "We could ask."

"Not a hope."

"They may have left it open because they know we haven't been paid, and—"

"Dreamer!"

"Cynic! Why do you suppose it's open, then?"

"If certain persons weren't always in such a rush to be first out of there every night, they would know that the postern's usually left open for an hour or two. The laird may be out riding, or men have gone fishing, or something. A blanket wearer like you would have to fight his way in."

"Blanket wearer?" Hamish said in outrage. *"Blanket wearer?"* he screeched. "Is that what they call us?"

"Haven't you heard them? It's no worse than—" But Toby was already running.

Someone had cried out in the shadows ahead where the road bent. He could not see what was there, but he had heard enough—a deep voice angry, a shriller one being cut off suddenly. . . . His feet pounded on the dirt. It might just be two boys telling each other dirty stories, in which case he would just look foolish and no harm done. Or it might be dirty deeds, in which case the quicker the better.

Fast as he ran, his mind raced faster. Everything was sharp and clear. It was not going to be boys telling stories. It was going to be rape and it was going to be a Sassenach doing it. Even as he came around the corner, the man forced the woman to her knees. Her efforts to scream were muffled by his hand over her mouth. He had his back to Toby, but was starting to turn to see who was coming. Moonlight flashed on his helmet.

How did an unarmed man fight a soldier? Those doublets were so thickly padded they were virtually armor. Even Toby could punch at that until his knuckles fell off and not damage his opponent much. Fusiliers' helmets lacked face pieces, so there would be a chin to aim at, but that would be about all.

How did an unarmed man fight a soldier? One thing he did not do was argue. Give the man a moment and he could draw his pistol or his dagger or his sword, and that would be the end of it. Toby did not have as much as a stick, but he could put his fist through a plank door. He must knock the man down with his first punch and hope to run off into the night with the woman. It was not a very noble prospect, but a safe flight into the darkness was the best he could hope for.

The soldier was still partly stooped over her, but his head was coming around and Toby knew him. He also knew he outweighed Fusilier Godwin Forrester considerably. He shot a straight left to the jaw.

It didn't work as planned.

Meg screamed, "Toby! Get him, Toby darling!"

Meg? He half-turned to her voice. Forrester ducked his head to offer his helmet. Toby pulled the punch before he smashed his knuckles. He careened into his opponent like a runaway wagon. They went down together. Although Toby was on top, he was winded more than his victim, landing on powder horn, pistol, bandolier—innumerable hard and sharp things stabbing at his chest. From helmet to breeches, Forrester was well padded. He was also a veteran fighter. His free hand clawed at Toby's face, fingers reaching for eyes. That tactic was not in the rules recognized by the glen.

To save his sight, Toby had to bring up his hands. Forrester butted them with the metal brim of his helmet and jerked up his knee—a move that would have disabled a smaller man completely. Fortunately he misjudged and struck Toby's hipbone instead. One moment Toby had been on top and the aggressor, half a second later, he was rolling free, struggling to defend himself. He was a boxer, not a wrestler.

Forrester lunged to his feet, his sword screeching out of its scabbard. Toby scrambled to rise, and his hand touched the musket lying on the grass. Before he was upright, the blade flashed at his head. He ducked under the stroke and sprang up holding the matchlock by its barrel. To fire it was out of the question—he did not know how, he had no powder and shot, he lacked the time. All the same, it was a usable weapon, a massive club of wood and steel longer than the saber. He parried the second slash: *clang!* The soldier had not expected that. The impact must have jarred his arm just enough to throw him off balance. Using his greater reach, Toby rammed the butt into the man's chest. The Sassenach went over like a weed.

Forrester's limbs thrashed, but even flat on his back he could aim a slash at Toby's legs. Fortunately, it was slow and clumsy. Toby dodged it. His only hope now was to stun his opponent, grab the woman, and run like demons.

The soldier rolled over, began to rise. Toby aimed at the helmet, swung with all his strength. At the last moment, pulling his legs under him, Forrester bent his head. The butt struck his neck with an impact that jarred Toby's teeth. Had he been using an ax, he would have cut the man's head clean off and buried the blade in the turf—but his victim would have died no faster.

Evil had come to the glen. He had gotten into a fight, and terrible things were going to happen.

TWO

A Night to Remember

1

"Rapist!" Meg screamed, kicking furiously at the corpse. "Coward! Pick on a woman, would you, but you won't get up and fight with a man?" *Kick, kick, kick . . .* "Get up and fight!"

Hamish stood like an icicle, his arms wrapped around himself and his face a white glimmer in the gloom. Hamish knew that Forrester's neck was smashed.

"Meg!" Toby said.

Meg went on yelling and kicking. There wasn't much of Meg Tanner, but she had a temper as big as Ben More. She could be louder than thunder at times, and this was one of those times. Her bonnet had fallen off, her two long braids swung like whips around her head as she kicked. "Tell him to get up, Toby! Pick him up and hit him! Show him!"

Men were shouting in the distance. This bend in the road was not a blind spot for watchers in the castle, for it lay almost directly under the battlements. There was light enough yet, and the moon sailed in and out of the clouds. Then a bugle . . . The fight had been heard and seen, and the Royal Fusiliers would be here in minutes.

Toby Strangerson had killed a Sassenach and terrible things would happen. He did not care. Let them happen! Filthy rapists! He had arrived in time, saved the woman. The toad had not had time to drop his breeches and Meg still had her clothes on, although her dress had been ripped open to the waist.

Not a woman at all, just Meg Tanner, Vik's sister, only a kid. How could that putrid louse have tried to force himself on a child? Even if he'd only been trying to kiss her—and maybe that was all he had intended at first, because Forrester had never seemed like a monster—now he was dead. But he had ripped her dress, and that wasn't kissing. He had scared her out of her wits, and that wasn't kissing.

"Come *on,* Toby!" Hamish was tugging at his arm. "We've got to get *out* of here!"

Toby reached for Meg. "He's dead, Meg. Stop doing that."

"Dead?" She shuddered and stopped doing that. Her chest heaved. Her chest was more visible than it ought to be and there wasn't much more than chest there. She was so little! Funny that this morning Vik had accused him of being involved with Meg and tonight he had saved her from, well, from whatever Godwin Forrester had been up to.

Meg realized her dress hung open. She gasped and clutched it tight. "Dead? Well, good riddance! Serves him right! Monster! Bully!"

"What are you doing here, Meg?" Just Meg? He still could hardly believe that a man would pick on a child like Meg.

Hamish wailed. "Toby, they're coming!"

Meg blinked. "Doing? I came to see you. Came to warn you."

"Toby, come *on!*"

"Warn me of what?"

"Colin! Vik's given him a knife, it's full moon, I think he set him onto you. . . . I came to warn you, silly!"

"You promised I could hang on the same gibbet," Hamish said shrilly.

Demons, oh demons! Toby glanced up at the silver globe floating through the clouds. Full moon. Well, he had much worse things to worry about than Crazy Colin, who was probably off in the hills somewhere, cutting up sheep.

Lights, torches coming, voices . . .

"Come on!" he said, and began to run, hauling Meg along with him. They would have to leave the road soon, but it would give them a start.

Meg! Stupid, stupid little Meg! This would not be the first time she had turned up at the castle at sunset. He had walked her home more than once. He had not connected . . . Vik had noticed and he hadn't. Meg was a sweet kid, but only a kid—scrap of a thing, didn't come up to his shoulder, probably no older than Hamish, breasts like two muffins, wore her hair in long braids . . .

Stupid kid!

They ran down the road, stumbling and reeling. He was almost carrying her, with a hand around her arm—his fingers closed around it.

Had the Sassenachs found the body yet?

He was a dead man for certain.

"This way!" Hamish shouted, veering to the left, onto the path to Murray MacDougal's croft. They left the road. The moonlight faded out. They slowed down of necessity—no use breaking an ankle now.

He had killed an English soldier. No traitor now. Even Vik . . . Damn Vik! Terrible things. Worry about his own neck. No escape from the glen. The Sassenachs would ride him down in the hills. Who would look after Granny Nan?

"Stop!" he said. They stopped. A moonlit glimmer ahead must be smoke from MacDougal's chimney. "Hamish, take Meg home . . . Be quiet, Meg! Explain what's happened. You weren't there, friend. You didn't arrive until I'd done it, all right?"

"They'll hang me anyway. Take me with you! Don't leave me to—"

"No. Tell Meg's folks exactly what happened. Then go and tell your pa. Tell everything. The glen will stand behind you."

It wouldn't stand behind Toby Strangerson, though. If he wasn't handed over right away, the Sassenachs would take hostages. Hamish was just a kid. Kids were hanged, too, of course, but if Hamish could disappear into hiding for a few weeks, until the English wrath subsided a bit, they might decide they would look foolish raising a hue and cry over a stripling like him and accusing him of hurting Forrester. Big brute Strangerson was a different matter. Granny Nan . . .

He forced his wits to come to order. "Hamish, take Meg home. Now! I have to go, and it's best you don't know where I'm going. Run, both of you."

"Crazy Colin!" Meg squealed.

"Never mind him! I'll give him what I gave the Sassenach. Now off with you! Thanks, Hamish. Good man. Relying on you."

Right on cue, the moon floated into a lagoon between the clouds, and Toby began to run.

He needn't go through the village. He could cut across country. Going home was rank stupid, but he must say good-bye to Granny Nan. He could survive a night in the hills in just his plaid at this time of year. The English would head for the cottage, but he could probably get there before them. They wouldn't push their horses in the dark; they'd stay on the road. He could go around.

He knew the landscape like a spider knew its web. He followed trails from cottage to cottage, short-cutting over the fields, hurdling the fieldstone walls, jumping the burn, ramming through gorse thickets, alarming sheep, setting dogs to barking. Everyone would think it was Crazy Colin up to his tricks. The moon dipped in and out of the clouds.

Rapist! Rotten Sassenach rapist scum! He thought of the other Meg and would have laughed had he the breath for it. So there was justice in the world sometimes? Nineteen years ago the English brutes had imprisoned one Meg Campbell and used her as their plaything for the winter. Now her bastard spawn had rescued another Meg Campbell. Justice! He had avenged his mother.

There was a silver lining to all this—he must leave the glen now. However much Grannie Nan still needed him, he could be of no further help to her. Escape was what he had really wanted, wasn't it? Now he had it. Now he need not worry about the steward's slimy betting schemes.

Go where? South, to lose himself in the crowded

Lowlands? There was only one road south, and they would picket that first. Curse the moon!

Or hide out for a day or two? There was one place in the glen where he might find sanctuary and no one would dare come hunting him. No one else would dare hide in the hob's grove, but the hob might agree to take him in if Granny Nan asked it. It might also forget who the intruder was, of course, and turn on him.

Soon he needed all his brain just to keep moving, and could no longer work on the greater problems. The one thought that remained was that Granny Nan's hands couldn't grasp anymore. She couldn't milk Bossie. The first thing he must do when he got home was milk Bossie.

2

The trees around Lightning Rock were almost the only trees in the glen. No one cut the hob's wood except Toby Strangerson, and he took only what Granny Nan told him to take, not a twig more. The cottage cowered on the edge of the copse, glowering under its shaggy sod roof and half hidden in broom. Shaking and panting, with the wind cold in his soaking hair, he staggered around, looking for Bossie. Even if she'd dragged her tether, she ought to be there in her shed, bellowing to be milked. There was no sign of her anywhere. He looked in the pens: no pig, no poultry. Just silence.

Thinking was an impossible effort. He wanted to fall on the ground and sleep for weeks. No Bossie. The Sassenachs couldn't have gotten here yet. They wouldn't have taken the cow—not yet anyway.

The shutter was closed. He could smell no smoke. With rising alarm, he lifted the latch and ducked through the doorway. A tiny fire glowed on the hearth, giving barely any light at all. It was just enough to show her white hair. She was huddled in her chair with her shawl over her lap. He fell gasping on his knees at her side, peering anxiously at her face.

Her voice came softer than falling leaves. "It was a just fight."

No need to tell; no need to explain or apologize. He dropped his head on her lap and panted. She laid a hand on his sweaty hair. The shutter rattled gently in the wind. Slowly his heart found peace.

Once she murmured, "A good fight. You're a good man."

He did not feel like a good man. He felt like a lost boy.

How small she was!

When he had his breath back: "I can't find Bossie."

"Sold her to Bryce Twotrees. Sold the fowls."

He looked up in dismay. A twig flared on the hearth. He saw the wrinkles of extreme age, the silver hair loose to her shoulders, the sad, wise eyes, the withered sadness of a smile. She was in her wits, apparently. He was the confused one. . . .

"Why—"

"You must leave now."

"But—"

"Follow the others," she murmured. "So many leaving! Where do they all go? What happens to all the men? They leave the glen and they never return. The hob is worried."

The *hob* was worried? How could a hob worry? And how could a solitary, friendless fugitive ever hope to escape in a bleak land like this—a man without a clan? But he mustn't distress her by mentioning that problem. He started to speak, she shook her head and he fell silent. He did not understand, but he often did not understand—even now, after a lifetime. She was not acting strange in the way she did so often now. Not crazy. Odd, yes, but a witchwife would always be odd. She had seen his confusion and was amused.

"I made up a bundle for you. I put some money in it."

"But—"

"Shush!" Her voice strengthened. "You must hurry.

You have far to go, but I can't see where. Here, I have this for you. Take it with you, keep it safe."

He felt for her bony fingers, found something hard, about the size of the top joint of his thumb. It was cold, although she must have been clutching it. Her hand was cold, too. Firelight twinkled. It was one of her pretty stones.

He mumbled thanks and dropped it in his sporran.

"A just fight," she repeated. "Good man. I promised your mother. I've kept my promise."

"What promise?"

"Have to make your own name in the world. Your father didn't give you his. . . . Go now, boy. Good spirits preserve you, Toby! Hurry."

"I can't just leave you here like this."

"Hurry. I'll be taken care of. He'll be here soon."

"Who will?" He peered closer, saw tears glinting in her eyes. Granny Nan? Never before had he seen her weep, even when she'd delivered stillborn babies.

"You must go before he comes. They'll be after you! Go now!"

"You're leaving, too? Who's going to look after the hob?"

She chuckled. "I found someone! If the hob's happy, then you needn't worry, my little Toby, now need you?"

"But . . . listen! They'll be looking for me tonight. If I can hide out for a few days—maybe wait until there's fog, or rain, or no moon . . . Would the hob let me—"

"No! No! You mustn't!" She hissed and cocked her head. Then she pushed at his head. "Go! Go!"

He heard it now, a sound of hooves, many hooves.

Granny Nan wailed. "Too late!" she said. "Too late!"

The English had come. The time for being a lost boy was over; now he must be a man. He heaved himself to his feet, aching in every bone and shocked at how much he had stiffened up. He was too tired to run more. He had had time to say good-bye, so it had been worth it, but he could run no more. He bent and kissed her, trying to mumble something of what he felt, but the words wouldn't come. She kept insisting he go, becoming fretful.

Thinking this was the last time he would ever stoop under the lintel, he walked over to the door. Shivering in the cold air, he latched it behind him.

From the thunder and shaking of the earth, there must be at least ten horsemen coming. They ought to know better! Sergeant Farmer had marched a squad past the copse once with drums beating, and half the men had been stricken with cramps, rolling on the ground and screaming. Where the hob was concerned, any loud noise was dangerous.

Perhaps Toby ought to feel honored that they had sent so many, but he was too weary to feel anything at all. To run and be hunted down like an animal . . . no. He walked out into clear moonlight and stood with his hands raised to show he held no weapon. He had killed one of their own, and they would not be gentle.

They streamed in around both sides of the cottage as if they were charging a Burgundian artillery post. He half expected them to ride him down, but they encircled him, and when they halted, he stood within a cordon of angry eyes, steaming horses, jingling harnesses. Hands pointed wheel locks at him, and swords. He held his hands up and his head down. He said nothing—what was there to say?

They shackled his hands behind him and put chains on his ankles. They laid him facedown across a horse, like a hunter's trophy, and roped him there. They were not gentle, but they did not abuse him as much as he expected. It was the first time Toby Strangerson had ever been on a real horse. He watched the great hooves beat the road below him until he became too nauseated to concentrate. At least he was headed to a clean cell; he had cleaned it out himself. He hoped they would give him straw, but he thought that tonight he could sleep without it.

3

Hamish would call him a cynic, but Toby was genuinely surprised to arrive back at the castle alive. He had not been shot while trying to escape from the horse's back, nor had he accidentally smashed his skull on a gatepost in passing. Dizzy and sick from his head-down journey, he was even more surprised to be unloaded at the door of the big house. He had assumed he would be thrown down the dungeon stairs and left there until dawn, which was the traditional time for hangings. He gathered that the laird was going to hear his case right away.

He clinked and clattered up steps into a part of the building he had never seen before. Soldiers with lanterns went ahead, others followed behind. Luxuries he had only heard tell of loomed out of the darkness and then vanished again: paintings on the walls, tapestries, and fine furniture. He glimpsed wonders and could not linger to admire them. He heard sounds of music overhead and recognized the new reel the laird's piper had been rehearsing for days.

Then he had to climb a long flight of stairs with the lantern shadows leaping and dancing all around. Cynically he waited for an ankle to be jerked from under him, but perhaps his captors were reluctant to get blood on the treads. They had to wait a long time in a corridor before being allowed to proceed. He wriggled his toes on the smooth planks and listened to the music and sniffed the fragrance of beeswax candles, so different from the stinking tallow the villagers used when they must have light after sundown. Little things like that seemed important, as if he must store up memories to take with him.

He wondered why he had been brought up here at this time of night, disturbing the gentry's revels. Why not just leave him in the cell until morning, to be tried and hanged at a more convenient time?

His guards moved, making way, and a stooped old man shuffled through, tapping his cane. Surprised, Toby looked down into the eyes of Steward Bryce. They no longer made him think of dirks. They looked blurred and infinitely weary; Bryce Campbell of Crief seemed to have aged years since Toby had seen him in the afternoon.

His voice was a dry croak. "A baron's court can hang a man caught red-handed in manslaughter."

"Sir? I don't—"

"But murder is withheld. It's one of the four pleas of the crown. Murder goes to the justiciar's court." The steward smiled gruesomely, then turned himself around with care, and hobbled away again, back into the hall.

The soldiers growled. Perhaps they could make more sense out of that than Toby could, but it did sound as if he had been told to hold out for a murder charge. What matter? A man was just as dead whether he was hanged for murder or stealing a loaf of bread. Better to get it over with than languish in a dungeon all winter, waiting for the justiciar to arrive. If the steward still dreamed of having Toby participate in the Glen Games, so he could win a few shillings, then age had rotted his brain. Men in dungeons couldn't attend games. Men in chains had trouble boxing. . . . So what was worrying the old fool?

The music ended. The prisoner was led into court.

He could not tell how large the hall was, for most of it was in darkness. He had a vague impression of banners hanging overhead, and probably a gallery at the far end. An island of light filled the center, where a golden constellation of candle flames twinkled above a table, and it was there that all his attention went. The laird and his guests had just finished a meal. The men wore coats over their plaids, and the women furs, for the hall was cool. They all sparkled with jewels. They had gaudy feathers in their hats.

Toby knew most of them: Steward Bryce was a skeleton someone had dressed up and put there as a joke, Captain Tailor glaring hatred in full dress uniform, white ruff and puffed sleeves and all, his wife and the laird's wife, and the mysterious Lady Valda.

She made the other women look like frumps. She dominated the table—nay, she dominated the hall, the castle, the entire glen, as if everything revolved around her alone. She seemed completely unaware of the chill, for her arms and shoulders were bare. Her violet gown was cut lower than any neckline he had ever seen, displaying a breathtaking vision of firm white breasts. Had Strath Fillan ever known her like? Her hair was indeed black, as he had guessed. It was uncovered, elaborately dressed on top of her head, and she bore a starry coronet of diamonds in it. She was regarding him with austere and intent amusement. He had an insane impression that she had anticipated this scene when they first met, that she had known she would see him tonight, being led in like a beast on its way to the abattoir. Recalling Hamish's wild allegation that her cowled companions were hexers, he wondered if she might have arranged this meeting, or if the instant and unorthodox trial was being held here and now because she had demanded it.

He felt again that sense of evil, stronger than ever.

With a conscious effort he tore his eyes away to look at the laird beside her. By comparison, Ross Campbell seemed old and small—haggard, worried, disheveled. Wisps of white hair had escaped from under his bonnet. His baleful stare at the prisoner was a reminder of the conversation Toby had overheard that morning. The laird had called the glen a powder keg. Worse than what he had feared then had happened already. One of the soldiers had been slain, so one of the villagers must die in retribution, sparks around a powder keg.

"Oh, that one?" The laird glanced uneasily at his companion and seemed to ask a question.

Lady Valda continued to study the prisoner. There was something unholy about so great a lady displaying such interest in a chained convict, disheveled and worthless. She did not reply.

Toby wished he could rearrange the pleats and folds of his plaid.

"Yes, I've seen him around," the laird said. "Big laddie, isn't he? What did you say his name was?"

"My lord!" bellowed Sergeant Drake, somewhere close, but in the background. "The prisoner Toby Strangerson of Fillan, Your Lordship's vassal, accused of wilful murder in the death of His Majesty's servant, Godwin Forrester, enlisted man in the Royal Fusiliers."

"There were witnesses?"

"Yes, my lord."

Campbell of Fillan sighed. "What's your story, prisoner?"

Nothing Toby could say would make the slightest difference. They were going to try him and hang him, without even waiting for a justiciar to arrive. If he must die, he would rather die proudly, and anything he did say would sound like whining. The only reason to speak at all would be to find out why that sinister woman was watching him so intently. He would hate to die without having at least some sort of clue.

"My lord, I found a man attempting to rape a child. I stopped him. He drew his sword and attacked me. I defended myself. I did not intend to kill him." He had quite liked Godwin, but he could not say so now.

The laird pulled a face. "Take him away and secure him, then." He peered along the table. "Bailie, see you prepare a breeve—"

Captain Tailor barked, "No!" The soldier's bony features were flushed with anger, or possibly drink. "One of my men has died. This is a military matter!"

The bluff had been called.

"Rape is not a military matter," the laird protested feebly.

"My lord . . . does the prisoner have evidence that rape was intended? Does he have evidence that the woman was harmed?"

"Her dress was torn!" Toby protested.

"That could have happened when you attacked!" Tailor snapped.

Useless to argue. "The only reason I am here at all," Toby shouted, "is that my mother was abducted and unjustly imprisoned and subjected—"

The metal collar was yanked against his throat. He stumbled backward and was pushed upright, gagging and retching.

He expected to hear sentence being passed then, but

still the laird hesitated. He must fear the spark and the powder keg. Did he not realize that the prisoner was a bastard, an English mongrel, not even a Campbell? Did he really think the glen cared a spit what happened to that one?

"Steward?" he said. "You know this man?"

Old Bryce had been gazing down fixedly at the table in front of him. He looked up slowly.

"My lord, big as he is, he is still only a boy. He has grown visibly in the few months he has been working here. I doubt much that he knows his own strength. He has never caused trouble before . . . " His voice quavered away into silence.

Campbell of Fillan tapped fingertips on the table again. Then he seemed to conclude that he had no choice. "Captain, you—"

"My lord?" said another voice.

His head flicked around. "My lady?"

He seemed almost as frightened of Lady Valda as Toby had been when he first met her on the road. If she was King Nevil's mistress—or even if she had been once—then that was only to be expected.

She smiled, as if at some secret joke. "A woman feels a natural sympathy for a man who seeks to prevent a rape, my lord."

"Quite understandable, my lady!"

"And am I to understand that the prisoner attacked an armed warrior with his bare hands?"

She turned to Captain Tailor, who grimaced.

"Your Ladyship, he is bareknuckle champion of the glen! His fists are weapons."

Lady Valda somehow contrived to raise her exquisite eyebrows without wrinkling her forehead. "Champion, and so young? Would he have a future in the ring, if properly handled?"

"Steward? Have you seen him fight?"

The old man chewed his gums for a moment. "I have heard enough. He is almost a legend already. He has the size, as you can see. He has the strength of a bear and the courage of a cornered badger."

Everyone looked expectantly at the lady, who smiled demurely.

"I see no reason why a member of the gentler sex should not sponsor a prizefighter! We can run race-horses—why not pugilists? Suppose I take the boy into my service, giving my personal guarantee that he will accompany me to England? Of course I shall see to it that he remains law-abiding in future, confining his violent impulses to the Manly Art." Her dark gaze settled on Toby with a gleam of triumph.

Captain Tailor looked stunned at this unexpected development. The laird swelled and shed ten years. Obviously it would solve his problem. The glen would have no excuse to rise in revolt. The dead man had been in flagrant violation of orders, and his companions must see the implications.

"That is exceedingly generous of Your Ladyship! The steward will reaffirm his testimony regarding the man's good character?"

The steward glanced briefly at Tony, muttered something inaudible, and scowled down at the table before him.

"Strangerson," the laird said, "you have heard Lady Valda's beneficent offer. I must tell you that your life is presently forfeit, but her suggestion will not merely save it, but open splendid opportunities for you to advance yourself. Will you enter into her service, giving this court your solemn word that—"

"No!" Toby said. Valda had seized on prizefighting as an excuse for something else. Whatever her real purpose, he would rather hang than be that woman's *meat*.

His reply surprised the onlookers as much as it did him. The guards did not even jerk his tether. The ensuing silence was deadly. The only person who did not seem stunned by his insane denial was Lady Valda herself. She pursed her red lips as if to hide a smile. Toby did not know what she wanted of him, but she made his flesh crawl. Evil had come to the glen, and he wanted no part of it.

"Oh, dear," she said. "What a pity! Of course, as you explained to me this evening, Lord Ross, the men of Fillan are celebrated for their courage. Will you give him the rest of the night to think it over? Perhaps he will change his mind."

"Perhaps I will have him flogged, my lady!"

She considered the proposal for a moment, watching Toby carefully. "A tempting thought, but I think not. Just lock him up until after breakfast. We'll see how he feels then, shall we?"

The laird shrugged, clearly as puzzled as everyone else. "Take him away! Lock him up. This court is adjourned."

"Tell them not to damage him!" she said sharply. "I have no use for a cripple."

4

Six soldiers took Toby to the dungeon; they left him in no doubt that he was much in debt to Lady Valda. Without her final remark and the laird's resulting orders, they would have made him pay dearly for what he had done to Godwin Forrester. They did debate whether they should hang him up by his feet or his elbows, and outlined several other entertaining possibilities, also. They were obviously apprehensive of his strength, testing the shackles carefully, but in the end they merely attached his ankle chains to one wall and his neck chain to the wall opposite, leaving him sitting in the middle of the rock-hewn floor. Then they went away. The gate creaked and clanged. A lock clicked faraway at the top of the stairs.

He was alone in the dark and the silence and the bone-freezing cold. It could have been much worse. By no human contortion could he ever free himself, but he could sit up or he could lie down. As his hands were still fastened behind him and the chain from his collar dangled down his back, that was not the most comfortable of situations. There was not enough slack on his leg tethers for him to roll over, facedown, which was how he preferred to sleep, and he could not wrap himself up in his plaid. But he was still alive and uninjured.

As he shivered himself to sleep, he wondered briefly why the prospect of swearing loyalty to that woman should be so unthinkable. He concluded only that it was, and that strangling in a noose would be preferable. Whose man . . . Never hers! Perhaps in the morning he would change his mind.

Either a rattling of chain wakened him, or he became aware of the light. He could not have slept long, but his wits were muddled. He did not understand where he was, or why he was on his back with his arms twisted under him. He blinked in bewilderment at the robed, cowled figure holding the candle. Memory began to return. He looked the other way and saw two more of them. . . .

Argh! He tried to sit up and almost choked himself. The chain from his collar had been drawn tight; he was staked out, helpless.

"Who are you?" he mumbled with parched mouth. "What are you doing?"

The man did not respond. Although he was standing motionless, clasping a black candle before him, only a steady glitter of eyes showed within his cowl. Toby's hair rose on his scalp. "Who are you?" he screamed.

"They will not speak," Lady Valda said.

He twisted his head until he located her. She was standing at a small table near the stair, busily unpacking a metal casket. Her four cowled associates stood in a square around Toby. Each held a black candle, and the steadiness of the flames suggested that the men were not breathing.

"Who are you?"

"My name is of no importance to you," she said calmly, intent on what she was doing. "To be truthful, nothing is of importance to you anymore." She closed the lid and laid the box on the floor, then began rearranging the miscellaneous objects she had removed from it. He saw a golden bowl, a scroll, and a dagger, but there were other things, too.

He was shivering shamefully. There was a tight knot in his belly.

To scream would be useless. The guardroom would be deserted. The house was far away, its residents doubtless asleep. The sentries on the walls would neither hear nor come to investigate if they did.

He stared again at the four men. Four flames, eight eyes unblinking. Masks! They all had thick black beards and wore black masks above them. So they were mortal men and that was trickery. But he was not cynic enough to believe that it would all be trickery. Hamish had been wrong about these men being hexers, or not right enough. Lady Valda was the hexer. Toby's recognition of evil had been a true instinct.

"What do you want of me?" His voice emerged as a hoarse whisper.

"Your body, of course. I came hunting a stalwart young man and see what I caught!"

She came across to him, her shoes scraping softly on the rock, the hem of her gown whispering around her ankles. He thought it was the same garment she had worn earlier, although it looked darker in the dim light— that shameless neckline was breathtakingly memorable. Her breasts seemed even larger viewed from below, above an astonishingly narrow waist. Unbound hair floated in a sable cloud around her, almost to her waist.

She crouched down beside him and stroked his cheek. He twisted his head away and the rusty collar scraped his throat.

"Relax!" she purred. "You're a big, brave boy, remember? You'd rather die than serve me, and you have the courage of a cornered badger."

He could see the burning evil behind the mockery dancing in her eyes. He tried to speak in a normal voice. "What are you going to do?"

"Conjure, of course. But you needn't worry. You will

not be eaten by demons. You will not even see a demon, I promise you, not the teeniest, wispiest demon. You will feel no pain—or only a very tiny amount, nothing a strong young lad can't grit his teeth through. And when we are done, you will walk out of here a free man! Now, isn't that an exciting prospect?"

"I don't believe you!" His heart raced in terror and yet he was conscious of her closeness, her musky perfume. He was a man and a desirable woman had a hand on his neck. He noted the long, deep crease between her milk-white breasts.

Seeing his gaze wander, she chuckled. "Not that exciting prospect, boy! Admire, by all means, but those are not for you. To work! All I require of you is that you lie there and be silent. I repeat—you will not be hurt, even by this." She raised a dagger above his eyes. Its blade shone steely blue and was long enough to reach all the way through him. She unpinned his plaid to lay bare his chest, then stroked it playfully with soft fingers.

"I need you conscious, but silent. Must I gag you, or can you be trusted?"

He hesitated and the soft fingers curled. Nails dug into his flesh. "You will be silent! If you cause me trouble, I shall make you endure such agony as you have never imagined. Is that clear, Toby?"

"Yes," he whispered.

"You do believe me now?"

"Yes."

"Good. Remember that you are destined to hang. I am saving your life. Cooperation will cost you nothing except minor indignity." Her scarlet lips curled in mockery. "And you have so very little dignity left!"

With a chuckle of satisfaction, she rose and returned to her table. The four men showed no sign that they had heard a word.

Demonic possession? As a kid, he had believed stories of demons taking over people's bodies. Later he'd decided that being possessed by a demon would make an excellent excuse for doing anything at all, so he'd stopped believing. Now he wasn't so sure. When the hexer said he would not see the demon, she implied that she was going to conjure it inside him. In the morning Toby Strangerson might inform the laird that he had changed his mind and would be a loyal servant to Lady Valda; the laird would let him depart as a free man—but how free? And would he be a man at all? What were these four voiceless, masked figures? Were they really human? Would he be another of those?

Lady Valda returned, clutching a vellum scroll. "Hold your breath and lie still." She placed a shod foot on his chest and put her weight on it.

He heaved with his shoulders and dislodged her. She stepped down hurriedly to regain her balance. She made a *tutting* sound of annoyance. "Don't be foolish, boy. This is your last chance! If you do not cooperate, I shall make you scream at the top of your lungs for a solid hour. A husky lad like you can endure my weight for a few minutes."

She stepped up and stood full on his chest. She weighed less than he had expected. He could breathe. The manacles dug into his wrists and back, but the pain was bearable, if it did not last too long.

She unrolled the scroll. She read out a proclamation in a guttural language he did not know. It went on for several minutes, the words rolling around the chamber, raising a deep echo he had not noticed before. When she finished, the silence returned. Could a silence grow *denser*?

She stepped off him and walked back to her table. He drew a long breath. He had a horrible suspicion that his living body had just been dedicated as a sacrifice to . . . something.

For a while after that, she did not touch him. She walked around him several times, sprinkling various powders from small vials, each time repeating a formula in that same harsh tongue. The flames on the four candles seemed to grow longer. The four human candlesticks never moved. If they blinked, Toby did not catch them at it. She placed a pinch of powder on each of his shoulders, on his heart, his forehead, his sporran. After her next visit to the table, she knelt down beside him, heedless of the damage the rough rock floor could do to her fine gown. She laid the little golden bowl on his chest as if he were a table, and he sensed that the preliminaries were over. How could a man be so cold and still sweat so much? Evil had come to the glen. Terrible things were about to happen.

She had brought the dagger back, too. The quillons were silver, elaborately inlaid with dark red stone. The pommel was a startling yellow gem as big as the top joint of his thumb. She raised both arms as high as she could, clasping the dagger by its quillons, point down. If she dropped it from there, it would go straight into his heart. Her lips moved, but this time she made no sound. She seemed to be addressing the weapon itself, or offering it to some unseen presence near the roof. The jewel on the pommel glittered, reflecting the candlelight. Her victim listened helplessly to his own breath and the thud of his heart.

He noticed . . . No, he refused to believe . . . Admit it! The chamber was growing brighter. The vault of the roof was in clear view and parts of the rock walls shone wetly. The candle flames had become almost invisible and the jewel no longer glittered. It was the source of the new light, glowing with an impossible internal brightness. Everything he had seen until now could be cynically dismissed as mere playacting, but that baleful radiance blazing from the dagger could not be denied. It was uncanny. This was real gramarye. Soon the gem was too bright to look upon, illuminating the whole chamber to the farthest corner.

The hexer completed her silent incantation and leaned over him. He wondered what horror was coming next. He saw mad exultation in her eyes, but she seemed unaware of him now. He was only part of the furnishings, an altar for her art. She slipped her left breast out of her dress. Holding it steady with one hand, she cut it with the dagger—an easy, offhand slash at the underside, almost contemptuous. She showed no sign of pain, indeed she watched the blood trickling into the golden bowl with a smile of childlike pleasure.

He felt the warmth of it through the metal. He shuddered and closed his eyes. His heart pounded. His head pounded, too. He wondered if he was about to faint. That could not be just his heart he was hearing. Faint and far away, a drum had begun to tap.

Was that part of her gramarye, or could it possibly be a hope of rescue? Had the laird guessed what sort of guest had infested his house? Or perhaps the shrewd old steward, who had seemed so glum? *Dum . . . Dum . . .* Someone was sounding a tattoo. Rousing the guard to rout the evil from Lochy Castle?

Toby felt the bowl being removed from his chest and opened his eyes quickly. Valda had covered herself, but a spreading dark stain on her bodice showed that the wound still bled. She was holding the bowl in one hand, making passes over it with the dagger, mouthing silently. When she was done, she set the dagger aside by laying it on his belly, as the nearest convenient shelf. He tried not to move at all then.

The drum drew closer, but it did not come from the stairway. It seemed to be inside his head. It could never be the fusiliers. That drummer was not of his world. Sweat trickled across his forehead and along his ribs.

"Aha!" The hexer was gazing at him. Her eyes shone with insane excitement, her red lips were drawn back. "You feel it already?"

She dipped two fingers in the blood and drew a mark on his chest. It felt cold as ice. Another dip, another mark. . . . She was concentrating hard, tongue between her teeth, inscribing some arcane symbol on him. The cold of it burned his skin. A steady yellow light blazed from the dagger, but he could feel no heat, only the winter cold of the sigil. She worked outward—around his nipples, curving down his ribs, up to his collar bones, down almost to his navel.

Dum . . . Dum . . . Thundering, the drumming filled

the chamber with its relentless steady beat, and now he knew it for the thump of his own heart, magnified to madness. Was this the sound of death? Why so loud? And why so slow? *Dum . . . Dum . . . Dum . . .* Stop! Stop!

"There!" The hexer cried out in triumph, yet she was barely audible through the pulsing beat. She set the bowl aside. "You hear me, my love? It is almost done!"

She took up the dagger with her bloody hand. Whatever else she said, Toby heard only the grotesque drumming of his heart. He tried to move and his muscles failed to obey him. Nothing happened at all. He could only stare at the woman's lips moving as she lowered the dagger. She laid the point on the sigil she had drawn on his chest and added another line, cutting his skin to add his blood to hers. He did not feel it. Another . . . he saw her eyes widen in sudden dismay. She raised the dagger as if to strike.

Shift . . .

A boy lay chained on a rock-carved floor—a huge and husky boy, but still only a boy, his eyes and mouth stretched wide in terror. He was bare-chested, his body inscribed with obscene demonic heraldry that flickered and glowed as if it were some foul living fire. Beside him knelt a woman in a rich gown, clutching a dagger whose pommel also flamed with loathsome internal light. Standing guard around them, four shrouded figures that were men and yet not men. The hands clutching the candles were human, the eyes were human, but within the robes swirled darkness like living smoke.

The boy's shoulders heaved and his hands came free, a few links of rusty chain dangling from manacles around his wrists. Even for his size, those hands were big, the hands of one who had milked cows in his youth. A massive fist slammed the woman aside as if swatting a bug. She sprawled bodily; the dagger flew off and its yellow light went out.

The drum thundered on; there was no sound but the inexorable beat of the drum. *Dum . . . Dum . . . Dum . . .*

The boy reached up and gripped the collar around

his neck. One of the robed *things* dropped its candle and dived for the dagger. It leaped back across the chamber in a single bound, robe flapping like bat wings, landing on its knees beside the boy in a move that would have crippled a human. It raised the dagger to strike at his heart.

The boy had snapped the collar. One of his hands moved impossibly fast. It caught the attacker's wrist and jerked it forward. The robed figure sprawled prone over him, the dagger striking the floor beyond. The hand shifted to the thing's bearded chin, its mate came down on its shoulders . . . there was a momentary pause, and then the cowled head bent back at an impossible angle. The roiling internal darkness shriveled and waned. The hands hurled the carcass away like a discarded pillow.

All light disappeared as the other three watchers dropped their candles and fled to the stairs. Pitch blackness filled the cellar, yet somehow it was visible. Every stone in the barrel ceiling showed in the dark, and dampness shone on the ancient chisel marks of the rock walls as if revealed by bright moonlight or the eerie lavender of a frozen lightning flash.

The boy sat up and reached down to his right ankle. Fingers gripped the steel fetter, muscle bulged, tendons flexed. The cuff snapped open. The hands moved over and freed the other ankle also. Those were Toby Strangerson's hands and arms, but they had more than Toby Strangerson's strength, more than mortal strength.

The drumming pursued its steady, unhurried beat. The boy was on his feet, flashing across the floor in pursuit even as the last cowled figure was disappearing up the stairs. He caught the robe, dragged its occupant back. He lifted the thing, swung it, shattered its head against the wall, dropped the body, and stepped over it to follow the others. He raced up the stairs without a change in the overriding beat: *Dum . . . Dum . . .*

The last two robed henchmen slammed the metal gate from the far side. That should have made a noise to rouse the entire castle, but it was inaudible under the irresistible drumming. The men collided with table and benches as they struggled to reach the guardroom door.

The boy took hold of the gate. The thick bars resisted, the arms swelled, iron bent. The gate changed shape, came loose bodily in a shower of rust and fragments of stone. The cowled men had gone, leaving the door open. As the boy passed the mirror, he turned his head and paused to look at his reflection—large, curly-haired, bare from the waist up, rusty bangles on his wrists. Bleeding scratches adorned his neck and ankles. The arcane sigil on his chest had gone dark and become merely a pattern drawn in blood. His juvenile face bore an idiotic simper of satisfaction, the face of one who had no worries and never would have.

Toby Strangerson stared out of the mirror in horror.

The boy swung a fist to meet another fist and the mirror shattered between them. He trotted forward, out the door.

The courtyard, also, was bright with the mysterious lavender radiance. The two cowled things were struggling to open the postern gate, but the boy ignored them and crossed to the stables. All the horses and ponies should have been in turmoil, but they dozed in their stalls, paying no heed to the eldritch light or the drummer's deafening beat. The boy took a bridle from a peg and moved along the line to the laird's pride, the white stallion whose name was Falcon.

Toby Strangerson had no experience with horses. He had ridden ponies a few times and watched the fusiliers at their dressage, but that was the limit of his experience. The stallion jerked its head up and rolled its eyes, then calmed at a touch on its neck. It took the bit without resistance. It let itself be backed out of its stall and led from the stable, ignoring the thunder of the urgent drum. There was no other sound in the world: *Dum* . . . *Dum* . . .

The postern gate stood open. A flash on the battlements released a puff of smoke, but the range was far too great for a pistol. Where the ball went was immaterial.

Falcon stepped through the gate. The boy sprang lightly to its back.

With his sure hand steadying its reins, the stallion raced down the road, leaving the castle far behind. Responding to the touch of knees and bare feet, it turned aside and made its way across country, soaring over walls, never faltering, never putting a foot wrong. The landscape rushed past, illuminated partly by fitful moonlight, but much more by that demonic blue glow, while an irresistible drummer beat slow time.

5

Reality returned with a crash. The drumming stopped. The light cut out like a snuffed candle. Toby awoke from his trance to instant darkness, full of motion and sound and an icy wind. Starting to slide, he grabbed at the horse's mane with both hands. Falcon shrilled in terror, stopped dead, and sent its rider spinning through the air. He smashed to the turf with a jarring impact. The horse kicked and bucked for a few moments, then thundered away across the fields.

Toby lay and stared at the whirling moon. Where was he? How had he come there? The events in the cellar and his departure from the castle seemed like the most improbable of nightmares. He had watched himself from the outside, yet what he had seen was so sharp and clear in his mind that he could not doubt it. Obviously Lady Valda's conjuration had gone seriously awry, resulting in the escape of her stalwart victim, who now lay flat on his back and half stunned, somewhere in Strath Fillan.

The moon steadied in the sky—the clouds had almost gone and a pale misty ring in the sky told of frost. He felt cold seeping into his body. It brought welcome relief from a collection of aches and pains he could not begin to catalogue. He might have just lain there, slowly freezing into a blessed numbness, had not his teeth begun to chatter noisily. Grunting, he checked that all his limbs moved, that he was still breathing, if only just. He heaved himself upright and looked around. He saw stony pasture, silver with hoarfrost, but right ahead of him was the grove, with the jagged spire of Lightning Rock glittering in the moonlight.

Well, of course! Although he was already shivering hard enough to fall apart, Toby laughed aloud. That was what had gone wrong with Lady Valda's conjuration—she had been messing with the witchwife's little lad! The hob had taken offense at a demon intruding in its glen. The hob had intervened. It had demolished her gramarye, brought the boy home. He had Granny Nan to thank, undoubtedly, but he must thank the hob itself, too. He had money now, so he could buy it some shiny trinket as a token of his gratitude.

First, he must head for the cottage. Even if the soldiers came looking for him again—and that was by no means certain—they could not possibly arrive soon. No mortal rider would travel as fast as he just had. That had not been Toby Strangerson on the horse.

He was a mortal man again now, though, and he had urgent troubles: biting cold for one, outlawry for another. He was still liable to be hanged for murder, and when the carnage in the dungeon was discovered, he could expect to be impaled as a demon, as well. Most urgent of all was the loathsome sigil on his chest. He supposed that it must be the demon's way of identifying him, or its password for entry. He had no wish to be repossessed. Tearing up handfuls of frosty grass, he wiped at the bloodstains until the marks were well smeared and the sign was illegible. If demonology was at all logical, then that ought to block any effort by the demon to return. He found two shallow cuts, but they were nothing to worry about.

Standing upright was.

Even when he was on his feet, it took more effort to straighten. He had lost his bonnet when the Sassenachs threw him onto the horse's back, and now he had lost his pin as well. Pulling his plaid over arms and shoulders, he set off around the copse at a stumbling run.

Granny Nan had said she was leaving. Whether or not she had gone, the door would not be locked, for it had no lock. He could blow up the fire or light another. From the position of the moon, sunrise was still a few hours off. He had a small start on the inevitable hue and cry. The Sassenachs would be looking for a man on horseback until Falcon calmed down and went home or was found in the morning. They might not come looking for him at Granny Nan's right away. He felt light-headed and battered, as if he'd fought two bouts in quick succession. What he needed most was sleep, about three days' solid sleep. Or a square meal and then sleep. If he ever sat down—if he ever got warm again—he would just fall over and snore. In the morning the soldiers would find him there, still snoring.

Would the soldiers come looking for him? Lady Valda had been killed or stunned. The cellar was full of evidence of her black art. Two of her adherents had been slain, chains snapped, an iron gate mangled like a string bag. An untrained farm lad had taken the wildest horse in the stable and ridden off bareback—*there* was real gramarye! The castle would be in an uproar of terror.

He wondered if Lady Valda was now shackled in the dungeon in his stead. It was an appealing thought, if not a very probable one. Lady Valda might be dead. Or Lady Valda might be alive and using more gramarye to reassert her control over the laird and the garrison. Did she still have a need for the stalwart young man? Spirits knew! To try and outguess the hexer was ridiculous. Or outguess a demon, either. Blocked in its efforts to possess Toby, it might have settled for Lady Valda. He did not even know if there were male and female demons, or whether it mattered. There were all sorts of possibilities.

Assume, though, that Lady Valda was not in control. What would the laird do to counter an outbreak of diabolism in the glen? He would believe the witnesses who had seen the demon ride off in Toby Strangerson's body, so he would order it hunted down and an iron spike driven through its heart. Most likely he would also send to a sanctuary—Dumbarton or Fort William or even Glasgow—for an adept to come and exorcise the castle. Whether the exorcism would succeed, of course, was another matter. Cowshed or palace, if a demon took up residence in a place, it usually had to be abandoned. Many a deserted ruin in the Highlands testified to the truth of that.

Even from Fort William, an acolyte would not arrive for a few days. In the short term, the laird would seek advice closer to hand. The local authority in such matters was the glen's witchwife, Granny Nan.

Toby decided that the situation held some interesting irony.

But he still had not solved the problem of where he could seek refuge, or even hide out until another night gave him a slim chance of escaping from the glen. He was an outlaw, a murderer, and credibly believed possessed. No one would dare shelter him. He bore the scars of fetters on his ankles and neck; he had rusty metal cuffs on his wrists.

He wondered if he was still under the protection of the hob. Its influence would not extend beyond the limits of the glen, and it might have forgotten about him already. Hobs were fickle, not to be trusted. All the same, it was a hope to cling to. It was all he had.

Twigs crackled underfoot as he neared the door. Then his heart lurched. Dismay! Moonlight shone on wraiths of smoke coiling up from the chimney—far more smoke than would come from any fire Granny Nan ever set. She must have company, or intruders.

For a moment he dithered in despair. Then he decided that whoever had come visiting, it could not be the English. If it was a bunch of Campbell neighbors and they decided to turn him in, then he could have a little enjoyable exercise. He limped over to the door, lifted the latch, and ducked in under the lintel.

There was no one there. The extravagant fire crackled and sparked, shedding a joyful light. The warmth of it reached out to him like a lover's arms, or what he supposed lovers' arms would feel like. But there was no one there. He shuffled across to the hearth and eased himself to the floor. At once he began to shiver and shudder and break out all over in more goosebumps than he would have believed possible. He rubbed his feet, trying to work some life back into them.

Granny Nan's chair was empty. Her bed was empty. The bundle she had prepared for him lay in the corner where he slept. Nothing seemed to be missing: the kettle on the ingle, the two black pots hung by the chimney, the crocks on their shelf, the loom. A list of everything in the room would not fill one sheet of paper. Ah! Her bonnet hung on its peg, but her cloak was gone. And his bonnet was hung in its place! That was the most welcome sight he had seen all night. Granny Nan must have found it after the soldiers left. But where could she be?

She had said she was going away. None of the villagers were rich, but they cherished their witchwife. She had pulled most of them from their mothers' wombs. She had tended their sicknesses. If she had announced that she needed care in her last years, then someone would have agreed to take her in, no question. Someone would have come with a cart to fetch her—Iain the miller, or Rae the butcher, or someone.

Someone had put logs on the fire not very long ago, someone accustomed to burning peat or broom, not wood, so perhaps the glen had a new witchwife. Until tonight Granny Nan had never mentioned choosing a successor, but she had been acting so strange these last few months. . . . Other women had taken over the midwifery. The glen did not lack for widows. One of them must have agreed to serve.

She would not have gone far without her bonnet. The logical conclusion was that she had slipped over to visit the hob—perhaps introducing the new witchwife, or inducting her, doing whatever was required. She was taking a long time about it. Toby must go and find her.

He should also find the salve she used for scrapes and cuts, but he lacked the energy to move. His thawing limbs ached and throbbed, which was the penalty for coming back to life. He was also starting to feel intensely sleepy. His eyelids were as heavy as rocks. He must not sleep! He turned around to roast his back and stretch his legs. First, he must find another pin for his plaid, and he thought Granny Nan had a spare somewhere. Then find her and thank the hob. Then decide where to run and start running. The idea was an impossibility, but his only alternative was death.

He was still facing the door when it opened and the men came in with drawn swords. Their eyes were filled with the same hatred and accusation he had seen earlier that night in the eyes of the soldiers.

6

Plaid-clad Campbells crowded the cottage. The first in was Iain Miller, faintly coated in flour so that he seemed like a fat ghost in the firelight. His plump hand looked absurd holding a sword, but that same hand had wielded that same blade at Leethoul with deadly effect. No eyes more deserved to be called piggy, but they glinted with the same dangerous shrewdness as a boar's.

Behind him came Eric Smith, who was broader but shorter, whose arms shamed even Toby's. No one would question his right to hold a sword—his hand was crooked and twisted from long years of hammering, but the smith was the strongest man in the glen. He had been bareknuckle champion for ten years and could still be, if he wished. When words led to deeds, it was usually Eric who took the combatants by the scruffs of their necks and dunked them in the burn.

Then came Rae Butcher . . . bushy black brows, shaggy black mustache, usually a hearty smile and a joyous greeting, but somber now.

These three were understandable, for they were the

unofficial leaders, men who would take charge whenever there was trouble that did not involve the laird—especially in these troubled times when the laird was a stranger and a suspect traitor. Toby thought of them as Brains, Brawn, and Blarney.

Surprisingly, there was a fourth: the peg-legged Kenneth Tanner, leaning on his cane. Nobody thought much of that souse, so why was he here?

Toby pulled up his knees and dragged his plaid over his shoulder again, resisting the temptation to stand. He was taller than any of them. They were armed; down on the floor he was less likely to provoke violence.

"What's happened?" he demanded sharply. "Where's Granny Nan?"

"Suppose you tell us," Iain Miller said.

Toby raised his hands to show the manacles. "I don't know! I escaped. I just got back here."

"The Sassenachs did not take her?"

"Of course not! Even English must know better than to meddle with a witchwife."

"Then where is she?"

"I don't know. She was here when I left. She said she was going away, that someone was coming to fetch her." With rising panic, Toby stared at the blankly accusing faces. "She knew I would have to leave the glen. I thought someone in the village . . ."

"News to me," the miller said.

Fear touched Toby with icy fingers. If there was to be a change of witchwife in the glen, these men would know of it. He began to rise, and again decided to stay where he was. They did not trust him any more than he trusted them. "Tell me what happened!"

Fat Iain glanced uncertainly at his companions, but none of them offered any help. "We came looking for you, but we were too late. We saw the horses' tracks. We decided to talk with the witchwife. She wasn't here. We've been waiting, looking . . ." He wasn't close to the fire, yet his fat face was moist. Iain Miller was worried half out of his wits.

"She'll be with the hob!"

"She's a long time about it."

"Did you go to the grotto?" It was a foolish question. They would not have dared. That was what witchwives were for. Hobs were touchy and unpredictable.

"We called out," the smith muttered. "She didn't answer."

"I'll go see, then," Toby said. Granny Nan took him to visit the hob sometimes—or she had when he was a child. He could assume that he was in its favor since it had saved him from Lady Valda's demon. He must go and thank it for its help anyway.

"Just tell us how you came back," the miller demanded suspiciously.

Toby scrambled to his feet and the men backed away from his fury. Right there by the fire, the roof was just high enough to let him stand upright. Groggy with fatigue, he leaned a hand against the chimney to steady himself and glared down at them all.

"I told you!" he shouted. "I escaped! They accused me of killing a soldier. I admitted it. They locked me up. I broke out. Are you suggesting I did something to Granny Nan? That's crazy! No one can have hurt her!"

He saw the answer in their eyes. No one could harm the witchwife—not here, so near to the hob—except perhaps Toby himself. He, too, lived close to the hob's grotto. Perhaps in their minds he had taken on some of the uncanniness that hung around those who consorted with elementals. In the last few years the orphan bastard had shot up to become the biggest man in the glen. Today he had killed a soldier, and yet here he was, home again.

Swords or not, they were frightened of him.

He gripped hard on his temper. "Well? If you're accusing me of something, say so. Yes, I killed a Sassenach tonight, and I don't care overmuch. What else is bothering you?"

The men exchanged unsure glances, like children in school when the teacher behaves unpredictably. Toby waited for one of them to ask about the blood on his chest, but he had so many other scrapes that the smears escaped notice.

"I think he's telling the truth," Rae Butcher announced loudly.

Smith and miller nodded with less confidence.

Tanner scowled. "I want to know how a man escapes from Lochy Castle." His voice was slurred.

Toby could not, must not, tell them how he had escaped. If they even suspected he was possessed, they would run a sword through his heart instantly, probably three swords. He tried to invent a plausible explanation and realized that there wasn't one. "I stole a horse." That was the best he could do.

Pause . . . Then the smith chuckled. "Before that? Rusty chains and the second best shoulders in the glen, I'm thinking." He was trying to break the tension.

"What do you mean *second* best?" asked the butcher. "I know quality beef when I see it."

The smith and the miller laughed very heartily. They all sheathed their swords. Toby Strangerson had been found not guilty in his second trial of the night—for the time being, at least—and now everyone was friends and everything was sweet and beautiful . . . for the time being.

"Stole a horse?" The miller's lardy face rolled itself into a smile. "Good for you! We're not accusing you of anything, lad, except being a true Scotsman, and Sassenachs' horses are another fine tradition in the glen, I'm thinking. We're all proud of what you did tonight!"

Oh, really?

The fat man turned to the tanner. "Kenneth? You have something to say to this man?"

"Aye." The flabby tanner lurched forward on his wooden leg. He stuck his melancholy face up at Toby's. It needed shaving and it brought a strong odor of liquor. "Thank you," he said sourly. "We're real grateful, the wife and me. And Meg herself, of course." He thrust out a hand, which Toby stared at uncomprehendingly.

"It was a brave deed," Rae boomed, "worthy of a Campbell."

Oh, that? One of the better murders! Toby shook the tanner's hand without enthusiasm. "Any man would have done the same." Why should they expect him to be different?

"Not any man, only a very brave one."

Brave was stupid. He did not trust their sudden change of heart. What were they doing here anyway? Where was Granny Nan? "You said you came here looking for me? Why?"

He put the question to the miller, but with the swords out of the way, the slick-tongued butcher had taken over. He rubbed his gorse-bush mustache. "To help you, of course. To get you away before the Sassenachs catch you."

Or to hand him over before the English began reprisals for Forrester's death? Toby Strangerson was not fool enough to expect help from the glen. It had never shown him any affection in the past.

"And just how do you expect to achieve that? They'll take hostages."

Rae Butcher raised his thick brows. "Then they'll regret it! They're outnumbered twenty to one. We have friends we can call on. Don't worry about that, lad."

"They'll watch the roads, send word—"

"We've made arrangements," said the miller.

"I don't think I like the sound of that."

The men rolled eyes at one another.

"Annie Bridge," the butcher explained soothingly. "She'll put you up until dark. We'll have a guide to get you out by ways the English don't know." He smiled knowingly. "And there's a noble lord who can use good fighting men."

Toby took the statements one at a time. Annie had lost her husband at Leethoul and sons at both Norford Bridge and Parline. No one hated the Sassenachs more than Annie did. If he could trust anyone, he could trust Annie. Her croft stood near to the mouth of Glen Orchy, which was supposed to be blocked by impassable bog and implacable bogy. If there was a safe way through that, then the English were not the only ones who had never heard of it. The lord was Fergan, of course. Because the village bastard had killed an Englishman they assumed he wanted to join the rebels. He had not intended to kill Godwin. He had done what he did because of Meg, not for King Fergan. He had better not go into that.

They were the laird's men, but he would have to trust them, or at least pretend to trust them. He could not hope to escape from the glen if these men turned against him. They might support a Sassenach-killer, a potential rebel recruit, but by morning the details of his escape from the cell would be common knowledge. Their sudden enthusiasm for Toby Strangerson would not extend to a resident demon.

"Young Hamish's going, too," the butcher said. "He was with you when it happened, so the Sassenach bast— The Sassenach scum, I mean. They may pick on him."

Something nudged the back of Toby's mind until he remembered young Hamish's bright-eyed appeal on the way to Bridge of Orchy: *Take me with you.* The boy might hang on the same gibbet yet.

"He's a good kid," he said, and realized that to these men he was only a kid himself.

"And Meg, too," Tanner mumbled. "The wife's having fits."

Considering the ordeal she had endured in her youth, Elly Tanner had every right to throw a few hysterics over her daughter's narrow escape, but even so . . . "You don't think they'll take it out on Meg?" Toby protested.

"It's a hard world, lad," the miller said cynically. "Not the laird, of course. But it's best for the lass to leave."

Not the laird, nor even Captain Tailor, but some of Godwin Forrester's friends might seek out the girl and see she got what she had missed.

"Elly has family over Oban way," Tanner stated, with the exaggerated precision of a drunk who had realized he was slurring his words. "Vik will see Meg there safely."

Fat Vik?

"Oh, no!" Toby straightened up and felt his hair brush the roof. "You let me near Vik Tanner and there'll be another murder in the glen."

He must have looked as if he meant it, because the

men made shocked noises and began to protest. He didn't hear. He was remembering what had started all the trouble and his blood froze in his veins. *Where was Granny Nan?* It wasn't possible, was it? The hob would have protected her?

Apparently they were waiting for him to put it into words.

"That lout gave Crazy Colin a knife—on the night of the full moon, too! He set him onto killing me."

Vik's father yelled, "No! That's not true!" The accusation had not surprised him, though, and the other men shrugged. Why had they brought him here? How likely was it that the tanner would limp all this distance just to shake Toby's hand?

"It is true. That's what your daughter came to tell me. That's why she came to the castle—because of your precious son! And where is Granny Nan all this time? Out of my way!" He pushed past them to look in Granny Nan's sewing bag, where he might find a spare pin for his plaid.

"Kenneth," said the smith, "the fewer people who go, the better. You could trust Strangerson to see your girl safely to her cousins in Oban, yes?"

Silence. Toby had tipped the bag out on the clay floor, but now he looked up. The men were waiting on the tanner, and even in the shadows, he seemed to have been shocked sober.

"You'd take good care of her, lad?" he said uncertainly.

The night grew madder and madder. Yes, it would be a good idea for Meg to disappear until the affair blew over and that no-good half-brother of hers would be worse than useless anyway. But to trust her to a murderer and a hunted outlaw . . . Of course, if they were asking whether he would take advantage of the child, then the answer was easy. "I'd guard her like a sister, but . . ."

The tanner nodded and looked away.

"That's arranged, then?" the miller said.

"Aye." Tanner nodded. Then he added, apparently more to himself than anyone else, "I'm thinking I got the wrong one."

The smith grinned at the butcher and the miller smiled knowingly. If that was a joke, Toby had missed the point completely: wrong what?

He found the pin and rose to adjust his plaid. Again he pushed by the visitors—the cottage was cramped when there was only him in it. He knelt to unpack the bundle Granny Nan had made up for him, wrapped in a square of tartan. He found his razor in there, his tinderbox, a metal pan, a knife, a new bonnet that she'd promised to make for him, a pair of gloves he had not seen before, a bag of meal, a lump of salt—and her little leather purse. It was fatter than he remembered, surprisingly heavy. He pulled the drawstring and took a look. He had given her what he'd been earning in the castle all summer, but he'd had to buy a new belt, and the rest could not amount to this much. Here was Bossie, and the poultry, and a lifetime's savings. Some of it was his, though, and probably all of it, because she wanted him to have it, because she had no use for money and he was going to. He slipped the two shiniest coppers into his sporran, then rolled the bag up in the cloth with the other treasures.

"Come on!" he said, and ducked out the door ahead of the village elders.

7

He was stiff and his feet still hurt from his walk to Bridge of Orchy. He limped slowly along the path, letting his eyes adjust to the darkness, letting the other men keep up. The moon was low in the west, still encircled by her misty wreath. His breath smoked in the cold.

He had never visited the hob by night. He could have brought a torch, of course, but fire would get the hob excited. The hob was excited easily, especially by thunderstorms. Any storm that visited Strath Fillan inevitably spent most of its time there directly over Lightning Rock, blasting trees and the rock itself in a continuous orgy of fire and sound, rolling echoes off the hills. For days afterward, milk would sour all over the glen, calves be stillborn, children fall sick, until the witchwife could get the hob calmed down again. A few weeks later, it would become annoyed at the blackened trunks disfiguring its grove; then it would let Granny Nan have them for firewood and she would send Toby to chop them down.

One of the men coughed nervously. Toby realized that they were at the copse itself.

"Why don't you wait here?" That was what he was supposed to say.

"Well . . . If you don't need us?" Miller said, feigning reluctance.

"Just one of us might be best. Don't want to make it snarly."

They all agreed it would not do to make the hob snarly.

Toby went on alone, climbing the narrow path. He wondered if the hob would be more or less visible by night than it was by day. The most he had ever seen of it was a faint silver shimmer, a sort of glow in the trees, as if all the leaves were twinkling and the air was sweeter. Usually it stayed in its grotto, but sometimes it would come and watch him chop wood. Very rarely, he had detected it elsewhere in the glen. It never spoke to him, only to the witchwife. He was not at all sure that it could speak to anyone else, or that anyone would understand it if it did. He suspected that it had very little intelligence in any human sense. Granny Nan rarely talked about the hob, even to him. She sang to it, and gave it pretty things, and kept it happy.

The path ended abruptly. Granny Nan was quite obviously not there. Directly ahead, a shaft of moonlight illuminated the side of Lightning Rock and the little open crack that was the hob's grotto.

Toby knelt down on the moss. He bent his head, glancing around surreptitiously. He saw nothing, except bright things twinkling inside the hole—offerings of pretty stones, mostly. People with troubles would bring little offerings to Granny Nan and she would take them to the hob and pass on the requests: Gerda Murray's cow is drying up . . . the pain in Lachlan Field's back keeps him from earning his bread . . .

He decided to begin by introducing himself, just in case it did not remember him. "I am Toby Strangerson, the boy from the cottage, the witchwife's boy." He felt oddly stupid, as if he were talking to himself. "I am very grateful to you for saving me from the demon tonight, and bringing me home safely." Almost safely—no bones broken, anyway.

He fumbled for the two coins, and found something small and sharp also. He remembered that Granny Nan had given him a pretty stone. He left the pebble in his sporran and brought out the money.

"I brought these for you. I hope you like them." He tossed them into the grotto. They clinked on the gravel.

Silence. No sound, no wind. Nothing.

He was suddenly quite certain that the hob was not there. He was talking to himself.

Somewhere a twig cracked.

His heart jumped madly. He peered around, waited, heard nothing.

"We can't find Granny Nan." He spoke faster. "We are worried about her, because she is frail and the night is cold. Will you lead me to her, please? Or send her home?"

Behind him, somebody chuckled.

He was on his feet in an instant, staring into the darkness, aware that he must be visible against the patch of moonlight. His heart thumped in his chest . . . *Dum* . . . *Dum* . . . Somebody sniggered, giggled.

Crazy Colin!

Crazy Colin Campbell was here in the grove, and he would still have the knife.

Shift . . .

The trunks of the trees gleamed with a frosty light, every leaf and twig clearly visible. The mad drum beat steady time. Off to the left, Granny Nan's body was a tiny crumpled heap in the shrubbery. A man was creeping up the path, knife glittering, teeth bared in an ecstasy of blood lust. He could not hear the drummer, could not see the eerie blue glow.

The husky boy stepped into shade, out of the moon-light. While he watched the killer come, he gripped the rusty bangle on his left wrist, pulled at it until the lock snapped. He tossed it away.

The man jumped and peered around to see where the sound had come from.

The boy worked on the right cuff. That was harder. Blood oozed from his wrist before the foul thing yielded. This time the madman heard the breaking and located the noise. He started forward again, panting with excite-ment and making little circles in the air with the point of his knife.

When he was within reach, the waiting boy shot out a hand to grip the knife arm; he took the man by the throat with the other. He squeezed until the arm bones crumbled and the blade fell to the ground. Then he crushed the lunatic's throat as a man might crack a flea, watching him die—eyes bulging, mouth open, making no sound audible through the relentless, all-pervading rhythm: *Dum . . . Dum . . .* Later he tossed the twitching corpse away like an empty eggshell.

8

Granny Nan had been dead for hours. Her body was cold and stiff, and it weighed no more than a bundle of branches. Toby cradled it in his arms as he strode down the path, trying not to see the loathsome gash across her throat, black with dried blood.

He went by the waiting men without pause, heading for the cottage, hearing them muttering angrily among them-selves as they followed. Quick though he was, they would have seen the tears coursing down his cheeks. It was shameful for a grown man to weep, but he hardly cared.

A murderer weeping? He had killed again. For the fourth time in one night his hands had killed, and this time he had slain the wrong man. The corpse stiffening in the copse should be Fat Vik, not Colin. Crazy Colin had been born faulty. Whether that was the hob's doing or mere chance, it had certainly not been Crazy Colin's choice. The terror and slaughter at Norford Bridge had spoked his wheels completely, yet the war had not been his fault either. The guilt was Vik's, who had put the knife in his fist.

Who had slain Crazy Colin? Toby Strangerson or the demon? He could no longer deny that he had a demon in his heart. He could no longer believe that the hob had saved him in the dungeon. That had not been the hob taking him over just now to commit another murder, for the hob worked more directly. When the soldiers' drums had annoyed it, the men had been felled by cramps. Years ago, a wandering tinker had tried to chop firewood in the copse; his ax had turned in his hand, slashing his leg, and he had bled to death. Stealing another mortal's body to be executioner was demon stuff, not the hob's style.

The drumming heart and the ghostly blue light were symptoms of the demon. It had taken control of Toby in the castle and led him safely home, but it had not abandoned him then; it had merely dropped the reins for a while. When danger loomed again, it had reasserted its control. The demon must be just as concerned with Toby Strangerson's well-being as he was himself, because now they shared the same body. Crazy Colin had been a threat, so the demon had killed him. It had solved the problem and again withdrawn, like a man turning a warhorse loose in the pasture to frolic and graze. When next the trumpet sounded, the rider would mount the steed once more.

Whose man was he now? He belonged to a demon.

He had sensed that the hob was absent—had it fled when his demon approached its grotto? But then why had it not saved Granny Nan earlier? Perhaps it had known of Lady Valda's arrival and quit the glen altogether. Useless to try and guess . . . no mortal could understand an elemental.

So twice Toby Strangerson had been possessed. The demon had overlooked the manacles the first time. It must have learned from his thoughts that they would be a problem, so it had disposed of them, knowing that he could not do so by himself. Therefore the demon knew what he was thinking and doing, even when he was not aware of its presence. It was doubtless reading his mind even now, chortling to itself in whatever fashion demons showed mirth. It was learning. It was growing more proficient at using the human body it had stolen.

What would happen next? Who would he kill next? What horrors might he find himself committing? He ought to cut his own throat first, or turn himself in for impalement. Men possessed often took their own lives—like the gravedigger's apprentice in Oban two years ago, who had run amok with a mattock, butchering women and children. They'd found him in bed with his wrists slashed. Could Toby Strangerson do that? Would his hands obey him if he tried? Would suicide be release, or just a victory for the demon?

He kicked the cottage door open, hearing the latch splinter. The fire had crumbled to embers, but his eyes were well adjusted to darkness. There was enough light for him to carry Granny Nan over to the bed and lay her there. He sank to his knees, laid his head on his arms, and let the sobs come until he gasped for breath and his throat ached.

The door thumped shut at his back.

"Go away!"

"No, lad," said the smith. "It is you who must go."

Toby looked around angrily. Old Eric stood there as solid as his own anvil, but the others had remained outside. Shrewd! If Toby had to trust one of them, it would be this one; they had known that.

"We'll see that she is laid to rest," the big man growled, "and the hob will care for her soul. She's been dead a long while. No one will blame you for it."

No, it had not been Toby's hand holding the knife, but if he had heeded Granny Nan's warning, if he had avoided the fight with Forrester, if he had hidden out in the copse instead of letting the soldiers take him . . . any of those *ifs* and he could have been here to save her from Crazy Colin.

Why had the hob not defended her, or at least warned her? Why, after all these years, had it proved so fickle?

The other death did not matter. The madman's body would not be found for months or years. No one would mourn Colin, and likely the killing would be attributed to the hob's vengeance anyway.

"The Sassenachs will come soon." Smith moved closer. "Can you make it as far as Annie's, lad? Or must we fetch a donkey?"

Toby on a donkey? He heaved himself to his feet, although the effort took every fragment of strength he had left. He leaned his head against a rafter for support, feeling its cold roughness. "I'm not a child! I can walk!"

"Then go. Take your bundle and—" The smith's hand flashed out and seized Toby's wrist.

Toby tried to jerk away, but the man's grip was as tight as his smithy tongs. For a moment they faced off, the two best sets of shoulders in the glen, jaws set. . . . Then the younger man yielded. He would not have been taking the weight-lifting crown this year.

"You're bleeding!" The smith peered at the scrapes. "The hob's doing?"

The hob had not been there, but to say so would provoke unanswerable questions.

"You think I pulled them off by myself?"

Pause for thought . . . then Eric released him. "No. No man could do that." His scarred and weathered face peered up at Toby appraisingly. "You have been working strange wonders tonight, lad."

Toby looked down at the tiny body on the bed. "Not wonders enough," he whispered.

A heavy hand squeezed his shoulder. "She had more time than most. She was old when I was a pup and when my father was, too. The glen will miss her. She did not say who was to care for the hob after she had gone?"

"No. She said someone would, but she did not say who."

"Well, we'll find out in good time, I'm thinking. Go to Annie, now. She's expecting you, and it's almost dawn already. Stay on the dirt as much as you can, boy, so you don't leave tracks in the frost. We'll get you safely out of the glen."

There was something that should be said now. Oh, yes. "Thank you." Why was that such an effort? Why did he feel so resentful for their help?

"It is we who are grateful," the smith said. "You raised your fist to a swordsman. Courage is a fine thing in a man, but by rights you should have died, lad. Even big men bleed. Don't make a habit of being reckless. Play the odds when you can."

A Campbell of Fillan counseling discretion? Truly, the skies would be full of flying pigs tomorrow. There was nothing more to say. Toby stooped and went to fetch his bundle. As an afterthought, he found Granny Nan's jar of salve. Then he headed for the door. Annie's croft was close to Bridge of Orchy. He could walk another couple of hours without dying of exhaustion; it was no worse than prizefighting.

As he bent for the lintel, the smith said, "May good spirits care for you, *Toby of Fillan.*"

He stopped and looked around, leaning against the jamb. He could still dredge anger from his pit of fatigue, and his resolve had been forged long since. "Oh, no! I will have a new name. I will make my own name in the world, Master Campbell. But it will never be that one."

The big man's jaw clenched at this affront to his beloved glen. "Choose what name you want, then, bastard. Will you have the world love it or hate it?"

"Fear it!" Toby said, leaving his birthplace forever.

THREE

Guiding Light

1

Annie Bridge was one of four Annie Campbells in the glen. Her cottage was among the largest, with two sizable rooms. Here she had raised three strapping sons after her husband died at Leethoul. When King Fergan had abjured his allegiance to the English in 1511, the oldest had marched off to avenge his father. When Fergan had escaped from captivity in London in 1516 and returned to the Highlands to light the beacon on the hills again, the other two had followed the laird to Parline Field. For the last three years, Annie had lived alone.

She was a gaunt, white-haired woman with all the softness and compassion of a grindstone. Her face and hands were dried to brown leather by a lifetime's toil and weather. She was stooped but unbending, and she peered menacingly at the world as if daring it to try anything more. She detested the English with passion, and she would do anything at all for a man who had killed one of them. She was also an excellent cook.

Toby had slept, eaten, slept again, washed, and shaved. Every muscle in his body ached and his joints were stiff as gateposts. Normally he enjoyed that familiar feeling—it was a sign of growth and progress and greater strength in future. Now he could find no satisfaction in it. About this same time yesterday, he had prided himself on perfecting the powerful body he had been born with, but then he had watched his own hands crush the life out of men and twist iron bars like dough. Strength was no longer a virtue. The demon had made a mockery of his ambitions.

With sunset angering the western sky, he was eating another meal. The table in the front room held more food than even he could have consumed in a week, although Helga Burnside always told him he ate more than the entire Sassenach garrison. He felt very odd, struggling to come to terms with the sudden shift in his life. He kept picturing ice on a burn—the sudden thaw that turned a smooth white pavement into a foaming torrent. Toby Strangerson's world had just broken up like that, with him not very far across yet.

He should be mourning Granny Nan. He should be worrying about the demon in his heart, the English hunting him, the dangerous passage through Glen Orchy, even the rebels who were probably waiting to recruit him at the far end—and yet all he could feel was a shivering excitement that he was leaving the glen at last to seek his fortune in the world. He chewed, and he wondered.

Seated in the doorway to catch the light, Annie sewed with quick, deft strokes. She turned her head to see how he was faring. "Take more of that beef! And of the goose. The fat'll keep you warm in the hills."

Toby reached out to slice the beef. Fall was the best time of year for eating, the time when the cattle were slaughtered and even the poor could hope to eat meat. Annie snapped at him to stop being so picky, take a decent helping.

"I'll beggar you!" he protested.

For a fleeting moment, something lit her craggy face as a ray of sun on a snowy day turned drabness to diamonds. "Boy, you don't know what it means to me to feed a man again. It warms my old heart to see you put it away. Empty the board and I'll keep filling it gladly."

What was a man to do but keep eating?

Ask a few discreet questions with his mouth full?

For instance: "Any word from the castle?"

Annie lifted her work to her teeth and bit off a thread. "Aye. The Sassenachs have been in a pretty turmoil, I'm glad to say. They've put guards on the roads, and they're riding the hills."

Toby chewed for a while, waiting for more. Then he asked, "Not searching the village or threatening to take hostages?"

"Now why would they be doing that?" Annie raised a needle to eye level and squinted to thread it. "Why would they be looking in the village when there's a horse missing?"

"Oh. The horse hasn't been found?"

"Well, they've not thought to look under Murray MacDougal's bed yet."

Fortunately Toby was not trying to swallow anything just at that moment. He laughed. He laughed the laugh that Granny Nan always said was worse than a clap of thunder and would excite the hob. He felt guilty at being able to laugh already, with her not a full day dead yet.

If Falcon was still missing, then the Sassenachs must assume their quarry had ridden off to join the rebels. Annie's serene approval suggested that he might risk other, more dangerous questions.

"And how do they account for my escape from the dungeon?"

The old woman looked at him sharply. "You were there, weren't you?"

"But what I remember and what they tell may not walk hand in hand."

She nodded, stitching again. "It was that fool woman, they say—the one that wanted to hire you. She went down to the cells to persuade you to change your mind about entering her service." The old woman's voice changed timbre. "That's what they're saying she was after, and I don't want to hear any details if it's not the case. They say you knifed her. They're calling you a mad beast and very dangerous."

Toby chewed, marveling that he could speak so easily with old Annie. Usually his tongue froze solid when there were women nearby. He realized she had not mentioned any dead bodies in the dungeon.

"I don't hold with ladies being knifed," Annie added. "As a rule. But there's rules and there's rules, and if that one is what they say she is, then it's a true shame you didn't do a better job while you were at it."

So Valda had explained the wound in her breast.

How had she accounted for the table, the scroll, the blood-stained bowl, and all the other gear of her gramarye? Perhaps she had hexed them out of sight, but what had become of the bodies . . . or had there been no bodies? Toby had brained one man and broken another's neck. His demon vision had seen the four as other than human, and the lack of mention of bodies was unwelcome confirmation. The bodies had recovered and walked away. If someone now broke Toby Strangerson's neck . . . would he do the same?

Again Annie bit a thread. "Here, try them on."

He rose and went to accept the trews she had been making. She ostentatiously turned her back to observe the sunset, but Toby turned his back, too. He removed his belt, letting his plaid hang from his shoulder while he pulled the trews on. The new tweed was pleasantly rough on his legs and came with its own fresh peaty smell, but he hated the thought of having to wear such a restrictive garment. He laced up the embarrassing flap in the front and then let Annie inspect the result.

"They're fine," he said. "Perfect fit. I don't know how to—"

"Bend over. Yes, they'll do. I wish there was time for me to make you a shirt, too, and a jerkin. Couldn't manage boots, of course . . . "

"You've done more than enough already. But you'll excuse me if I stay with the plaid for now?" He stepped by her and went outside, round to the back of the house in search of an area large enough to dress in.

He was unhappy at the thought of giving up his plaid. Legs and arms covered? Feet crammed into boots? But if he was going off to the Lowlands and other foreign parts, Annie had insisted, then he would have to dress like a Sassenach. The same idea had evidently occurred to others. Neighbors had delivered two shirts, a tabard, and a pair of boots—curiosities that had found their way to the glen years ago by one way or another and been lying in clothes chests ever since. None of them had come close to fitting him.

It was troubling—were these tributes rewards for killing Godwin Forrester, blood money? Or did the glen really care about Toby Strangerson after all? Likely he was just being handed his fare out of town and good riddance.

He returned with the trews over his arm. Annie took them as he returned to the table.

"I'll put them in with your things." She fussed with his bundle, which she seemed to have been adding to all day. "You'd best be putting this in your sporran for safekeeping." She dropped Grannie Nan's purse in front of him.

As he obeyed, his fingers found something in there already. He took it out and looked at it properly for the first time. It was clear and angular, one end broken and the other perfectly faceted, gleaming in rich purple—amethyst, obviously, for amethyst was common in the glen. A wandering tinker might pay a couple of pennies for a good crystal like that.

Annie's sharp eyes had noticed.

He tucked it away again quickly. "It was a present from Granny Nan. You know how she was always looking for pretty things to take to the hob, but lately she grew quite odd about it, worrying, hunting and hunting. And last night . . . saying good-bye . . . think she confused me with the hob . . . Just want to keep it for a while . . . " That was enough explanation. Annie wouldn't tell anyone, and why should it matter if she did? He took a very large bite of fresh bap, not as good as Granny Nan's, but quite adequate.

Annie nodded solemnly. "When Eric left, I gave him a new plaid. The old one's still hanging on the peg, waiting to be washed." She gathered up her sewing bag. She paused on her way by the table. "What's wrong?"

"Nothing," he mumbled. Her husband had died before Toby was born.

"You were giving me an awful funny look, Toby Strangerson!"

He felt his face redden from his chin to his hair. "I

was just thinking that I never suspected you of being a sentimental person. And I was wondering why you told me about the plaid."

She went on her way, out of his sight. "You've got some growing up to do yet. You're a cynical lad, Toby. Understandable, of course. There's a sword ben the house that you are to take with you."

"Sword? I can't use a sword!"

She appeared at his side again, dangling a bucket in each hand. "And who's ever going to find out? The likes of you wearing a sword will not meet many challenges, I doubt. One look and they'll be tipping their hats to you. Old Bran Westburn sent it. He says it's drunk much English blood in its time, but it's getting thirsty again. So you'll take it. I'm off to milk."

"I can do that for you!"

"You stay here!" Annie snapped. "Eat until you can eat no more. Then take the sword and your bundle and be on your way like I said. We'll have no good-byes."

Toby started to rise.

"Eat!" she barked.

He sank back on the stool. He was completely full, but he reached for the meat again to please her. How to put his gratitude into words? He was a tangle-tongue, with no gift for speeches. "I don't know how to begin to—"

"Then don't. I want no thanks from you, Toby Strangerson." She paused in the doorway. "You're a nice enough lad, but I'm glad you're leaving, more glad than I can say. The whole glen will be cheering to see you gone and the only pity is that you aren't taking the no-good Vik Tanner with you. We'll get him out somehow, though, or some husband'll knife him, and that'll be all of you."

Stunned, he said, "All . . . ?"

Her face was shadowed, but her voice was bitter as sloe berries. "Married off over the hills or wandered away. Don't you understand? You've been the shame of the glen all these years. Did no one ever tell you? Did you never hear of the Taming? Oh, they tamed us, I can tell you, tamed us well! All the strong young men had gone and few returned, but there were still men here. They had things between their legs, anyway, so they claimed to be men. But they didn't burn the castle when the Sassenachs took the women. After a month or so, when the English had tired of the six, they offered to exchange them. No grandmothers, they said, but we younger ones could take their place, spell them off. Do you suppose we lined up at the gates?"

He could only shake his head, his throat knotting painfully.

"You're very right!" Annie grew louder. "We didn't. Of course I had three wee ones to care for, so I couldn't go, could I now? We all had some excuse. Children. Husbands and fathers who locked us up. Who was going to be first to volunteer to be a harlot? Who wanted to satisfy a squad of Sassenachs every night? All those widows . . . but we all had excuses. Men and women both, we had our excuses. And this way there could only be six Sassenach bastards, no more. That was important. No more than six. Well, six there were of you, and every day since you were born, Toby Strangerson, the sight of you has been a cut across the eyes for us, a reminder of our shame, a reminder that *we were too cowardly to help our own!* So leave the glen. Take your rotten half-brother with you—I wish you would. When you've all gone, then perhaps we can start to forget."

She marched out the door with her buckets, firing a final shot: "I want no thanks from you." Then she had gone.

Toby rose. He had lost his appetite; he wanted no more of her hospitality on those terms. Providing a meal and some clothes was certainly easier than whoring for Sassenachs all winter.

It helped, though. He need feel no guilt for accepting help.

So much for the Campbells' friendship.

So much for their famous courage.

2

He was almost out the door when he decided that there could be no harm in *looking* at the sword. He went through to the other room. Annie had not picked a very good hiding place—he could see right away that there was something under the pallet. It would certainly not be very comfortable to sleep on. He knelt down and reached for it.

It was a two-handed broadsword, double-edged and almost as long as he was. It seemed both old and of poor quality, probably made right here in the glen. The guard was a simple crosspiece, and there was a weight on the pommel for balance. In the hands of a strong man it would have had value against a knight too much armored to move nimbly, but knights did not fight like that anymore. Nowadays the gentry stood behind the guns and directed the cannon. Even on a rainy day, when firearms were unreliable, a shield and short claymore or a musket with a bayonet would be a safer weapon. The blade was well nicked by use, but had been sharpened and greased recently, probably that very morning. The scabbard was a crude thing of wood and leather that looked ready to fall apart.

He had no use for a sword like that! It was heavier than a sack of oats. It would attract attention to him, and he was not much over a mile from the Sassenachs at Bridge of Orchy. Common sense told him to put it back where he had found it and leave without it, but the feel of the worn leather binding on the hilt and the sense of power as he hefted its weight sent shivers all through him and filled him with a hateful, irresistible longing. A blade like that would make him a man to reckon with—a big man with a big sword.

He slipped the strap over his shoulder. If he found it too heavy, he could always throw it away in the bog, yes? He slung his bundle over his other shoulder and walked out into the dusk.

There was no road where he was going. Beinn Inverveigh on his right and Beinn Bhreac-liath on his left were masses of darkness against a stormy sky. Glen Orchy closed in around him, narrow and eerie. The moon would be up soon, but meanwhile he stumbled on the rough ground, stubbing his toes. He passed four or five cottages at a distance and twice dogs barked, but no one came to the doorways to wave. Now he knew what the Campbells thought of his departure—*good riddance!*

The feeling was mutual.

Going to see the world. Going to seek his fortune.

With a sword! Why did he covet that great blade so strongly? Was it Toby Strangerson who felt that way, or the demon? In a few minutes he would meet up with his companions. Then perhaps a thunder of diabolic heartbeat and his arms would take over, the sword would whistle through the air, slicing heads clean off. He ought to throw the horrible thing in a patch of bracken and go on without it.

He didn't—or couldn't.

He wondered why, during his two episodes of possession, he had heard his own heartbeat drowning out all other sounds. He was not normally conscious of his heart, although obviously it had been pumping away since his birth and would continue until the exact moment of his death. An immortal might find that constant thumping very strange, or even annoying. It was almost as if he had been forced to listen to what the demon heard. The cure for possession was a blade through the heart.

He heard a shout behind him and turned.

"Toby! Toby!" Hamish came staggering over the moor, slim and stooped under a pack almost as large as himself. "You keep your promises, Toby!" The boy's dark-tanned face was an excited gleam of eyes and teeth. He was panting with exertion or excitement.

No monster heartbeat; no sinister glow brightening the twilight . . . the sword stayed in its scabbard. Toby breathed again.

"I'll keep the one about the gallows, too." They fell into step, Toby shortening his stride. "I take it you're looking forward to this?"

"Oh, yes!" The kid gasped his agreement. "This is a real adventure, going off over the hills with you, Toby! Friends in adversity? We're outlaws together, aren't we! Mates?" He looked up hopefully.

As a friend, little Hamish would be less use than the broadsword. Hamish didn't want a friend, anyway; he wanted a hero. The sort of friend Toby needed was . . .

He didn't. Some men were strong enough to manage by themselves, so they had no need of friends. He was one of those men. He'd gotten along well with Hamish's brother Eric, but even they had never been close—no boy had wanted to be seen consorting with the bastard very often. Toby Strangerson had been a loner all his life, and he would stay that way.

Mustn't upset the kid, though. "Friends," he agreed.

With a sigh of relief, Hamish heaved his monstrous pack higher on his shoulders. "You worried about the bogy?"

"Not as long as you're with me."

Hamish chuckled with jittery glee, not realizing that Toby was serious. If the Campbells wanted to dispose of him by feeding him to the bogy, they would not have sent Hamish along.

"Where're you going, Toby?"

"I promised I'd see Meg as far as Oban. And you?"

"Pa says I must go and stay with Cousin Murray."

"Who's Cousin Murray?"

"Murray Campbell of Glen Shira. I'm to stay with him until Pa sends word that it's safe to come home. He sounds old and cranky, but Pa says he should have books. Pa met him once, years ago. Where are you going after Oban, though?"

"Try to get a boat there, I suppose." Toby tried to shrug, but the sword wouldn't let him and Hamish wouldn't see anyway. "After that, I don't know. Travel the world."

"You're not going to join the Black Feathers?" The boy sounded both shocked and disappointed.

Not if he could help it, Toby wasn't. The rebellion had

been dragging on for years and showed no signs of success. The first thing he needed was an exorcism, and a town like Oban must have a sanctuary—but would the demon let itself be exorcised? If he tried to go there, would his feet obey him? Would his tongue explain the problem?

"The Sassenachs will be putting a price on your head, Pa says. How much do you think they'll . . . Not that anyone will take their silver, of course," Hamish added hastily, "but—"

"But it would be nice to know what I'm worth, you mean?"

"Pa says it might be as much as ten marks!" He sounded quite impressed that a friend of his would command a price that high. It was certainly more than the five shillings the steward had offered yesterday.

The moon was rising at their backs. The wind had fallen strangely silent. Glen Orchy was ominously still. Toby listened for the music he had been told to head for, but all he could hear was a trickle of the burn and Hamish's endless prattle. . . .

"What?"

"Cousin Murray's the keeper," Hamish repeated.

"Keeper of a shrine? A holy man, then? An acolyte?"

"Sort of. A shrine isn't a sanctuary."

"But it has a tutelary?"

"Just a spirit." Hamish heaved his pack higher on his shoulders. He chuckled. "More than a hob."

The night was already cold. The ground was squashy underfoot. Not a breath of air moved, yet there was a sound . . . right at the limit of hearing, a lute was playing a plaintive melody. That was the sign they had been told to listen for, where they would meet with Meg Tanner and their unnamed guide. He veered toward it. If Vik was there with her, Toby would let his demon try out the sword. He shivered at his own black humor.

He was being unfair. He had been entrusted with two youngsters' lives, and he wasn't trustworthy any longer. He could not even rely on himself, so why expect them to? He ought to warn Hamish . . .

But he had not killed the boy on sight. He had not harmed those pompous village elders in the night, nor old Annie. So far his private demon had behaved itself when in well-behaved company. It had acted only when he was in danger—a curiously helpful and nonaggressive demon! If he told Hamish about it, Hamish would flee. He would run back and tell the whole glen. Then every man's hand would be against Toby Strangerson, not just the Sassenachs'. Did all traitors rationalize their betrayals so easily?

"What sort of work will you look for, Toby?"

"Needlework."

"You mean swords?"

"I mean needles. Embroidery."

"Eric used to say you had no sense of humor."

"That's not true! He did not say that!"

"He did," Hamish muttered, "but I think only when he'd just done something especially stupid that you hadn't joined in. I know he said you were the last man to take to a party and the first one to want in a tight spot."

Thinking that would make a fair epitaph, Toby said, "Ah! Listen!"

In the darkness ahead a woman was singing "The Flower of the Hill," with the lute weaving rainbows of music around her voice. It was a strangely moving sound in this lonely, haunted glen.

Wee Hamish Campbell was a walking library. Toby Strangerson was a muscle-bound dolt . . .

"You know, this must sound funny. I mean, I was raised by a witchwife, but I don't really know the difference between an adept and an acolyte, or a keeper of a shrine. Granny Nan never spoke of such things."

"Don't suppose she knew. I mean, I'm not trying to—"

"Granny Nan never read a book in her life."

"And reading is all I have ever done!" Hamish's laugh was a nervous twitter of sparrows. "An adept is someone who has studied the occult. I suppose acolytes are adepts, too, but usually 'adept' is used in the bad sense, like the black arts. A witchwife like Granny Nan wouldn't know any ritual or gramarye. She just kept the hob happy. Self-taught. A natural."

Like Toby Strangerson swinging a broadsword, as opposed to a trained fencer like Captain Tailor. "You mean a spirit is a hob, but bigger, sort of?"

"Sort of." Sounding uneasy, Hamish dropped his voice. "A hob's an elemental—mischievous, unpredictable. The books say that a spirit is . . . bigger, I suppose. Benevolent. A tutelary has a sanctuary, with acolytes and worshipers making offerings. A shrine is in between, with a keeper or two. People make pilgrimages to shrines, though, if the spirit is well thought of."

Toby sounded them in his mind: hobs, spirits, tutelaries. Witchwives, keepers, acolytes. Grotto, shrine, sanctuary. Elementals, adepts. Demons, hexers . . . were these all just words in the night? Could they ever mean anything to an ignorant country lad?

"And demons?"

"They're bad!"

"I know that. Are they much the same, though? Bad spirits?"

Still the woman and her lute sang of sorrow and loneliness in the night. She had a gorgeous clear voice. Toby had never dreamed that his guide would turn out to be a woman.

Hamish had been thinking, anxious to impress his big friend, flattered by his attention. "There's differences. An acolyte worships and tends a tutelary, just like a witchwife and her hob—serves it. Hexers compel demons and use gramarye to force them to do their bidding. Any spirit is local, whether it's a tutelary or just a hob. Demons are not attached to one place. Well, sometimes they are. Mostly demons are attached to *things*."

"Or people?" Toby said.

"Sometimes people, yes—husks, they're called, or creatures. More often jewels, though. I read in a book that hexers imprison demons in jewels."

That explained Lady Valda's dagger.

"Thanks, Littledirk. You know something?"

"What?" Hamish asked warily.

"You've taught me as much in the last minute as your pa did in five years of schooling."

Hamish chuckled, much pleased. "More, I expect, from the way he still talks about you."

3

Two people sat on a boulder in the moonlight. The small one, with her hair dangling in two long braids below her bonnet and bare feet showing under the pleats of her dress, was easily recognizable as Meg.

The second was a youngish man of no great height but notably wide shoulders. He had a clean-shaven face with a high, angular nose. The sword at his belt was a basket-handled short claymore, nothing like Toby's cumbersome broadsword. He wore a tartan shirt under his plaid; he had on hose and shoes. He stood up, still holding his lute.

As there was no one else present, the singer must have been Meg Tanner. Toby was surprised, yet not sure why—so strong a voice from so small a person, perhaps.

"Campbells are the most notorious liars in all Scotland," the man announced cheerfully. "They said you were big."

"I'm not?"

"Understatement can be carried to deceptive extremes. Still, you are the chivalrous chevalier who saved the damsel and slaughtered the unsavory Sassenach, so I will shake your hand."

Toby left his fists at his sides, not sure what to make of this stranger in the night. His voice was an odd mixture of Highland burr and English drawl. The fancy words indicated that he was not an ignorant peasant—and implied that Toby was.

"Sir, I'll shake your hand when I know who you are."

"Names can be dangerous. I have several." The stranger chuckled and glanced at Meg as if sharing a joke, meanwhile removing his bonnet to scratch at a head of sandy hair braided at the back into a stubby pigtail. The move was slickly done, for when he replaced the bonnet and adjusted it, whatever emblem he had been wearing on it had disappeared. "How about 'Rory'? Rory MacDonald of Glencoe. Will that satisfy you, Toby Strangerson?"

It had better. There was nothing uncommon about sporting an emblem to show whose man you were, but Toby had a niggling half-recollection that in Rory's case it had been a silver badge. A silver badge meant either a chief or heir to a chief.

Toby accepted the handclasp. Of course, what Rory MacDonald wore in a deserted glen at night and what Rory MacDonald dared to wear in daylight might not be peas from the same pod. His palm was smooth, but there was no frailty in his grip. He studied Toby's face for a moment with steady pale eyes, then turned to his companion. "What by the demons of Delia have you got there, boy? Been looting the castle, have you?"

Hamish had lowered his burden to the ground with grunts of relief. "Food, sir, mostly. Clothes. Ma thought—"

"Mothers always do. You'll sink out of sight with that load. A true Highlander carries one day's rations and nothing more, so throw all the rest away." He aimed an arrogant finger at the broadsword. "And you, Strangerson? What foul monstrosities are you planning to slaughter with that thing?"

"Lutists."

MacDonald stared at Toby for several seconds before making a small noise that might indicate amusement or just surprise. "Well, I suppose you can handle the weight. We'll be wading, remember."

Toby had concluded that he did not like Rory MacDonald of Glencoe. He turned to Meg, who was standing beside him—quite close beside him, eyes downcast. "Hello, Meg."

She looked up eagerly. "Toby?"

"I loved your singing. I didn't know you could sing like that."

"Did you ever ask me?"

"No . . . You're all right?"

"Thanks to you." She seemed to be waiting for something more.

He waited also, puzzled.

She bit her lip and turned away. "I did not have a chance to thank you properly, Master Strangerson, for your dauntless gallantry. It was very brave of you to rescue me like that."

Toby said, "Any man would have done the same."

Rory and Hamish were on their knees together, hauling objects out of Hamish's bundle. "Books? Why in the world do you need . . . "

Meg tossed her head without looking around. "Your courage is exceeded only by your modesty and does you great honor, sir. I was indeed fortunate that you were at hand to succor me in my moment of peril."

She must have got that out of a book, or else she had been infected by that Rory man's flowery way of talking. In Strath Fillan, words were short and meant what they said.

"Considering how stupid you were to be there by yourself, you certainly were fortunate."

She whirled around, braids dancing. "Stupid? I came to warn you of danger!" Her breath was a pearly mist in the frosty moonlight.

Toby laid his sword and pack on the ground and knelt to inspect the supplies Annie had added to it. Despite his superior airs, the Rory man made sense when he said that carrying unnecessary weight would be folly. Yet nothing in Toby's collection seemed superfluous. He could carry it all without tiring. He decided to leave the bundle as it was.

Meg's bare feet were still there, one of them tapping angrily on the stony ground. She was riled because he had called her stupid. So she was! Her folly had caused the deaths of Granny Nan and four men. It had led to Toby being possessed by a demon and driven from his home—even if he did not much mind the last bit. Still, he could hardly upset the kid by telling her all that. He looked up and smiled at her.

"It was a kind thought," he said gently. "But I can look after myself better than you can. You must realize that you're close to being a woman now. Soon men will begin to lust after you. You should have sent a man with the message, if you thought it was that important."

"Or a real woman, perhaps?"

The moon was behind her. He could not see her face under the brim of her bonnet.

"A man, of course. A woman would have had the same trouble."

The foot tapped faster. She heaved her cloak higher on her shoulders. "I was doubly fortunate that you recognized me in time, though."

He looked up, puzzled by her tone. "Recognized you? I didn't. I didn't know it was you."

Meg said, *"Oh!"* very violently. "You crude, oversized, shambling ox, Toby Strangerson! What does it take to get an idea into that lump of granite you call a head? Why don't you ever even *try?*" She whirled in a dance of braids and stalked away.

He shrugged to himself, remembering that last night's experience would have been terrifying for a child and this wild flight into the unknown could hardly be helping calm her down. He should have swallowed his stupid pride and let her rotten brother accompany her . . . Fat Vik: her half-brother and probably his, too. She would have felt safer with someone she could trust. Now, if he could fasten the bundle to the hilt of the sword, he would have both hands free . . .

"Do it this way," Rory said, kneeling beside him. "Fine lass, that one."

"She's a nice kid."

"You think so?" Rory chuckled softly. "Feisty, I'd call her. There, try that. So you are leaving home, Toby Strangerson? It may be a long whiles before you are able to return safely."

"When the Fillan flows up Beinn Bheag will be soon enough."

The pale eyes regarded him steadily, shining in the

moonlight. "What of the grieving friends you leave behind?"

"They'll survive." In truth—no friends.

"Och, but they will mourn!" Master MacDonald shook his head in sorrow. "And surely there is some small window with a candle lit for you! You have left your heart in trust?"

To admit that there was no one at all who cared whether Toby Strangerson lived or died would be a statement of cold fact. It proved curiously difficult to say out loud. He could easily lie, of course, but lying would itself be a confession that the truth hurt, and it didn't. He had accepted long ago that a strong man must stand alone. He had no need of friends and he would find a woman to love when he had something more to offer than the shame of bastardy and an empty sporran. He had no need to explain all that to this stranger in the night. Besides, he had begun to wonder if the man already knew the answers and was making fun of him. He just shook his head.

Rory sprang to his feet. "We'll be on our way, then. You'll all do exactly as I tell you, because Glen Orchy is no romp in a featherbed."

"Just how does one get across the bog?"

"You talk nice to the wisp, of course."

Hamish said, "The *what?*" very squeakily.

"The wisp. The bogy, if you prefer. Bogy, boggle, wisp . . . a wild hob. It's not malicious as a rule. It won't meddle with you if you don't meddle with it, but it can get playful, like a bear cub. Come on." Rory hung his lute on his back and turned to go. "Bring the rope, Longdirk."

"Take it yourself."

Meg and Hamish gasped aloud. Toby had surprised even himself. He should not be refusing orders from a man of rank, and especially not one armed with a sword. Darkness and remoteness did not matter—he would be in mortal danger in a crowded street now.

"Indeed?" said the sandy-haired man softly. "Whose man are you, then, that speaks to me so? Who must I deal with when I have taught you your manners, little laddie?"

Toby Strangerson was an addlebrained idiot! His bundle hung on the hilt of his sword. By the time he had disposed of that and drawn the monster blade from its ramshackle scabbard, Rory would have put more holes in him than a charge of grapeshot. Even if Rory sportingly waited until they were both armed and ready, he could still win easily.

Himself, Toby did not need this self-proclaimed MacDonald of Glencoe. Himself, he would brave the hills and take his chances on starvation or freezing or betrayal, but he had given his word to Kenneth Tanner. He had Meg to consider, was responsible for Meg. Hamish Teacher would be no protector for her with Toby lying dead in the bog. He must back down, and quickly, and count himself lucky if he did not get his tongue slit anyway. Yet the apology stuck in his throat.

"Just don't call me that!" he said.

Rory made an incredulous sound. "I'll call you anything I want, boy. You'd rather be Toby the Bastard? I said, *'Bring the rope, Longdirk!'"*

In silence, Toby went for the rope and slung it over his shoulder.

"When I give you an order, Longdirk, you answer, 'Yes, sir!'"

"Yes, sir."

"And *run,* Longdirk."

"Yes, sir."

"Remember in future, Longdirk. Come along, everyone. May I carry your pack, Miss Campbell? Will you stroll with me this evening?"

Toby stalked off with the rope. He did not know what use it was going to be and would rather not know any sooner than he had to. He wondered why he had been so surly and pigheaded. He certainly did not care about his name. He was determined to find himself a new one, so why insist on the old? That was just dimwitted. And why had he made the snippy remark about lutists earlier? Why had he taken such a dislike to Rory of Glencoe?

He was not usually so childish. Boys of his own age

had spurned him, but by the time he was twelve, he had been looking most adults straight in the eye. He had learned that if he acted his size instead of his age, he would often be accepted as one of them. Now the Rory man was here to help him in his time of trouble—a gentleman, probably a noble, well-educated, and wise in the ways of the world. His fancy talk might have been an offer of friendship by gentry ways. So why was Toby Strangerson behaving so loutishly?

Perhaps because he was sure that the stranger was one of King Fergan's Black Feather rebels and intended to enlist another. If the help was conditional on that, then things were going to be tricky.

A few moments later, he was annoyed but not at all surprised to find Rory walking at his side, with the two kids following. The questions began:

"Tell me about your fight with the Sassenach."

"It was nothing much."

"Tell me anyway."

Toby considered his options. If he again challenged the man's right to give him orders, then dawn might find him still trapped in the glen, or lying dead on the heather. He had responsibilities to Meg and in lesser amounts to Hamish. He must cooperate.

"There wasn't much to it. He was pestering the girl. I knocked him down, he drew his sword, I found his musket lying in the grass, I hit him with it, but too hard. I didn't mean to kill him."

"Just like that? It's beautiful! And how did you escape from the castle?"

"Their manacles were old and rusty. I managed to free myself in the cell. Then Lady Valda came down to—"

"*Who?*"

"I'm told that's her name. Her emblem's a black crescent on purple. She rode in from Fort William."

"Spirits preserve us!" MacDonald muttered. "Black crescent? Black hair and a face to drive men insane?"

"Black hair, yes. Beautiful, certainly, but not my type."

"No?" Rory said skeptically. "Lad, if she decided *you*

were *her* type, then nothing would save you! You'd howl outside her window for the rest of your life. What exactly . . . Roughly, what did she want of you?"

"She said she wanted to sponsor me as a prize-fighter. I didn't believe that was what she really wanted. I knocked her men down, got out, stole a horse, and rode home."

Put like that, it was gibberish. He wondered how in the world he could expect to be believed. He wasn't.

"A singular narrative!" Rory MacDonald of Glencoe faked a yawn. "Can you add a few plausible details to undermine my native skepticism?"

"Only that I was raised by the witchwife. I think she enlisted the hob to rescue me."

"Ah! Now that helps. That does help. Just because hobs aren't smart, people assume that they aren't power-ful, but if a hob ever gets truly riled about something, it can be deadly. I know of one that shook down a castle and had boulders rolling off the hills. I wonder if it took a dislike to Lady Valda? Would I be completely crazy if I decided to believe you?"

The footing was very marshy now and there was a boggy scent in the air. Tendrils of faint white mist drifted close to the ground.

Toby had just been called a liar, but that was danger-ous bait. He ignored it. "Tell me about Lady Valda—sir."

"She was Nevil's favorite." Rory glanced around to make sure the youngsters were keeping up. "That's a courtly way of saying mistress. She was a hexer even then. She disappeared about ten years ago. Nevil put a price on her head, but she was never found."

Feet made sucking noises in the moss.

"King Nevil offered a reward for her? Why?"

"He didn't tell me. It was a hefty one."

"So what's she doing in the Highlands? Is she par-doned now?"

"I very much doubt it," Rory said firmly. "Wherever she's been, it was beyond Nevil's clutches, probably abroad."

"Perhaps she hid from him by gramarye."

"Do you think she's the only hexer in England? The king himself is an adept of renown. I cannot imagine why any woman would masquerade as her, though, so you are probably correct. I suppose I must let you live after all."

"What do you mean?" Toby growled.

"What I say. Your account of the fight agrees fairly well with Meg's—allowing for your touching modesty and her romantic fancies. I can't see how the encounter could have been faked, or set up in advance. But that flying-pig-singing-fish tale of your escape from the dungeon is pure malarkey. You're bait, my boy. You've been set up as a lure to lead the Sassenachs to my friends. The question now is whether you know it or not."

Toby stumbled, not entirely because the footing had just changed to bare rock.

Rory steadied his elbow with a disconcertingly powerful grip. "We're there. This is where we enter the bog. I'll lead you across alive."

Toby looked down at him angrily.

His guide beamed benevolently. "I mean it. Do you doubt that I would kill you? Do you doubt that I could?"

If he was a competent swordsman, which he probably was, then he was certainly capable of spitting Toby Strangerson. He might, of course, find himself with the same diabolical problems Crazy Colin had run into.

"If you can catch me."

Rory laughed, a flash of white teeth in the moonlight. "We're going to be roped together! But you have my word: I'll see you safely through."

"This is a change of plan?"

"Possibly a temporary one. You've made me curious. You're either a spy or a lure. If the Sassenachs set you up, then you're a traitor and a spy. You wouldn't be the first man to buy his life with a few solemn oaths. If Lady Valda is behind it, then there's gramarye involved. Since she's not on Nevil's side, I don't know what game you're playing. No, that's not right. What I mean is, I don't know who's using you, or how. Somebody is. Until I find out who and how, I'll let you live, Little Man." Rory turned to include the two kids in the conversation. "This is the edge of the bogy's bog."

4

"I came through last night," Rory continued, **"and it** never reached my knees, but we could go in up to our waists—icy water and mud. We'll be roped together, because the wisp may try to separate us in the mist."

Hamish moaned. The mist was closing in already.

"A wisp's just a sort of hob." Perhaps Rory meant that remark to be comforting. "I'd prefer that you go blindfolded, but you can look if you want. Just don't believe anything your eyes tell you. You'll see lights and strange shapes in the fog. Some of them may be ghoulies, trying to scare you off the path. Pay no attention to those—dead people are the least dangerous sort. Most of what you'll see will be only the wisp's idea of fun."

The wisp was not the only one with a nasty sense of humor, Toby decided. "And what if it leads us to our deaths?"

"It may," Rory said seriously. "I warned you this would be tricky. Fortunately, it likes music. I had no trouble last night; of course, there was only one of me." He kicked off his shoes and tucked them into the folds of his plaid. He left his hose on. "I can't guarantee that my lute will stay in tune in the damp, but the wisp doesn't seem to mind a few twangs. Hitch your dress up, Miss Campbell, as far as your modesty allows. Plaids, too."

The clammy fog was growing thicker, muffling the moonlight. Meg plucked up her dress and somehow tucked it into her belt. Toby hitched his plaid up until the hem was above his knees.

Rory began looping the rope under their arms. "I'll go first. We'll put this wee fellow next, because he's the strongest. Normally, we'd go in single file, but I'm going to tie both of you to him. Hold your tethers in front of you with a little slack in them, so if one of us falls, we don't drag the rest under, too. There's holes in the muck you can't see."

"I hope the wisp can hear your music over the noise of my teeth chattering, sir," Hamish said bravely. Meg was saying nothing at all, hovering close to Toby.

Rory hung his lute around his neck. "We'll find out."

"How can you tell which way to go?" With the others all strung to him, Toby felt like a spiderweb.

"That's up to the wisp!" Rory strummed strings to check the pitch. "Should do." He began to play a cheerful, jigging tune.

For long, shivery minutes, nothing seemed to happen. Then Toby realized that the mist had become patchy. Behind him, it remained solid, but over the marsh it was breaking up into pillars and sheets, opening gaps. Soon a faint glow flickered in the distance, a tiny candle burning on the water.

"There we are!" Rory said cheerfully and strode forward. "Our guiding beacon!" The others followed him, stepping down from the rock onto moss—soft, cold, and squelchy.

The moon must be shining somewhere overhead, but its light was diffused by the fog. The way led between pools and channels so dark that they seemed like empty space, between tufts of sedge and clumps of tall, spiky bulrushes, and through the slowly shifting coils and wraiths of mist. The twinkle of light ahead shifted; Rory changed direction. Soon it shifted again.

Somebody's teeth were chattering, providing a counterpoint to the jangle of the lute.

The muck underfoot grew softer, treacherous to walk on. Water came up over Toby's ankles, agonizingly cold. Hamish was the first to slip, going down on his seat with a splash and a cry. His rope jerked on Toby's chest. He scrambled to his feet again and they continued to trudge forward, heading for that illusive beacon glow. It receded before them, leading them on. Leading them where? Following a bogy into a bog was not a traditional mark of sanity.

The mist had begun to take on nightmare shapes: women writhing in slow and silent dances, giant faces, vague hints of ghoulies or bogeymen. They gleamed with an eldritch light of their own. Toby wondered how much was his own imagination and how much the wisp's reported sense of humor. Tangles caught at ankles, bulrushes brushed with wet fingers on shivering legs. The world had shrunk to the size of Granny Nan's cottage, enclosed in silvery fog monsters. Mud sucked harder around his feet, and slowly the cruel cold climbed higher on his shins. The footing was sludge or moss or tangled grasses, and never sure. Every step involved hauling a foot straight up before it could be moved forward. The light kept changing position until he lost all sense of direction.

Could the wisp detect his demon? Would it resent the diabolic intruder? He was sure that the hob had been gone from its grotto when he went to look for Granny Nan. If the wisp reacted that way, then Rory might march them in circles until they all froze to death. On the other hand, the demon had proved it would protect Toby Strangerson, so it was not likely to let him freeze or drown. Which was stronger—Lady Valda's demon or the bogy of Glen Orchy?

Meg cried out and disappeared completely. Toby hauled on the rope until he could grasp her arm and drag her upright, spluttering.

"All right?" Stupid, stupid question! His feet were sinking deeper as he stood there. Rory had turned to see, still strumming vigorously.

Meg shuddered. "Yes! Keep g-g-going!" Her sodden dress had fallen out of its tuck and was clinging to her slender legs.

The journey resumed, curving to the left. Water lapped around Toby's thighs and mud sucked at his feet. He was a beetle wading through cold porridge. Everyone's teeth were chattering now.

Rory's suggestion that Lady Valda had expected Toby to escape was an unwelcome complication that he should have thought of for himself. It was certainly plausible, for surely a hexer as powerful as everyone said she was ought not to have botched a conjuration so badly.

She had not explained her real motives. He had no idea why she had gone to all the trouble of demonizing him. To believe that she wanted him as an incubus would be stupid vanity, and he did not doubt Rory's statement that she could bewitch any man she wanted. Surely love charms did not require daggers and self-mutilation and bowls of blood—those must be gramarye of deeper, darker purpose. Why go to so much trouble over the big Highland lad? She must have been playing for higher stakes than just a prizefighter or a very questionable gigolo.

Tendrils of mist floated over the water like glowing fingers. Here and there they seemed brighter than they should be, and not matched to their reflections in the dark mirrored surface below. He could see three or four lights now, and he wondered how Rory knew which one to follow.

The water was up to his crotch. He glanced back and saw both Meg and Hamish waist-deep and struggling. The cold was making his whole body tremble. The lute sang a wild lament.

Rory had hinted that there might be a hex on Toby, but had he guessed about a demon? Predictably, he was fleeing from the glen, heading for the rebels in the hills. In a sense, he was a loaded gun that could fire at any moment. Who was the intended target? King Fergan?

Without warning, his feet slid from under him and he plunged into icy, inky blackness. He struggled upright, coughing and cursing and spitting. His mouth tasted of swamp and the water hurt in his nose. Now he was wet all over—his hair, his pack. He rescued his bonnet and tucked it in his belt. Cold was driving deep into his body, and he was the largest of all of them. How much of this could little Meg stand?

Two eyes glowed at him. He shied away and almost

fell again before he remembered Rory's warning. The wisp was playing tricks. The eyes drifted apart and became just two globes of fire. Then three. A dark shape threatened amid the bulrushes. Giant worms writhed, pallid faces grimaced.

"Go faster!" he shouted. "We're all freezing!"

"Daren't!" Rory shouted, still strumming. "If I fall, we're done for."

Splash, splish . . . The lute sang discordantly, hitting unexpected pitches, dissonant trills. A face with glowing red eyes and green teeth loomed out of the mist. Toby waved an arm through it, dissolving it into streamers.

Silence. Rory had stopped moving and stopped playing. The water was up to his waist. "This is bad! In case you haven't guessed, we're in deep trouble."

"We're getting deeper just standing here!" Toby snapped. "Play on. Move!"

Their leader was barely visible in the darkness. "I was never this deep last night. The wisp is playing with us!"

Or the wisp was trying to kill them. It didn't like demons in its swamp? Monstrous white shapes moved in the darkness, glowing with more than moonlight. The very silence was menacing.

"We haven't much t-t-time, sir," Hamish wailed.

"Which light do you fancy? That one? Or that one? Let's try the green one, shall we?" Rory shrugged and began playing again, picking his way forward through the cruel, cold water.

The mud sucked harder. Their progress had slowed to a snail's crawl. Every step was a struggle to pull up a foot, balance in the sludge on the other leg, move the foot forward without tipping over, find bottom again . . . Toby could not feel his toes at all, which did not help.

Meg submerged with hardly a splash, but he felt the tug. He hauled in the line, dragging her to him. He scooped her up in his arms. She and her pack together weighed more than he expected, but she was a frozen, trembling waif. She coughed and gasped and clung to him. Now he could no longer keep a grip on the line to

Rory. He sank deeper with every step. The muddy bottom sucked at his knees. Hamish's head went under and then reappeared, gasping that it was all right.

The music twanged painfully and stopped. Rory had gone. Toby almost overbalanced as the rope yanked him forward.

Then Rory came up right in front of him, his face plastered with mud and wet hair. "That's it!" he said hoarsely, between coughs. "I've lost the lute. The wisp won't cooperate without music. Sorry, children, but there's going to be four more ghoulies playing in the fog."

The glittering marsh monsters drifted closer. Every direction looked the same, the stars were hidden, and the cold was eating into bones. No sound except chattering teeth and thumping heart . . .

Demon! I'm dying!

Dum . . . Dum . . . Faint and muffled by the reeds, lost in the water sounds whenever anyone moved . . . It might be only his own normal heartbeat, but he thought it was coming from outside him, from *over there,* and in that case it must be a signal.

"Well, we can go faster without that damnable lute!" he said. "Follow me. Swim, or float on your backs. I'll tow you." *Demon? Which way?* Taking the lines over his shoulders, he plunged forward without waiting for argument.

He turned to the sound of the beat, clawing through sedge and bulrushes. No occult lavender glow came to lighten his path. The wisp's mocking beacons twinkled in red and green and blue, but he could barely see anything for the vegetation splattering water in his eyes. He felt no surge of demonic strength—this was Toby Strangerson fighting this battle, fighting for his life. Every few minutes he would pause and listen, locating that elusive thump, but to stop moving was to freeze, to sink deeper. Weeds clutched at his legs; the combined burden of Meg and his broadsword was driving him down. Rory and Hamish struggled along behind him, half wading, half floating, offering little resistance except when he had to pull them through tangles of sedge.

Dum . . . Dum . . . Why so faint? Why no demonic power? Was the bogy keeping the demon at bay? Were the two spirits locked in battle? Or was he imagining some foolish echo of his heart, struggling around in circles in the dark? Glowing faces bared fangs at him. His blood coursed and his lungs were bursting, but at least he must be warmer than the others. Would he arrive at the shore towing three corpses?

Ah! The ground was firmer and the water was down to his waist. The mist brightened overhead, taking on a sheen of moonlight.

"Almost there!" he yelled, and lost his footing as he trod on a painfully sharp stick. He went down in a bed of knives, it seemed, swallowed half the swamp, and struggled to his feet, helping Meg up. As he wiped the water from his eyes he saw the guards, a crowd of skeletal shapes looming out of the haze, arms spread to bar mortal intruders.

Rory was upright, teeth chattering wildly. "I know this part, it's a drowned forest. It's near the west shore, but we'll never get through it. Which way round? Left or right?"

Toby listened. Silence?

Rory cupped his hands and bellowed into the darkness: *"Jeral? Cruachan!"*

"Shut up!" Toby barked. "Be quiet."

More silence, just Hamish's chattering teeth—no, a faint *dum . . . Dum . . .*

"This way. Come on!" He scooped Meg up and set off again, letting the others wade behind or float as they could. The cold seemed to burn, it hurt so much. The water was below his waist now, yet he could move no faster, for the bottom was a tangle of branches and roots, hard and sharp. Deeper water would have helped to support his weight. Every muscle shuddered convulsively. Moonlight glowed brighter; pale wraiths floated between the dead white trees. The guardians seemed intent on barring the way to shore until the intruders froze to death, and surely that ending could not be many minutes off.

Almost without realizing, he had left the swamp and was scrabbling over a litter of driftwood, stumbling up a shingle bank, dragging the others behind him. Fire! He must have fire! If the water had penetrated his tinderbox, they were all going to die anyway.

Then his head came level with the land, and he saw light in the darkness—real flames, and none of the wisp's fox fire. A few hundred paces or so along the shore, someone was waving a lantern.

Rory shouted, "Cruachan!" again, and a faint cry responded, "Cruachan!"

5

The cottage was very small, just four dry-stone walls roofed with branches and sod. Meg was the only one who could stand erect in it. There was no chimney, no covering for the doorway, and one corner of the roof had collapsed, but a heap of peat glowed in the center, giving at least the illusion of warmth. At some time in the past it had been used for livestock, yet it was shelter from the night, and the travelers huddled gratefully around the fire to thaw.

The man named Jeral had disappeared. Rory had sent him off somewhere, and Toby found that troublesome. Someone had cleaned out this little hovel and covered the floor with rushes to make it habitable, but not recently. That was even more worrying.

Four faces gleamed faintly in the firelight. The shivering had mostly stopped. Wet wool steamed.

"Are we safe from the bogy here, sir?" Meg inquired.

"Probably." Rory eyed Toby thoughtfully. "I expect it's busy burying my lute. It's probably forgotten all about us, and it never worries overmuch about dry land things anyway. I would like to know why it took such a scunner to us."

Meg missed the implications of that dangerous question. "Where are we, then?"

"We're in Glen Orchy, still. A few miles down we'll get to Strath of Orchy and Dalmally, but we can worry about that in the morning."

Poor Master Rory had lost his fine shoes; his feet stuck out of the remains of his socks. Pity poor Master Rory!

Toby was thinking about trees. There were trees here. Trees implied an absence of people to turn them into lumber or firewood. No people meant no roads, no traffic. No one came through the haunted glen. But Rory did, and Rory now wore a black feather in his bonnet. The rebels had a shelter here that the English did not know about. The Jeral man had been sent off somewhere—possibly to fetch help.

Secrets were dangerous in time of war.

"I've been to Strath of Orchy!" Hamish announced. "That's where Kilchurn Castle is, and the laird's name is Hamish!"

Rory grunted. "*Lord* Hamish—Hamish Campbell, foster brother to the earl of Argyll."

The boy pulled a face. "How will you get by Kilchurn Castle, then, sir? It guards Pass of Brander, where the road's squeezed between the cliffs and the water—"

"We begin by hoping there are no Sassenachs there. Then we worry about Campbell traitors."

"But . . . you can see Ben Cruachan from Dalmally."

That innocent-seeming remark caused MacDonald of Glencoe to turn and stare at the boy. "What of it?"

Hamish flinched. "Nothing, sir! . . . Ma says I talk too much."

"Sensible woman."

Hamish subsided, shooting one of his owlish looks at Toby—meaning he thought he knew something that Toby was too stupid to work out for himself.

Rory turned his attention back to Toby. "You haven't explained how you managed to lead us out of the bog."

"I have a good sense of direction."

"A superhuman sense of direction? You escape from dungeons, from hexers, from bogies? You have more lives than a cat!"

"I hope so."

The rebel wanted to know what had vexed the wisp, how a mortal man had found his way out in the dark. Was the young fugitive merely a spy, or was he one of Lady Valda's demonic creatures? Let him wonder! Toby did not know the answers himself.

Hamish yawned. Meg caught the infection.

"May as well sleep," Rory announced, but he did not move. "Miss Campbell is bound for Oban. You, lad?"

"Pa told me to go and stay with Cousin Murray in Glen Shira. The keeper of the shrine of Glen Shira."

Rory snorted. "Old Murray Campbell? You know him?"

"No, sir."

"You have an interesting experience in store, then. And you, Man Mountain? Wither goest thou, Big Man?" He raised sandy eyebrows, waiting for Toby's reaction. He was not actually sneering; he just seemed to, because of his eagle-beak nose.

"I promised to see Meg safely to Oban, and then—"

"That was very rash of you, Longdirk. You're not really up to being a reliable protector with your history of blundering into trouble." Rory was still dropping hints about demons, but he wasn't sure. "Suppose I come along to hold your hand and we get her there between us, what then?"

Yesterday morning, Vik Tanner had tried to make Toby lose his temper. Baiting had not worked then. It would not work now.

"Then I'm going to travel and see the world."

Be a prizefighter and win large amounts of money.

"Mm? Travel where? To the Lowlands? To England? There must be a price on your head by now, you know. An insultingly small one, I expect, but every penny counts, as they say. You're not the sort to disappear into a crowd—not unless you walk on your knees, that is. How do you plan to feed that oversized carcass of yours?"

"Honest work."

"Digging ditches?" The sneer was undeniable now. "You're an ignorant country lout who won't last a week in the real world."

Meg looked shocked, Hamish owlishly worried.

"That isn't your problem," Toby said steadily. Demons would be, though.

"Lady Valda is. Besides, you intrigue me, Shoulders. The Sassenachs are hunting you; you killed one of them. You seem to have courage, unless it's all stupidity. Why aren't you planning to join Fergan, your rightful king?"

Toby eyed the fingers of red fire caressing the peat. "The brave Black Feathers? Tell me what you're fighting for."

Rory MacDonald considered Toby for a long moment before he answered. "For freedom. To clear our land of the oppressors. For our own ways, for our families, for justice."

Toby adopted what he hoped was an expression of amused cynicism. "Freedom, you say? One lord is much like another. I have no land, I have no family, and I'll believe in justice when I see it. Your fight is not mine, Rory MacDonald of Glencoe." He could add much more— that King Fergan was a rebel only because he had broken the oath of allegiance to King Nevil; that the wars were always started by the Scots and won by the English; that the English paid their troops, which the rebels did not . . . but he had said more than enough already.

The rebel was scowling. "You support the English?"

"No. Just a neutral."

"There are no neutrals in this war."

"My father was an Englishman."

"From what I was told, you can never know who your father was."

Evidently Meg had been yattering.

Toby turned himself so he had space to lie down— there would not be much room for four. He unfastened his pin and rearranged his damp plaid into a bedroll. Hamish copied him. Meg began fussing with her cloak with the same end in view. Only Rory continued to sit upright, apparently waiting for an answer.

The argument was a waste of breath. Toby was not about to lose his temper and neither of them would ever change the other's mind. "That's true—I am no man's son. So I'm free to make my own decisions, aren't I? I can think what I want, not what my pa tells me to think. I will never be King Fergan's man, Master Glencoe."

"We'll see about that." The rebel smiled thinly. "Again I tell you: there are no neutrals in this war."

Toby rolled over, facedown, and went to sleep—for the first time . . .

6

It had begun again. He was in darkness—utter, total, impenetrable darkness, as if he had sunk to the bottom of the bog. He was in silence. It always began with darkness and silence.

He could not move. His hands were behind him and his feet apart, as they had been in the dungeon. He could breathe, so he was not in the marsh. He was vertical, but he could feel no floor under his feet or wall at his back, no shackles binding his limbs. He was not conscious of cold or pain, but he was aware he had no clothes on. He floated in nothing, and waited.

The first time, or the first few times, he had assumed that he was dead. He hardly remembered the first times, except through a vague certainty that he had been here before, that this had happened before. There was someone else here also. Someone was hunting for him in the darkness, wandering, searching. At times he could hear her. She was calling to him, calling him by name; the name she was using was not his name, but he knew that he was the one she sought.

Soon the light . . . Yes, the light was coming now. It began as a very faint milky glow, no more than starlight glimmering on ghostly mist-shapes all around him, with darkness beyond. It grew brighter, but slowly, very slowly, while the filmy haze writhed, grew more definite, then faded again, dancing and twirling in endless variations of shape, glowing in indefinable colors like the lights a man saw when his eyes were closed. His were open. He caught occasional glimpses of a dark and shiny floor, perhaps water, but it was a long way below his feet. He sensed the huntress gliding to and fro. He saw no shadows—how could he, when *he himself was the source of the light!*

The first few times, he had awakened screaming when he had realized this. Yes, he was asleep, but the vision was real, and dangerous. Demons could take men in their sleep. Sleep was no defense. To waken would be to escape, but he could not force himself awake, and he was in peril.

Wherever he was, wherever this nothing-place might be, he was being hunted in it. She could not find him— indeed, she seemed to be more visible to him than he was to her—but she could make him reveal himself. The light was her doing. He shone in the foggy darkness, and as his glow brightened she drew closer, her voice became clearer.

As the unmeasured time crept past, as his silvery glow brightened, he sensed that other essence—moving, searching, seeking him, calling him. Not his name, but a name meant to be his, and other words in a tongue he did not know. Yet their meaning grew clearer: *Lord? Beloved? Master?*

This was worse than before. This was the first time he had made out words. What was that name she was calling?

The danger was becoming more imminent, the huntress questing ever nearer, a pale and sinister presence in the mists. *Beloved, why do you hide from me?* He wanted to run, to flee to the ends of the world, and he could not as much as blink. He was alive, for his heart was beating. He burned brighter.

Waken, fool, waken!

The hunter, a huntress, Lady Valda, of course . . . he could see her wandering through the roiling mists, searching. Why could he not awaken, as he had awakened the other times—screaming and sweating, but unharmed? She had never come so close in the earlier dreams . . . approaching, receding, returning. Blurred in the fog— pale arms outstretched, delicate hands feeling in the mist, dark hair, white body. His heart thundered faster. Each return brought her nearer to where he was and revealed more detail: dark eyes, red lips, the great round nipples, the fascination of the black triangular patch that he tried not to see and could not ignore. There were stories. Young men had dreams, but no dream could equal what he saw now. Oh, the beauty of her!

She had seen her quarry. She peered, frowning, as if barely able to make him out, or dazzled by his brilliance. Her lips moved, her red tongue stroked them. She approached, heading straight for him, not walking, just floating, shining brighter in his radiance.

Waken, waken! The dream had never gone this far before.

He could not swallow, could not move except for the beat of his heart. *Dum . . . Dum . . .* Faster than before. His body was responding to hers. He felt desire as he never had.

There was no wound in her breast. Her breasts were perfect, her body was perfect—her limbs, also. There was not a mark on her anywhere. Her flesh was alabaster, with faint blue veins under the skin. He could see the texture of her nipples, her lashes, the tiny hairs in her eyebrows. He was aware of her perfume, as he had been in the dungeon.

She smiled. She was close enough to touch or be touched. *Beloved! Lord! I have found you. I have come to you. Speak to me.*

She waited eagerly. Waited for what? He could not move to seize her in his arms. He could not compel his lips to curse her. She drifted closer, until her breasts were almost touching his chest, until he could feel her warmth. The scent of her was maddening. Her dark eyes stared directly into his, but watering as if his brightness pained them.

"I restored you," she whispered. "See the fine young body I found for you, my love, my adored master! What pleasure we shall have together with it! What joys will it bring us?"

Her fingers touched his chest as they had in the dungeon. He could not feel them—not quite. Soon, though? He shivered, and felt the shiver. His arms were coming around. She was drawing him into her world, making him real to her, making them real to each other. He blazed like a sun and she basked in his warmth, yet he shivered convulsively.

"Where did you go, my love? You have already traveled farther than I expected. I have searched and searched. But I have you now. Will you not return to me, my love? There is nothing to fear. Rhym cannot know."

The ghostly fingers stroked his cheek, his neck, his flanks, and their touch was almost, *almost* perceptible—swansdown, gossamer on his skin.

"So strong, my love! What shall we call you?" Scarlet lips pursed in a coy smile: "Shall I call you Longdirk? Why do you not yield to me? Do you not know what I have suffered these long years? Suffered to bring you back to me?"

Valda, glorious, irresistible, beauty to drive a man insane . . .

Triumph! "I have you now!" she cried. Her fingers caressed his cheek, and this time they were warm and smooth. His body came to life at her touch. His arms fell free, reached out to take her. She leaned her lips forward to his, her hair brushing his shoulders.

The apparition changed. It shrank, darkened, writhed. Hair became scant and silver, the skin shriveled, the breasts sagged. Wounds and scars and hideous . . .

He screamed. He awakened

FOUR

◆—◆

Over the Hills and Far Away

1

The long, long night was over. Toby shivered as he
adjusted the folds of his plaid. Daylight seeped through
a swampy gray sky. A rising wind promised rain and
combed a steady shower of leaves from the wasted
foliage of the trees. The glen was less than a mile wide,
its sides rising steeply to vanish in cloud, but dawn had
told him which way was west, so he knew his road to
Dalmally. He needed no further guidance from Master
Rory MacDonald of Glencoe.

He was less sure of his way back to the shelter.
After he had awakened screaming for the second time,
he had stumbled off into the woods to sleep by himself.
Now he had to find his way back—preferably without
having to yell for help. He peered around at the trees.
There could be more than one dwelling hidden here.

There could be a whole army. The haunted glen
might be a major rebel base, and King Fergan himself
on hand to extract Toby's oath of allegiance with a dirk
under his chin, as Iain Miller had predicted.

He wanted breakfast, although long habit made him
feel that he ought to milk Bossie first. He stamped his
feet and blew smoky breath through reddened fingers.
Which way to go? Northeast, probably. If he did not find
the others in that direction, he would come to the bog
very shortly. The hovel had not been far from there,
although everything would look different in daylight.

Then he heard Meg laughing, surprisingly close.
Relieved, he strode in that direction, crunching dead
leaves underfoot and combing them out of his hair with
his fingers.

His companions were picnicking outside the hut.

They looked up as he arrived, but only two of them smiled. Their ears and noses were red. Meg was huddled in her cloak, and Hamish had pulled his plaid over both shoulders and was heaped like a tartan-wrapped parcel on the grass.

Rory sat on a boulder as if it were a throne. He was younger than he had seemed in the night, his sandy hair looked lighter, the stubble on his chin had a reddish tint, and his eyes were a pale, silvery gray. The permanent sneer was more evident; his failure in the bog had obviously caused him to lose none of his superior airs. With the sword on his belt and the dirk just visible under the fold of his plaid, he could probably be as deadly as he chose to be. The crow's feather still jutted from his bonnet.

Hamish had one, too.

"Toby!" Meg exclaimed. "Hungry?"

"Starving." He knelt down and inspected the fare. It had come from his bundle—Annie Bridge's offerings—and had been well looted. He chose a hunk of blood sausage and bit into it eagerly.

"Do you always sleep so loudly, Longdirk?" Rory inquired.

"No. I'm sorry I woke you all."

"A clear conscience is a great advantage. I did hear you letting rip a few more times. Will you tell us what troubled you?"

"No."

"Was it the bogy?" Hamish inquired solemnly.

Toby shook his head. He would not describe his visions of Lady Valda to anyone.

"I slept like a log!" Meg proclaimed. She seemed to be in very good spirits, considering the ordeal she had been through. Either she was still buoyed up by the excitement of the adventure or else she was one of those vexing people who came awake chirruping like birds. "What do we do now, Master Glencoe? Head on to Dalmally, I suppose? And then Oban?"

Rory chewed for a moment. "We wait here. I'm expecting a friend."

Or several friends.

But poor Master Rory had lost his shoes in the bog, and poor Master Rory was not accustomed to walking on bare feet.

"There's no need for you to trouble yourself further on our account, sir," Toby remarked with his mouth full. "We are grateful for all your help, but we can be on our way now."

"My friend and I are coming with you."

"No, that won't be necessary," Toby said sweetly. "We can manage by ourselves now. Of course, we do appreciate the way you guided us through the bog."

Amused to see Rory's silver eyes narrow at the gibe, he turned to Hamish. "How far to Oban, do you suppose?"

Unlike Meg, Hamish had noted the dangerous undertow. He glanced uneasily at Rory, then said, "Twenty-five or thirty miles."

"Then we must be on our way." Toby laid his sausage on the ground and began repacking his bundle. "Should make it before dark."

"I think we ought to wait for Master Glencoe's friend!" Meg declared firmly. "Traveling with company is more fun. Please, Toby?"

She smiled appealingly at him.

He was disconcerted. She was a distraction from deadly serious business.

Hamish was amused, Rory openly smirking.

Very funny! In the long sleepless ordeal of the night, Toby had realized that Fat Vik's accusations were not entirely baseless. Meg's presence at the castle that evening had been part of a pattern. He had been running into Meg Tanner quite often lately. He had not been pursuing Meg, but she had been pursuing him.

Stupid kid! His only asset was his size. A child might fall for a man just because he was big, but mature women knew that large Highlanders just made easier targets. Meg had been hanging around in his path for weeks, and the dramatic rescue from the fusilier must have confirmed all her romantic fancies. When he had met up with her the previous evening, she had expected him to kiss her.

Small wonder the other two were laughing. She was

pretty enough in a childlike way, but by any standards she was small; she had a tiny, upturned nose, a pointed chin, and dark eyebrows. Muffled in her cloak, she seemed younger than ever: a starry-eyed kid with a juvenile crush on Strangerson, the big bastard.

He'd promised her father he would guard her like a sister. He must not encourage her romantic notions.

"No, let's go." Toby looked around—the others' bundles were in evidence, but not his broadsword. He rose to fetch it.

Rory sprang up and blocked his path. Moving with deliberation, he drew.

Toby tensed—here came the violence. Most likely, he was about to be given the choice of swearing to bleed for the rebels at some time in the future, or bleeding on his own account right now.

The rebel's silver eyes glinted. "You'll never make it to Oban, boy." He tossed his sword, hilt-first, so that it landed at Hamish's feet. "You'll never get by Dalmally. There's only three ways out of Fillan—think the English can't count?" Then he pulled his dirk. "I told you last night you wouldn't last a week in the real world, and I tell you now you won't live out the day without my help. From now on, you take my orders." Dirk followed sword.

Well! So it was to be fisticuffs was it? Toby folded his arms and looked down at Rory MacDonald with fresh confidence. "I'm not your man."

"You're nobody's man—at the moment. That makes you fair game."

"Not this way, sir. I'm bareknuckle champion of Fillan."

Rory smiled. "So Meg said. Show me." He raised his fists and put his left foot forward.

On the face of it, he was being suicidal. Granted he had fair shoulders, Toby had a full head advantage in height and probably weighed half again as much. So there was some other game in play that Toby hadn't worked out yet. If Rory was trying to keep Toby here until his friends arrived, then why discard the blades?

The smell of a trap was too strong—and in the background Hamish was shaking his head violently.

"No."

"Oh, you *are* a gentle giant, aren't you? Hit me. Try! Just try!"

"No."

"Won't you spare the maiden's blushes and even pretend to be a man for her?"

"She knows what I can do when it's needed."

Rory put his fists on his hips and sighed in exasperation. "I hate explaining! Let me put it this way—you don't know how to use your strength. If I had stumbled on that Sassenach getting out of line, he would have wakened up an hour later with a sore neck, and there would have been no further trouble. Now be your age, sonny. Get mad! Hit me!"

Again Toby said, "No. I might hurt a little man worse than I meant to."

The rebel did not enjoy being called a little man. "I order you!"

"I am not your man."

"Then defend yourself." MacDonald shot a couple of very fast lefts at Toby's face, followed by a right. Toby's arms blocked of their own accord. Rory came in under his guard, hammered him twice in the midriff, and danced back out of reach. He was fast, very fast. The blows stung, but that was all. A small man's speed might help compensate for a big man's strength, but nothing could counterbalance the bigger man's ability to absorb punishment. Toby could take fifty such blows and then win with one.

He had not had to move his feet. He frowned and scratched his stubbly chin. "If you're trying to rile me, sir, you'll have to hit me a lot harder than that."

"I will." Rory came dancing back and swung a deliberate low blow—one that Toby was certainly not willing to absorb. In blocking it, he put himself off-balance, feet wrong, hands too low. Rory grabbed his wrist and . . . *flip!* Caught by a cross-buttock throw, Toby hit the ground with his entire length. *Ooof!* The sky spun and steadied . . .

"I could kick your head in now," Rory said calmly. "Would that be hard enough? Ready for Lesson Two?"

Toby scrambled up and raised his fists, keeping a firm grip on his temper. He was a boxer, not a wrestler, as Steward Bryce had warned him. The glen followed the Fancy's Rules very strictly, and discouraged throwing. Like a fool he had been expecting Rory to fight as he did. Well, now he was ready. . . .

Rory's bare foot shot up and struck his elbow, jarring his entire arm. "With a shoe on, I could have disabled you. Lesson Three?"

Toby blocked a fusillade of jabs, felt his wrist caught again and hit the ground again with his face in the dirt and his opponent on his back, holding him in a painful arm lock. He discovered that there were angles at which muscle made no difference.

"I could dislocate your shoulder, you understand," Rory murmured in his ear. "Ready for Lesson Four?" He broke loose.

The bareknuckle champion of Strath Fillan staggered up again and looked at the mocking silvery eyes through a red fog of fury. The desire to flatten that arrogant nose had become one of the world's most urgent concerns.

As his opponent came dancing in again, he ignored defense, feinted with his left, and threw a right cross that slammed into Rory's shirtfront like a cannonball demolishing a castle. Against an opponent of equal size, it would have been a wasted blow and possibly costly. Perhaps its very clumsiness caught Rory unprepared. Certainly poor wee Rory could never have been swatted like that before. He struck the grass spread-eagled and skidded before he came to a stop; he lay there, dazed, gasping, and comically astonished.

"I could jump on your guts now!" Toby bellowed. "Lesson Five . . . Get up!"

"No!" Meg screamed, rushing between the two of them. "That is enough! I won't have it! Put your fists down, Toby Strangerson!" She knelt to help poor Rory.

Toby forced his hands to his sides, quivering with

fury. He wrestled his anger back in its cage, took a couple of very deep breaths, and turned on his heel. He stalked away into the trees, boiling. So he was the stronger—who would have questioned that? Rory was the better fighter. The uppity little runt had beaten him three times. The real world would offer no fourth chances. His one talent had betrayed him. He needed lessons in fighting.

2

He might have stormed off and fallen into the bog, or become lost in the woods, had he not come face-to-face with another man heading toward him. They both halted, staring at each other with mutual surprise.

He was small and plump, of middle years. The top of his head had been shaved, leaving bare scalp surrounded by a black-and-silver tonsure. He wore a heavy wool robe, ostensibly white, although now bedraggled and smeared with grass stains, and he held a cloth-wrapped parcel under one arm. On the extreme end of his pudgy nose perched a pair of glass lenses in a contraption of gold wire that hooked over his ears. Toby had heard of eyeglasses, but never seen any before.

The newcomer peered up at him over them and demanded urgently, "Was she wearing any jewelry?" His voice was high-pitched and squeaky.

Toby blinked. "Who?"

"The Valda woman, of course, the one you think was Valda."

"Er. No. Well, she had a sort of crown thing on her head at table. It was sparkly, so I suppose—"

"But no rings? No pendants?"

"No . . . A big gem on the pommel of a dagger?"

"Ah! What color?"

With distaste, Toby concluded that the older man was either drunk or mentally deranged, and the only thing to do was humor him. "Yellow."

The little man shook his head as if that was a wrong answer, then quickly raised a finger to push his glasses higher, although he continued to peer over them instead of through them. "Black crescent emblem? You're sure? Curved left or right?"

"Um. No. Hamish saw it."

"Tell me everything you saw, then."

"Why?"

At Toby's back, Rory laughed. "You'll have to take it slowly, Father. Short, simple words. Toby of Fillan— Father Lachlan of Glasgow."

Toby noted that the robe had a hood and remembered what Hamish had told him. "You're an adept?"

Father Lachlan twitched angrily and again caught his spectacles before they slipped off. "I prefer to be described as an acolyte, although I am on leave from my office at present. I am also a friar of the Galilean Order. I must hear all about this Valda woman."

"Why?"

The little man seemed to find the question incomprehensible. "Because she is dangerous, of course! And evil, if she is who you think she is. Now sit yourself . . . " He peered around as if looking for a chair. "Right here will do, I suppose." He flopped down on the loam, adjusted his spectacles again, and addressed Toby's sporran. "I must hear everything you saw, everything you heard."

"Why?"

Rory laughed again. "He's trying to help you, Baby Beef."

Toby almost asked, "Why?" again. What reason could a total stranger have to aid him? On the other hand, he had a demon in his heart and had resolved to seek out a sanctuary. Although he distrusted any friend of Rory's on principle, he would have to ask help from somebody. He stared down uncertainly at the shiny bald scalp.

"You can talk on the way, Father," Rory said. "Are those my shoes?"

"Oh . . . yes, of course."

Rory helped the little man rise and took the parcel,

which comprised a pair of silver-buckled shoes wrapped in thick tartan socks. "You don't *need* that, Man Mountain!"

Meg and Hamish had arrived also, and Hamish was solemnly offering Toby his broadsword.

He said, "Thanks!" and put it on. Then he accepted his bundle also. Meg looked cross, Hamish uncertainly amused.

"I said, you don't need it!" Rory repeated angrily. "It makes you stand out like Beinn Bhreac-liath. It's liable to get you shot on sight."

"I am not your man!" Toby snapped. "Go away. We don't need your help to walk to Oban."

Rory scowled, unconsciously rubbing his chest as if it hurt. "You need someone's help, Longdirk. All right—carry the horrible thing if you want. Now tell Father Lachlan the whole story, everything you can remember, every detail. And don't forget your dreams in the night."

He waved for Hamish and Meg to accompany him and marched off through the trees in his shoes.

The acolyte had been ignoring the bickering, looking mostly impatient. He put a hand on Toby's arm to urge him forward. "Come along, my son. Tell me about the woman. Did you have dreams of her in the night—vivid dreams, I mean?"

"Yes, sir. Very vivid. I . . . I think she conjured . . . " He clenched his fists and said it: "I think I may be possessed."

The little man shrugged. "That's what we fear, of course. Tell me everything, and we'll see. It's possible, but there are other possibilities." He peered quizzically at Toby and then smiled. "I'm not about to stick a knife in your heart! Even if what you fear is true, there is still hope! But you must give me all the facts. Did you, um, couple with the woman?"

"Certainly not!"

"Even in the dreams?"

"No."

"That's good. I'm sure that helps. Now, begin at the beginning."

Trying to have faith that he was not dealing with a lunatic, Toby began at the beginning, the hob's warning. Father Lachlan displayed a talent for asking penetrating questions and proved to be a concerned and attentive listener, despite his distracted manner. Much to his surprise, Toby found himself telling everything.

Rory seemed to know where he was going, although the woods were totally bereft of landmarks—it would be difficult to become seriously lost in a gorge like Glen Orchy. He strode on confidently, chatting with Meg and keeping Hamish at hand, so he did not linger and eavesdrop on the conversation proceeding in the rear.

Toby's tale had progressed only to the laird's dinner when he saw that the others had stopped. Rain had begun to fall, a fine misty rain sifting down from the brooding morass of gray clouds. Meg was arranging her cloak over her head. Hamish and Rory were similarly adjusting their plaids. The waxed wool would resist the rain, at least for a while.

Toby began to follow suit and at once ran into difficulties with his broadsword. Rory watched his struggles with open scorn. "Throw it away, Longshanks! It's worse than useless!"

True. But to throw it away now would be to admit that he had been wrong all along. So he wasn't going to.

Gaining no response, the rebel frowned. "This is irrational! Why? Do you think you look romantic with it? Do you expect Miss Campbell to swoon when she looks at you? Even you can't swagger with a thing that size."

Still Toby did not reply. He did not know why he was keeping the sword. He hoped he was motivated only by pride and mulish stubbornness, not by demonic possession, but the great weapon still gave him the same seductive thrill he had felt when he first handled it in Annie's cottage. He wanted to part the air with it, hear it whistle. A fast blow, and torrents of blood . . . When the others moved off again, he followed with the broadsword back in place over his plaid, its straps threatening to rub holes in his shoulder.

Father Lachlan had pulled up the hood of his robe, but it forced him to crane his neck to look up at Toby, so he soon let it fall back again. He was fascinated by Toby's account of having seen himself from the outside. "That must have been a strange experience! Were you looking at yourself from one direction, or from all around?"

Toby thought about it. "From all around, I think. I could see the signs painted on my chest and the marks the manacles had made on my back, too."

"At the same time?"

"Um . . . Think so. I'm not sure."

"Remarkable, though! What color was the light? . . . " He caught his spectacles just before they fell off.

The trees were thinning out, giving way to settled countryside, with crofts, and cattle, and dry-stone pens. The glen itself was widening into a strath and starting to look familiar. The hills to the left were still cloud-capped, but the precipitous slope on the right must be Beinn Donachain. Soon the travelers would reach the Glen Lochy road, with Dalmally no more than a couple of miles ahead.

This was the heart of Campbell country. Were the weather better, Ben Cruachan itself would be visible from here, as Hamish had annoyed Rory by mentioning. "Cruachan!" was the war cry of the Campbells, and Rory had shouted it to attract Jeral's attention when they escaped from the bog. Therefore Rory was certainly no MacDonald and not from Glencoe.

So who was he? Why would he go to such trouble to assist three young fugitives who had absolutely no claim on him? Toby would dearly like to know what his real motives were. His only failure so far had been with the wisp, and that could be blamed on Toby's resident demon.

He told himself to stop being a sourpuss and just be grateful for the unearned and unexpected help. Trouble was, he was not good at gratitude; he lacked experience.

* * *

3

Drizzle grew to downpour. Toby completed the story of his adventures and then described his loathsome dreams also. The rising wind threw rain to cool the flush on his face and snatched the hateful words from his mouth. Father Lachlan listened in silence, nodding and pursing his lips, but otherwise showing no reaction until the story was ended.

Then he sighed. "That's all? You don't remember the name she was calling you?"

"No, sir. I think it was a woman's name . . . but I'm not sure. It was only a dream, not real."

"Never mind, then. Can you remember anything you've left out? Anything at all you didn't mention because it didn't seem important?"

"No, sir—Father. I think I've told you everything."

He was astonished that he had so easily confided his troubles to a total stranger and even more surprised that he should feel such a sense of relief at having done so. Now he waited anxiously to hear what the acolyte concluded, but Father Lachlan just plodded on, staring blankly at the watery landscape, biting his lip. The movement repeatedly caused his eyeglasses to slide down his nose, and he would push them back up again with one finger.

At last Toby could stand it no longer. "I wondered if the hob helped me escape."

"Something did," the acolyte muttered absently. "But what? And escape from what?"

"Am I possessed?"

"Mm?" Father Lachlan looked up as if surprised. Then he smiled faintly and reached overhead to pat Toby's shoulder. "I don't know, my son, but you do! If you had a demon, you would know it, because you would be caged up in a tiny corner of your mind, unable to do anything but watch. A demon enjoys tormenting its host by letting him see what horrors his body is performing. I don't think that is what you are experiencing—is it?"

"No, but that's how it began, and then—"

"Demons do not go away of their own accord!"

"Not even . . ." Toby wished he was better at explaining things. "I thought it might be like owning a horse. Sometimes the owner rides the horse, other times he lets it run in the pasture."

Father Lachlan chuckled and shook his head. "Never heard of a demon dismounting, not even for a minute! Demons enjoy tormenting their hosts as much as hurting other people. Granted, possession can be hard for outsiders to detect if the demon is wily, but the victim knows the truth. Sometimes possession is completely obvious, of course. Those two you think you killed in the dungeon, for example—were they men or demons? Well, the test in their case is whether they are truly dead, or if their bodies are still walking around."

More than the lashing rain made Toby shiver. "That's really possible?"

"Oh, yes. Only for a few days, then the flesh decays too far to sustain even a demon. But that's not a test we are about to apply to you!"

Others might not be so well-intentioned. How could a man prove that he was not possessed without dying? Father Lachlan's opinion would be comforting, if Toby had any reason at all to believe he was telling the truth.

"Do you not have powers to find out?"

The little man blinked at him. "Powers? My son, I have no powers!"

"None?"

"None at all! I have some knowledge of matters spiritual and demonic. I obey the precepts of my order, and I serve the Glasgow tutelary, which has on occasion granted my petitions, so it would seem to approve of my efforts, but—"

"Efforts to do what?" Toby said angrily.

"To aid others. This is my vocation—to help others."

"Help how?"

"As an acolyte, by interceding with the tutelary on their behalf. As a friar, by giving comfort, by spreading the philosophy and ethics of the great founder of my order."

"You even help strangers?"

"Why not?" Father Lachlan smiled gently. "Anyone will help his friends and family! You are troubled and I am honestly trying to be of assistance. Why do you suppose I have been asking so many questions, my son? Just out of nosiness?"

Toby shuffled his feet in the grass. "I'm sorry. I never met an acolyte before. I thought . . . I wondered if you were just one of Rory's men."

"Whose? Oh, Rory! Yes, Rory. Well, I support the cause, of course—whatever else I am, I am also a true Scotsman! But I would still help you if you were an Englishman. Even if you were King Nevil himself, I . . . " The little man fell silent, as if struck by a novel idea. He chewed his lip, repeatedly adjusted his eyeglasses, and made no sound except for the wild flapping of his gown.

Toby considered picking him up and shaking him like a riddle—perhaps an answer or two would fall out. There was an interruption, then, as they reached a wide and boggy burn. The other three were already across, heading over the pasture toward a group of three cottages. Toby jumped over it and turned to hold out a hand for his companion, but Father Lachlan hitched up his robe and made a surprisingly agile leap. Toby snatched the spectacles out of the air and returned them to him.

"Thank you," the acolyte said calmly, replacing them on the end of his nose.

"Rory knows who lives here?" Toby demanded. He could see no living thing except shaggy cattle, but a dog was barking. He realized that unexpected visitors could no more hope to pass unobserved through Strath of Orchy than through Strath Fillan. Someone would challenge.

"He knows just about everyone!" Father Lachlan said cheerfully, resuming the journey. "Where were we? Oh, yes. The most reliable evidence of possession is superhuman power, of course."

Despair! "Then I am possessed!"

"Why do you say so?"

"I twisted iron bars like string! I broke men's necks, I—"

"Mmph! Your feats of physical strength do not impress me."

"They impressed me!"

"Oh, no. In emergencies, people can often display astonishing strength. You are probably far more powerful than you realize. Your ability to see in the dark is more worrisome."

"Only sometimes! And what of the way I rode the horse, Falcon? And finding my way out of the bog?"

"Yes, yes, yes!" Father Lachlan said in his squeaky, fussy voice. "You have displayed some superhuman abilities, but possession is not the only possible explanation of those. Lady Valda may just have put a hex upon you. I can think of a hundred things it might be. . . . She may have planned to send you out as an assassin, for example, to hunt down King Fergan and slay him. Or King Nevil, for that matter. She seems to have selected you for your size and strength. Having chosen a doughty vessel for her perfidy, she may have granted you some demonic abilities to aid you in your task." He beamed encouragingly at Toby.

"Do you believe that?"

He sighed. "Not much. But it is possible; and I don't believe you have a demon! If you do, then it is the most subtle, sophisticated demon I ever heard of. It is making you seem and sound like a very likable young man. You rescued your friends and, ah, Rory, from the bogy."

Toby could not recall anyone ever describing him as *likable* before. He wasn't sure he approved. "I had to rescue myself and they were tied to me."

"Paw! You could have snapped those ropes like darning wool, couldn't you?"

"I suppose so." He had twisted iron bars.

"No, you rescued three mortals you could have left to drown, and that simple little altruism would be beyond almost any demon, no matter what the stakes. You must remember," Father Lachlan told him sternly, "that demons are motivated only by hate. Originally, they were just primitive earth spirits, elementals. Such entities have enormous powers, but very little inclination to use them. A village hob, like the one you knew, has acquired a rudimentary concept of morality, but completely undomesticated elementals have none at all—good and evil come from mortals. Hexers know ways to enslave elementals, ripping them from their natural haunts and imprisoning them in objects, usually gems. By gramarye, the adept compels the demon to do his bidding."

"Could he not do good with the demon instead of evil?"

Father Lachlan adjusted his eyeglasses. "Perhaps some of them have such designs initially, but remember that they begin with an act of great cruelty. I don't suppose *pain* is an adequate description of whatever a demon feels, but to tear it away from its natural locale is itself a form of rape. How can such a person have good intentions? How can the demon itself be well-disposed toward mortals after that, or while it is caged and deprived of its freedom? Lady Valda was reputed always to wear three great gems: a ruby, a sapphire, and an emerald. She was therefore assumed to own three demons. From what you tell me, I suspect that she has since gained two more and transferred four of them into the hooded bodies you saw, demonic creatures."

And the yellow gem on the dagger was the fifth? "Then she tried to do the same to me? But why?"

"Perhaps that was what she was trying." The acolyte pulled a face. "As to why . . . who knows how such a mind works? It depends on what she plans, I suppose. To invoke the powers of a bottled demon takes time. It involves ritual—conjuring—gramarye. You witnessed her at work, so you know the sort of rites she must use. An incarnate demon is more easily biddable. Its powers are not as great, but it can act faster, obey simple orders. It is more dangerous in a sense, and more demonic. If it felt pain before, now it must also learn fear, because it has become to some extent mortal." He shook his head and hastily caught his spectacles. "The result can only be evil, my son, never good. A demon is always driven by hatred."

Toby would enjoy taking Rory down a peg, and he was convinced that Fat Vik deserved a thorough thrashing, but only that. He had no desire to murder anyone. He could spare no tears for Colin and very few for Godwin Forrester—but he still could not believe he was driven by hatred.

"So what roused the wisp against you?" the acolyte murmured. "What provoked the robed man to try and put a dagger through your heart? He must be on Valda's side, so whose side did he think you were on? It's all very murky, my son! I have never met a more complex case. The best we can do is get you to a sanctuary as quickly as possible—preferably before you sleep again, although that does not seem possible, does it? A tutelary can detect possession and sometimes cure it. Even a spirit may be able to help, and the closest shrine happens to be in Glen Shira, whither we are bound anyway."

"We are? I thought we were going to Oban!"

"There is no tutelary at Oban, now," the acolyte said sadly. "There was once, but York sacked the town, remember."

More history . . . the English army under the duke of York had rampaged through the west in one of the previous wars. Toby could not recall which one, and did not care. "Why does that matter? It was rebuilt, wasn't it?"

"The town was, yes. But a tutelary will not let you sack its town! It isn't just firearms that give the Sassenachs their victories, my son. They use gramarye, too. I suspect that this is why, er, Rory is so interested in you, because—" He stopped and caught at Toby's arm as he was about to scramble over a dry-stone wall. "I think we should wait here a minute."

A hundred paces ahead, Rory, Meg, and Hamish had been challenged by four men from the cottages. Trouble?

Toby's hand reached for the hilt of his sword.

"Wait? Why?"

The acolyte chuckled. He sat down on the wall and

turned his face away from the wind. "Because it will be easier for them. If they are questioned, they can admit to speaking with a man and two children. They need not mention a friar and a young giant carrying a broadsword."

"Oh." Perhaps Rory was necessary, after all. The waiting men had obviously recognized him. They were pulling off their bonnets and bowing. What did that say about the self-styled Master MacDonald?

Toby turned back to Father Lachlan. "Why Glen Shira? I promised Meg's father I would guide her to Oban." What were these two up to—Rory and his pet acolyte?

The little man smiled reprovingly. "She might make it, my son, although she would be questioned. You cannot go that way—not directly. Remember, there are three groups hunting you. Laird Ross and his men will pretend to cooperate with the Sassenachs, while doing everything they safely can to frustrate them. The Sassenachs themselves are much more dangerous. They will have blocked the three main roads—north by Bridge of Orchy, south through Crianlarich, and west through Dalmally and Pass of Brander. We are not far from Lochy Castle, you know." He waved a chubby hand at Glen Lochy, which had now come into view.

Toby hitched his sword to a marginally less uncomfortable position and wished he could hear what was being said at that meeting up ahead.

"So how do we go to Glen Shira? And how do we get from there to Oban?"

"We go on down the Shira. When we reach Loch Fyne, we take a boat. Outwitting the soldiers will not be difficult."

"Who pays for the boat? Who will sail around the Mull of Kintyre at this time of year?" It must be nice to be a trusting sort of person, who did not see betrayal in every cock-and-bull story.

"Or we can cut inland to Loch Lomond."

"And Lady Valda?"

Father Lachlan sighed and studied Toby for a moment with a disconcerting stare. "If she is pursuing you also, my son, then I fear for you—body and soul."

The only comforting thought then was that he would not have said so if he doubted Toby's courage.

Rory had finished his consultation with the locals. They turned and ran off, one to the cottages and the other three in other directions. Father Lachlan rose to clamber over the dike. About to vault it, Toby remembered his sword and took a more cautious approach. He would rather not fall flat on his face with Meg and Rory watching.

"The hunt is on," Rory announced when they reached him. He looked annoyed. Hamish looked owlish. Meg was blue-lipped and shivering. "The Sassenachs have set guards on the Pass of Brander."

"Where did your friends go?" Toby demanded. "And where are *they* off to?" A stream of youths and leggy boys had begun emerging from the cottages and haring off over the pastures, one after the other. Six . . . seven . . .

Rory's silver eyes were as cold as the weather. "To make arrangements. Certain persons will be discouraged from seeing certain things. We will be advised when it is safe to cross the road. And so on." He obviously had no doubts as to who was in command of the expedition.

"No word of the lady?" Father Lachlan inquired.

"Not so far."

Toby had promised Kenneth Tanner that he would deliver Meg safely to her relatives in Oban, but to stick to the letter of his promise now would be to break it in spirit. He represented the greatest danger she would ever face. He must reconsider his duty in the light of circumstances, even though that meant putting trust in strangers—never Rory, but an acolyte ought to be reliable if any man was.

"Wait!" he said. "It's me the Sassenachs are after. They have no quarrel with any of you. You all go on. I won't—"

"Not a chance, Longdirk." Rory spoke softly but emphatically. "Firstly, that's not true. And we're all in this together, anyway."

"Don't be crazy! You all go on; I'll take to the hills. Father Lachlan, will you pledge to see Meg Campbell safely to her cousins' place? I promised her—"

"You're wasting breath, young man," the acolyte said, pulling up his hood and lacing it under his chin. "I am determined to find out what that Valda woman is up to, and I shall be much happier having you where I can keep an eye on you. Now let us be on our way."

Rory made an *ahem!* noise. "Can you give us a few general clues as to what's going on, Father?"

"I wish I could." The little man pondered for a moment, and then spoke with an authority and decisiveness he had not shown before. "I do think Hamish Campbell was right, and the mysterious woman is the infamous Lady Valda—" Hamish beamed. "There can't be many female hexers on the loose, and her appearance here may explain Oreste."

Rory nodded. "Ah!"

Toby said, "Oreste?"

"We are worried about Baron Oreste." *We* meant all the rebels, presumably. "He is one of Nevil's closest cronies and a notorious hexer, a most evil man. He arrived in Scotland a couple of weeks ago and is still lurking around Edinburgh, as far as we know. We have been wondering what could be so important as to require his attention here."

"Could he be hunting for King Fergan, sir?" Hamish said, looking as worried as if the Oreste problem were all his fault.

"We thought that," Father Lachlan murmured. "Now the timing suggests he may have come in search of the lady. As to what happened . . . apparently she tried some sort of conjuration involving Master Strangerson, but I don't know what. It seems to have failed, or produced unexpected results—that's my guess. She may pursue him, and it is up to all of us to keep him out of her clutches. I do not believe he is possessed—if he were, you would be dead by now."

"I would, certainly," Rory said cheerfully, rubbing his chest. "I baited him a little this morning. He displayed remarkable self-control for one of such tender years—almost bovine."

That was what Rory had been up to—testing.

Hamish gulped. "Oh! You thought he might . . . Wasn't that rash of you, sir?"

The rebel shrugged. "As a mortal, he presented an interesting challenge. As a demon . . . Well, my father is always telling me I am destined to be roasted with hellfire or ripped to pieces. I thought I could find out if he was correct."

Father Lachlan frowned disapprovingly. "You don't know what fear is, do you?"

Rory looked modest. Toby gritted his teeth and wished he could teach him.

"So how did our oversized friend escape from the castle, Father?"

"You must ask him. Anything he told me was in confidence."

Toby had been watching Meg's horrified eyes growing wider and wider. "Tell them, Father—I don't care. If I am a danger to them, they should be aware of it. They know about the Sassenachs, they should hear of Lady Valda, too. Won't her powers enable her to track me down?"

"Powers?" the acolyte said disapprovingly. "I told you. She has no powers, my son, only evil skills that enable her to command demons. She herself has only knowledge—evil knowledge, and evil designs." The little man began to move away. "Pray that one day one of her demonic minions will turn on her."

Toby raised his voice. "Can her demons track me down for her, then?"

Father Lachlan stopped and looked around and adjusted his eyeglasses. "Well, yes. Of course they can. From what you told me, two of them are probably in poor condition at the moment, but one would be enough."

With a macabre chuckle, Rory slapped Toby on the back. "If they get within range, Longdirk, they'll nail your feet to the rocks. We must move."

"What is their range?"

"Good question! Father?"

"Impossible to say, my son. Some demons are more

powerful than others, or more biddable, perhaps—it depends on their training. A bottled demon . . . Well, I am sure than Baron Oreste in Edinburgh can communicate with King Nevil in London, if that is where he is. Demons incarnate, as Lady Valda's are presently, are much more restricted—but I don't think we should let them get any closer than we have to."

4

Rory called a halt for lunch in the lee of a dry-stone dike. If those were dry stones, Hamish remarked, then he had forgotten what the word meant. The five fugitives hunkered down to pool their remaining supplies. There were no trees to provide better shelter from the downpour, but why not a haystack or a cattle barn? Rory insisted on the wall. He wanted to keep an eye on the road.

He seemed oddly concerned about crossing the road. Some of the locals, he admitted, were unreliable, and Sassenach patrols had been sighted. The road itself, running from Glen Lochy to Dalmally, barely deserved to be called a track. It wandered from house to house, fording burns, detouring around bogs and peat cuts, frequently offering the traveler a choice of several ways, none of them appealing. Strath of Orchy was wide, flat, and marshy, but it was inhabited. No one could cross it by day unobserved.

"The rain helps, though, doesn't it?" Hamish demanded, wolfing the last of Annie Bridge's blood sausage—he had freely handed out his mother's stale baps in exchange. Rain was marching gray armies along the glen, ghostly giants.

"It helps blind the Sassenachs. I doubt it will stop demons."

Hamish gulped on a mouthful.

"So what are you planning, Master MacDonald?" Meg asked attentively.

"I've got patrols of my own out." He did not elaborate.

Just who was Rory MacDonald of Glencoe? Father Lachlan knew him by some other name, and although the younger man treated the older with diffidence, there was no question that the younger was the leader. The cottagers had doffed their bonnets to him, and Highlanders did that for few men.

What motivated these two? Meg and Hamish were here by necessity, but Rory and Father Lachlan would be far better off indoors, sharpening swords by the fireside, than struggling through storm-racked hills for no evident advantage. It was Strangerson whom Valda pursued, so why not just give the young bastard a head start and let him lead the hexer into someone else's shire?

The road—or the nearest branch of it—was only a few hundred paces away, and no one had come along it in the last quarter hour. Beyond it flowed the Lochy, which they would have to ford.

"That's where we're going, isn't it?" Hamish asked, peering into the murk. "That gap? The valley of the Eas a Ghail?"

"And the magnificent mountain to the left of it is Ben Lui," Meg snapped. "You can't see that, either."

"I can see the bottom of it. Going to be steep going, sir?" As Eas a Ghail meant "White Waterfall," he was making a reasonable assumption.

"Steep enough," Rory said. "Ah!"

Three men were approaching from the east, leading a pony loaded with broom, winter fuel. A few minutes later, two others came into sight from the west, with another pony similarly laden. The two groups paused for a brief word, almost opposite the watchers. Then they continued on their respective ways—having unobtrusively exchanged ponies.

"That's it!" Rory said with obvious satisfaction. "The all-clear signal. No patrols. Let's go."

Leaving only some crushed grass and not a single crust to mark where they had been, the travelers scrambled over the dike and hurried toward the road. The men with the ponies never looked around.

Toby found Hamish at his side.

"You don't mind if I use you as a windbreak?" His plaid was already sodden. His lips were blue, his fingers bone-white, but he was grinning happily. He was an outlaw and wore a black feather. Incredibly, the kid was actually enjoying himself!

"Be my guest." Toby suspected that the rain was starting to show signs of whiteness. "When we get higher, we're going to be in snow, and then we'll leave a trail."

"I d-d-don't think demons need snow to t-t-track people."

"Perhaps not."

After a moment, Hamish said, "Who do you think Rory really is?" He was shouting over the wind, but his manner implied that he was whispering. His dark eyes gleamed conspiratorially.

"I have no idea."

"He speaks the Gaelic like a Sassenach."

"Yes he does."

"You think he might have lived in England when he was a kid? Prince Fergan was a hostage in England during the Taming, after the Battle of Leethoul."

Toby shrugged, feeling the wet plaid rubbing his skin under the weight of his sword. "You think Rory is King Fergan?"

"No," Hamish said reluctantly, obviously wishing that he did. "He's too young. A lot of chiefs' sons were taken, too. He may be a chief's son, or even . . . No, he mentioned his father, so he's not a chief yet. He may be a chief's son!"

"What if he is?" He probably was.

Hamish stumbled along in silence for a while. They crossed the muddy trail, then waded across the foamy brown Lochy, following Rory and Father Lachlan and Meg, who was chattering as if they were all old friends.

"Toby . . . do you like Meg?"

Toby looked down coldly—which was not difficult under the circumstances. "She's a nice kid."

The boy grinned impishly. "She's madly in love with you!"

"No, she's . . . Well, she may think she is, but she's not old enough to be really in love."

"She's older than I am!" Hamish said indignantly. "Girls grow up faster than boys do, and she's only a few months younger than you are."

"She is? But . . ." Toby thought for a moment and then said, "Oh." School memories were no help, because boys were taught in the morning and girls in the afternoon. Meg had been around for as far back as he could remember. She might not be much younger than he was, after all.

Maybe that did make a difference.

Hamish grinned triumphantly. "She's in love with you!"

"How do you know?"

"Everyone knows. The other girls all tease her about it, because she's so little and you're so big."

Did that explain some of her brother's enmity? "I'm also an outlaw, and I'm probably bewitched. She ought to find a better prospect."

"Tell her that!"

"You tell her, if you think it's any of your business."

Hamish shot Toby a wary look. "Father Lachlan's a Galilean, did you know? He was telling me some of their teachings and he says they don't contradict what Pa taught in school, which is mostly Stoic, because there's more Stoics in Scotland than any others—Pa uses some of their tracts—but I know the Socratics have a chapter in Glasgow, and of course the Tartars favor the Arabic . . ."

Toby listened to the prattle with less than half an ear and mulled over the implications of what he had been told about Meg. The idea was oddly worrying. He liked little Meg. He did not want to hurt her feelings, and he had probably done so already. A man could tell a woman that he loved her and risk being rejected—that was part of the burden of being male. A woman must be more careful, lest she seem brazen. If she dropped a few hints and the man was too stupid to notice, what more could she do? That must make things very difficult for her. He had never really thought of that before.

He certainly couldn't start falling in love now—not with Meg, not with anyone. Until he had been purged of his demon, or hex, or whatever Valda had done to him, he was not fit for human society. And even after that, he would still be an outlaw, and a homeless wanderer with no trade, no money, no prospects. Love would have to wait a long time.

Besides, he had promised Kenneth Tanner that he would treat Meg as a sister.

"Down!" Rory shouted. "Down, you big oaf!"

Hamish grabbed Toby's plaid and tugged. Hamish was already down—they all were. He had been daydreaming. He dropped to the wet moss.

They had come about half a mile from the road. A band of riders had emerged from the mist, heading east, coming fast.

"Toby!" Hamish squealed. "It's them! It's Valda!"

They were too far off to be certain, of course, but horses like those were rare. It was not a military patrol, certainly. Six . . . the lady, her maid, four demons . . . ? If Valda had used Toby's dreams to locate him, then she would have had no need to detour around by Bridge of Orchy. She could cut him off by taking the Glen Lochy road.

Then what? What could demons do? Could they smell his tracks like bloodhounds? With sick apprehension he watched the sinister cavalcade draw near the point where he had crossed, expecting any minute to see the horses reined in, the hunt turn south in pursuit.

It seemed unfair that demons could travel the world while benevolent spirits like tutelaries remained in one place. Why should forces of evil have such an advantage over the good?

But the riders kept going, onward to the west, and in a few more minutes the rain hid them from sight. Hamish released a loud gasp of relief, speaking for all of them. He scrambled to his knees.

"What happens when she gets to Pass of Brander and finds out Toby can't have gone that way? She'll turn back!"

"Come on!" Rory shouted, jumping up. "We're easy meat on the flats. Let's get into the hills."

5

The land steepened into pasture, then bare hillside. A faint trail climbed the valley of the chattering, frothing Eas a Ghail. Toby discovered that he was alone with Meg for the first time. He wasn't sure if she had arranged this, or he had. It didn't matter. Hamish had gone scurrying on ahead. Father Lachlan and Rory were deep in conversation at the rear.

Her cheeks were bright red; her braids dangled from under a brown bonnet. She looked up expectantly, blinking as the rain blew into her eyes. He smiled. She smiled back—so if she blamed him for her present troubles, she was not going to say so.

Smiling was fine. Talk . . . he felt totally tongue-tied. Meg had never affected him like that before. He could recall the nights she had turned up at the castle and he had walked her home . . . he could remember himself chattering like a flock of magpies—like Hamish, even— but now he had no idea what about.

"Er . . . Um . . . How're you managing?"

"Fine."

"Cold?"

"Yes."

Oh.

Pause.

"Meg . . . I'm sorry. I mean, I'm sorry to have dragged you into all this danger."

Her slender eyebrows almost disappeared into her cap. "It wasn't your fault, Master Strangerson. It was my fault for being so stupid, remember?"

"I'm sorry about that."

"You're sorry I was stupid?"

"No! I'm sorry I said that."

"But if a person is stupid, it must be a kindness to tell her so, so that she won't be stupid in future."

Why was talking with women so much harder than talking with men? Why did words seem to change their meanings and simple sentences turn around to bite the tongue that spoke them? Why did humor always become insult and criticism poison?

"You weren't stupid. I was stupid to say you were stupid."

"Then you didn't mean what you said when you said I will soon be a woman and men will start to lust after me?"

Demons! "Did I say that?"

"Indeed you did, sir."

"Then I was wrong."

"Oh?" Danger crackled somewhere in that monosyllable. Bonfires blazing on the mountain . . .

"I mean, men lust after you already."

"Such as who?"

"Any man!" Toby dearly wished Lady Valda and her demons would descend on him immediately and carry him off. Since that did not happen and he was already in over his head, he snapped, "Me, for instance."

Meg's eyes opened wider than normal. "Truly?" Then she tossed her head so that her braids danced. "I mean . . . Toby Strangerson, that's a terrible thing to say! How dare you say such a thing! What does she look like?"

"Who?"

"Lady Valda. Describe her!"

What had Toby Strangerson ever done to deserve this? He described Lady Valda. Having totally taken leave of his senses, he went on to relate how she had bared her breast in the dungeon. Then the wind felt icy on his heated face, but it was warm compared with Meg Campbell's expression.

"And you dream of her now, I understand?"

Oh, demons! "Never mind about that!" he said hastily. Fortunately, they had caught up with Hamish, who had reached a fork in the river and was sheltering against a boulder, waiting for directions. Toby had never been more pleased to see anyone.

He grinned at them with chattering teeth. "Having fun?"

"Fun?" Meg said. "Hamish Campbell, you haven't got the brains of a peewit! Freezing in a storm on a mountain, being hunted by Sassenach soldiers and Sassenach demons, and why would you think we're having fun?"

"Why else would you be holding hands? Helping Big Toby up the hill?"

Meg snapped that she would clip his ear. Toby wondered how long he'd been holding her hand and why he hadn't been aware that he was. He realized, too, that Meg regarded Hamish as he did—as just a kid. That meant she was more than a kid, didn't it? How long *had* he been holding her hand? Helping her up a steep bit, then not letting go . . . Had he ever held her hand walking home from Lochy Castle? If this was the first time, why hadn't he been more aware of it? Because he had always thought of her as a child?

"Right fork," Rory said, coming up behind. "I do wish you'd tell me what you're going to do with that sword, boy. How are you faring, Miss Campbell? I wish we did not have to subject a lady to such uncongenial circumstance."

Meg simpered, but she had not released Toby's hand. "Oh, I fare well, thank you, sir! Are we not like the mother plover, who feigns a broken wing and so leads the foe away from her nestlings? We have drawn the hexer away from Fillan!"

"So you have! A very poetic allusion!"

"The plover runs toward danger, not away from it!" Toby said.

Meg looked up at him with disgust.

Rory laughed.

The track soon disappeared altogether. The entire world disappeared behind walls of sleet and draperies of rain. Reality was reduced to rocks, grass, patches of heather, fading swiftly to gray in all directions. It moved underfoot, but never arrived anywhere or changed significantly. The journey had become an endurance test. The only hints of excitement came from the little stream, whose peaty brown waters already frothed at the lip of the banks. The wind buffeted, snatching away breath, trying to freeze any flesh it could reach, turning even raindrops into needles. Rory decreed the way with undiminished confidence, although Toby was hard put to believe he could possibly know where he was.

Hamish lost some of his enthusiasm, no longer questing ahead like a hound. He was the most agile, with Meg a close second, hampered by her long dress. Father Lachlan kept up a steady pace. Toby cursed his outrageous sword and himself for being such a fool. He could not admit defeat and discard it now, of course. A man had pride.

The way grew steeper. Snow swirled in the air now, starting to coat the ground. Only Rory had shoes. Toby had never worn such sissy things in his life, although he had kept a couple of leathers he would wrap around his feet when he attended to the chores in winter. In really bad weather he just stayed home. True Highlanders prided themselves on being hardy, but even true Highlanders had to make concessions to the rigors of their climate sometimes. With a regular job at the castle and his feet grown to full size—they *couldn't* be going to get any bigger!—he had been reconciling himself to acquiring a pair of shoes and probably a leather cape. He could use them now. . . .

"Can't bring horses up here!" Hamish crowed, scrambling on hands and knees up a scree slope. "This'll stop the demons! Won't it, Father?"

"I expect it will," Rory said cheerfully. "We'll find them waiting for us at the top."

"Is that possible?" Meg asked.

Father Lachlan just nodded grimly and kept on plodding.

Once they came to an overhanging rocky wall that had even Hamish looking baffled. Toby cupped his hands and hoisted him overhead until he found a handhold and scrambled up. Meg smiled gratefully and offered a foot. Then it was Father Lachlan's turn—Hamish and Meg grabbed his arms and pulled him after them.

Rory beamed royally and raised a muddy shoe. Scowling, Toby cupped his hands once more. That left him alone, but he jumped, caught a grip, and swung himself up unaided, sword and all. He found Rory waiting for him, while the other three had moved on ahead.

"You are definitely useful, Muscles." The silver eyes twinkled devilishly. "Too good to waste."

"What does that mean?"

"It means you are promising material. You have strength and a certain raw brute courage, even if your brains leave much to be desired. I'll turn you into a rebel yet! Field craft, horsemanship, swordsmanship, unarmed combat—a month or two should do it. We'll make you the terror of the Sassenachs from the Mull of Galloway to John o' Groat's."

"I'll choose my own enemies, thank you. And my own friends."

MacDonald shook his head. "Lummox, you have already chosen your enemies, and they plan to hang you. Now you need friends, don't you?"

Toby scowled and said nothing. Some men were strong enough to stand alone.

"You don't want any *more* enemies, do you?"

"Is that a threat?"

"Could be."

It was time to change the subject. "Listen. I've been thinking."

"A novel experience?"

Toby's fists clenched. "If you're so smart, Master MacDonald of Glencoe, then explain something to me. Ten years ago, King Nevil put a price on Lady Valda's head. Has she ever been pardoned?"

"Not as far as I know."

"Then if she's not on Nevil's side, perhaps she's on your side—the rebels' side."

Rory sobered. "Never! She's the sort of help that nobody needs." He strode in silence for a moment, as if choosing his words carefully. "All right—here's how I see it. Any hexer is inherently evil. Valda may still be opposed to Nevil, but Oreste certainly isn't. In that case, he's come hunting her for his master and you're mixed up in some sort of demonic duel. If she's made her peace with the king of England, then she's hand in glove with Oreste, which is even worse."

"Doing what?"

"I wish I knew! Hunting down Fergan? That would not be difficult for them. Either of them could find him easily, and then destroy him. Demons are his worst danger. It's no secret—the reason we Scots tend to lose when we fight the English is not just that they have more men and better guns. The Sassenachs often use gramarye, too, and we've never had many hexers in the hills. Theirs is the sort of help you're better off without. Fergan feels that way, or I assume he does, because of the way his father died. You know about that?"

"King Malcolm died at Leethoul, the Battle of the Century." Toby had managed to forget most of the history Hamish's father had taught him; that fragment must have escaped.

"Eyewitnesses claimed he drew his dirk as the fighting started and cut his own throat. Perhaps it's not true, but it could well be. A single demon can't destroy a whole army bodily, but it can swing a battle!

"So even if Valda has dreams of raising an army here to carry on her fight with Nevil, whatever that fight is, I don't want anything to do with her, and I'm certain that Fergan doesn't either. If we won with her help, we'd probably end up wishing we hadn't, and be in a worse state than before." Rory wiped rain from his face. He was very familiar with his king's thinking.

"I don't know what she's up to, but I'm sure I would hate it. One possibility is that she's come to the Highlands to harvest some more demons. Father Lachlan says she has at least four already. With that much power at her command, she can enslave any elemental she can locate, understand? And not just elementals—spirits, even tutelaries!"

"Tutelaries aren't demons!"

"They can be made into demons! They can be enslaved, ripped from their locales . . . And tutelaries are more . . . I suppose 'sophisticated' would be the right word—Father Lachlan can explain this better than I can. He says when tutelaries are perverted they make even deadlier demons than simple elementals do. Just because we've never had many adepts here in the hills, we still have more native spirits than the more populated parts of Europe do. You've heard of the siege of Oban? It wasn't the armies that decided that—it was when York's demons overcame the tutelary that the town fell, and the demons roamed the streets, burning people and tearing them apart. So Valda and Oreste between them can do more damage around the Highlands than whole regiments of fusiliers. I just hope they are enemies still, and not partners!"

Toby almost wished he had not asked, but it was a pleasant change to have the rebel drop his flippancy and address him as an adult. It tied in with some of what Father Lachlan had hinted about his motives. Meg had stopped and was waiting for them, but he asked anyway:

"So what's your interest in me, sir? Where do I come into this?"

Rory cocked an eyebrow at him. "Valda wants you as a lover, of course! Lucky lad! Are you willing?"

"Never!"

"No? Quite certain? Don't you lust at all to fondle that pale aristocratic flesh?"

"No!"

"Ha! Any woman scorned can be a dangerous enemy, Longdirk, and that one is hell in a basket! You seem to have a knack for collecting enemies. Don't you think you need all the friends you can get?" With a laugh, the rebel pushed on up the slope to rejoin Father Lachlan.

"Isn't he wonderful?" Meg sighed.

"Wonderful?" That was not a word Toby would have used to describe the man in question.

"Oh, yes! He's a real gentleman!"

"And Lady Valda is a real lady!" Toby snapped.

6

The snow had turned back to sleet and then to mere rain. The travelers had reached the pass, a windswept moor flanked by steep hills on either hand. Clouds streamed low overhead, and wind thrashed the heather.

"See the burn?" Hamish exclaimed. "It's flowing the same way we're going! It's leading us!"

"I wish I could move that fast!" Meg sighed.

"Well, it means we're going downhill. . . . Toby? What'ch you looking at?"

Toby had stopped. Everyone looked where he was staring. "Those rocks? You see anything odd there?"

No one commented until Father Lachlan said:

"What do you see, my son?"

"I think I see a hob."

"Indeed? I see nothing, but my eyes are not as good as they were. Anyone else see it?"

"Just rocks," Rory said. "What does a hob look like?"

"Nothing at all when I look straight," Toby admitted. "But out of the corner of my eye . . . a sort of shimmer. It's right by that pointed one at the moment. It's the way the hob looks, back in the glen."

Hamish squeaked. "I never saw the hob in the glen!"

"I did, sometimes."

"Where?" His eyes were wide, not wanting to disbelieve his hero, but worried that he was being kidded.

"Several places. Outside the schoolhouse a few times. At the games, once—finding out what we were all up to, I suppose. It's nosy!"

"If that one's just watching us," Father Lachlan said, "then I think we should just proceed. Staring may alarm it."

He shepherded them onward. They moved faster than before, edging away from the rocks. The shimmer flitted to another boulder.

"I expect it's merely curious," the friar continued soothingly. "It won't be a hob, not up here, just a wild elemental. They're usually called specters in mountains. Those that inhabit groves of trees are dryads. Bogies in bogs, naiads when they live in water . . . I doubt if there's any significant difference between the various types."

"Why not a hob?" Toby asked

"Hobs have some experience with people. But to see any immortal is unusual. This is very interesting! Of course Fillan knew you, so it let you see it. But a wild elemental is another matter altogether! I am truly surprised that you can see it, my son, and more surprised that it is interested in you, because it obviously must be. Most curious."

Toby had to turn his head to watch now, for they had gone by. "Could I go and speak with it? If I gave it an offering, would it help me? Ask it to stop Lady Valda—"

"No, lad," Father Lachlan said sadly. "First, you can never trust a wild elemental. It might turn on you or betray you to the hexer instead of aiding you—remember the wisp? Secondly, to make it understand what you wanted of it would be almost impossible; and then it would probably forget the whole affair as soon as you left. Thirdly, adepts like Lady Valda are constantly on the lookout for more demonic slaves. If she detects that one, she may seek to entrap it—if not now, then later, when she is not pressed for time. That is why I am surprised that it has allowed you to see it. Elementals are naturally distrustful of mortals for that very reason."

"Valda can't be following us!" Hamish protested. "*No one* could get horses up that hill!"

Father Lachlan did not reply, but Toby was sure he disagreed. Hamish began speaking in Latin with him. The old man responded, seeming to spend more time correcting his grammar than telling him anything.

Quite soon after that, the way pitched downward.

The wind was still vicious, but the world grew larger: life began to seem more tolerable. Green hillsides dotted with cattle came into view below the thick flannel sky. The glen ahead was narrow and steep-sided, and apparently almost uninhabited.

Toby was sore, hungry, and soaked to the skin, and he knew none of his companions were in any better shape. The idiotic broadsword had bruised his backbone and made his shoulders ache—but everyone else must be in just as bad a mess, and he felt better being able to see where he was going.

This was new country for him, his first glimpse of the world waiting for him outside the glen. It wasn't much different, except for the absence of cottages.

Hamish had noted that also. "Why aren't there more people?" he demanded of Father Lachlan. The three of them were together at the head of the parade.

"You'd best ask Master Rory about that." The acolyte had pulled his hood back, seemingly oblivious to the drizzle. "I think the earl reserves Glen Shira for hunting."

"Nice for the deer."

Father Lachlan chuckled. "Until he comes for them! Another reason may be Loch Fyne. People would rather live close to the water." A gleam of eyes over glasses suggested that the remark was intended as a question.

"So they can get about in boats."

"Right you are."

"And Loch Fyne is a sea loch, of course, and the sea is the greatest highway of them all. You can sail from Loch Fyne to anywhere in the world, can't you, Father?"

"If you have a ship."

"France," Hamish said. "Castile, Flanders, Aquitaine, the Kingdom of the Two Sicilies . . . "

"You'd like that, would you?" Toby asked.

He was granted a cheeky grin. "What I'd like most right now would be a warm fire, a dry plaid, and a dead cow on a spit."

"Add one for me," said Father Lachlan, "and two more for Master Toby."

They were both bearing up very well, the boy and the older man. And so was Meg. Toby glanced back. Rory was yattering his head off at her. That was beginning to seem serious! She was very young. That ax-nosed smoothie was trying to impress her with his smarmy manners. Toby had promised her pa he would look after her, but he couldn't handle Rory. Rory could tie him in knots, even without drawing his sword. . . .

"I beg your pardon, Father?"

The little man smiled up at him over his spectacles. "I said I think that one has her head on straight."

Hamish had run off to inspect the river, perhaps hoping to find a suicidal trout to tickle.

"Uh? Who? Meg?"

"Meg Campbell. I don't think she's any more fickle than most young ladies. You don't need to be jealous yet."

"Jealous? Me jealous? I . . . " Toby decided not to explain. Let the old man think what he liked.

"Master Glencoe is a better friend than an enemy, my son."

"Friend? The likes of him can never be friends with a churl like me."

"That's not true, my son," the acolyte said gently. "He outranks you, yes, but if you think that prevents him from being your friend, you don't understand the duties of a chief. The relationship between man and master is a very close one. Many legal systems regard it as the closest tie of all, even closer than marriage. My order disagrees, but others do not. A good chief cares very deeply about his men, for they have wagered their lives upon his judgment—as he wagers his upon their courage and loyalty. He values his followers ahead of anything else."

Toby said nothing.

After a moment, Father Lachlan continued even more softly, as if musing more to himself than his companion. "You are not of Clan Campbell, of course, and Fillan lost its hereditary laird. Perhaps that is the trouble?" He peered up shrewdly over his glasses. "We must all take the world as it is, Tobias, and make what we can of it.

Everyone owes loyalty to someone. If you own land, you need men to defend it. If you do not, you need a leader to defend you. Soldiers obey their officers, lairds obey their kings. Even kings do homage to the Khan. A good master is beyond price. The law should protect everyone, high or low, but in practice it inevitably favors the great. You will never find happiness or security in these troubled times until you find a good master and give him your heart."

Obviously Toby must now say something tactful. "I admit that I would rather be Rory's man than Lady Valda's. Can you describe this hex you think she put on me, Father?"

The acolyte sighed and pushed his spectacles up his nose so far that he had to pull them down again to see over them. "Not easily. Remember what I said about powers—hexers have no powers of their own. All Valda can do is use gramarye to compel her demons to carry out her wishes, so what she would have done—if she did it, and remember that we are only guessing—is order one of them to force you—or whoever she wanted to put a hex on, that is—to do whatever it is she wants doing." He frowned as if he had confused even himself with that statement. "And a demon's range is not unlimited. It depends on the training it has had and the hexer's skill. Incarnated demons are less potent than those confined in material objects, like gems." He chuckled squeakily. "The irreverent refer to those as 'bottled' demons, by the way."

Toby had a strong impression that his question had not been answered at all. He took another look back at Meg.

He cried out.

In the far distance, a line of riders was coming in pursuit.

FIVE

Events in Glen Shira

1

"Run!" Rory bellowed. **"Take off that accursed sword,** drop your bundle, and run for your life!"

They were all shouting at him to run. Toby stood with his arms folded and stared over their heads, ignoring them. Run away? Absurd! He couldn't leave Meg. Or Hamish. Or even old Father Lachlan. Rory MacDonald could look out for himself, but the others could not be abandoned to the demons. He must stay and fight. It would be two swordsmen against four, and the four were not only mounted but also superhuman. Even so, he could not run away.

Hamish was squealing, shriller than ever. "You told me it was stupid to give your life—"

"This isn't that," he said quickly. This wasn't bravado, show-off Campbell-of-Fillan courage. This was a question of manhood.

"Toby Strangerson!" Meg shouted. "You are being mulish. I hate you when you act stupid!"

The riders had disappeared into a slight dip, but they would still be coming.

Father Lachlan yelled, "Quiet!" and the babble stopped. "You must run, Tobias! It is you they are after. We shall be much safer if we are not with you. We can take cover under the riverbank, and they will go past us. It is our only hope."

"I promised I would look after Meg!"

"And this is the best thing you can do for Meg! I'm sure you can run faster than any of us. Leave the sword and head for the shrine. It is only a mile or so. If you can reach it, you will be safe—or at least safer than you are now. Pray for us to the spirit. Now go!"

"Drop the sword, Strangerson!" Rory snapped.

"No!"

They all started yapping again like a litter of puppies. This time it was Rory MacDonald who shouted them down, flushed with anger, silver eyes blazing. "Is that a demon sword? Is that why you won't be parted from it?"

"Huh? What's a demon sword?"

"No, it isn't!" said Father Lachlan. "It's just a sword. A neighbor gave it to him, after all the trouble started. We'll take care of your sword, my son. You have my word. Now, hurry!"

The riders came into view, much closer, seeming to move faster than before.

"My sword will be of more use against horsemen than yours will, Master Rory," Toby remarked.

"Bonehead! You think demons will let you draw it? They'll turn you to stone."

"Please, Toby!" Meg said. "The mother plover, remember? You must draw the demons away from us. Please? For my sake?"

Oh! Put like that, running away did not seem so unthinkable. Reluctantly, he dragged the scabbard strap from his shoulder. Rory took the sword. The relief from the weight was extraordinary.

Toby turned and began to run.

It felt all wrong. He almost stopped and went back, but then he found his stride and it was too late. Mother plover: draw the danger away from the nestlings. Faking a broken wing would not be required in this case. They knew he couldn't fly.

He was built for sprinting, not for distance. The shrine was a horribly long way off.

The glen ran straight as a pike, narrow and bare. The right side, beyond the Shira, was precipitously steep. This side was gentler. At the limit of sight in the rain a wooded bluff marked the Shrine of Shira—so Father Lachlan and MacDonald had said. That was where the buildings were; the shrine itself was in a cave, a little higher up the hill.

They were assuming that the spirit would grant him

asylum—*if* it didn't object to the demon in his heart as the bogy had done, *if* it was strong enough to resist Valda and her pack, *if* Valda and her pack didn't come into range and freeze him first. What was their range? They might be close enough already. The hexer might be just enjoying the chase, knowing that she had her trophy in the game bag.

His feet slapped in the mud of the track. Rain blew in his face. He pushed himself as hard as he dared.

Demon! Demon, I need you now!

His appeal went unanswered. His heart thumped madly, but he did not hear the mysterious *dum . . . dum . . .* he had heard before. No weird light, no superhuman strength to fly him down the road. *Demon, demon!*

He glanced back. His companions were hurrying to the river. The riders were almost level with them but still coming after him. Hiding from demons was crazy. Valda had brought horses up the Eas a Ghail.

The shrine seemed as distant as ever. His heart was thundering, his lungs bursting. No use keeping anything in reserve—it was win the race or die. His waterlogged plaid weighed more than a cartload of meal. He fumbled with his belt buckle, dropped the load, and raced on, wearing only his bonnet.

There was an isolated croft off to his left. A man stood in the doorway, staring at this strange race disturbing his solitude. Toby wanted to yell at him to hide, to warn him that those were demonic creatures pursuing him, but he lacked the breath.

Where was his demon protector now, the presence that had saved him from the bogy, from Crazy Colin, from Valda in the dungeon? If that had not been a demon, but only a hex, as Father Lachlan suggested, then perhaps Valda had corrected her mistake and removed it.

He glanced over his shoulder. His companions had disappeared, but the pursuers had not tarried to deal with them—all six were still following. That was good! The plover had led the danger away from the nest. He need not be ashamed of his decision, then. But the race was almost over. Valda was in the lead, and she was already passing the sad little bundle of his plaid lying in the track.

He turned his face forward again, blinking through the rain. The shrine was closer, yes. He wasn't going to make it. Even if he reached the bluff, he would still have to run up to the buildings in the grove, and then on to the shrine itself. Hopeless!

His head was about to burst. The world was disappearing behind a black fog. There was a taste of iron in his mouth. He could hear the slapping of his feet and the rough gasps of his breathing . . . and now he could hear hooves, also. They had him.

He started to look around, missed his footing, sprawled headlong into the mud.

Almost before he landed, his hands came down to push him up again. He raised his head . . . he froze. Every muscle turned to stone. He lay helpless at the mercy of his pursuers, staring fixedly along the road ahead—a road he was destined never to walk as a free man. The shrine was half a mile away, farther than the moon. Valda had him now . . . naked and helpless as a newborn babe.

Hooves beat nearer.

And kept coming.

The ground shook, mud splattered all over him. A horse thundered by him, its iron feet missing his hand by inches. Lady Valda, robed and riding sidesaddle, but hunched forward as she pursued a prey that lay unseen behind her.

More tumultuous hoofbeats, mud spraying—one by one, the four hooded demonic creatures followed their mistress. But the last two . . . their heads were wrong. One was canted forward, chin on chest, and the other flopped horribly to one side, bouncing in time with the horse's stride. And finally went the lady's maid, alone.

They all rode on without a backward glance. They had not turned, had not looked down, had not seen their quarry in plain view beneath them. Valda, the first two demons, then the two corpses, the maid—all went galloping along the highway and dwindled rapidly into the distance. The sound of hooves faded away into the steady hiss of rain and the rustle of wind in the heather. What did they think they were pursuing?

Finding himself no longer petrified, Toby scrambled to his feet. His companions were coming back into sight, climbing the riverbank. He was plastered all over with mud, and he had scraped himself when he fell. His plaid still lay in the road. He pushed himself to a weary trot toward it, so he could take it to the river and make both it and himself respectable before the others reached him.

2

He was shocked to see how exhausted they all were. It had been an arduous day and night would come early. The light was already fading.

Hamish had been set to carrying the sword. Not being tall enough to wear it, he held it over his shoulder. He was canted sideways under its weight, but he had a grin to match its size.

"The spirit!" he yelled. "It saved us! This is its territory. Thanks to Father Lachlan!"

"Oh, I doubt if I made any difference," the acolyte said. "I think the spirit understands the problem much better than I do—but it never hurts to ask." He adjusted his glasses and beamed benevolently. "Shira has placed us under its protection. Now we must go and give formal thanks."

Rory's pale eyes shone improbably bright in the twilight. "That's certainly one possible explanation."

"What's the other?" Toby demanded angrily.

"Why ask me? You seem to have contrived another of your astonishing escapes—you tell us."

"I don't know!" Toby glared around at his companions, all suddenly so quiet that he could hear his heart again: *Dum . . . Dum . . .* Balderdash! Everybody's heart beat! Just because he could hear his heart doing its steady slow thump did not mean that his demon had pulled off another rescue. It had been nothing like as loud as he'd heard it in the dungeon or by the hob's grotto. More like Glen Orchy. And he did not recall hearing it like that when he'd been lying naked in the road.

Whatever had saved him—the spirit of Shira or a personal guardian demon—it certainly had shown no interest in maintaining his self-respect.

"Don't look at me like that!" he yelled, girding on his sword again. "I don't know any more than you do, any of you! *I* certainly didn't do anything, if that's what you're wondering. I just fell flat on my face. Will they be back, Father?"

The acolyte shrugged wearily. "I don't think so. The spirit has shown it can blind the hexer; I am sure she will not dare a direct assault on it. I hope it will enlighten us. . . . Have faith, children! Evil has been balked, that is what matters."

"You're not hurt?" Meg asked. She looked worried, as well she might. She had not run into Toby's arms to welcome him. Why had he expected her to?

"I deserve to be." Certainly his pride was hurt. What must she think of him? Great, clumsy oaf—some protector her father had chosen for her! Demons pursued him and he tripped over his own feet.

Rory snorted. "Let's walk. We need the exercise."

As they set off, Toby said, "Father? What's a demon sword?"

The tubby little man peered at him and then at the hilt behind Toby's shoulder. "A blade that has slain a demon—an incarnate demon, of course. The blow through the husk's heart, you know? The blades are supposed to possess power against demons." He glanced apologetically at Rory. "With all due respect . . . I don't believe in them."

The rebel shrugged. "One hears stories. I never met one myself."

"Oh, I have met them. Men bring them to the sanctuary and ask the tutelary to authenticate them. They always turn out to be perfectly ordinary blades. The whole notion is pernicious!" The acolyte had abandoned his normal calm and become quite fervent. "This foolish superstition has killed far too many innocent people! A touch of brain fever, a mysterious accident, or just plain spite . . . someone gets accused of being possessed and is promptly stabbed through the heart so the killer can claim to own a demon sword—which he will sell to you for a price, of course! I see no reason to believe that Master Strangerson's blade is anything out of the ordinary."

"It's a load of scrap iron," Rory agreed solemnly.

The little man pushed his eyeglasses up his nose. "And the whole idea of stabbing demons through the heart is nonsense! It's ridiculous! How can anyone expect them to stand still for that? You take a sword to a demonic creature, and I'll tell you which one of you is going to die!"

"I'd much rather not." If Rory was amused by the acolyte's ardor, he was keeping an admirably straight face.

"Can't you creep up behind them?" Hamish looked so concerned that he must be planning to take up demon-stabbing as a sport.

"Of course not! The demon could hear you thinking!" Father Lachlan wagged a finger at him. "I don't suppose there are a dozen genuine demon swords in all the realms of the Golden Horde, or ever have been! So who can know anything about their supposed powers?"

Abashed, Hamish walked on in silence for a moment, then: "What can you do about demons if you can't impale them?"

"Head to the nearest shrine or sanctuary and pray, of course. Which is exactly what we are doing now."

So Toby's sword was just a sword, and not even much of one. He was not surprised. He had acquired it after he became hexed, so for it to be hexed as well would require an absurd coincidence. The curious fascination the great bull-sticker held for him was not caused by the sword; it came from some perversion in himself.

Swords didn't kill people; swordsmen did.

3

Dark was falling by the time the travelers reached the buildings. They were uninviting—old and gloomy, with stone walls and black slate roofs huddled under dripping trees. Some of the roofs had collapsed. The tiny windows were all dark. The overgrown yard looked as if it had been deserted for years, without dogs or chickens, or any signs of life at all.

"Let me see now," Father Lachlan said fussily. "It's years since I was here, but I doubt if anything's changed. Which one is the keeper's house, do you recall?"

"The one at the end," Rory said curtly.

"Whose are the rest, sir?" Hamish looked worried, very worried.

Rory just growled.

The acolyte said, "They are for pilgrims—doesn't look as if we have any company."

"Understandable!" Rory was glaring around him. "Who would want to visit a sty like this?"

Father Lachlan made a tactful, soothing noise. "I shall go and inform the keeper of our arrival. I fear it is too late for us to visit the spirit tonight." He plodded off through the weeds.

"Let's try this one first!" Rory headed for a cottage with the others at his heels.

Just to get under cover and out of the rain was a huge relief. The prospects were not encouraging otherwise. Only rusty hinges remained to show where the door and shutters had once hung. The interior was dark, but the rebel soon located a lantern with a stub of tallow in it. No other man could possibly have produced dry tinder after such a day, but in seconds he had the lantern lit.

The central hearth had no chimney; rain had been entering through the smoke hole above it, but the roof seemed fairly sound otherwise. Clearly the hut had not been used for months or years, and the last tenants had not cleaned up before they left. The only furniture was a flattened heap of straw that reminded Toby of the dungeon at Lochy Castle. On this dank fall evening the place reeked of rot and neglect.

Rory growled again, louder and fiercer. "It's a disgrace, an absolute outrage!"

"Who is supposed to look after it, sir?" Hamish asked in a very small voice.

"The keeper, of course! The Reverend Murray Campbell. Your dear cousin is a first-class miser. All pilgrims make offerings to the spirit, but most leave money for the upkeep of the shrine, too. He must have a king's ransom buried somewhere, but he won't spend a farthing of it." Rory had dropped his frivolous manner; for once he sounded as if he really cared about something other than his precious rebellion.

"But, sir . . . doesn't the laird have any say in how the shrine is maintained? Doesn't it reflect on the whole glen?"

"Mind your tongue, lad! Remember who's laird here."

Toby was no Campbell. "Just because a man's an earl doesn't mean he isn't a fool."

Rory swung around violently, his hand snaking to the hilt of his sword.

"Does it?" Toby added, putting his fists on his hips.

Rory seemed to consider a little punitive bloodletting and then decide against it. "I know more fools who aren't earls. I also know that the Campbell has more than once sent workmen to restore this shrine. The keeper scares them away by telling them they are annoying the spirit. I assume he then uses the lumber for firewood, or sells it. Have you any helpful suggestions to offer?"

It was a fair question, more than fair. They were all tired and hungry and short-tempered. "No, sir. And I will apologize to His Lordship . . . when I meet him."

"You do that!" Rory said, releasing his sword.

Hamish said, "Um?"

"Yes?"

"If the laird were to allow the keeper to charge pilgrims for the use of the repaired cottages, sir?"

Rory stared at him for a moment, and then chuckled. "Ingenious! Suggest that to the earl . . . when you meet him!"

"Yes, sir." Hamish grinned, but briefly. He was understandably more depressed than any of them by this first sight of his new home. "What about food, and fires, and dry clothes?"

"Ha! What do you think? Pilgrims are supposed to bring their own. You've never met your esteemed cousin?"

"No, sir."

"Ah! Well, Murray can be awkward. He's more or less a hermit. He hates men, and women terrify him. I'm not sure how he reacts to boys. Take that feather out of your cap before he sees it." The rebel had become ominously sympathetic all of a sudden.

"Do I call him 'Father'?"

"If you want. He's not a full acolyte, so you'll be flattering him. You can call the spirit a tutelary, too. Again, that's just a courtesy."

Toby had removed his sword and was stretching his shoulders luxuriously. "What's the difference between a spirit and a tutelary? Strength?"

Rory hesitated. "Strength? No, not at all. Talk with Father Lachlan if you want to discuss theological niceties. You will not go too far wrong if you think of a hob as a child, a spirit as an adolescent, and a tutelary as an adult. It has nothing to do with age, because they are all immortal. Just . . . experience." There was warning in his eyes.

"Oh—thanks!" Being familiar with the Fillan hob's

tantrums, Toby should not have asked such a question here in the precincts of the shrine. Hobs could be touchy and unpredictable, even dangerous. So could adolescents.

Rory turned his attention back to Hamish, who was looking more apprehensive than ever.

"Did you bring any money, laddie?"

"Pa gave me some."

"Hang on to it! Murray has never learned that the stuff can be spent, too. Go and see if any of the other cottages are any more habitable. Brawny laddie, you go find some firewood."

Toby shrugged and followed Hamish out into the rain. He strode over to the cottage that had been named as the keeper's. Finding a miserably small woodpile there, he began stacking logs on his arm.

The door opened and Father Lachlan emerged. He said, "Oh!" Then he said, "No one there, I'm afraid." He had taken a surprisingly long time to hunt for a man in a one-room cottage, and his guilty air showed that he thought that Toby thought that.

Toby said, "Would you mind giving me a hand, Father?"

He held out both arms so the acolyte could load logs on them.

"No fire lit, but the house is inhabited. I was trying to establish how long the keeper has been gone. One always worries that he might have fallen sick or had an accident."

One always thought, Toby thought, that the spirit would take care of the keeper. He couldn't think of anything tactful to say, so he said nothing. He assumed that acolytes were capable of being nosy, like anyone else. Father Lachlan had likely just been measuring the staleness of crusts and estimating the thickness of dust.

Bearing a good third of the woodpile, Toby returned to the cottage. Hamish and Meg were sweeping the floor with handfuls of broom, while Rory knelt at the hearth, nurturing a seedling of fire. He glanced up, apparently back in his usual irreverent good humor.

"Any signs of the holy Murray?"

"No fire lit," Father Lachlan said. "From the warmth of the fireplace, he must have been here last night. He may have gone down to the loch for supplies."

"Then we shouldn't expect him back tonight. Can we raid his larder?" Rory bent to blow on his fledgling blaze.

"Larder? I saw no larder! Fasting purifies the soul." The acolyte beamed cheerfully over his spectacles.

"My tastes run more to cannibalism. Shall we draw lots?"

A shadow darkened the doorway. *"Oh it's you, is it?"* roared a new voice. "I might have guessed."

Everyone jumped, except Rory, who rose, beaming amiably. "All good spirits be with you, Father Murray."

"Trouble! You always bring trouble." The newcomer lumbered forward into the pale flicker of the lantern. He leaned on a thick, gnarled staff, moving as if his joints hurt. He was old and gaunt, even skinnier than Hamish—it must run in the family. His faded, waterlogged plaid revealed arms and legs like twigs. His face was a craggy construction, all nose and high cheekbones and protruding jaw, its weathered texture visible through wispy white whiskers. Streaks of silver hair had escaped from under his bonnet, plastered to his face by the wet.

Hamish's mouth had fallen open and his eyes showed white all around the irises.

"Trouble is the lot of us mortals, is it not?" Clearly, Rory was intent on being insufferably angelic. "You know the Reverend Father Lachlan of Glasgow, of course. You will also recall that my name is Rory of Glen—"

"Your name is Trouble!"

"Thank you. Rory of Trouble, I must remember that. I am also happy to present—"

"Who are you fleeing from this time?" The old man's voice creaked like Iain Campbell's mill. "I saw you running to hide down by the road. Who was that after you? Where are they? English, I'll be bound, ready to hang you at last. Outlaw!"

Rory sighed. "I am so sorry to disappoint you, Father. Yes, we were pursued. No, they were not

Sassenachs. Most of them were not mortal. They were demons, led by a notorious hexer."

The keeper thumped his staff on the muck-littered floor. "Balderdash!"

"Father Lachlan?"

"I'm afraid he speaks the truth, Father."

Obviously Father Murray's worst suspicions had fallen short of the mark. For a moment he just chewed, his craggy face writhing as if about to fall apart from sheer outrage.

"Shira itself diverted them and thus gave us refuge," Rory said sweetly. "I suggest you check with it before you order us out of here. Now, may I present—"

"Where's your gear, huh? No victuals, no bedding? I suppose you expect me to provide those? You think you'll empty my larder and burn up all my firewood to dry yourselves? I'm an old man to be chopping firewood while young ne'er-do-wells take whatever they fancy without thought of payment. . . ."

The angrier he grew, the wider became Rory's smile.

"Firewood shall be no problem, Father." He waved a languid hand in Toby's direction. "The boy there will chop all you need. Food, yes, we shall be happy to take advantage of your renowned Glen Shira hospitality, and money we do have—this time." He jingled his pouch. "We shall amply replace what we eat. Now, I am trying to introduce you to your kinsman, Master Hamish Campbell of Tyndrum."

The fearsome old man rounded on Hamish, who backed away a pace and said, "Cousin?" in a thin whisper.

"Kinsman?" the keeper barked. "Not close! Neal Teacher's youngest? Very distant kin! What're you doing running with these rebel dogs, boy?"

Hamish shot an agonized glance at Rory, then at Toby. "I had to leave the glen for a while . . . Father."

"Fleeing from demons?"

"Er . . . Well, no. From the Sassenachs, sir."

"Ha!" Murray Keeper glared triumphantly at Rory. "Now we draw closer to the truth?"

"I am always truthful, Father! Last but most certainly not least . . . " Rory held out a hand to Meg.

As she stepped forward to the lantern, the old man recoiled with a startled cry. "A woman!" His expression of horror suggested that this was the worst news yet.

"Correct! And none other than the famous Lady Esther, youngest daughter of the Lord Provost of Lossiemouth, whose fabled beauty is the toast of Scotland. She takes after him, as you can see. My lady, may I present Murray Campbell, keeper of the Shira shrine? Do not be daunted by his rough exterior, for it conceals a natural shyness and . . . Oh, he's gone! Hurrying off to prepare a feast for you, I expect."

4

With Rory barking orders, the pilgrims located another habitable cottage and set fires in both to warm them. They swept the floors and plugged the windows with makeshift basketwork shutters of ferns and branches. Rory repeatedly denounced the hermit as a slatternly miser; Father Lachlan's efforts to defend him were notably half-hearted. The only furnishings they could find were a few rotted heaps of ferns, which nobody fancied. Rory himself went off to confront the old man; angry shouts echoed through the glade. He returned with a tight jaw and a threadbare blanket for Meg.

Leaving her to manage as best she could, the men resorted to the other cottage to toast themselves and wring out their plaids. No matter that the blaze Rory had built would have roasted a team of oxen, those bulky wool garments would never be dry that night.

Toby smeared Granny Nan's salve on his various scrapes. His back, Rory informed him acidly, was one enormous bruise from the broadsword's bouncing. He could have guessed that.

Four bare men knelt around the fire, smelling

strongly of wet. In the golden firelight, Father Lachlan was soft and pleated, Hamish lean as a board. Rory was all taut muscle, but the reddish hair on his chest failed to conceal a purple bruise there. He scowled when he saw Toby admiring it. Rain beat down on the trees and dripped steadily into a lake of mud in one corner. Someone yawned. Then they all did.

"Don't go to sleep yet," Rory said. "Aren't you hungry?"

Hamish brightened. "The keeper will feed us?"

"He said he would. I showed him gold and he twitched like a dowser's twig." Rory sighed and glanced sideways at Father Lachlan. "Don't judge all holy men by Murray, lads. Father Lachlan is more typical."

The acolyte sighed. "But no more worthy. He has dedicated his life to serving the spirit. Loneliness is a burden."

"He was probably nuttier than a squirrel's hole when he started!" Rory heaved himself upright. "What harm does a keeper like that do to an immortal? What twisted ways of thinking does he teach it? What dubious ethics? Tell me that!"

"The spirit has known scores of keepers and will know plenty more."

Rory did not pursue the argument. "Let's get dressed. Then we'll collect Lady Esther and go see what our host has prepared."

The others rose also and began to drape themselves in wet plaids, all moving stiffly.

"One bright spot in the gloom," he continued cheerfully, "is that Master Hamish will not be bored this winter. The Reverend Murray has never been known to give anybody anything before, but I am sure he will give his willing and industrious cousin more than enough work to keep him busy till the heather blooms. His wages—"

"I'm not staying here!" Hamish howled.

"Those were your father's orders, were they not?"

"Yes, but—"

"Must obey one's parents!" Rory said sternly. "So mine are always telling me, anyway. Here you are, here you stay."

Father Lachlan chuckled. "You're not afraid of hard work, are you? Joking apart, my son, Master Rory is right. Our mission is fraught with considerable risk. You will be safer remaining here."

Hamish turned a stare of abject horror on Toby.

Zits! Toby had given his word to the tanner, but not to the teacher. The boy was not his concern, and the men were undoubtedly right—this was no outing for juveniles. On the other hand, he had made some glib promises to Hamish himself. He had not meant them to be taken seriously, but he had said the words. Now Hamish was going to throw them back in his face. Hamish was going to appeal to friendship.

Where was honor? Where was friendship? A true friend would grit his teeth and tell the kid to be sensible about this. . . . Hamish was not his friend, anyway. He had no friends. He didn't need friends, right? He certainly didn't need Hamish, and Hamish did not need him and his troubles, whatever the kid thought at the moment.

But a man must stand by his word, and the expression on the lad's face would make a demon weep.

"Father?" Toby said. "How many books does the keeper own?"

The acolyte looked at him in bewilderment. "I don't recall seeing any. Why?"

"In that case we may have a serious problem! If Master Campbell is deprived of books for more than two days, he starts having fits. He twitches. He foams at the mouth."

"That's too bad!" Rory snapped. "He can just foam."

"Really? When you were fifteen, Master Glencoe, if someone had told you that a stalwart young Highlander like yourself must stay out of danger by settling in here to work as an unpaid lackey for a deranged miser—how would you have reacted?"

Rory frowned, looked at Hamish, then Father Lachlan, Toby. "I'd have cut out his guts and strangled him with them! Why do you ask?" The familiar silver twinkle was back in his eyes, but for once he was smiling *with* Toby and not *at* him, seeming almost likable.

Toby smiled back. "Just curious. Why don't we go and see what's for dinner?"

Hamish beamed relief and gratitude at his hero.

The keeper's idea of a meal turned out to be scraps of stale bread, raw onions, and one boiled egg per customer. He distributed the salt himself in tiny pinches. Rory restrained his tongue, but he threw the whole log pile on the hearth and handed out a second round of onions from the net of them that hung from the rafters. Had there been anything else edible in sight, he might have pirated that, too, but there wasn't. The hermit glared murder at him.

His cottage was no larger than Granny Nan's, more sparsely furnished, and a great deal dirtier. The host sat on his own tottery chair, Meg on the straw mattress, and the others spread themselves around the open hearth. The only light came from the fire; books were conspicuously absent. The little room was thick with smoke. Toby's eyelids grew impossibly heavy. Meg sank back on the pallet and went to sleep.

The keeper clearly detested Rory, probably with good reason, and yet seemed wary of him. He was respectful to Father Lachlan, ignored the youths, and never once glanced in Meg's direction. As the urgent crunch of onions died away, though, he straightened up on his chair and demanded to know what the supplicants wanted of the spirit of Shira.

Father Lachlan looked to Toby for permission. Toby shrugged sleepily. The acolyte told the story, but without mentioning how he and Rory had become involved, or where they had come from.

Murray Campbell's haggard face reddened steadily. When the tale ended with the miracle on the trail, even that did not mollify his anger. "You have led evil to this holy place!" He sprayed spit in his agitation. "You risk even Shira itself! Four demons, you say that hexer controls—"

"I think you slander the spirit!" Lachlan said sharply. "It has already shown that it can overrule her forces."

The hermit turned a glittering gaze on Toby. "If that

was its doing! But if this man is one of the hexer's creatures which has somehow managed to escape from her compulsions, then he . . . it . . . may have contrived that evasion, not Holy Shira."

His voice was deep and strident. Father Lachlan's was shrill and squeaky, yet it carried more authority.

"You argue in circles, brother. First you fear that the hexer's four demons may endanger the spirit, and then you fear that one demon is stronger than the four. I have faith that Shira is invincible here at its shrine. I do not believe this young man is possessed anyway. I am gambling my life and soul on that. Remember that Valda's army is in disarray. Two of her creatures' husks are dead, so she must soon find new bodies to reincarnate those demons, new victims. If she wishes to bring her full power to bear, she must bottle them instead, even bottle all four of them. This will take time—several days, I hope."

"And while she is doing that, she will be vulnerable to attack by the spirit," added Rory, who had been staying unusually quiet in the background.

Murray swung around to glare at him. "You must leave as soon as you have visited the shrine, my lord!"

"Oh, no! We have used up half your winter supply of firewood. My stalwart retainer there will need two or three days to chop you a replacement—won't you, Longdirk?"

Toby decided he enjoyed the rebel's humor when it was not directed at him. "I don't dare sleep, so I may as well chop wood all night."

The hermit scowled as if believing he was serious.

"I am sure you can sleep safely here, my son," Father Lachlan said. "And sleep sounds like an excellent idea."

It did indeed. Hamish's head was nodding. Toby's jaw would not stay closed. Even a wet plaid on a dirty floor would satisfy him tonight. Let the rain beat on the trees and drip through the dilapidated roofs! Let the logs crackle and smoke. He would sleep soundly if Valda danced naked round the cabin blowing a bugle. . . .

"Wait," Rory said softly. For once the silvery eyes seemed deadly serious. "I have a question. Perhaps you holy men can answer it. But first . . . Tobias, you said that the woman in your dream spoke to you as a lover?"

Toby stopped yawning. He glanced apprehensively at the bed, but Meg seemed to be asleep. He nodded.

"And she called you by name, but not your own name?"

"That's correct. I can't remember what it was."

"A woman's name? Was it by any chance . . . *Susie?*"

A cold shudder ran fingernails down Toby's back and suddenly he was wide awake. "Yes! Yes, I think it was!"

Rory frowned. Everyone was waiting expectantly, even Hamish.

"Here's my question, then, Fathers. When a man is possessed, what happens to his soul?"

"It is still there," Father Lachlan said, "imprisoned with the demon."

"Always?"

Keeper and acolyte exchanged glances.

"Perhaps not always." Father Lachlan adjusted his spectacles. "I have heard of cases where the demon was exorcised but the husk remained inanimate and soon died—as if the mortal soul had gone. When that might happen, I don't know. Would it be displaced at the moment of possession, or expelled by the exorcism? I can't venture to guess. I can't even guess how one could find out. Why? What are you implying?"

"Bear with me!" Rory stretched and made himself more comfortable, raising his knees to lean his arms on them. "I shall have to tell you a story. Could 'Susie' be the name of a demon?"

The acolyte displayed signs of annoyance. "Anything could be the name of a demon—who ever speaks with them? In the lore, they are identified by the names of the places they are thought to have been collected, but I'm sure that is mostly guesswork. In common parlance, to say that you know a demon's name means that you know how to conjure it, but that is not a name in the usual sense, just the formula by which that particular demon is controlled, the words of command."

"Quite," Rory said, evidently satisfied. "Well . . . the story. It's quite long—perhaps it should wait until another day? No? As you please. Well, when I was a mere cub, even cuter than I am now, I was carted off south as a hostage. I know I talk like a Sassenach. I can't help it—I spent my childhood in England. That's why I hate the bast—scum . . . so much. Part of the time I even lived at court. I knew Lady Valda."

5

No one said a word. The fire crackled, the trees thrashed in the storm, but no one spoke.

Rory yawned, enjoying the reaction. "Not intimately, of course, much as I . . . I never spoke with her, and I'm sure she didn't know I existed. I knew her only as one of the ranking courtiers and the most beautiful woman in the land. Men drooled as she went by. The palace floors were permanently soaked. The rugs rotted. Unfortunately, I was at a very impressionable age. I swear my whiskers grew in two years early because of her. You can't begin to imagine how I suffered."

"Get to the point!" old Murray growled, looming over the guests clustered around his hearth.

Rory looked up at him with bland stupidity, an effect spoiled by the golden flames dancing in his silver eyes. "Why? We have all night to talk."

The hermit stretched out his large and horny feet to toast at the fire. "Then I shall narrate the circumstances of your last visit to the spirit."

"Demons, no! Not in front of these innocent young gentlemen!" Rory did not seem very worried, though. He rose. Yawning, he stepped over to the bed and turned the free end of the blanket to cover Meg. He came back to the fire and settled again on the floor with the other three, closer to the fire than before. He grinned, admitting that he was playing tricks with them.

"All right, I'll get to the point. The point is that I was at court when Valda was banished. Now that was a very curious affair! It has never been properly explained.

"I'd spent years taking dancing lessons on an estate near Guildford, in Surrey. A group of us were brought to court at Greenwich in March 1509, to learn some civilized manners. Edwin was still king then. Edwin was a *big* man. Not big like our bareknuckle friend here, although he was beefy enough—big in the sense of domineering. He could be cruel and ruthless, but he was never mean. Edwin might stamp you into the ground, but he wouldn't knife you first. He was a bugle of a man—loud, resolute, overbearing. Early in his rule, he'd been suzerain for a while, and I think he did a fair job of satisfying the Tartars without grinding the peasants of Europe too badly. He fell afoul of some political infighting. The Khan deposed him and appointed the king of Burgundy in his place, but I don't think that had anything to do with Edwin's performance.

"His son Bryton was much the same sort of hard-riding, hard-wenching, crude-but-rather-likable ruffian. Another bugle, but not quite as strident. The middle son, Idris, was quieter, devious, persuasive. A violin, maybe.

"Then there was Nevil. Nevil's mother was Queen Jocelin, Edwin's second wife. There's no question she dabbled in gramarye, and it was generally assumed that she'd snared the old boy by putting a hex on him. Potentates usually keep mistresses, you see, and he didn't. When a top dog does nothing in the nighttime, that's always regarded as curious behavior. No matter . . . Jocelin still had a sexual glow to her, and the old rascal certainly seemed content."

Toby smothered a yawn. Everyone else appeared to be far more engrossed in this irrelevant rigmarole than he was. Hamish's eyes were big as mushrooms. He wouldn't find this in any book.

"Nevil had been absent from court for a year or so—officially studying law at Oxford, although everyone assumed that he was studying gramarye. I'm sure he was, because Oxford is notorious for it. He reappeared in the palace just a month or two after I arrived there. The value of a good school is not what you learn but the friends you make there, yes? Nevil turned up with Lady Valda on his arm. He already had a wife and child, but they were not in evidence and were never mentioned. This was the summer of 1509."

Ten years ago—Rory must be in his middle twenties now. Fair men often looked younger than they really were.

"Nevil was just nineteen, slim, dark. Valda seemed . . . ageless. If Bryton was another bugle and Idris a violin, then Nevil was a harp. He spoke very softly, and there always seemed to be overtones of meaning shimmering behind the main refrain. . . . I'm getting fanciful. He was sweet and he was sinister. He was boyishly young and yet gave the impression of being well seasoned in evil. He was moonlight to Lady Valda's noonday sun.

"Valda hit the court like a charge of gunpowder. No one doubted for an instant that she was a hexer, and everyone waited to see what would happen between her and Queen Jocelin. Well, they had one thing in common—they both wanted to see Nevil on the throne. Within three months, Bryton died of a fever and Idris in a hunting accident. In January, in a fit of total sobriety, Daddy Edwin jumped from a high window and Prince Nevil was King Nevil. It really wasn't difficult at all, now was it?"

Rory glanced around. Father Lachlan nodded, everyone else looked blank. Meg mumbled and rolled over on her side, pulling her legs up. Straw crackled. Father Murray's craggy jaw clenched, but he did not turn his head. Rory caught Toby's eye and grinned faintly.

"Of course, he wasn't officially king until he had made the required visit to Sarai to do homage to the Khan and have his accession confirmed. He never did.

Queen Jocelin left court within a week—probably the wisest move possible under the circumstances. The court gossiped, as courts always do. The courtiers wondered if Valda would be content to remain royal harlot or if she craved royal honors, and what would happen to Nevil's existing queen if she did. They wondered if her powers would extend to making him suzerain. They wondered what France and Burgundy would do—whenever a monarch dies, it's regarded as good manners for his neighbors to invade as soon as possible and grab off whatever they can before his successor gets settled in. Nevil was smart enough and subtle, he just didn't seem strong enough to be an effective ruler. The question was whether Valda could rule through him, or so the gossip went. Then came the infamous Night of the Masked Ball."

Rory glanced around as if to see who already knew about the Night of the Masked Ball. Everyone except Toby was nodding understanding.

"No one knows exactly what happened that night. The king did not attend the ball, and neither did Valda. In fact, Valda was never seen again. He put a price on her head the next day."

"Ten thousand marks," Father Lachlan muttered.

"That came later. It was less to begin with. Nevil himself was changed after that night, dramatically changed. Everyone noticed. Oh, he looked just the same, and he had the same gentle manners and soft voice, but something fundamental was different. He was nothing like a harp anymore, more of a bass drum. He began raising taxes, raising men, planning for war. One of the first things he did was to call us all in—the Scottish hostages his father had collected—and send us home."

Rory's face darkened and he stared at the fire for a moment. "Before we left, he made us swear allegiance at a grand public ceremony in Westminster Hall. I've told you how old I was, and I was not the only madcap youngster in the group. We agreed we were utterly determined to die rather than betray our beloved Scotland. We were going to smuggle knives into the hall, we were going leap out windows in a mass suicide . . . and so on. Of course none of us did anything of the sort. Nevil demanded the full Tartar obeisance, and we kowtowed and touched our faces to the floor and laid the king's foot on our heads and all that, just as we were supposed to. Well-trained dogs!"

He fell silent and continued to scowl at the embers for so long that Hamish plucked up the courage to whisper, "He used gramarye on you?"

Rory turned an eagle glare on him. "Would I admit this if he hadn't? I mean, would I ever admit he hadn't hexed me, when I confess to treason?"

The kid shriveled about three years younger, shaking his head vigorously.

Rory relented with a bitter smile. "Nine years ago and it still rankles! It didn't last, of course. Away from the source demon, hexes soon fade. Or go to any sanctuary and the spirit will take it off you. And in compensation, we were going home! We were all ecstatic at the prospect of seeing the Highlands again—at least we all said we were, but some of us had been prisoners for years and could barely remember our homeland.

"What we couldn't understand was what had come over Nevil. All those hostages his father had used to keep Scotland quiet for a decade—why was he letting us go? The court thought he'd gone crazy. As soon as we were safely home, the Highlands exploded, with every ex-hostage right out in front, screaming to enlist and prove his patriotism. The Lowlands followed. We knew what was going to happen. Everyone knew what was going to happen. It was inevitable. But Nevil knew what he was doing." He grinned. "Well, lad? Have you any suggestions?"

Again Hamish shook his head. "I don't know, sir." He was as intent on the story as a toddler hearing a favorite bedtime fairy tale.

Toby was bored. He stretched his long arms and yawned luxuriously. "Practice! Nevil's father wanted peace. Nevil wanted war. He used the Scottish campaign to temper the army he was raising. The Battle of Norford Bridge, June, 1511 . . . it was an English training bout."

Hamish gaped at him as if he'd grown wings.

Rory laughed. "Muscles," he said, "you are acting out of character! Who told you that?"

"Don't remember." In fact he'd worked it out for himself, at the time, while the Fillan survivors were still limping home. He must have been a horribly cynical little boy to have seen that. He'd even been cynical enough not to speak such blasphemy in the glen, for he'd never told anyone.

"Well, you're absolutely right, although of course it wasn't apparent at the time. It's obvious enough in hindsight." Rory shot a reproving glance at Hamish, who shrugged bashfully. "Nevil was a different man after Valda's disappearance, and a military genius in particular. The French invaded the English enclaves in Brittany and Aquitaine. He invaded France. He didn't merely beat them back and rough them up as he was supposed to under the usual rules. He conquered France, annexed it, and had himself crowned at Reims. Then he went on to grander things. He has never lost a battle, never failed to hold a field or take a city."

"He hasn't conquered the Highlands!" Hamish protested.

"Hasn't he?" growled the keeper from his lofty perch. Rory scowled at the fire and did not answer.

"Admit it!" said the keeper. "He has! He strangled you. Scotland has never been able to throw out the English without the backing of France or Flanders. Now Nevil rules both of them, and half of Europe besides. You have no money, my lord, no guns, no prospects."

Still watching the dancing flames, Rory said, "That's true. At the moment at least, that's true."

Hamish had subsided into horror-stricken silence.

"But?" said Father Lachlan. "If I were King Fergan, which I am not, then I might be thinking of other allies—such as the Tartars themselves." He smirked mischievously, firelight flashing on his eyeglasses.

"Dangerous talk!" Rory snapped.

"Oh, nonsense! If a peaceable old man like me can work it out for himself, then don't you think the English can? I've never heard of the Khan taking any interest in Scotland at all, I admit, but he must be getting seriously worried about Nevil."

The rebel did not want to talk about that.

"What has all this got to do with me?" Toby demanded. "Who was Susie?"

Rory turned thoughtful silver eyes on him. "Do you understand how the Golden Horde runs Europe, how government works?"

"The kings are vassals of the Khan."

"In theory. But in practice? You know the English have to reconquer Scotland all over again every few years. The Tartars haven't brought an army across the Vistula in two hundred years, and yet all of Europe still pays tribute to the Khan. Do you think the Golden Horde's hexers are so much better than ours that they do it with demons?"

"I never really thought about it," Toby admitted, shifting position. He hated being lectured at any time, and it had been a long day.

Hamish chuckled. "It's no use asking Toby about history, sir. My pa could never beat any history into him."

"Couldn't he?" Rory studied Toby again for a minute. "Or couldn't he beat it out of him?"

The boy frowned. "How do you mean?"

"I'll bet it went like this: *Teacher says:* 'Strangerson, the Tartars overran England in 1244. When did the Tartars overrun England?' *Horror Child says:* 'Sir, I don't remember!' He does, but he won't admit it. So your pa reaches for his birch and tries to beat the answer out of him. I would guess that, in this case, he usually lost and Horror Child won. Am I right, Longshanks?"

"No. I never called him 'Sir.' "

Rory chuckled. "And you're still not admitting you know anything, are you? The khanate runs the continent on a simple divide-and-rule system. Whichever monarch is current suzerain grows rich, because he gets to collect and remit the tribute, and he can also call on the others to make war on his personal enemies in the Khan's name. They all want to be the next suzerain, and that keeps them licking the Khan's boots. They know that as soon as the present one begins to get out of line, the Khan will depose him and appoint another.

"But now Nevil is turning the system upside down. He's deposed three suzerains and is about to start on a fourth."

Father Lachlan pushed his glasses up his nose. "I cannot understand why the Tartars haven't marched against him already."

Rory shrugged. "Because the khanate is old and decadent, probably. When they do come, they'll come like a tide. Or else they're waiting for Nevil to cross the Vistula, so they can take him on their home ground. That's when we . . ." He yawned. "Never mind. It's getting late, and this is an odd place to be discussing world politics."

"I thought you were going to tell us about Susie," said Toby.

"So I was, Longsword, so I was. You don't know what a palace is like. It's like a school, with one teacher and hundreds of children. Courtiers are stupid, worthless people. They're idle, useless, and bored. They live in circles, grouped around the ruler, and all they ever worry about is which circle they're in and how they can move closer to the center. Their lives are an endless game."

He shifted, leaning on his left arm and pulling his feet around. His eyes were suddenly very intent on Toby. "They have childish habits."

Toby decided he did not like that stare. "Such as?"

"Such as nicknames," Rory said softly. "Each circle, each little coterie, has its own codewords, its own signals. It's a great honor to be able to address someone of higher rank by his pet name, and of course everyone is always gossiping. The secret names are common knowledge, although just because you know that a senior minister is Wooky to his friends doesn't give you the right to get familiar. As Father Lachlan says, names can be words of power. Names are dangerous—I told you that."

"You're not telling me much now. Who was Susie?"

Hamish gulped.

Rory did not look at him. He kept his eyes on Toby and his free hand hovered close to his dirk. "Got it?"

"Suzerain?" Hamish whispered.

"Right, lad. Susie for short. *Susie* was the innermost secret codeword for King Nevil. That was probably what Valda called him in bed. Your oversized friend used to be Toby Strangerson. He says he still is, but Lady Valda calls him Susie."

6

Morning came, cold and dark, rainy and hungry. The Reverend Murray Campbell hammered on the cabin wall to rouse the men and must have then found the courage to go and waken the fearsome Meg, for they heard him beating on the other cabin also.

Toby moved and groaned aloud. All his joints had frozen and all his muscles petrified. The fire had gone out. He had slept, though, slept like a boulder. The hexer had not haunted his dreams—he had been much too tired to dream.

"Breakfast first, please," said a subdued whisper from Hamish's direction. "A hot breakfast and a blazing fire and dry clothes . . ."

"If we are to break our fast here," Father Lachlan remarked squeakily from Toby's other side, "which I doubt—then it will not be until after we have visited the shrine." His voice changed. "We are one short!"

Toby sat up sharply. Rory was missing.

More trouble? How could there possibly be more trouble than there was already?

"I didn't hear him go. Perhaps he went to the market."

"I just hope he didn't go up to the shrine by himself!" The acolyte found his eyeglasses and put them on, looking worried.

"Is that dangerous?"

"Er . . . not usually. But it would be a grave affront to the keeper."

Toby did not care eggshells for the keeper's feelings, and he thought Rory was more capable of looking after himself than any man he had ever met. He shivered out of his blanket and began pleating it into day wear.

Ten minutes later, he was starting up the path to the shrine. Apparently it was correct procedure to attend to one's devotions on an empty stomach; it seemed disrespectful not to shave first, yet when he had suggested it, Father Lachlan had told him not to bother.

Rain was beating the trees harder than ever. The keeper limped ahead, leaning on his staff. Father Lachlan and Hamish followed him, deep in talk. Toby brought up the rear with Meg. Huddled in her cloak, she was just as irksomely chirrupy as she had been the previous morning, but worrying about Rory.

"He can't have gone far," she said.

"I expect he'll be waiting for us up at the shrine."

Had he wanted to ask the spirit a few private questions?

"I'm not very happy about the shrine," Meg said. "It's easy for you—you were brought up with a hob—but I'm nervous!"

Did she think he wasn't? He was scared to a jelly, but he would die before saying so. The idea of an adolescent hob was very unsettling.

"Don't worry! It isn't going to *do* anything. We're just going to thank it for saving us from Lady Valda and ask it some questions."

Toby supposed he wanted to hear the answers.

They walked on in silence. He could think of nothing to say. What did one say to girls? Meg's crush on him was flattering, and also very disturbing. He was not experienced in friendship, let alone love.

Meg raised her head to peer at him, blinking as the rain fell in her eyes. "Are you going to ask if you're really King Nevil?"

"I thought you were asleep."

"I heard some of it. Are you?"

"No."

"Pity. I would like to be friends with a king." She looked down quickly.

"Not that one, surely?" World traveling must already have made Toby bolder, for he added, "Don't you like me just as myself?"

"Oh! Yes . . . of course."

Good. What was the right thing to say next? Meg made him feel like a clumsy, lumbering ox, but if she didn't mind being seen with a man who must weigh twice—or three times—what she did, then why should he mind? She was a jewel: small and sparkly and full of fire. If he tried to say so, she would laugh her head off. Men couldn't say such things.

"When I am restored to my throne, you can be the belle of the court." Coward! Humor was cowardice. He took her hand. It was icy. She did not pull it away. He closed his great paw over her tiny fist to warm it.

"Does Master Glencoe really think you are Nevil?"

"No, I don't think so. He was just talking nonsense. It's rubbish."

But . . . There were *buts*.

Meg plodded on in silence.

"There's no reason to believe it," Toby protested. But that name, Susie . . . He had not told Rory that; Rory had told him. "Nobody can explain what happened between Nevil and Valda. If she demonized him, then why did she disappear? Why did he banish her?"

"Something went wrong with the gramarye. Or the demon possessed Nevil and then turned on her." Either the tanner's daughter had overheard most of the arguments, or she had been giving the matter much thought on her own.

"Maybe," he admitted. "But then why has she come back now? Why wait ten years?"

"She lost all her demon slaves and had to go hunt down more? Or she has been gathering more gramarye somewhere, learning how to restore him. I mean, she still had Nevil's soul bottled in a jewel, and she chose you to be . . . to . . . A very good choice, of course."

"Thank you." He remembered her words in the dream: *See the fine young body I found for you, my love.* More than the cold trickle of rain inside his plaid made him shiver. "But Father Lachlan says he's never heard of anyone being possessed by a mortal soul."

"He also admitted that Lady Valda must have forgotten more evil than he's ever known, didn't he? He wouldn't say it was impossible."

Yes, Miss Campbell had been listening! "He also said that a man possessed by a demon has superhuman powers that a man possessed by a mortal soul couldn't have."

"And you do?" Meg asked quietly.

"I . . . No, of course not." *But* he had found the way out of the bog. *But* he had bent iron bars to escape from the dungeon. "Even Rory had to admit that Nevil was a superlative horseman and I ride like a sack of coal." *But* that first time, bareback on Falcon, hurtling across country by moonlight . . . Too many *buts*. There was a hex on him, or a demon inside him. He felt soiled, unclean.

"You heard Hamish, didn't you?" he protested. "He asked me all sorts of things about the glen—the names of Dougal Potter's children, what Rae Butcher's shop looks like . . . I answered correctly. I'm Toby Strangerson, not King Nevil!"

But he might be both.

"Do you think I'm not me?" he demanded miserably.

"You never held my hand before it happened."

"Is that a sign of evil?"

"No. It's a big improvement!" She grinned up at him and he discovered he was smiling.

"I'm sorry."

"Sorry for not doing it before or sorry for doing it now?"

"Um . . . sorry I can't hold both of them."

That won him another smile. Her smiles were lovely. He seemed to be doing all right.

Talking with girls was not all that much harder than talking with boys.

7

At close quarters, the cliff was as rotten as old deadfall, pitted with numerous holes. The path led to the largest: the shrine.

Rory was sitting on a rock just inside the mouth of the cave, munching an apple. He tossed the core away without explaining where it had come from. He ignored the keeper's angry glares, smiling blissfully. He looked well rested, but at some point in the small hours he had found time and opportunity to shave. He also looked drenched to the skin, and he had not achieved that inside a cave.

"Morning all! Fine day for a battle—wet the Sassenachs' powder. Longbones, why did you bring that preposterous sword?"

"For the battle, of course." Again Toby cursed himself for cracking jokes. The rebel would guess how nervous he was.

It wasn't just the spirit that was making him nervous, either. He had not meant to bring the sword. He hadn't even realized that he'd strapped it on his back until it thumped on his bruises. Then he'd wanted to take it off—and hadn't got around to it. He could believe he was possessed when he thought of the sword, or else that it was a demon sword and had hexed him.

Rory glanced around the group. "It's customary to make an offering. If you don't have anything suitable, I can lend you some money. That's always acceptable— isn't it, Father?"

He had addressed Keeper Murray, but Father Lachlan spoke up hastily.

"Of course. I brought a book of poems by Wilkin MacRobb."

Meg produced a small brooch. Hamish hesitated and then pulled out a tiny penknife in a leather sheath. Toby would have wagered real silver that it had been a going-away present from his mother, a hint to write often. As for Toby himself, he knew what he would offer. He met the inquiring glance blandly and shrugged.

Rory stood up. "I suggest you be our spokesman, Father Lachlan. The rest of you—stay silent unless you are addressed directly."

So spirits, unlike hobs, spoke to people?

The little acolyte seemed ominously worried, fiddling constantly with his spectacles. "Father Murray and I were discussing . . . We do not plan . . . Even if the spirit does determine that Tobias is possessed . . . as you know, I do not expect that . . . but we do not intend to ask for an exorcism, unless the spirit offers one." His smile at Toby might have been intended as reassurance but wasn't.

The implication was that a country doctor might be allowed to diagnose Toby's sickness, but treatment would require the services of a skilled surgeon in a city. Suppose the spirit decided to try its hand anyway? Did an adolescent elemental yearn to be a big, grown-up tutelary?

Rory gestured to the keeper. "Lead on, then."

Father Lachlan said, "Wait!" He wrung his hands. "Tobias, I must warn you that you may be going into danger. A spirit is not like a wisp. The wisp can be mischievous or spiteful; it cares only for its own whims. The spirit knows the difference between good and evil. It is benevolent. It means well. It looks after the glen and cares for its people. That is the problem! If it detects evil in you, then it may . . . It may take drastic action."

Toby felt all his muscles knot up. His fears were not groundless. He heard his voice come out very harsh: "It may protect you by killing me, you mean?" Unclean!

The dumpy little man nodded unhappily. "I do not

expect this, my son, but you should know that the possibility exists. If you do not wish to enter the shrine, then we shall understand."

One morning, years ago, a little orphan bastard had called in at the tanner's shop in Tyndrum on an errand for old Mara Ford. Kenneth Campbell had been very drunk. He kept the boy there for hours, babbling about Leethoul, the Battle of the Century, how he had taken a musket ball through his leg, and how he had almost bled to death before he was brought to the surgeons. In the next few days the leg had turned black and begun to rot. Horrified, disgusted, fascinated, the boy had stayed to listen.

"They made me decide!" the tanner said, between his incoherent mumbles. "They said if they left it on, it would poison me, and I would die. They said I had lost so much blood already that if they cut it off I would probably die anyway. Then they asked me what I wanted them to do. They had a great butcher's saw there, and men standing around waiting to hold me down. Can't go near Rae's shop without seeing the saws and thinking of that day."

"And you told them to cut it off?" the boy asked horrified.

"I did. I told them I couldn't stand the smell of it. And it still hurts! It isn't there, but I feel its ghost, and it hurts, hurts all the time . . . "

Now the boy was a man and it was his turn to make a decision.

Everyone was waiting. Meg and Hamish were aghast; even Rory was frowning. Murray Campbell's face was a granite outcrop.

"If I am possessed," Toby said, "then isn't a quick death the best thing I can hope for?"

Father Lachlan blinked over his spectacles. "Well, unless the demon can be removed . . . "

"Would it let itself be exorcised? Would it let me approach a sanctuary? I think I can walk into that cave— let me go and ask the spirit!"

"Very well, my son," the acolyte murmured, nodding to the keeper.

The keeper limped forward without a word and the others followed in single file into darkness.

Toby waited until the end, but Rory waved him ahead, bringing up the rear.

He might be going to his death. He might never walk out of this hole.

Why? Why was he doing this? Was it courage? He did not feel very brave. Or was it cowardice? Was he craven like Kenneth Tanner, who had chosen mutilation over the chance to remain a whole man? Was he just afraid to live with uncertainty, desperate for superhuman reassurance that he was only mortal?

This would be his third trial in three days. The Laird of Fillan had tried him for the murder of Godwin Forrester and found him guilty. The elders of the village had tried him for the murder of Granny Nan and acquitted him. Now an immortal would try him for the crime of being possessed.

The still air felt warmer than the wind outside. It had a dead, stony odor, but the absence of rain was a real joy. Someone, at some time, had leveled a path, which wound to and fro like a snake, gently descending into the hill. A rail had been spiked to the wall to guide supplicants; the wood was worn to silky smoothness by the rubbing of countless fingers. He could see nothing ahead except Meg's cap, which was a paler shade than her plaid. He could hear only a faint shuffle of feet and rustle of cloth. There was no echo at all. He sensed that the roof was rising and the tunnel spreading, and he decided that the walls he felt nearby were probably only fallen boulders.

He wondered how safe the roof was, and whether the spirit ever dropped rocks on unwelcome visitors.

Then the others were stopping, edging into a line abreast, silhouetted against a faint glimmer of light ahead. The path had widened into a smooth floor. He stood with Meg on his left and Rory on his right. Taking their cue from the adepts, they all knelt. The rock was flat as ice on a bucket.

His eyes adjusted with maddening slowness. The cavern was huge—far larger than he had expected. He began to make out marble columns and carvings, a strange white stonescape of incredible beauty. Curtains of ice draped the walls. Pointed pillars hung from the roof, masking the source of light, which must be a shaft leading eventually through to daylight. Other columns rose from the floor, except that there was no real floor. He was suspended halfway up the side of the chamber. Overhead hung the toothed ceiling, but downward the chamber was equally rugged, with great white fangs fringing a funnel-shaped pit, from whose heart poured even more light than came from above. It was like nothing he had ever seen or imagined. The spirit must have worked for centuries to make this unearthly abode for itself.

Somewhere water was dripping.

Meg's hand found his, tiny in his grasp. Her fingers were shaking. He squeezed to convey a comfort he did not feel.

The shelf was completely flat and level. It ran all around the cavern, sometimes wide, sometimes very narrow. It was incredibly thin—how could anything so frail even support its own weight, let alone the weight of the worshipers kneeling on it?

Water dripped irregularly: *Plop . . . plip, plop . . . plop . . . plip, plip, plop . . . plop . . .*

Suddenly the lower half of the chamber *rippled* in spreading circles and Toby's head swam with vertigo. He was looking at a pool, a small lake—kneeling on a shore, not a shelf. Crystal-clear water lay exactly level with it, reflecting the roof. The light from below was the light from the chimney above, bent back by the mirror.

"Great Spirit of Shira!" cried Murray's raucous voice. "I bring you supplicants, who come in reverence and good will!" He was at the far end of the line. He had drawn a flap of his plaid over his head to conceal his face. The cavern swallowed his voice without a hint of echo.

"Hear our prayers, Spirit!"

There it was. At the far side of the lake, just over the water—a shimmer. It was a mist, a shower of faint sparkles, a hint of smoke, but not unlike the hob at Lightning Rock. Toby's skin broke out in sweat and goosepimples.

"They bring you offerings!" the keeper screeched. "First, Lachlan of Glasgow, whom you know, a holy man!"

Father Lachlan tossed his book out into the pool. It landed with a splash, sending circles floating outward, rippling the phantom reflections. For a moment it bobbed and floated, and then sank in silence.

But while the surface was disturbed, Toby saw through it. The pool was very shallow, paved everywhere with ancient offerings. He saw all sorts of things: shoes, tools, candlesticks, bowls and goblets, carved figures, little precious things that worshipers had been able to bring with them and dedicate to the presiding spirit. Now they were all white stone. For centuries the immortal must have accepted offerings and preserved them by turning them into white stone to match the rest of its shrine.

The water stilled, the shiny surface again hiding the hoard beneath, but now the ghostly shimmer hovered over the place where Father Lachlan's book had submerged, as if the spirit was examining the sacrifice.

"Hamish Campbell of Fillan, a distant kinsman of my own."

Hamish's penknife made a tiny plop, sinking instantly. The ghostly glimmer of the spirit moved to inspect it. Toby could only just detect it, and he wondered if anyone else had noticed it at all. Meg did not seem to be looking in that direction.

He leaned forward a little. Staring almost straight down, he could see the bottom through the illusion of space. He made out a baby's shoe of pure white marble. What story could that tell?

"Meg Campbell of Fillan."

Meg tossed her brooch only a little way and the glimmer drifted closer.

"Tobias Strangerson of Fillan."

Now! Toby reached up and dragged the straps over his head. He took the great sword in both hands . . . and froze.

This is right! I must be rid of this thing before it perverts me utterly and I wreak devastation with it.

But it had been a gift . . . it would not be right to throw away a gift. If he was possessed, then throwing it away would solve nothing. One sword would do as well as another.

He hugged the blade and its clumsy wooden scabbard to his chest, unwilling to part with it, unable to make the effort.

This is a massacre sword. My arms and strength could do infinite damage with a blade like this. Give the terrible thing to the shrine, and it will never kill anyone again.

If he was only human, then the sword was meaningless. If he was a demon, then he could easily find another. Throwing it away would be a foolish gesture, perhaps even a deception. That might even make him relax his guard, thinking he had disposed of the problem when it was really still there. His fascination with the crude broadsword was a constant warning, and he would be safer keeping it by him as a reminder. . . .

Plop . . . plip, plop . . . plop, plip . . .

Do it now! Quickly!

He raised it overhead with both hands.

Plop, plop, plop . . .

Sweat trickled down his face. The others must all be watching in bewilderment. How long could he hold that weight up there?

Hours, probably. The spirit . . . He thought it was watching him, and such delusions were the toes of madness.

Help me, please!

He heard no answer but he knew what the answer must be: *Help yourself!*

He swayed back to throw and again his muscles locked.

If I do not do this thing now, then I am damned!

So go ahead and be damned! Start by chopping off Rory's head. Then run Meg through and . . . Ugh! *Demon sword!*

He jerked forward, hurling the monster from him like a deadly snake. A spasm of pain almost pitched him face-first into the pool. *Done it!*

The sword spun across the lake, struck the rock wall on the far side, and seemed to fly apart as the scabbard broke open. Water flew up, splashing over the stone draperies and cornices. Tiny waves rushed out, lapping over the edges of the platform. Two narrow planks of wood floated, but the blade had gone.

The spirit stayed where it was, a misty glimmer hovering above the surface a few feet away from him.

"And one already known to you!" Murray cried.

Rory tossed something into the pool without taking his eyes off Toby. There was not enough light to reveal his expression.

"Accept these, their humble tokens!" the keeper brayed. "Guide them in goodness. Holy Shira, hear their prayer!"

The shimmer drifted toward him.

"Most Holy Spirit," Father Lachlan squeaked, an octave higher. "We thank you for rescuing us last night from the evil that pursued us. We thank you for giving us sanctuary here. We come seeking guidance. There is one among us who is grievously troubled."

The cave fell silent. Then:

"Lachlan, Lachlan!" said a new voice. "Why does a man of peace consort with men of violence?"

It could have been the voice of a woman, or an adolescent boy. It was soft, tuneful, appealing. It came from Father Murray, but it was emphatically not his voice. He knelt very still, head bowed, face concealed. He was enveloped in the shimmer of the immortal.

Father Lachlan grunted, and took a moment to frame his reply. "They are not evil men, Holy Shira—no more evil than others. They would gladly go home to their wives and children and be at peace, if only their enemies would do the same."

"We see," said the spirit, through the keeper. "And how do their enemies feel?"

"I think they feel the same."

"Tell us, then, why do they not do this?"

"If the English will go away to their homes, then the war will end. If the rebels go to theirs first, then the English will kill them."

"So why do the English remain here?" asked the haunting, insinuating, inhuman whisper. It might be genuinely seeking knowledge on a tricky ethical problem, or it might be trying to make Father Lachlan admit that he was supporting an evil cause—Toby could not tell.

He did not care overmuch. He had won a victory of some sort. His heart ached for that splendid giant sword, but he was jubilant at having found the strength to discard it—he was not damned yet! But why had it been such an effort? What had the others thought? What had Meg thought?

Then he realized that Father Lachlan's ordeal had ended and the conversation had turned to him.

"Let him speak for himself," said whatever spoke through Murray's mouth. "Ask us what you would know, Tobias."

"Am I possessed by a demon?"

"You are in great danger. Two dangers. The hexer and her demon host await you. She will not trespass here in search of you, but we cannot defend you at any great distance—and would not, anyway. You must go forth and face her."

So spirits were capable of evading issues? It had not answered the question.

"Will you tell me what she wants of me?"

"Your body and your soul."

No evasion there! He almost wished he had not asked. Before he could frame another question, the spirit put one of its own, in its calm, delicate voice:

"Why did you throw away the sword?"

"I could not stand the smell of it." Then Toby realized that Meg might recognize her father's words. She must have heard that story a thousand times. Too late to call them back. . . . "Is it a demon sword?"

"No more than any other sword," the spirit whispered. "Because you gave it to us, Tobias, and because we know what that giving cost you, we shall give you in return what hope we can. We do not fully understand the ethics of the burden you bear, so we shall leave it to others vaster in wisdom. If you can thwart the hexer, which will not be easy, then your troubles will be only starting. We see no great evil in you—not yet—but the possibility is there. So is the possibility of greatness. You are a gathering storm, and we cannot tell where or how you will strike. Be resolute and true to yourself and go with our blessing."

After a moment of silence, Toby realized that the spirit had departed.

"Advise us," Father Lachlan cried, "how best we may escape the woman and her unholy minions."

There was no answer, of course. Toby began to rise. Rory grabbed his shoulder to stop him.

Toby rose anyway. "It's gone."

"You could *see* it?"

"Yes. Let's get out of here!" He had learned nothing of any use. He had thrown away a valuable sword to no purpose.

"It is customary to wait for the keeper," Rory snapped. "He needs to recover . . . "

Murray stirred and raised his head. "What did you hear?" he mumbled in his normal coarse voice.

"Nothing much!" Toby reached down and lifted Meg bodily, setting her on her feet. "Let's go!"

"Take your hands off me!"

"Fine!" he said. "I'll wait outside." He turned and marched up the tunnel.

* * *

8

The rain seemed less and the day brighter, but that might just be after the dark of the cave. Toby was staring out at the rain and the narrow glen when the others came blinking into the daylight. They regarded him warily, as well they might. Gathering storm . . . ! Twaddle!

"I wish the spirit had advised us how best to proceed," Father Lachlan fussed. "But the fact that it did not shows that it has faith in our judgment."

"Or it doesn't know!" Toby growled.

"What?" The old man blinked, peering up over his glasses.

The spirit was frightened of Valda and had not answered Toby's questions because it had no answers. But to say so would just get him accused of blasphemy. Hamish had *Cynic!* written in his eyes.

"I promised I'd get Meg to Oban. Which way from here?"

Rory shrugged disdainfully. "Back the way we came yesterday and through Pass of Brander. The Sassenachs will still be there, I expect. Or you can go down the glen, but that takes you in the wrong direction, and you will have to get past Inverary. In case you don't know, that's the seat of the earl of Argyll, a traitor who never misses a chance to lick the Sassenachs' boots. You will be stopped and questioned."

Trapped!

"North it is, then," Toby said. "We'll try Pass of Brander at night. Come along, Meg." He stepped out into the rain and was alone. He turned.

She was standing very close to Rory with her chin up. "And suppose I don't want to come?"

What had made her so mad all of a sudden?

"Then I'll put you over my shoulder and carry you!" Couldn't they see? He had a hexer and four demons to worry about. The spirit had as good as told him he had to go and fight them. He could not keep running away. He must stop and fight—and he had no idea how to begin.

"You lay a finger on me, Toby Strangerson," Meg screamed, "and . . . "

"Yes?"

"Master Glencoe will defend me! Won't you, sir?"

Rory doffed his bonnet and clasped it to his heart. "My life is at your command, dear lady. I'm not sure I can defend you from Wee Willie, though—we are dealing with a gathering storm, remember. But I do have a suggestion. A mile or so down the glen lies the home of Sir Torquil Campbell, whose heart is as true to Scotland as the heather. He's also a friend of mine. I dropped in on him this morning and asked him to lay on a meal for eight hungry men. I meant us, you see, counting you as one and the Tyndrum Mauler there as four. Why don't we go and eat, and then perhaps we shall all feel a little more agreeable?"

Meg beamed.

Toby spun around and strode off down the track. Outsmarted again!

He was shortly joined by Hamish, red-faced, out of breath, and intent on leaving before anyone remembered that he was supposed to stay here.

Toby stopped at the cottages only long enough to snatch up his bundle. Common sense suggested he should wait there for the others to arrive, but he was too mad to listen to common sense.

He gained control of his temper when he reached the end of the trees and was faced with the heaviest cloudburst yet. He took shelter under a massive sycamore, leaning against the trunk to wait. At least he was no longer encumbered by a ton of scrap iron on his back.

Hamish was staring at him in solemn silence. The boy must be ill!

"So you don't want to be deputy keeper of the shrine? Where are you heading?"

Hamish bit his lip, looking uncomfortable. "Eric, I suppose. Glasgow. I can write to Pa and explain."

Toby nodded. Hamish could look after himself, which was more than anyone would say for Toby

Strangerson. Why had he gone and upset Meg like that? Worse, he wasn't even sure what he'd done wrong.

"And you, Toby? Oban?"

"Not sure . . . I wish I knew what Rory's up to. What's his interest in me?"

"He's . . . I don't know." The kid looked so owlish that he obviously thought he did.

"Guess."

"I think . . . Did you notice Cousin Murray call him 'my lord' a couple of times last night?"

Of course. And it had been right after the first time that Rory had launched into his tale of being imprisoned in London—sons of peasants were not held hostage in Greenwich Palace. But if Toby had worked that out, then Hamish must have.

"Fergan was a hostage, wasn't he?"

Hamish shivered and pulled his plaid tighter on his shoulders. "Rory's too young to be Fergan. Fergan's thirty-two."

"How'd you know that?"

"Read it in a book of course." He lowered his voice in case the trees overheard. "You want to know who I think Rory really is?"

The other three came scurrying and slithering down the steep path, huddled against the rain. Father Lachlan seemed lost in thought, but Meg and Rory were chattering busily together. All three went by without stopping.

"No," Toby said. "I don't want to know." Hamish had not answered his first question.

9

They walked a mile and saw no sign of Valda. They saw no one. They could barely see each other—the air was thick enough to swim through. Water danced on the mud and flowed over the fields in sheets. In places the road was ankle-deep.

Sir Torquil's house was a grand affair of two stories, surrounded by a retinue of trees, sheds, cottages, barns, and horse paddocks. It stood on the right bank of the Shira, the travelers stood on the left, and the river foamed betwixt. Bloated by the rain, it was lapping greedily over some of the stepping stones. Rory had stopped to consider the crossing. Toby and Hamish arrived at his back.

"It's risen since I was here earlier," he said. "If you want to wait a minute, Meg, I'm sure Torquil will send a horse as soon as he sees us."

That was funny. The river was considerably more deadly than the one at Tyndrum and the crossing longer, but the stones were closer together and more regular. Meg Tanner could hitch up her dress and skip across there with an agility Master MacDonald had lost years ago.

Meg turned around to Toby and said, "Carry me!"

There was absolutely no accounting for women.

Toby threw his bundle to Hamish and was on the third stepping stone with Meg in his arms before it hit. She looked up at him with a grin and sparkles of water on her eyelashes. He knew there was no use asking why she felt a need to be carried. Whatever the reason, he probably wouldn't understand it. Demons, who cared?

"You weigh more when you're waterlogged."

Her grin widened. "I'm sorry I snapped at you."

"I'm sure I deserved it. Don't try to explain what I did wrong, though. It would waste too much valuable time." Having reached the middle of the stream, Toby stopped. He would never get a better chance.

Devilry danced in her eyes like sunlight on water. "Valuable for what?"

"Toll."

"How much?"

"A kiss, of course."

"Long or short?"

"As long as you like." Then his heart failed him—decent women did not kiss men in public places. "If you don't mind?"

"You big lummox, that's what I wanted!"

Whatever Toby might have said then remained forever unspoken. . . .

It lasted much longer than he expected. He had believed that kisses were brief affairs. He should have picked a stone where the icy water was not running over his feet. He wondered what would happen if he swooned and fell off the boulder. Again, who cared? When it was over he opened his eyes, savoring the taste of her mouth. . . .

"There's two of us," he said hoarsely. "Passenger pays toll for both."

"He's waiting right behind you," Meg said softly. "We've made the point."

Pity. He made a long stride to the next stone. "What point?"

"If you don't know that, Tobias Strangerson, then you are a bigger fool than you pretend to be."

Another stone, leaving only three to go. "It's not pretending, Meg. I really am a fool. Less brains than an ox."

"But more muscle."

"Don't trust him, Meg. He's rich and probably noble—"

"And handsome, and I'm only a tanner's daughter, who can be sweet-talked into yielding her virtue and then be discarded. Have I got that right?"

"No, you haven't. He is not handsome." Another stone. One to go.

"Sorry, Toby darling. Yes, he is. You turned every girl's head in the glen, but Rory could turn them back again."

None to go—last stone. Toby could think of nothing more to say, so he kissed her again. She did not refuse him, and he twisted around so that Rory, waiting on the previous boulder, would have a clear and unobstructed view. It was only when Meg broke away that he realized he had an audience on the bank as well.

He set her down on the turf and stepped aside as Rory came ashore and the welcoming committee surged forward.

He had done it. He had kissed her.

Sir Torquil Campbell of Shira must rule a minor clan of his own. He was a loud, short, broad man with a flaming red beard. The woman at his side could be assumed to be his wife, and she had flaming red braids. They had brought a retinue of men, women, youths, maidens, boys, girls, toddlers, and babies. As every one of them was loud, short, broad, and afflicted with flaming red hair of varying amounts, they must all be related. Every one of them had been waiting in the rain, while Toby . . .

While Toby kissed his girl! Pipe bands and drumbeats! He had kissed her!

"Master," Sir Torquil exclaimed, "er, Rory, that is! And the good Father Lachlan! And who's the bonnie lass? You'll all be coming in out of the weather, it being a touch damp now."

The visitors were led indoors and upstairs. Meg was rushed away by the women into one room, and the men directed into another. It was a big chamber, with a ceiling so far above Toby's head that he could barely have touched it if he tried, but there was not much space for five men to stand between two chairs, several oaken chests, and a real bed—complete with feather mattress and curtains and bolsters and all.

Sir Torquil had followed them in. "Doff your wet things now. There's cloths there to dry yourselves, and dry plaids. You'll not mind that, Father, while the women see to your robe, now? And I've brought a dram of something to warm you. That's a terrible bruise on your chest, Master, er, Master Rory. Was it a horse kicking you?"

"It felt like that," Rory said.

He took a long swig from the flagon and handed it to the friar, who in turn passed it to Toby. Toby tilted it, but did not swallow. The trace of whisky he got in his mouth was enough to paralyze his tongue and dissolve his teeth. Eyes watering, he passed the bottle to Hamish in necessary silence.

Sir Torquil continued his soliloquy. "You'll be putting on these dry plaids now, Master—Rory. We have no robes here, I'm afraid, Father. I don't know about your man, there. He can just wrap himself in two of these for now, and we'll see what we can find for him after you've all come downstairs and—"

Hamish exploded.

Father Lachlan rescued the flagon; Rory and Toby took turns thumping the corpse on the back until it began breathing again.

"You'd best have another drink, lad," Sir Torquil said solicitously. "Like being thrown from a horse—a man has to get on again right away to show who's master."

"Very sound idea!" Rory agreed. "Don't you think so, Longdirk?"

"Two might be safer," Toby said.

Hamish looked at them despairingly with red and weeping eyes, then manfully took another sip.

Swathed in borrowed plaids, they went downstairs to eat.

The kitchen was almost as big as the one in Lochy Castle. Sir Torquil sat at the table with his guests and the rest of the space was filled by redheads, who stood around and stared. They varied in size from wet-nosed toddlers to pregnant mothers and thick-armed laborers smelling of cattle.

The food was superb. Before every guest was laid a slab of bread cut from loaves straight out of the oven; on that were piled beans, juicy hot meat, and fresh fish. There was whisky to drink, although the fainthearted might dilute it with water if they wished. The refugees from the Reverend Murray's meager hospitality fell to with avid purpose while Sir Torquil talked—of the weather, of the ships in the loch, of reports of fighting up near Banff, of rumors that the Sassenach king had razed another town in Europe somewhere with his customary fearful slaughter. His assembled clan stood with folded arms, listening, studying the visitors, and speaking only when their patriarch addressed them.

Toby did eat enough for four, but Hamish came a close second, and the others did not skimp. If a man was going to die, it was best to do so on a full stomach. The world mellowed to a kinder, easier place. He could forget for a little while that he might be possessed by a demon, that a notorious hexer was hunting him, that the Sassenachs had probably set a price on his head, that he was responsible for seeing Meg Campbell of Tyndrum safely to Oban. What matter? He had escaped from the prison of his childhood. He was no longer Toby the Bastard, he was making his way in the world. He was going to make his name also.

Toby of Tyndrum, Toby of Fillan? Never!

Toby of the Highlands? Too vague.

"Annie," Sir Torquil told one of the redheads, "Master Longdirk needs more beef."

"Nonsense, Father! He's got more beef than I've seen in years."

Toby heard his own laugh over all the rest.

Gradually the voids were filled and the eating slowed. Rory wiped his mouth with the back of a hand, licked his fingers, and folded his arms. He refused offers of more. He began to talk, ignoring the huge audience with apparent confidence that his words would never be reported to outsiders.

"What news of Lord Robert?"

"The Campbell's in Edinburgh still," Sir Torquil said cautiously, "with his lady. Attending Parliament."

Rory did not repeat his earlier description of the chief of Clan Campbell as a boot-licker—his hosts lived only an hour's walk from Inverary. He did not parrot the usual rebel description of the current parliament as a farce of traitor puppets.

"And the master?"

"He's gone hunting up Fort William way." The caution was even more marked. "So they say."

Rory nodded. "I gave Keeper Murray money for the wood we burned and the food we ate—the most expensive meal in the history of Scotland, that was. But he'll never spend it. Would you take a load of peat and—"

"I was planning to, soon as the rain stops. I do that every year."

"Good!" Rory reached for his sporran and his host growled like a dog at a bear-baiting.

Rory smiled thanks. "Apart from that, we have a couple of problems. The Sassenachs are after my man Longdirk, there, and you have a hexer loose in the district."

Sir Torquil nodded. "Aye, you told me. Nobody's seen any strangers."

"She's around."

"Well, you're safe here."

"But we can't stay!" Rory raised a hand to balk argument. "You're close enough to the shrine that the spirit will guard you, but if we hang around, we may endanger the spirit itself."

"Like that, is it?"

"Very much so. We need to decide where to go. Father?"

The little friar blinked, suppressing a burp. "Glasgow. Master, er, Longdirk, needs to visit the sanctuary. Failing that, Dumbarton. But we must get past Inverary."

"That can be arranged," Sir Torquil said, smiling yellow teeth in his red beard.

"Then we should go by Glen Kinglas, over to Loch Lomond. Two days should do it."

Rory nodded thoughtfully. "Hamish Campbell?"

"I go with Toby, sir." Hamish was very pink, fighting an attack of hiccups.

Rory's eyes turned to Meg. "You'll be safe here."

Meg glanced at Toby and then down at her hands.

"You're a Campbell with Campbells in the middle of Campbell country, miss!" Sir Torquil thumped a hairy fist on the table. "No one will lay a hand on her here, Master, er, Rory."

Except perhaps Campbells. Toby had already registered that there were many more males than females in this household. Several young faces were displaying interest already. If Meg wanted a husband, she would have a wide selection available in Glen Shira. Why should that prospect alarm him? It was no business of his, even if she had let him kiss her. She must stay and he must go, out of her life forever.

And what of the alleged MacDonald—the MacDonald

who gave orders to Campbells in the middle of Campbell country and had them obeyed instantly? The allegedly handsome smoothie?

He knew who Rory was now.

Still Meg said nothing.

Rory was looking at him expectantly.

Was he really to be allowed to make his own decision? He held the rebel's gaze for a moment while he straightened out his thoughts. He wished he were smarter. If he blundered, he would imperil not just his own life—which was worth very little at the moment—but the others' also. Meg, obviously, must not be taken into more danger. To insist on trying to protect her would be to expose her to Valda's demons. Meg would have to remain at Glen Shira, yes. It was the least of all evils.

"You heard what the spirit said, Master MacDonald." He noted the twitches of amusement in the audience. "It said I might thwart the hexer, although what that means, I don't know. I have to go out and face her. I don't fancy a life of endless miraculous escapes. If I stop running away and go on the offensive, perhaps I'll start enjoying miraculous victories?"

Rory showed none of his usual mocking contempt. "Or just stop escaping? How do you go on the offensive? You've thrown away your sword. What weapon will you use? Fingernails?"

"Boulders!" Hamish declaimed. "There's lots of battles in Scotland been fought by rolling boulders down on the enemy. Pass of Brander in . . . " His voice withered away under Rory's glare. *"Hic!"* he added quietly.

Toby sighed. "Why not boulders? I'll pick them up and throw them. Show me the Dumbarton road and I'll be on my way. The rest of you stay here."

Rory shook his head. "We'll come. We could try and find a boat to take us, of course, but not while the weather's doing what it's doing."

Toby thought about that. "No. If you're all trapped with me in a boat, you'll be too vulnerable. I'd rather walk where I can run."

"Walk it is, then. Not Miss Campbell, of course, but—"

"Me, too," Meg said quietly. "Where Toby goes, I go." She looked up, her face flushed. "He needs looking after!"

Some of the onlookers tittered, but then silence fell.

Rory's jaw was clenched. He was obviously about to exert a veto, and what the alleged MacDonald said here had the force of law.

"Yes," Toby said, "I do need looking after. Let's all go. When we sight Lady Valda, you turn back and I'll go on alone." If Meg was there, there would be less chance for heroics from any of the others—Hamish, or Father Lachlan. They would rally around Meg.

Rory drummed his fingers on the table. Then he shrugged. "We'll see you as far as Kinglas, then. Valda'll not likely try anything before that." He turned to Sir Torquil, who was looking deeply shocked. "Can you get us by Inverary without the earl's men questioning us?"

Their host smiled. "Aye, Master, I think we can that."

SIX

Dead or Alive

1

Sir Torquil had offered ponies, which Rory had
refused, much to his companions' relief, but half a
dozen young Campbells had ridden off, presumably to
clear the way. Leather capes were another matter—
Torquil had insisted on providing them, and no one had
argued very hard. He had wanted to donate shoes also,
muttering about walking on shingle. Everyone knew
that shoes would soon cramp feet unaccustomed to
them, so the shoes were declined with thanks.

A short walk brought them to Loch Fyne—forty
miles long, Hamish announced, reaching all the way to
the Mull of Kintyre and the Isle of Butte. As the rain hid
everything out of bowshot, Toby was not impressed by
the information. He had never seen the sea before, and
found even the smell of it intriguing. The tide was out,
exposing smooth gray rocks coated with strange weeds
and barnacles. He would have liked to see the ships
that Hamish insisted would be anchored off Inverary,
but had to be content with bobbing gulls and the little
boats that lay on the strand near every cottage, surrounded by intriguing tackle.

"Fishing nets," Hamish said, unnecessarily. "Lobster
creels. They dry fish on those racks, don't they, Master
MacDonald? And *see yon harpoon!*"

According to Rory, they passed within a mile of
Inverary Castle itself, but the rain obscured it totally.
Few folk were mad enough to be about in such weather,
and any who had reason to watch for strangers must
have been discouraged by the Campbells of Shira. The
fugitives saw hardly a soul.

Their way lay east, a crude trail where the hills met

the sea. At high tide, it might have been impassable. Hamish quartered like a questing hound, trotting back with shells and crabs and jellyfish to show.

The world was starting to offer novelty. With a cape to keep off the worst of the rain and free of his weighty sword, Toby was having a better day. Better was a relative term, of course.

They reached the mouth of the River Fyne and turned south, still following the shore. At the hamlet of Cairndow, two men emerged from the rain to interrogate the strangers. Rory stalked on ahead to speak with them, and they reacted in the now familiar fashion, doffing bonnets and bowing. The travelers were allowed to pass.

They crossed a river on stepping stones that were mostly underwater. They turned inland.

Miraculously, the rain had eased to a drizzle, revealing a straight glen ahead, almost narrow enough to be called a gorge. On the left, beyond the river, the hill was an imposing wall, soaring into the clouds without a break. It was not quite a cliff, although a man would need go up it on all fours. The near side was more gentle, although still too steep for any use but cattle. The river might be just a peaty burn most of the time, but days of rain had turned it into a roaring brown torrent, which had taken over the track in places and was washing it away in others. It frothed and thundered over boulders, setting Toby's teeth on edge with a sepulchral rumble of rocks rolling along its bed.

"Where is this?" he demanded after a while.

Rory said, "It's Glen Kinglas—" and stopped.

Toby looked back, seeing a glimpse of Loch Fyne framed in the glen mouth, with hints of the hill beyond like a wall of mist. "Then here we part."

Silence, except for rain and wind and the growling of the river.

He had calculated well in bringing Meg along. Now the moment of farewell had arrived, the other men were reluctant to desert him, even though they knew they could give him no aid.

"Go back," he said. "This is my battle. You have done more than was required, by many a mile, all of you."

"Just because you have escaped the woman before, Tobias . . ." Father Lachlan began, but he did not finish. What he meant was that there was no spirit of Glen Shira here, no hob of Fillan. Toby was alone.

He had always been alone. He always would be. Strong men could stand alone. The time for running away was over.

"Go back," he repeated, speaking to Rory's angry stare. "If you had a warband at your back, you could not help me now. Find a warm hearth down there in Cairndow, or somewhere. Or go back to Sir Torquil's."

"The tide is in!" Rory snapped. His pride was burning him alive. He was the leader. Sons of chiefs did not stay behind when their followers went into danger—he regarded Toby as his man, even if Toby refused to bend a knee to him.

"I am sure you have other friends close, to offer you shelter, Master . . . MacDonald."

That hint made the gray eyes glint dangerously. "Father Lachlan, you take the girl and the boy and—"

"No, my son," the friar said quietly. "This battle is not for you. Remember your grandfather."

"I'm going with you!" Hamish announced—bravely enough, although there was a strange whiteness around his eyes.

He was a puppy yapping at a bull, but Toby was touched. The courage of the Campbells of Fillan was very real to the teacher's son, and not to be mocked now. He squeezed the boy's shoulder. "Thanks, my friend. I know I promised you we would hang on the same gallows, but I'm not headed to the gallows today."

"Go with our prayers, Tobias," the friar said. "You can follow the trail without trouble, over Rest and be thankful—"

"What?"

"A pass. That's its name, Rest and be thankful. Then down into Glen Croe, between the Cobbler and the

Brack, to Arrochar. You'll be only a mile or two west of the Loch Lomond Road, then. When you get to Dumbarton, ask at the sanctuary for Father Gregor . . . "

If he got that far. Toby braced himself. He had never reneged on a promise before, but in this case it was a distasteful duty. "I must ask you for your oath, Father. Promise me that Meg Campbell—"

The friar cried out. "Where is Meg Campbell?"

Meg Campbell was a tiny figure in the distance, trudging along the road, indistinct in the rain. With a roar, Toby took off in pursuit. He heard feet slapping in the mud behind him. How had she managed to get so far without them noticing?

He caught up with her and grabbed her arm. She swung around furiously.

"Take your hands off me!"

He took his hands off her.

She started walking again. He tracked beside her, fuming. "What the demons are you doing?"

"Going where you go. I told you."

She was being so stupid that he didn't know where to start.

"Meg, I'm an outlawed murderer, a demonic husk, a penniless vagrant. I've got a price on my head, a hexer at my heels . . . "

She glanced back at the posse. "Yes, but I feel safer with you than I do with Rory. Oh, Toby, I can't explain . . . I trust you. I more than just trust you, I . . . "

"You what?"

"Never mind. Rory frightens me!" She smiled suddenly, seeing his shock. "I don't mean he threatens me. He's witty and charming and attentive. But . . . I am afraid when I'm with him. Not afraid of him, so much as afraid of *me!*"

"What does that mean?"

Again she glanced back at the pursuers. "I don't know. I mean, I don't know how to tell you without hurting you."

"Try me!" He had never seen fiery little Meg Campbell

so off-balance, so unsure of herself. Rory would be here in
seconds.

She bit her lip. "He's so devious! He could steal a
horse's shoes without lifting its feet."

"He's clever and I'm not, you mean?"

"Oh, you know that's not what I mean! He promises . . .
You really think he's a rebel?"

What in the world was she trying to say?

Then Rory came splashing up to them, obviously
furious that his followers were not following as he
expected. Hamish was close behind him, handicapped by
his bundle. Father Lachlan would come in a distant
fourth. Below his leather cape, the hem of his white robe
flapped madly, like a housewife's duster.

"Meg, you are being foolish!" Rory said sharply. "You
go on, Longdirk." He reached for Meg's arm.

Toby struck his hand away. "She goes with me if she
wants."

"To face Valda? And demons? Are you out of your
minds, both of you?" Again Rory reached for her arm.
"Come with us, Meg. You go on, Longdirk. We'll talk sense
into—"

Again Toby smacked the rebel's hand away. "I am
not your man and she is not your woman."

Rory stared at him incredulously and drew. "By
the demons of Delia, I have taken all I can from you,
you ignorant ox. Now I am going to teach you some
manners!"

Toby edged away from Meg, clutching his bundle in
both hands before him. It was the only weapon or shield
he had. He ought to drop to his knees and beg forgiveness, but he would rather drop dead.

"Armed, this time, my lord? The last lesson misfired,
didn't it? Your match was a little damp."

He had been a fool to rile a swordsman, a noble.
Rory would be within his rights in chopping off an ear or
two. Indeed, if Rory just ran the churl through, then who
would bring justice against him? Who would seek
vengeance for Toby Strangerson? He had no clan, he was

no man's man, whereas Rory was a very importan[t] personage indeed.

"Or are you just annoyed that an ignorant ox man[aged] to work out who you were? Managed to see throug[h] all the childish lies!"

Meg shouted, "No! Stop this!" She tried to mov[e] between them, but Rory dodged past her, pushing he[r] away.

"Stay out of this, woman!" He advanced slowly o[n] Toby again, lips white with fury, silver eyes shining, stee[l] glinting. Any moment he would leap forward and lunge.

Toby continued backing away. *Spirits, let me get i[n] one good punch! Let me just smash his nose, if I have t[o] run up his sword to do it. . . .* "If you're so good with [a] sword, Master MacDonald, then why didn't you draw o[n] the bogy? You didn't even hit it with your lute, did you[?] You were going to drown, Master—"

He stopped, his feet stuck. They looked all right, bu[t] they felt as if they were buried in mortar.

Rory, too, was staring down in dismay.

Hamish screamed, "Valda! It's the woman!"

About half a mile up the glen, a line of riders wa[s] advancing toward them. Five—no, six. Where had the[y] come from?

"Well!" Rory said, sheathing his sword. "Do you sup-pose that's just the local cattlemen's association holding its annual meeting?" He had switched instantly from fury to icy calm.

Meg cried, "Toby!"

Again Toby tried to move, but his feet stayed rooted to the road. Trapped! He glanced over his companions and saw that they were all transfixed. He had promised to guard Meg and then led her into more danger than her father could have dreamed in his worst nightmares. With a howl of fury he hurled his bundle away from him.

Shift . . .

He looked down at the five mortals. They stood in a loathsome pool of demonic power. He blew it away. Apart from that, they were unharmed.

Dum . . . Dum . . . Dum . . .

He looked up the glen. The mounted six trotting along the road . . . The hexer smiled gloatingly as she led her odious pack along the trail. Their horses were dead—ridden to death and beyond death. The other woman lived, but her mind had been tormented away to nothing. Two of the males were corpses, their resident demons fully occupied in running the decaying bodies they inhabited. They could contribute nothing. Of the other two, one was directing the horses and also had an overriding directive to protect the hexer. That left only one fully operational, and even that one was encumbered by shackles of gramarye.

Back to the five. . . . The big one, the witchwife's lad, the curly-haired one . . . he grew. He swelled to a giant, a mountain, looming over Glen Kinglas. Ignoring the clouds and the rain, he surveyed the hills: the trail, heading straight for big Beinn Ime and then bending right to find the pass, gentle Beinn an Lochain on the right, and the sheer, straight face of Binrein an Fhidhleir, soaring up two thousand feet without a break on the left.

Weapon?

Dum . . . Dum . . .

Roll boulders on them, the teacher's boy had said. Why not?

He reached out a cloud-sized arm and sank fingers into the slope above the riders, clawing at it. The soil was sodden and saturated by so much rain. It moved easily.

This game was fun! Too late, the one available demon sensed the opposing power. It rose like black smoke to give battle, and then paused with evil glee as it saw the ploy. The damage was already done, anyway.

The side of the hill slid away bodily. Green slope became a carpet of brown mud, slithering downward, ripping up bushes, tearing out rocks, picking up speed. The ground moved in waves. Unbearable sound filled the valley. A gale roared ahead of the landslide. Valda looked up and screamed. The demon fled back to aid her. On the far slope, long-horned cattle stampeded in terror.

The mud slide poured down the mountain, burying the river, burying the road, rushing partway up the opposite slope. In seconds, the heap rose like brown dough, filling the gorge, building a mountain, spreading out sideways along the trail. Boulders bounced free ahead of the advancing wall. The thunder was a palpable presence, paralyzing the mortals. They could do nothing but stare at the approaching cataclysm; and then the hurricane bowled them over, hurling them to the ground and rolling them—all except the big one, who leaned into the wind.

The mass steadied before it reached them, the muck bubbling and writhing like a giant slug as it settled in place, its deathly roar fading to a steady, comforting beat: *Dum . . . Dum . . .*

Fun! Fun! More! Farther up the glen were other wet slopes just waiting to roll down. . . .

2

"Toby! *Toby!* **Are you all right?"**

Dum . . . Dum . . .

The first thing he noticed was Meg's face, all black with mire around two white, staring eyes: comical. That had been Meg shouting. Her cape and dress were thick with mud. Rory and Hamish were helping Father Lachlan to his feet, and every one of them was slathered in it, like human pigsties. Funny.

He was all right, just wet.

"Are you all right?" Meg repeated urgently.

"Yes, I think so . . . " He was mortal again . . . merely mortal, back in the cold and the wind. He had a waning sense of loss, of heady power lost. Clouds mantled the hills again, but he could still taste the savage joy he had felt when he clawed down a mountainside to destroy a foe.

The glen had fallen silent. A wall of glistening mud

blocked it; the air reeked of wet soil. The river flowed no more.

Father Lachlan wiped his spectacles on the sleeve of his robe, and put them on again so he could peer at Toby over them.

"Was that your doing, my son?"

Toby looked down at his hand. There was no dirt under his nails, but he felt as if there should be. He could remember the strange sensation of digging his fingers into the hillside. He had soared with the eagles. He had looked *down* at the hills.

"Mine? How could I do that?"

"I suppose the rain could have set off the slide," the acolyte muttered uncertainly, as if trying to convince himself.

"It was a very fortuitous rescue," Rory remarked shakily. "Is she dead?"

Toby faced four incredulous stares. They were not fools, none of them. They were all smarter than he was. They could not have seen what he had seen—Toby Strangerson grown to the size of a mountain. If they had seen that, they would be fleeing in all directions. But they must have noticed him behaving oddly, and if he tried to explain, they would flee from him now. He was possessed, demonized, uncanny. Leper!

"Dead? Valda? How should I know?" He did not think she was dead. The demons had been trying to save her. Even if they had succeeded, though, she must be in disarray. No, she was not a threat now—but he dared not say so.

"So it was Valda?" Rory snapped.

Toby shrugged. "Your eyes are as good as mine."

"We had best get out of here!" Father Lachlan said. "There may be more slides ready to fall."

Not unless Toby arranged them. If Meg had not called him back when she did . . . He did not want to think about that.

"We'll have to turn back," Rory said. "The road's blocked. No reason not to now, is there?"

"Is the danger over?" Father Lachlan asked, still sounding shaky. He meant: *Is Valda still there?* He did not believe Toby's denials. None of them did.

Toby said, "We could get by. We can go on to Dumbarton."

"In this weather?" Rory growled. "There's no hurry anymore, is there? Demons, but I'd like to get out of this rain! I have friends here. I can lead us to a warm, dry house and some civilized comfort. I didn't dare go there as long as I thought there was a hexer after us. If we're safe now, then that's where we ought to go before we all freeze to death. We're not in a hurry, are we? Only Sassenachs to worry about now?"

He stared challengingly at Toby.

Toby looked at Meg. Her lips were white. She had done marvelously well. For two whole days, she had survived cold and wet and hunger and physical torment. To submit her to more days and nights of those would be deliberate cruelty. He had promised to look after her, and he must not gamble her life just to safeguard his own skin.

"All right!" he said. "All *right!* Yes, that was Valda. I don't think I killed her, but I probably destroyed her maid and at least two of her demons, possibly three. She's not going to be a problem for a while." He glowered at the horrified faces and waited for the panic.

Rory smiled at having his suspicions confirmed, but it was a sickly imitation of his customary smirk. "You brought down that slide?"

"My demon did."

Still the panic did not come. They all exchanged glances, but they did not flee in terror, as they should.

"Beautiful!" The rebel laughed. "Attaboy, Little Man! Oh, what we would have given to have had you at Parline Field, when the bowstrings broke in our fingers and our gunpowder turned to salt! Come on, then, all of you—I know where we can find dry beds tonight. Longdirk, you're a hexer after my own heart!"

He moved as if to go, expecting his followers to

follow, but everyone just stood. He frowned and folded his arms.

Hamish chewed his lip. "I don't think you're a hexer, Toby." He did not look very certain, though.

"I do," Toby said.

"Don't say that!" Meg screamed. "Don't even joke about it!"

Father Lachlan was adjusting his spectacles, waiting patiently.

"They were all dead!" Toby said. "Almost all! Dead already, I mean. The two men I killed earlier, and all the horses. And the other woman . . . she was breathing, but not . . . not thinking. Valda was laughing." His voice was becoming shrill. He felt sick.

"The spirit saw no evil in you, my son. Tell me what happened."

"What did you see?"

"Nothing. You just stood and stared."

"That's all?"

The acolyte pulled his hood up as the rain began to grow heavier again. "You did have a strange expression on your face."

"A grin? A sort of idiot simper?"

"I suppose so." He reached up to pat Toby's shoulder ineffectually. "You can tell me later. What matters is that you have chased the evil away, at least for a while. The spirit said you might, remember?"

It had also said that his troubles would be just beginning.

"It was different this time, somehow. It's never quite the same twice. The demon must be learning how to control me better!"

Father Lachlan frowned anxiously. "I still do not believe you are possessed, my son. You cannot be a hexer, for you do not use the rituals of gramarye and you have no demonic creatures at your command. I admit that I do not understand. You seem to fit none of the rules at all! I have studied the lore of demonology for a lifetime, but if an immortal could not fathom you, then

how can I hope to? Now we have won time to get you to
Glasgow. The tutelary is very benevolent, very wise. I am
sure it will help you."

Toby turned away. Did he even want to be helped?
He had *enjoyed* that brief blaze of omnipotence.

"Master!" Hamish shouted. Even under the mud, his
face showed alarm. "The river's stopped flowing!"

Rory glanced at the channel, silent pools in a night
mare of boulders. Then he looked at the barrier
upstream. "Well, of course it has! Tiny Tim, there, has
given Scotland a new loch! Loch Strangerson, the bastard
loch?"

"But, *sir!* That's just mud! This happened somewhere
down in the Borders a few years ago, didn't it? A slide?
Then, when the river runs over the top, or when it just
builds up behind . . . "

"Spirits save us!" Father Lachlan said. "The boy's
right! Near Roxburgh somewhere. If that dam bursts,
there's going to be a flood!"

Rory stiffened, then turned to look down the rainy
glen. "Cairndow! Demons! We must warn them! We must
get them out of there! Come on!" He started to run.

3

Iain lowered the sail and Rae held the tiller as the boat
drifted in to the jetty. Iain was a towhead, old Rae was
dark as a Castilian, but they would both be Campbells.
The pelting rain had turned the surface of the loch to
mist, so that it was hard to tell where the sea ended and
the air began. Water swilled around in the bottom of the
boat, glittering with fish scales.

The passengers sat along the sides. Father Lachlan
looked old and tired, although that might be just by way of
contrast with Hamish, who had not stopped jabbering
questions at the two sailors since they left Cairndow.
Toby faced them, with Meg beside him, not quite close

enough to be asking for an arm around her. He should have put an arm around her anyway, and all the way across the loch had been cursing himself as a coward for not doing so. But he was very conscious of Rory on her other side, and those deadly, silver eyes. He could throw their owner overboard if he wanted, but that would do no good—the arrogant louse could probably swim like a shark. To strangle him first would require fighting three Campbells at the same time, and probably Hamish as well.

Hamish was very impressed, even awed. He had confirmed from someone in Cairndow that Rory MacDonald was really Gregor Campbell, the master of Argyll. That ranked him just below the sun, and so far above Toby Strangerson that it was amazing they could even see each other. So what if he was? He sat down to shit like anyone else, didn't he?

They had sounded the alarm in the hamlet. The inhabitants had fled away from the river, carrying possessions, driving livestock. The master had commandeered a boat for the trip down to Inverary and met no argument. He had ordered his companions into it, never doubting that they would obey. They had obeyed. Only the sight of Meg, huddled and shivering, explained to Toby why he had come, but in truth he had had no alternative. He was totally at Rory's mercy now. Gregor's mercy. What mercy?

Inverary Castle loomed out of the rain, far larger and grander than Lochy, towering over a sprawl of buildings, cottages, animal paddocks, orchards, and vegetable gardens, a sizable village. One of the corner towers was framed in scaffolding, being repaired or still under construction. The Sassenachs would have spread the word. How big a garrison would they have placed in a fortress this size? Their warrant would be known here in Inverary.

Toby leaned around Meg. Rory stared back with dislike, raising a pale eyebrow.

Toby said, "Didn't you tell us that the earl of Argyll was a traitor who licked English boots?"

The helmsman overheard and gasped in horror.

Rory chuckled—doubtless for the eavesdropper's benefit—but there was murder in the silver eyes. He removed his bonnet, took the black feather from it, and placed it in his sporran. Then he put his bonnet on again. "One has to remain in character."

"And the Sassenachs want to hang me!"

The master's mouth twisted in a familiar sneer. "Who can blame them? Getting nervous, are you? Well, you have no cause to worry. Just because Lord Robert is such a notorious boot-licker, the English haven't posted a garrison on him. No fusiliers here! He's in Edinburgh, as you know. His mother, Lady Lora, is a most formidable lady, and a rabid patriot. And then there's me." He wasn't sure if his disguise had been penetrated. Getting no reaction, he smiled benevolently and added: "Nobody hangs one of my men without my permission."

"I am not your man!"

The boat jostled against stone steps. Rory shrugged. "Then I offer you hospitality as my guest, as I offer my home to your charming companion. Nobody hangs my guests, either. Not even me—it's bad manners. Miss Campbell?"

He handed Meg ashore, then offered help to Father Lachlan, who shot Toby a disapproving and warning frown.

Toby and Hamish were left to manage by themselves, following up a paved road to the castle, bent against the driving rain. The few people they met on the way all recognized their leader. Bonnets came off. Men bowed, women curtseyed.

Hamish walked at first in worried silence, clutching his muddy bundle. Then he muttered, "Toby, you'd better take care! He's the Campbell's son! He's the heir to Argyll—that's what 'master' means!"

"I know that! And I would still like to ram his teeth down his throat!"

"Toby!" Hamish's voice rose to a batlike squeak. "He'll have you beaten! Or branded! He can throw you in a dungeon."

"That's no way to treat guests, either. *And he wouldn't*

dare now!" That hurt more than anything—nobody would dare threaten the hexer who could haul down mountains. Inhuman! Leper! "You know what he wants of me, don't you?" Getting no reply except an unhappy nod, he said, "Well? He thinks I'm an adept. He wants me to hex the bloody Sassenachs for him!"

And what did he want of Meg?

Hamish mumbled, "Maybe."

"What else, then?"

"Earl Robert's one of King Nevil's strongest supporters in Scotland. What's his son doing running with rebels? And do we know that he is a rebel at all just because he wears a feather in his cap? Or is he trying to find Fergan and betray him?"

Toby thought about it as they hurried to the barbican. "You worry about that," he concluded. "I don't care either way."

By then, Hamish had forgotten the problem and was gaping up at the towers and battlements. "This is one of the strongest castles in Scotland. It's never been taken."

No Scottish lord had cannon to blast a way into a citadel like this, so of course the earl would be on the side of the English. And strongholds made good prisons. Toby saw the arch with its daunting portcullis like a giant mouth about to swallow him whole. He was an outlaw, with every man's hand against him. His only possessions were the sodden clothes on his back, a few coins, and a pretty stone in his sporran. It was too late to run, though, and he had nowhere to go.

"You suppose a great castle like this would have a *library?*" Hamish muttered.

More to the point, would it have a gallows?

The archway cut off the rain at last. Two guards stood in their path, but they were Highlanders in plaids and leathers, shoes and steel helmets; they held pikes and wore swords. They jumped to attention and saluted—which was a surprising courtesy to offer a band of mud-plastered vagrants—but they seemed more interested in Toby than in their chief's son. Why?

"Bran!" Rory said cheerfully. "How's Ella? The twins all right? Inform Lady Lora that her favorite headache has returned, will you? And Sir Malcolm." He glanced around at Toby and Hamish. "You'd better come along too. Leave your trash here."

4

The hall was larger by far than Castle Lochy's. It rose clear to the roof. The windows were tiny, but glazed, and on this miserable day they gave less light than the blazing pile of driftwood in the great stone fireplace. A long table for feasting occupied the center of the floor, flanked by benches. Chairs like thrones stood on either side of the hearth, but the visitors were all too muddy to sit in them. Meg and Father Lachlan and the master had gathered before the flames to warm themselves.

Toby and Hamish stood back at a respectful distance, wriggling their toes in the rushes. Hamish was gazing open-mouthed at the minstrel gallery, the banners hanging from the rafters, the collections of weapons adorning the stonework. Toby just watched Meg. She seemed content enough, smiling, laughing at Rory's banter, but he remembered what she had told him, and amid all the splendor he saw her as a tiny bird in a cage.

She had wits and spirit—she had her head on straight, as the acolyte had put it. All true, but she was only a tanner's daughter. Rory was master of Argyll, heir to power and wealth. *He promises,* she had said. *I'm not afraid of him, so much as afraid of me.* He could promise, he could even threaten, and no one would hold him to account for whatever happened. How long could a poor country lass resist him?

Why should it concern Toby Strangerson? There was nothing a penniless outlaw could do to deflect one of the most powerful men in Scotland—except try personal violence, and even that was unlikely to achieve anything except his own death. His promise to protect her was worthless against an opponent like the master of Argyll.

"Rory!" boomed a new voice, reverberating from the high stone walls. Astonishingly, it seemed to originate from the very small lady now sweeping into the hall with an escort at her heels. This must be Dowager Lady Lora, the earl's mother.

So "Rory" was a family pet name for Gregor. How cute!

"Just look at you, you terrible bairn!" It seemed impossible that so tiny a person could be so loud. Her hair shone pure silver, yet her face was barely wrinkled and she still displayed a delicate charm that testified to the beauty she must have been long years ago. She wore a gown of fine violet velvet; she had jewels on her fingers. Followed by maids, pages, and a dozen armed men—all of them much larger than herself—she was as unobtrusive as a volley of artillery.

"Father Lachlan! How wonderful to see you again! You honor our house."

Toby's attention settled on the man at her side. He was big, gruff, red-bearded, and solid as the castle walls. He wore a gleaming leather jerkin under his plaid. His helmet and sword were grander than the others'. He bore a pistol and powderhorn on his belt. He was appraising Toby with eyes like green pebbles, and with more than trivial curiosity.

Lady Lora turned to Meg and raised carefully tended brows.

"Miss Meg Campbell of Tyndrum, Grandmother," her grandson said, sweeping a bow. "Maiden in distress."

"You poor child, you must be frozen! Have you walked far? Trust that Rory . . . I am not surprised you are in distress if he has had anything to do with it. I'm sure you would like a hot tub and some fresh clothes and something to eat before . . . "

She registered Toby and the echoes died away into silence.

He overlooked every one of her burly warriors handily. She herself was no bigger than Meg.

"Toby Strangerson of Fillan," Rory said innocently. "Youth in distress. Lora, Dowager Countess of Argyll."

Toby bowed.

Lady Lora gave her grandson the sort of look a mother gives a tiresome two-year-old. Then she turned to the man at her side, as if he had emitted a silent warning. "Sir Malcolm?"

"We received a communication this morning concerning a man of that name, my lord." He produced a paper from his sporran.

Rory beckoned Toby with a nod of his head. Then he took the paper to read and his eyebrows rose.

Toby walked forward with Hamish at his heels. The warriors clasped the hilts of their swords. He bowed again.

Rory looked up, thunderously displeased. "How well did you know the Sassenachs at Lochy?"

"Fairly well, my lord."

"Is one of them an artist?"

"Gavin Mason can draw."

Rory nodded angrily. "Somebody can draw. This is a printed poster with a woodcut of your face on it. It's a fair likeness, except it makes look like a starving wolf. The description is clear enough: eighteen years old, over nineteen hands tall, heavily muscled, brown eyes, curly hair, and extremely dangerous. Fits you to a tee, doesn't it? A convicted murderer, suspected of conjuring demons. There's quite a price on your head, Longdirk—one hundred marks!"

"What?" Toby howled.

"Dead or alive. You're worth more than I expected."

The guards were smiling.

Rory shrugged. "This is the man, Malcolm. The official story lacks a few details, which I shall be happy to supply at a suitable time. Meanwhile—just to discourage gossip—perhaps his presence here should not be advertised."

"Lock him up, you mean?"

"Why, not at all! He deserves our famous Inverary hospitality. So does his accomplice. Grandmother—Hamish Campbell of Tyndrum."

Hamish bowed until his head almost vanished under his plaid.

Lady Lora boomed a laugh. "Welcome to Inverary, kinsman! Rory, trouble is your shadow. See to his men, will you, Malcolm? Come along, Father . . . and you, Miss Campbell."

The moment her back was turned, Toby found himself surrounded. No one barked orders, no one laid a hand on him or drew a weapon, and his attendants did not actually march him off—but he went without argument and he kept his fists at his sides. A hundred marks dead was easier to deliver than a hundred marks alive, especially when it stood nineteen hands tall. Hamish strode along, head high, smirking blissfully at having been described as one of Rory's *men*.

Their journey was short: out a side door and into a kitchen hardly smaller than the great hall. Its well-scrubbed tables would have fed half of Clan Campbell without crowding. Boot heels drumming on flagstones, they passed fires where two carcasses were already turning on spits in preparation for the evening's festivities and counters where women were chopping vegetables and kneading dough. Sir Malcolm led the way along a somber stone corridor, past many oaken, iron-studded doors. If their destination was not to be a dungeon, it would serve as well, Toby thought. Then a door was opened and steam gushed unexpectedly forth.

Their guide's green eyes had lost none of their vigilance or suspicion. "You will have the bathroom to yourselves at this time of day. The gentry have their own water, so use all you want. I'll send towels, plaids . . . We'll see what we can do about shoon." He looked Hamish over and turned to one of his men. "Come here, Ken."

One of the guards stepped forward, slipped off his boot, and laid his neatly socked foot alongside Hamish's muddy one.

"Aye, that's about the size. As for you . . ." He looked despairingly at Toby's feet and shook his head.

"Fishing boats?" said a whisper in the background.

Sir Malcolm obviously heard but pretended not to. "Go get the aches out, then, lads."

Toby lurched into the bathroom, mumbling thanks, too astonished to articulate properly. Through the fog he could see benches, peat glowing under a giant copper boiler, half a dozen wooden tubs large enough to launder a plaid. The garrison at Lochy enjoyed no such luxury. As the door closed, Hamish muttered, "Spirits!" and in one fast movement was naked.

One would get you twenty that guards stood in the corridor, but who cared? After what felt like a lifetime of wind and rain and cold, the warmth was sheer rapture.

Toby eyed the boiler uncertainly. "Do we climb into that?"

"I don't think so. I think we fill tubs and sit in them."

Hot water—enough to *bathe* in? Would that be healthy?

"Soap!" Hamish squealed. "Real soap! Smell it—lavender!"

Toby stripped to the skin, then almost stripped that off as well when he tried to fill a bucket with water and got a blast of scalding steam instead. He jumped back and let Hamish work out the mechanics of the taps. It was necessary to mix cold water with the hot to obtain a bearable mixture—more complicated than he had expected. No matter, they were soon kneeling in whole tubfuls of hot water, soaping themselves, basking in the sheer sensuous luxury of it.

A hundred marks would buy a herd or a cottage. The earl's men-at-arms lived better than the farmers and artisans of Fillan, but it would only take one, even if the master ordered them not to talk.

Without warning, Hamish burst into song. His treble voice was surprisingly tuneful, and the stone walls reverberated nicely.

> The lass I love lives up the glen,
> She entertains all sorts of men.
> She has no use for all the rest,
> Because she knows that I'm the best . . .

Toby gave him the verse about the piper and repeated the chorus. Hamish responded with the two shepherds. Toby was halfway through the improbable accomplishments of the three sailors when a guard came in, scowling through the steam. It was probably not just the quality of Toby's baritone that was upsetting him, because one of his colleagues stood watch in the doorway with a drawn sword. He deposited a pile of bleached cloths on one of the benches and backed out again, still watching the *extremely dangerous* outlaw.

Eventually the singers ran out of lovers for the promiscuous lass and just lay back, soaking blissfully, heads against the stone wall, arms and legs dangling over the sides of the tubs. Another man delivered a plaid, shirt, socks, shoes, bonnet. He said, "For you," to Hamish, but he, too, kept his attention on the murderer, and again another man stood by, ready to intervene if there was trouble. Trouble? The monster was almost asleep. Now if they would just commute his death sentence to life imprisonment and let him die of old age right here. . . .

A third man brought in two muddy bundles and dropped them distastefully on the floor.

Hot water, they found, had an annoying tendency to cool off. Hamish was up and yipping about the towels being real linen, and Toby still had to shave. He hauled himself from the tub and admitted that the towels were very enjoyable, whatever they were made of. Having dried himself as well as he could in the steamy air, he found his razor in his bundle and set to work reaping stubble. By then Hamish was dressed and eager to go exploring the castle in search of books. It would be interesting to see how far he was allowed to wander.

The door opened again, this time to admit the red-bearded Sir Malcolm himself. He closed it behind him, shutting himself in with a dangerous outlaw wielding a razor, but his green eyes smiled warmly. "Is everything satisfactory, Master Toby? Anything more you need?"

Toby was so startled by the change of attitude that

he almost cut off his upper lip. "Everything's fine, sir," he admitted.

"I'm Malcolm Campbell, the castellan. If there is anything we can do to make your stay here more enjoyable, see you ask me right away."

Bewildered, Toby glanced at Hamish for clues. He was wearing his owlish look, which meant he was a step or two ahead.

"Now the best I can do for wear for you at the moment, sir," the castellan continued, "are these." He laid his burden on a bench. "The shoon we think belonged to Wee Wilkin, a great warrior who fell at Parline. I'm sure he would be honored for you to have them. If you'll just leave your plaids here, the women will get them washed and dried by morning. I'm afraid the shirt'll be snug, but they can run up something for you by tomorrow, and we'll find furs if you need to go out."

This sudden change of heart must be some sort of trap, but Toby could not see how, or what, or why. Hamish, damn him . . . if he looked any more owlish, he would fly away and hunt mice.

"The evening meal's still an hour or so off," Malcolm proclaimed cheerfully. "But I expect you'd enjoy a little something to keep you going until then. Have you any preference in whisky, Master Toby?"

Toby shook his head, causing the soldier to nod his.

"Then I'll see something is laid out for you and, er . . . your friend. If you'll just come back to the mess whenever you're ready." He reached for the door.

"What do we do with the water?"

"Oh, it gets ladled back into the boiler. But don't you mind it—I'll send a lad."

The door closed.

Toby rounded on Hamish. "What by the demons of Delia is going on? Why this sudden back-slapping, nothing-too-good, long-lost-brothering?"

The owl blinked. "You don't trust him, do you?"

"Of course not!"

"Do you ever trust anyone, ever?"

"Tell me what's going on!"

"Why ask me? How can you trust what I tell you? I'm just . . . " Hamish's smirk wavered and he backed away as Toby advanced menacingly on him. "Well, think about it! They knew what you did."

"So?"

"Now Sir Malcolm knows how and why." With an impudent grin, the kid added, "You're a big hero, Longdirk!"

Toby resisted the urge to dunk the kid's head back in the bathwater. He was probably right, as usual. Any story coming from Meg would be well embroidered. Rory's might have no resemblance to the truth at all. He might as well go out and see what sort of trouble the two of them had gotten him into. Besides, it was a long time since breakfast at Sir Torquil's.

The shirt would have to go on first. He pulled it over his head and then tried to put an arm into a sleeve. The tussle ended in a sound of ripping as the stitches surrendered.

"You'd think the Campbell could afford better seamstresses!" Toby discarded the remains. Who needed a shirt? The plaid was smaller than his own and smelled unpleasantly of soap, but a plaid was an accommodating garment. Best of all, it was dry. He wiped mud off his belt and sporran with the remains of the shirt and struggled into the unfamiliar socks. Wee Wilkin's feet must have been longer and narrower than his, but the shoes would do if he did not have to walk far.

When the two still-faintly-damp visitors emerged from the corridor into the kitchen, at least fifty of the castle guards were assembled there, lounging around on the stools and benches. Sir Malcolm was waiting at the entrance. He took Toby's hand, but instead of shaking it, he raised it overhead. The men surged to their feet in a tattoo of boots and a fanfare of scraping furniture.

"Huzzah!" cried the castellan. The ensuing cheer rippled the banners overhead. "Huzzah!"

Toby felt his face going red, redder, reddest. He was being applauded because he had misjudged a blow and killed a man? That was ridiculous! This was rank hypocrisy.

No matter how lustily they shouted for him, some of them must be planning to become rich off him before tomorrow's dawn. Earl Robert was known to favor the English governor; his men could not possibly all support Fergan—a few perhaps, in secret, but not all of them! Yet here they were making public rejoicing at the death of an English fusilier. Some of the guard would certainly rat. It would only take one. And even if none of the guard did, what of the hundreds of servants in the castle? Where was their loyalty?

Phonies!

The cheering ended, the castellan conducted the guests to a table laden with food. Hamish set to with a will, but Toby was beset by men twice his age coming to shake his hand and laud his heroism in tackling an armed soldier with his bare hands. They made him feel like the biggest idiot in the history of the Highlands.

Eventually the procession of admirers ended. Most of the guard departed. At last he could do justice to the cold pheasant and blood sausage. He drank only water.

5

He was distracted by more scraping of boots as the remaining men again rose to their feet. This time they were acknowledging visitors. One of them was Rory, almost unrecognizable in the dandified dress of an English gentleman—hat, kid buskins, embroidered shirt, fur-trimmed, full-skirted surcoat, and his legs encased in stocks of contrasting colors, one blue, one striped red and green. The outrageous outfit must be the latest fashion in Sassenach-loving Edinburgh. Even a woman whose taste ran to popinjays would never class him as handsome, surely? Damn him!

And the lady on his arm . . . Demons! It was Meg, decked out as if she had just arrived from the court, looking five years older and a hand taller. How could she even stand up in all that material?—laces and stitchery, flounces and puffed sleeves, plumes and pleats. The braids had gone and her hair was gathered in a silver net. She was a child playing at dressing up—no woman could have a waist that slender! Realizing that he was the only man in the hall still sitting, Toby staggered to his feet as she approached on Rory's arm. That neckline? How did the dress make her look so, er, buxom? That night he had rescued her, he had seen . . . There must be some sort of padding to push her up like that.

She was certainly enjoying the attention. She simpered. She curtseyed. She had a brief struggle with her gown, and then perched on a stool.

At the far end of the mess, the kitchen staff decided the young lord was here to stay. They unobtrusively started work again as quietly as they could.

Rory took the end of a bench beside Meg and looked up reprovingly. "Longdirk," he murmured, "it is permissible to notice a lady, but that gawky ogle is overdoing things by far."

Toby was the only one still standing . . . he sank back on his stool.

"Better!" the master said. "Now close your mouth and dry your chin."

"You approve?" Meg asked, her cheeks bright pink.

Toby gulped and stammered helplessly. The only word he could find was, "Gorgeous!"

Rory frowned. "I came to issue a warning. Hello? Can you hear me?"

Toby tore his eyes away from Meg. "Yes."

"Sure? Noose? Gallows? One hundred marks, dead or alive, remember? We have a small problem."

"What sort of problem?"

"Grandmother has a house guest."

"What sort of house guest?"

"A gentleman, of course. Master Maxim Stringer—an English merchant. He owns an import business in Dumbarton. He may not take quite the same attitude toward outlaws as we natives do."

Reality began to seep into Toby's churning wits.

"The natives? Does one more matter? Somebody here is going to squeal to the Sassenachs."

"No."

"A hundred marks—"

"It's tempting," Rory said sharply. "One or two may be tempted, but the Campbells won't betray a guest. Lady Lora has already made her feelings known, and so has Sir Malcolm. Believe me, any man who tips off the English won't live long enough to enjoy his reward. So you needn't worry about the chief's men, nor the house staff. But Master Stringer may be different. He won't care as much for the money, you understand, but he is English, poor fellow. His servants are living on the ship or billeted in the village, so they're no problem. Just him."

"I should leave!"

The master shook his head impatiently. "And go where? You're posted on every tree now. Even the Campbells can't shield you in Oban or Glasgow or Dumbarton. You stand out like Ben Cruachan, laddie."

Toby clenched his teeth. "So I have to stay here?"

"Not indefinitely. When the weather clears, Master Stringer will be sailing back to Dumbarton. Other ships, too. Father Lachlan's convinced that he must get you to Glasgow before you start causing terrible damage."

"What? What sort of—"

Rory shrugged. "Ask him. I think he's floundering. But that doesn't solve the long-term problem, does it? You're an idiot, but an interesting idiot, and not unlikable. You saved my life in the bog, even if you did provoke the bogy's spite in the first place. I owe you a debt, and I pay my debts. I want to see you settled, Master Strangerson."

He smiled reassuringly at Meg. Oh, he was very sure of himself now, was Rory! No one could call him to account in Inverary, except his father, away on the far side of Scotland. He could even parade around in the motley of a court jester without making a mess hall full of Highlanders collapse in earthquakes of mirth. There had been grins, yes, but no more. He must have proved himself a demon of a fighter at some time to have earned such respect.

He had the woman he lusted for trapped in his web. He could afford to be generous to the serf who had assisted in arranging this desirable turn of events. He could patronize him now.

"Muscle is no substitute for clan or land, boy. The law says you're a vagrant, even without the price on your head."

So again Toby faced the question: *Whose man will you be?*

"Which side are you recruiting for today?"

His insolence brought a welcome flush to the master's handsome cheek, and a most unwelcome stare of dismay from Meg. Rory's voice did not waver, though. *He has charm,* she had said. There was no need for him to lose his temper now, no need to resort to swords to keep the foolish girl from running away.

"Do not discuss politics in this house! Never! Only the Campbell himself decides such matters. Clear?"

"Yes, Master."

"Good. I'm recruiting for Inverary. My father can adopt you into the clan. Sir Malcolm is always looking for strong young men. So you'll be Pikeman Toby Campbell of Inverary, and then the Sassenachs can stuff their warrant in a bombard and blow it to hell."

Hamish made a noise perilously close to a whistle of astonishment. Meg beamed ecstatically.

Everything a man needed: a name, a job, a home—a master.

"Just pikeman? Not official Clan Hexer?"

Rory stared at him through a long silence. "Can you?"

"No. Whatever wonders happen around me are not my doing. I don't call them."

"That limits your value, but I won't believe it's all just luck. If I was marching into battle, Longdirk, I'd rather have you at my side than all the MacDonalds in the Isles."

"Wouldn't he be better protection in front?" said Meg.

Toby winced. The ice in her eyes said he was being unnecessarily mulish.

The master guffawed at her humor and then returned to business. "It's time to make up your mind! Whose man do you want to be?" He adjusted a lace cuff thoughtfully. "Of course, you are the king's man. Every man is the king's man first. Every bond of manrent excludes fealty to His Majesty."

Toby could only nod. In theory that was true, although it did not prevent the earl of Argyll from deciding which king his people would support.

"Which king, Longdirk?"

The tables had been turned.

"You just told me not to discuss politics here, my lord."

"May I intrude?" Meg asked, intruding. "When an ox can't be led, it can sometimes be driven. Lord Gregor has made you an incredibly generous offer, Toby. You spurn it. What do you *want*?"

He scratched his head. "You safe in Oban, to start with."

Rory smiled like a well-fed wolf. "You need worry no more about Meg. My grandmother is even now writing a note to her parents, and it will go by runner tomorrow. They will know that she is safe."

Safe from whom? Meg had lowered her gaze to the forgotten food on the boards. Her parents would be enraptured at the news. The tanner was a rich man in Tyndrum, but the humblest scullery job in Inverary Castle would be a great advancement for his daughter. Toby was relieved of his promise.

"Next wish, Longdirk?"

"To be free of my hex, or demon, or whatever it is."

"That means Glasgow. And after that?"

The ox was being driven. "I don't think Valda's dead." Mindful of Meg's reproach, Toby added, "That's why I can't accept your offer, my lord. If I stay here, she'll find me, and I may not be the only one who suffers then." That was true, if only part of the truth.

"It would have been tactful to say so sooner," Rory murmured. "I told you I'm grateful. So *what* do you *want?* What will you be when you grow up, Little Toby? Soldier? Farmhand? Miner? Shepherd? Highwayman?"

The barn door closed. He said the words he'd never spoken aloud before. "I'm going to be a prizefighter." He saw Meg shudder. "It's all I've got! I'm big, and I can box. I can't do anything else. There's good money to be made in the ring in England."

Even Rory seemed disappointed. "There's also gambling, and cheating, and criminals. A very low crowd."

"Making a living by hurting people?" Meg said. "Breaking bones, smashing faces? And what do they do to you? In a few years you'll be a pug-ugly, shambling hulk with no brains at all!"

"Note that I refrain from making funny remarks here," Rory said airily. "Prizefighting sponsors I cannot produce. The best I can do is to refer you to Sir Malcolm. He has some of the finest trainers in Scotland. No boxing instructors, so far as I know, but you can brush up on your holds and throws. They need work."

He rose, graceful as a swallow. "Come, Miss Campbell. We must leave the lads to their meal and go see what Grandmother has provided for us. Our solar is greatly praised, but your beauty will transform it." He offered her a hand. "Hamish—you want books? I'll show you the library."

Hamish sprang to his feet, food forgotten. "That would be wonderful, my lord!"

"There's about a thousand volumes, I'm told. Reading is not my favorite pastime. Help yourself. You, Knuckles, have to keep under cover. Master Stringer is another idiot, but stay out of his way if you value your cervical vertebrae."

Toby's nails dug into his palms. "For how long?"

"Until the storm blows over and the boats can leave. Then we'll ship you and Father Lachlan off down to Dumbarton. It's a good idea to let a hue and cry die down—people always assume after a week or two that the fugitive has fled to foreign parts, and they forget. Do keep your mouth shut."

Rory nodded a mocking farewell and departed, with Hamish tagging at his heels like a puppy and Meg on his arm in her courtly gown.

Damn him! Damn him! Damn him!

6

Toby was trapped. Even if he was allowed to leave the castle, he would never escape from Campbell country against Rory's will. In any case, he could not desert Meg, although she had not asked for his help and probably never would. He must just accept the master at his word and wait for the Atlantic to stop throwing gales at the coast. Then, if Rory were to be trusted, he could risk his neck in Dumbarton, seeking an exorcism at the sanctuary.

So he had time to kill. The Campbells were respectful but distant; he must not talk politics with them and he had nothing else to discuss. Meg and Rory and Father Lachlan could float amid the gentry, hobnobbing with Master Stringer and dining with Her Ladyship. Hamish would be happy to eat, drink, breathe, live, and sleep books. Not Toby! Reading had always been torment for him, one plodding word at a time.

Much as he disliked admitting a debt to Rory, the idea of wrestling lessons had a strong appeal. The next morning, he accosted Sir Malcolm.

The castellan scratched his red beard as if perplexed, but a twinkle in his eye hinted he had already been warned. "Just wrestling? How about a few of the other manly arts as well? Fencing? Musketry? We can't do much on archery or horsemanship without going outdoors. That's true of artillery, too."

"All of them!"

"Then all of them you shall have. If you'll just come with me, Master Toby." Sir Malcolm led him upstairs.

Toby followed, wondering if he had been overly rash. He might have chopped down more than he could saw up. "This is very kind of you, Castellan."

"Not at all. Good for the lads. I always tell them that instructing's one of the best ways of learning, because it shows you what you thought you knew and don't really. This is the armory. The man with the shoulders is our wrestling champion, Neal Big, and that antiquated spider over there is Gavin the Grim, who can still chop any man into sausage filling in the twinkle of an eye."

Thereupon Sir Malcolm set the entire Campbell warband onto Toby, or so it seemed. Baby-faced recruits no older than Hamish knew more about swords and guns than he did, while the old-timers knew more about everything than he could ever dream of knowing. Every man in the castle could teach him something and seemed eager to do so. He intrigued them—he was a hero, a fugitive, and a baby giant. They came at him in relays. The day became a blur of locks and throws . . . longbow and crossbow . . . pistol and musket . . . saber, rapier, and short sword . . . matchlock and wheel lock.

He soon realized that they were making a game of it, seeing who could work him to exhaustion. Fine—just let them try! They couldn't, of course. He had the stamina of a mule, always ready to go again as soon as he caught his breath. With blades he won polite praise and a few heady compliments about being a natural athlete, but he lacked the speed ever to be a top fencer. He could already handle a quarterstaff, and he took to wrestling like a bat to bugs. Along about what felt like noon, he realized that night was falling already. By the time he retired to the little tower room he shared with Hamish, the candles were burning low and his roommate lay fast asleep, flat on his back with an open book spread on his chest.

Morning dawned in one solid ache, but the first ten minutes on the mat with Neal Big limbered him up again.

That afternoon, as he hammered short swords with Gavin, he observed the dumpy shape of Father Lachlan perched on an empty powder keg in a corner of the armory. When the fencing paused for a breather, Toby trotted over and dropped on one knee beside him, panting.

The acolyte beamed at him over his spectacles. "From the breadth of your grin, I take it you are enjoying yourself, my son?"

He nodded, that being easier than speaking.

"No bad dreams?"

Head shake.

"You are certainly working hard enough. Do you know, Tobias, from one cause or another, I don't think I have ever seen you totally dry?"

Toby chuckled. "What . . . you mean when . . . told Rory . . . I might . . . cause terrible damage?"

"Ah." The little man frowned. "I am concerned. You have displayed superhuman powers, but they are not under your conscious control, are they? You don't will them to happen. So far they have been restricted to effecting miraculous escapes, but can we count on that always being the case? Suppose Sir Malcolm and his men try to arrest you?"

That was an uncomfortable thought. He wiped his forehead with an arm. "I might hurt them?"

"Perhaps. You might just disappear out of their reach, or you might haul down the castle on their heads. I don't know, and neither do you." Father Lachlan pushed his glasses up his nose. "Listen to this, as a theory: Lady Valda attempted to put a hex on you, and something went wrong. The arts she practices are very dangerous, so that's not too surprising. As I told you, she cannot compel you directly. She would order a demon to make you do whatever it was she wanted of you. She might have included instructions to the demon to protect you from outside interference, right? And somehow those orders have taken precedence, so that the demon defends you even from her? Frankly, Tobias, I don't believe you are in any great danger from the sentence of death that has been passed on you—but I think anyone who tries to carry it out may be very surprised indeed!"

There were flaws in that theory, surely. Where did "Susie" come into it?

The old man saw his hesitation. "It is only a suggestion, and I admit objections. Demonic powers have a limited range. If the demon she invoked was imprisoned in the jewel on the dagger, then she must have planned to give you the dagger to carry with you—but she didn't, did she? So where is the demon? How does it stay close to you?"

"I don't know, Father."

"Neither do I! But I still believe that we must get you to a sanctuary as soon as possible, before something bad happens. Now I see that poor old man is waiting for you to stop shirking."

" 'Poor old man?' Gavin? He's got more stamina than a billy goat!" Toby went back to fencing.

The next day he was pleased to see that the weather was worse than ever. He had begun to worry about Meg, wondering why she was not coming to see him, as he could not seek her out. He determined to ask Hamish, but he did not see Hamish all day, either.

The two of them shared a small circular room at the top of one of the towers. It was drafty and furnished with nothing but two straw mattresses, but none the worse for that. That night, as he was turning his plaid into a blanket, he heard a sleepy murmur of greeting, the contented purr of a bookworm who has spent a whole day digesting books and expects to spend more days doing so.

"Awake?"

"Mmph!" Meaning no.

"Hamish, do you know how they corn gunpowder?"

"Mmph!" Meaning yes.

Toby rolled himself into a bundle. "Do you know how an arrow is tuned to a bow?"

There was a pause. Then a slightly more alert boy said, "Yes, again. Why? Why do you want to know?"

"I don't. I know already." He stared miserably at the darkness.

Hamish misunderstood, which was not surprising. He yawned extensively. "Go ahead and tell me if you want to, but I read about it once."

"I don't want to tell you."

A note of irritation. "You woke me up to tell me you don't want to tell me how an arrow is tuned to a bow? Have you been planning this for long, or did it just come to you on the spur of the moment?"

"Sorry. Have you seen Meg?"

"Not to speak to. She went walking with Lady Lora this afternoon, when the sun came out. I've heard her singing in the hall." Yawn. "She's fine."

"Oh. Good. I was just wondering. Sorry to wake you. Go to sleep."

"Sleep, is it? Go to sleep? Now? After you start acting . . . "

"Start acting what?"

"Oh, nothing. G'night, Toby."

The room was small. Toby leaned a long arm across and took an ear between finger and thumb. "Do you want this? It feels loose."

"Owww!"

"Should I pull and see?"

"All right! Let go! Thank you. What do I have to talk about?"

"You were about to tell me about noticing me acting strange."

"Oh, I would never be that crazy!" Straw rustled and Hamish chuckled from the relative safety of the far side of his pallet. "I've hardly seen you since we got here! But . . . why did you ask about corning and the arrow thing?"

"They're interesting," Toby said stubbornly.

"But it's not like you to find 'why' sorts of things interesting. I'm the scholar; you're a doer." He fell silent for a moment, then turned a white blur of a face in the dark. "That's what you meant, isn't it?"

"Yes," Toby admitted. "They tell me things—and I *remember* them! I even care! I never did before. Your pa used to say I was the worst student he'd ever had."

Hamish laughed aloud. "That's a ridiculous understatement! I'll never forget my first day in school! I must have been five. You would have been about eight, right? I know you were the biggest boy in the school even then, and that day Pa was trying to teach you the four-times table. I knew it already, of course—I could read when I was three—and I couldn't believe a boy as big as you could be finding it so difficult. Neither could Pa! I had never seen him really angry before. I hardly knew him. I was weeping because my pa was behaving like that— screaming and yelling at you, cuffing you, beating you. All the kids in the village were sitting there, waiting to be taught, and he spent more time on you than on all of the rest of us together, but I don't think you knew one more fact at the end of the morning than you had when you walked in late, and you'd had at least a dozen strokes of the birch."

"Only a dozen? I always felt I'd wasted the day if I couldn't drive him up to twenty." He was bragging, of course, but not by much. "Five years of struggle! I kept hoping he'd admit I was unteachable and expel me."

"But he knew you were faking, so he wouldn't. I don't know how you stood it, though."

"I knew how he used to go home and weep—Eric told me. That kept me going—knowing that he wept and I never did. I still sleep facedown, even now, just out of habit."

"When you left school, Pa said you'd won, he hadn't taught you a thing."

That was gratifying! "Oh, he got a few facts into me," Toby said modestly. English, for example—even as a child, he'd known that English mattered, so he had let himself be taught it. That was what the school was for, why the government decreed it. "But I soon managed to forget them. Now look at me! I'm remembering things! I'm learning things! That's not like me! I must be hexed."

"I don't think it's that," Hamish said sleepily. "You never wanted to know what Pa was trying to tell you. Anytime you learned something, you felt you'd failed, right? But what they're telling you here are things you want to know. So when you learn something, you feel you've won. That makes all the difference in the world! I'm interested in almost anything, especially if I can read it in a book—all 'cept family. Anytime Ma tries to teach me her cousinries, I turn stupid. Stupid as Toby Strangerson, she says."

"Really? Is that what they say?" It would be nice to think he still had that reputation in the schoolteacher's household after all these years.

"It's what everyone says. Your ignorance is a byword in the glen, big man! But I think you're just very choosy in what you want to learn. You're not stupid; you only learn what you want to know."

Toby said, "Mmph!" into the pallet. That was a far-fetched notion. It would be very odd to think of himself as not stupid. A few moments later, Hamish said something more, but he was too far away to hear. . . .

The next morning the rain had stopped, but a north-wester was raising whitecaps on the loch. Sir Malcolm suggested riding lessons. Toby exchanged plaid for trews and jerkin and accompanied him to the stables. By lunchtime, he was clearing five-foot gates.

"Totally fearless," the castellan said.

Toby hadn't the heart to tell him it was just lack of imagination. There were advantages to being stupid.

When he hobbled into the mess hall, he saw Meg sitting at a table with half a dozen of the younger guards buzzing around her like flies at a cowpat. She was smiling tautly up at them: Pretty Will and Iain of Clachan and others. Toby strode over at a moderate gallop and came up behind them. He stumbled into Will, jabbed an elbow in Iain's kidneys, and accidentally trod on Robb Long's toe.

"Sorry," he remarked. "I'm not usually so clumsy."

They took a thoughtful look at his face and made their apologies and went off to another table. He sat down.

"It's good to see you, Meg. . . . What are you glaring like that for?"

"I am not glaring!"

Oh, yes, she was.

Her dress was much simpler than the fantastic court own he had seen her in before, just plain green wool ith pleats and no sleeves. Her hair was back in braids. he was a country lass again—but oh, she was lovely!

While he was out of breath, a great sweaty cart orse. He was also tongue-tied. "I've been worried about ou."

"Oh? Well, you knew where I was, didn't you?"

"Yes, but . . . Well, I have to stay in the barracks."

"There are a thousand pages. You could have written note if you wanted to speak with me."

"Never thought of it."

"What are you worrying about?"

He was so pleased to see her—why was she looking t him like that? "Just wondering if you were all right."

"All right?" Meg said with a shrill laugh. "All right? iving like a lady in a castle? How could I not be all right? he only thing that isn't all right is that one day I'll have o wake up and be the tanner's daughter again and go ack to scraping hides."

"Enjoy it while it lasts!" He was. "Is Rory behaving imself?"

"Oh, that's it? Lord Gregor is a perfect gentleman."

Which was exactly what he was afraid of. She had urned her head away, but he saw a wash of pink on her heek.

"What's wrong? I mean, if there's something trou-ling you, I . . . " I what? He was as much of a prisoner as he was. He couldn't do anything.

"Toby," she whispered, suddenly sounding not at all ike Meg Tanner. "He says he loves me!"

"You don't believe him, I hope?"

"No other man has ever told me that."

Oh, zits! He leaned his elbows on the table and put his forehead on his palms so he had to look down and wouldn't stare at her. "Meg," he told his biceps, "dear Meg! I can make a lot of money prizefighting in England.

I'll save it all. In a few years—before I get the few brain
I've got knocked out of me—I'll come back to Scotlan
and rent a few acres, and buy a horse and a plow. The
I'll find me a girl, and marry her, and make her ver
happy. I've never had family. I want people to love: a wif
and lots of children. I would be the best husband an
father I could be. I'm strong. I could do the work of thre
men and prosper. And I won't be anyone's man, excep
my wife's, and I'll always be true to her. But at th
moment I can't ask any girl to believe in that dream."

"How many years? Five?"

He looked up. Why were her eyes so shiny? Did sh
want him to talk of love? He didn't even know wha
friendship was, let alone love.

"At least," he said. "Maybe ten. Sorry—I'm not th
one for the fancy speeches."

"What do you mean by that, Toby Strangerson?"

"I mean he's a glib-tongued rascal. He was brough
up at court, and you know what sort of morals they have
You told me he was devious yourself. He's out to trap
you. He'll try to . . . I mean, he'll talk you into . . . You
don't know anything about him!"

She tossed her head, snapping braids like whips.
"Yes, I do! I know he's a gentleman, which is more than
know about you. He's a courteous, educated—"

"Oh, is he?" He shouted her down. "And I'm just a big
safe lout who's handy to rescue you when some man
you're teasing gets violent, but not rich and sweet-talking
and able to dress you up in fancy clothes?"

Meg stared at him in utter silence.

"I shouldn't have said that," he muttered.

She stood up. "No, you shouldn't."

"But you know what he'll do, Meg! He'll get what he
wants from you and then toss you aside because you're
not good enough. That's all he wants, just to . . . you
know."

Meg said, "*Oh!* Oh, you *are* a boor, Toby Strangerson
A brainless boor!" Her voice shrilled across the tables.

"Don't take any more bastards back to the glen, Meg!"

"What? How *dare* you say such things about me?"

"I didn't mean—"

"Yes, you did! You called me a loose woman!"

"No, I didn't!" He, too, was yelling at the top of his lungs. They would hear him in Fillan. "Any woman is loose if . . . I mean can be . . . you know a man turns her head with words and talks her into . . . Oh, demons! I promised your pa I would look after you!"

"That's why you're taking musketry lessons, I suppose? And playing swords all day? You smell like a stable."

"You're crying!"

"No, I'm not!" She spun on her heel and flounced out of the mess.

There were grins everywhere.

He ate without noticing what he was eating.

He found Hamish by himself in a corner, eating and reading at the same time. He sat down on the same bench.

"I want to write a letter!"

Hamish looked up in amazement. "Did I just hear—"

"Can you get me a piece of paper and a quill?"

"Steal paper?" Hamish said doubtfully. "Paper costs money!"

"And wax. And ink, too."

Hamish dutifully went off to the library and returned with a sheet of paper and writing tools. Toby turned down more fencing lessons and wasted the whole afternoon struggling over a letter. In the end he had five blots, six scorings-out, and three sentences: *I am sorry about I was a boor. I was just am worried if you might get hurted and hoping you forgiving me. Your good friend, Tobias Strangerson.*

He sealed it with the wax and handed it to a page to deliver. Then he ran up to the gym and threw Neal Big around like a sack of oats.

The next day the sun was shining, but no one came to summon him to the loch. They tried him on archery. In an hour he was putting his shafts alongside the gold at two hundred paces with a hundred-pound bow. In the afternoon he learned that he had a fair eye for firearms, although he knew most of his success stemmed from sheer brute strength, guns being cumbersome things that out-kicked any mule.

There was no reply from Meg—not that day, nor the day after.

He had no way of knowing if his letter had reached her.

7

It was another morning. Toby had been wrestling, so he was wearing trews. He had added a mask and plastron to fence short swords with Gavin the Grim, who had gained his name from his unchanging gentle smile— who had to be at least fifty but was still spry as a grasshopper and could wield a blade better than any man in Scotland. They were just about to face off for the second time . . .

Gavin said, "Break!"

Toby hauled off his mask and turned to see Rory, resplendent in full Highland regalia, from the silver badge in his bonnet to his shiny shoes and the black knife in his stocking that meant he was otherwise unarmed.

Gavin murmured "My lord," and tactfully departed.

Rory led the way over to a window. "I'm impressed, really impressed! You were giving the old boy a serious match there!"

That remark felt so good that Toby ground his teeth to stop himself smiling. He unbuckled the plastron and took it off with a sigh of relief—it was so tight on him he could hardly breathe in it. "I can't touch him. I was trying to wear him down."

Rory laughed disbelievingly. "That's all? Even I can't do that to old Gavin! Never mind, I have news."

"Good or bad?" *Have you managed to seduce Meg yet?*

"Good. But first . . . have you changed your mind? If not Pikeman Toby, how about Serjeant? Malcolm says he'll shoot any six men at random if he can have you."

Toby shook his head. He had been expecting something like this. *Have you broken her heart yet?* They had reached the window, well away from eavesdroppers. The old devilry was back in the silver eyes and he braced himself for treachery.

Rory shrugged. "I said I couldn't deliver a sponsor or a prizefighter, but I was being too modest, as usual. I've found you one. He's on his way here now."

"Who is?"

"Stringer."

"Coming to claim the reward?"

"I hope not." Rory spoke as if the matter was trivial. "A hundred marks isn't all that much to him. Listen *carefully!* Stringer's a trader. He buys here and ships back south. He's heading home for the winter in another week. He's rich enough and important enough that he won't be questioned at the docks the way you would be if you tried to board a ship. If we can get him to take you with him, you'll be free and clear, right?"

Away to England? That had always been Toby's ambition, hadn't it? Why did it feel so wrong now?

"Yes, but—"

"You can see Cruachan this morning. Unless the wind veers, the ships will be leaving on the next ebb, so there isn't much time. At breakfast this morning he happened to mention that he dabbles in the ring. And then he went on to relate that he has a pugilist of his own, and the man travels with him as a bodyguard. He's here in Inverary! Zing! Lightning struck!"

"Struck what?" Toby asked warily.

"My slow wits, I suppose. I should have discovered this sooner. Stringer is one of the Fancy, you numbskull! He promotes fighters. He was bragging about the money he would make this winter off this Randal of his. I told him I knew a Highland lad who could knock Randal's stuffing out and spit on it." Silver eyes gleamed.

"Oh, you did, did you?" Toby said, feeling somethin stir in his gut. "How big is Randal?"

"No idea. I just spoke up on principle—he can't b any bigger than you, can he? I offered to lay money o you, of course."

"That was very rash of you."

Rory was smiling dangerously. "Nonsense! Th champion of Strath Fillan against a pansy Sassenach You won't make a liar of me, will you?"

"I haven't seen him, this Randal."

"Stringer's gone to fetch him."

Sudden changes of plan suggested sudden change of circumstance, and a chance remark at breakfast di not seem quite sufficient. Perhaps it did to gentry. "Wha about the dead-or-alive business? I thought I was hidin from Stringer so he wouldn't find out about that."

"A hundred marks is chicken feed compared to wha Stringer will think he can make off you if you can beat hi man." Rory raised his eyebrows. "I understood this wa. your ambition? He's your meal ticket, my bareknuckl friend! He'll take you south and promote you—train you line you up with fights. If you want to rat out on him onc. you're there, of course, that's your business."

"I couldn't do that!"

The rebel snorted. "That's up to you. What I'm say ing is that you fight his man today and make a goo showing. . . . You don't even need to win, just sho promise. You're young yet. Stringer can spirit you out o Scotland better than anyone. Here he comes now. Are you game or not?"

It seemed to make sense. It was a challenge a ma could understand, one Toby Strangerson could no refuse and did not want to. Best of all, it was a chance t do something for himself instead of depending on Ror or Lady Lora or even Father Lachlan. When it came t fists, he knew what he was at.

"I'm always game."

"Good lad!" Rory switched to English. "Max, ol chap—this is the man."

Toby turned around, then bowed to the gentleman.

Master Maxim Stringer was well named, being almost as tall as Toby himself and extremely thin. He wore hose and knickerbockers, a fur-trimmed doublet over a frilly shirt. The hair on the top of his head was set in elaborate curls as a vain effort to hide a thinning crown, and his pigtail was wound with silver thread. He had an excessively long upper lip but no chin worthy of the name, and he looked Toby up and down with disdain.

"Frightfully young, isn't he? You'll break a foal's spirit if you run it too soon, you know."

"His spirit's as sound as his wind," Rory said cheerfully. "Name the stakes."

The man at Stringer's back laughed, displaying a wide absence of teeth. He was broad and bald and at least forty—not short by most standards, but shorter than Toby. He might weigh almost as much, though, for he was thick, bulging over his belt. His nose had been pounded flat, one of his ears was several times the size of the other. His face had a leathery look, like one big scar. This must be Randal.

So Toby had wind and reach on his side. He would have to keep the older man at a distance and just wear him down. He tried to see what shape the man's hands were in, but Randal was keeping them out of sight.

Randal wore a sleeveless shirt and short breeches, and his feet were bare. He had an anchor tattooed on his arm—there was room to engrave a whole navy on those arms—and his pigtail was tarred. He was a sailor, which did not exactly disprove Rory's tale, but didn't quite fit with it, either.

Master Stringer reached in a pocket and produced a single piece of glass on a ribbon. He contorted his face to insert this in his right eye and then walked all around Toby, as if Toby were a nag in a horse market. Rory took the foil and plastron away to display him better.

The armory was filling up. Word of the proposed match must be out already, for a continuous line of men lounged along the far wall. Hamish was one of them, looking as if he had just seen a ghost—or someone wh[o] might be a ghost very shortly, perhaps?

"Mm. Promising!" Stringer admitted. "The arms ar[e] especially impressive. But too young—his gristle isn't se[t] yet. What do you think, Randal?"

"I'll break him like a twig, sir."

"I'm sure you will. But, if you're quite serious, Rory . . [.] say four hundred pounds?"

"Make it five," Rory said cheerfully. "It's a nice roun[d] number."

Toby gulped at the thought of so much money ridin[g] on his ability to punch—and withstand pain, of course[.] That was the hard part. There ought to be a purse for th[e] fighters themselves, but in a sense he would be fightin[g] for his life, so he could hardly ask for cash as well.

"Five then!" Stringer drawled. "And I have anothe[r] hundred says the boy won't be there for the tent[h] round."

"And if he is, another two hundred for the twentieth?"

"If you like."

"And three hundred for the thirtieth and so on?"

Even Stringer looked startled at that. He glanced a[t] Randal.

"Take it, sir," the pug growled. "It's sugar fro[m] babies. I'll put him to sleep in three rounds."

Toby was trying to work out the numbers. Som[e] fights lasted seventy rounds or more, although he'[d] never gone more than nine, when he'd been knocked ou[t] by Ross MacLachlan, four years ago. One hundred plu[s] two hundred was three. Plus three . . . Um, six? If h[e] could stand up for fifty or sixty rounds, he was going t[o] make Rory a fortune. Or lose him one, of course, if he go[t] knocked out sooner.

With a sickening twinge of doubt, Toby realized tha[t] he wasn't certain of winning. He thought he could, an[d] he certainly had a good chance, but he wasn't quite sure[.] He'd never doubted himself before, and it was a bad feel[-] ing. Perhaps life in the outside world had already begu[n] to teach him discretion. In Fillan he'd always been u[p] against country lads like himself. This Randal, sailor or not, looked like a bareknuckle expert, a pro—hard, solid. Prizefighting was never about hitting hardest or fastest, it was about taking punishment and coming back for more. He suspected that he could punch Randal until his fists fell off and the man would still be there.

"Sounds good!" Rory said. "You still game for a fight, Longdirk?"

"Of course!" Toby snapped, laying his left foot forward and raising his fists. Randal jumped and backed away a step.

"Not yet!" Rory laughed. "You see the mustard in him, Max? He's a real killer."

Not funny!

"Where?" asked Stringer.

"Out in the paddock. Can't fight on stone!"

"Oh, absolutely not! Grass is best. Always prefer grass. Makes the blood look redder, what?"

When Rory had described Stringer as an idiot, he had been unusually accurate. The man seemed quite witless.

"And why not right now?" Rory said airily. "Let's go and get the lads started. How about Sir Malcolm for referee?"

"Splendid choice. And we'll need a timekeeper and umpires . . . " The Englishman's drawl faded away as Rory led him off.

"Kid," said Randal, "you're crazy! Don't make me do this to you."

"I'm not worried!" Toby turned round and headed for the door. His blood was starting to race as the prospect sank in. A real prizefight! And good money! Damned good money to ride on a tyro.

The sailor was growling at his heels. "You really are crazy, lad. I've been a pugilist for twenty-three years. I know every trick there is and I've stood up to most of the best in my time. I went thirty-seven rounds against Crusher Fishmonger, and not two men in England can say the same. I took the Exeter Butcher in sixty-five rounds and he never walked straight again. Bryton Fletcher was only twenty-four, poor fellow, and I put his left eye out in the thirtieth round, but he insisted on going on, and he lost the other one, too. He barely knew night from day after that. You're not bad looking, boy, but there's no way you can put a face back together after I've worked on it. The girls won't love you if you look like a pudding. Let me tell you—"

His hand barely settled on Toby's shoulder—Toby spun around and struck it off just in time. A week's training might not have made him an expert wrestler, but it had taught him some of the pressure points and he knew where those twisted, powerful fingers had been heading.

"Here!" Randal barked indignantly. "What's all this hitting before the match?"

"Save it!" growled old Gavin, sliding between them. "Keep your paws to yourself, old man. And keep your lies to yourself, too. Need a second, lad?"

Randal shrugged his great shoulders and rolled away.

"I'd be honored," Toby said. "Unless my sponsor wants to second me himself." It felt good to have a sponsor to talk about. As for Gavin, the spidery old fencing instructor felt right. True, he was volunteering, but if he'd been bribed already, it had been extremely fast work. He was older than Randal, though, and the memory of his stamina with the swords was a warning not to take anything for granted. . . . Toby's mind was flitting like a butterfly. *Calm down! It's only a fight.*

"And bottleholder?"

"This one," Toby said, watching Hamish's anxious face approach through the crowd. He could trust Hamish not to fill him full of liquor when he expected water, or water when he needed liquor to deaden the pain. The gym was almost empty now, the audience having siphoned itself off to the paddock to preempt the ringside positions.

Hamish failed to return Toby's cheerful grin. Hamish was poking at something in his left hand, which turned out to be money. He looked up, worried and distracted. "Got any coins, Toby?"

"Some." Toby stalked over to where he had left his plaid and retrieved his sporran. "Here, bet it all."

"What? No, that wasn't what I meant!" He lowered his voice. "I just want to look at them."

Toby had no time to unravel the lad's high-flying fancies, whatever they were. "Well, take care of that for me anyway. Will you be my bottleholder?"

Hamish blinked several times. "Your what?"

"Bottleholder. There's going to be a fight."

"Oh? Is there? Who're you fighting?"

Hamish must have been at the bottle already.

SEVEN

Knockout

1

The sponsors had chosen a corner of one of the paddocks where the turf was in good shape. Ropes and stakes were being hurriedly arranged to form the other two sides of the ring, eight paces a side, and already there were two or three hundred people gathered, with more coming all the time. Word must have spread through the village and even reached the ships. The crowd buzzed like summer wasps. Meg was there, behind the fences, with Lady Lora and the whole population of the castle. Servants were placing chairs in a wagon to make a grandstand for the ladies and gentlemen.

Rory and Stringer leaned on the wooden rails nearby, chatting quietly, neither of them displaying concern at the horrible stakes they were risking. The two umpires they had chosen were seeking out a third to act as tie-breaker. Ben Cruachan was certainly in view, white with snow, but the sun had brought no warmth. The wind raised goosebumps on Toby's skin. He jogged in place, eager to get started. His opponent stood with massive arms folded, scowling at him contemptuously.

A stable boy was painting the Scratch on the turf. Apart from him, there were six men in the ring, waiting for the referee to arrive and start the fight—the two bare-chested combatants, their seconds and bottleholders. Randal's second was another tar-queued sailor with an equally battered appearance. The bottleholder was a wiry ferret of a man with a shrill voice. The other two were leaving the jeering to him, but he lacked imagination—*bastard* and *uppity kid* were about the best he could manage, apart from a few improbable obscenities.

Hamish had now recovered his wits and was doing

better, deriding Randal as a punch-drunk antique has-been, whose wits had all been knocked out of him years ago and whose face showed that he couldn't stop a fly-swat. The crowd listened appreciatively and shouted out its own comments. Except for some of the sailors, every-one favored the Scotsman, of course. They would have put their money on him if he'd been missing an arm. He mustn't fail them!

Without his shirt, Randal seemed larger than before. As if to compensate for his bald scalp, his thick body was a forest of grizzled hair, like a bearskin stretched over a barrel. His breeches displayed very bandy legs. There was nothing wrong with his shoulders, but it was the depth of his chest that Toby found worrisome. Hitting that heap of muscle would do no good at all.

"Keep the rounds short," Gavin muttered at his side. "Go down every chance you get. Helps to keep one leg half-bent."

"That's not very sporting!"

"Never mind sporting! You're doing this for money now, lad. And look out for teeth. He's still got some teeth, and a fist full of broken teeth isn't any good for hitting with. Stay away from his mouth."

Toby caught Meg's eye and waved cheerfully. She returned the wave, but she looked worried. She had seen him fight in the past, so why should she be worried? Nice that she was, though. He wouldn't let her down, either.

He flexed his arms. Even Stringer had called them impressive!

One good thing about this battle was that he wouldn't be fighting someone he knew. He wouldn't care so much about hurting a stranger. His right cross was his weapon. He'd won seven fights in the last three games, and every one of them with his right cross. He would keep his left fist in Randal's face until he got an opening and then bring in his timber-splitting right. Just one to the chin might do it. Even at half-power it had floored Rory.

"Remember," Gavin said, "keep your head covered!

You've got five fingers on him in height, easy. Body blows just hurt; it's the head that does the job and he's got to come up to you."

Rory excused himself, vaulted the fence nimbly, and strode toward Toby, smiling confidently. Behind him, Sir Malcolm clambered in over the rails. The stable boy trotted off with his paint bucket.

"All set?" Rory said breezily.

Toby flexed his shoulders. "Ready."

"Good man! You know the wagers—if you can come up to Scratch for the thirtieth round, we can't lose!"

"I plan to finish him off a lot sooner than that."

The silver eyes smiled cynically. "Please yourself! Master Stringer and I have put up a purse of fifty marks."

"That's generous! Thank you." Toby had hoped for a share of the winnings, but fifty marks was still money. Real money!

"Plus a tenth of my winnings for you. So the longer you make it last, the more you earn," Rory added pointedly. "Give us a good show. Don't let Scotland down."

A tremor of warning ran over the skin on Toby's back. He glanced quickly at Hamish and saw a reflection of his own sudden unease. Rory had arranged the wagers so that Toby had every incentive to spin out the butchery as long as possible. Why? He had told Stringer that this match was for sport and a wager. He had told Toby that he was fighting to earn an escape from the law. Could he have other motives as well?

And what other parties might take an interest in the match? There was no denying that prizefighting was dangerous. Men died in the ring every year.

"One question," Toby said. "Suppose my opponent gets struck by lightning? What do the Fancy Rules have to say about that?"

Rory glanced covertly at Gavin, doubtless wondering how he would take that unusual query. Then he chuckled.

"Well, it'll be an interesting match, won't it? Thunder to startle him you might get away with, but I suspect lightning would class as cheating." His silver eyes gleamed joyfully as he thumped Toby's shoulder. "This is your big chance, Longdirk. Murder the bast—I do beg your pardon! Murder the *beast,* I mean. Miss Campbell and I will be cheering every punch."

He turned and sauntered back to the fence as Sir Malcolm shouted for the fighters.

The combatants advanced to Scratch. Their handlers followed, continuing their baiting until the referee barked at them for silence. He looked the two contestants over with no discernible feelings. "Under what names do you fight, gentlemen?" he said quietly.

"Randal the Ripper."

Toby opened his mouth—and wavered. To use his own name in front of this crowd would be rank insanity, when it was posted all over Scotland. He had not foreseen the problem, and yet this was his first professional fight, so the name he used now would be his permanent name.

"He's the Baby Bastard," Randal said, and his two seconds laughed.

"Longdirk of the Hills!" Hamish shrilled.

Sir Malcolm opened his mouth above a flaming beard and let forth a bellow. *"My lords, ladies, and gentlemen!* For a purse of fifty silver marks, an unlimited match under the Fancy Rules, between *Randal the Ripper* in the brown trews, and *Longdirk of the Hills* in the green and black."

The crowd roared for the Campbell colors.

"This fight will continue until one man concedes."

An even louder cheer.

"And may the best man win!"

The referee spoke in lower tones. "Fancy Rules means no hitting when you're down, and no kicking. You'll get one warning only. Going down without a blow disqualifies and I'll give no warning on that. Each round ends when one of you touches the ground with anything except feet. After each round, you will have one half minute to come up to Scratch or forfeit the fight. Is that clear?"

"Let me at the brat," Randal growled.

"This is your last fight, old man!" Toby settled his left foot at Scratch and raised his fists. He must use his advantage in reach, keep Randal at a distance.

"Round one!" shouted the timekeeper.

The two men collided in a blizzard of blows. Randal came in under Toby's guard, left-jabbing his ribs mercilessly. Toby backed and fell to one knee, gasping.

"Time out!" the timekeeper called.

Zits! The man was a hundred times faster than he had expected. How many blinks had that taken? Red welts burned on his chest—good! It always took a few thumps to get him mad. He tried to rise and Gavin leaned on his shoulder.

"Take your break. Have a drink."

"I don't want a drink!" he snarled, pushing Hamish's bottle away. "He tripped me! Let me at the sonofabitch!"

He marched to Scratch and raised his fists again.

"Round Two!"

This time Toby blocked the assault, taking the blows on his arms. For a minute he did nothing else, then he began jabbing at Randal's right eye. Soon he saw his chance and swung his thunderbolt right cross at his opponent's chin. It slid harmlessly by. Demons, the man was quick! Again he saw an opening. Again he failed to connect. A fist smashed into his face, sending him reeling.

Randal followed, grinning. He had identified Toby's favorite blow and he could avoid it. The crowd booed: dodging was cowardice. Randal would not care. He did not signal his own punches at all—watching his eyes was useless. He seemed to have no favorite punch. He was good with both hands, and he was delivering real punishment. Toby saw a chance for an uppercut, but it was another trap and left him open. A cannonball left slammed him just above the belt. He hit the turf bodily, choking for air. No man could hit that hard! Impossible!

Oh, dungheaps! What had he let himself in for?

Hamish splashed water on his face and Gavin wiped

it. "Take your time, lad. Use your height. Work on his face. Up you get."

Already? Toby hauled himself upright and felt Gavin's hand urge him forward. Two rounds gone and he had hardly landed a blow. Crap! He was going to get slaughtered! Randal had a faint red mark near his eye. The man was a human millstone.

They were at Scratch. "Round Three!"

Again Toby concentrated on blocking, backing steadily. Randal came after him, fists windmilling. The handlers leaped clear. He's older, needs a quick win . . . Make him work, wear him out . . .

That noise? The crowd booing! Boy wonder was running away, was being chased around the ring. Toby registered the hateful grin on the older man's face and threw caution to the winds. He slammed a left hook at his opponent's eye, then tried another right cross. The brute came in under his guard. He took the punishment while pounding both fists at eyes and nose. Then he switched and landed a one-two on the man's gut and it was like punching an oak door. He tried a cross-buttock throw—Randal got him in the kidneys with a haymaker. They both went down together and their seconds rushed in.

Through the waves of pain, Toby could hear Hamish screaming that he had really hurt the swine that time. But he was hurting, too. There was no air in the world. And it was time for more.

Randal's face was bloody. The timekeeper barely had time to call the round before they both went at it. No running this time—they stood toe to toe and slugged. The crowd roared approval. This was what they wanted: butchery! Jab, hook, feint, block, pain, blood. Randal tried to close, but Toby drummed fists on his ribs until the referee pulled them apart. Randal went down.

So did Toby. He drank from the bottle Hamish thrust at him, spat blood, drank again. His face was a swelling furnace, his chest a huge agony. That noise was his own breathing. Up again.

He must end this soon. He couldn't take much more of this.

But he couldn't end it. It just went on and on and nothing he did seemed to make any difference. The rounds blurred. His arms were all ache; they were tiring and he wouldn't be able to keep them up much longer. He had almost closed Randal's left eye and damaged his right, but his own were no better. Both men's noses and ears were battered and bloody, their bodies smeared with mud and gore.

Once Randal caught him by the hair and held him for four brutal punches before Sir Malcolm broke it up.

Once Toby found himself backed against the fence and had just enough wit to go down before he could be nailed there and pounded to jelly. Once he landed a right cross to the jaw that spread the older man on his back. Oh, that felt good! But his strength was failing and even his best punch was not enough now.

Randal must have done much the same to him, because he found Hamish and Gavin running him forward between them to get him up to Scratch in time for the next round. His ears rang and he couldn't focus well. His fists were falling apart. The world shrank to that hateful, battered face, and he pounded and pounded at it, ignoring what was happening to him. He went down. Randal went down. It was Round Thirteen or Fourteen, so he had won the first side bet. He was sitting on Hamish's knee while Gavin wiped blood from his eyes. He was being helped up from the grass. He was at Scratch and his knees were wavering. Now Randal was backing. Toby followed blindly, pounding, blocking, pounding. He got Randal on the fence and landed a half-dozen killers before the referee hauled him away.

The crowd screamed in fury. Gavin began to appeal to the umpires, then stopped when he realized that Toby needed extra time as much as Randal did.

One round lasted only one punch, but it was Toby who fell. An earthquake of pain in his chest . . . He doubled over, clutching himself.

"Think you've broken some ribs," Hamish wailed. Gavin snarled at him to shut his mouth, but it was too late—the opposition had heard. Seconds later they were at Scratch again, and Randal went straight for those ribs. Toby tried to shield them. A farm-boy uppercut to the chin floored him.

Water in his face . . .

"You've done good, kid," Gavin said. "It's time to throw in the towel."

"No!" Fail in his first real fight? *Never!* His mouth was so swollen and his chest so sore that he could barely speak. He had lost a tooth or two, and he suspected his jaw was at least cracked, if not broken. "Get me up there. I'm going to murder the scum."

The ribs were bad. Again and again he got hit there and the world blossomed in red glares of pain. Fortunately Randal had not noticed the jaw, while he himself had a broken cheekbone that gave him his own defense problems. Toby worked hard on that, because every time he got in a good hit, Randal went down. Neither man was punching as he had before. Their fists were pulp. There was less footwork now, more slugging. Neither could see very well, neither had much breath, so they both just stood and hammered, trading blows like madmen. The crowd screamed in delight.

Once Randal went down and Sir Malcolm shouted that there had been no punch. Randal's second appealed to the umpires. They had an argument, yelling at one another over the howls of fury from the crowd. In the end, the castellan was overruled and the fight went on.

"This is Round Twenty," Gavin said as he and Hamish helped Toby to his feet again. "One punch, go down, and we throw in the sponge."

Toby gasped, "No!" Let Meg see him beaten? Worse, let *Rory* see him beaten? "Never!"

"You're taking serious damage, lad."

With a supreme effort Toby forced out the words. "Never! Promise me! Keep me up there whatever it takes!"

He thought Hamish was sobbing, but it might have been him. There was straight whisky in the bottle now.

"Promise!" he insisted as they dragged him up to Scratch.

"We promise," Gavin said grimly. "He can't last much longer either."

Oh, yes, he could! Hours. Days. Life was only pain and struggle and hate, bone on bone. The grass was red mud. How much blood could a man lose? How long until his eyes closed altogether? *Kill* the sonofabitch! But the worst was over; now the rounds were ending with him on his feet, which was good, yet they kept bringing Randal back for more. Toby gave him more, ignoring the man's feeble efforts to respond, whirling a blizzard of fists, getting in as much damage as he could before his victim fell again. Pound, pound, pound . . . *Give up, damn you!* Why wouldn't he give up?

He was at Scratch and there was no one else there, just a bloody towel on the mud. His arms sank lower. Sir Malcolm grabbed one and raised it overhead. The crowd screamed hysterically. Randal's supporters weren't even working on him. He was flat on his back—the bugger couldn't even sit up, let alone stand.

He had won!

He sobbed for breath as the joy registered. He wasn't going to be hit anymore. Won! No demon lightnings, just knuckles, just pain—and finally just butchery. Hamish spread a plaid over his shoulders. Winning should have more triumph, should be one big haymaker punch—not this dismal nothing-left-to-hit. There was terrible noise, not all in his head . . . the crowd? He had won. He wasn't going to be hit any more! They were shouting, *Longdirk! Longdirk!* They were paying off bets. He forced his arms up again to acknowledge the cheers and his plaid fell. Someone put it back. Gavin was trying to tend to his battered hands. Hamish was passing the hat.

Rory, using both hands to clasp one of Toby's fists; Rory smirking . . . sort of smirking.

Toby took a swallow from the bottle. He had shown

him! He had shown all of them. "How many rounds?"
Hard to speak with lips like muffins.

"This was twenty-nine."

"Twenty-nine? Needed one more. Scum cheated us!"

"Not really," Rory said.

He peered around the circle. Meg, chalky pale . . .
Lady Lora . . . Others . . . smiling, but not happy.

Here was Stringer, with a face long as a carrot, and
Randal's second and bottleholder, come to congratulate
the victor. Tears? They had tears in their eyes! Where
was the loser? Toby rose on his toes and looked over the
crowd. Randal still lay on the grass. They had given him
a plaid, too. They had covered him with a plaid.

Stringer babbling: "Well fought, Master Longdirk!
Jolly great fight! Best fight I've seen in years."

Ignoring him, Toby tried to grab Rory with bloody
fists, almost fell as Rory shied away from them.

"Where's the loser?"

Rory shrugged sadly.

Toby choked. Nobody covered an injured man's *face!*

He turned to look for Meg, but Meg was walking away
with Lady Lora.

2

They cleaned him, washed his cuts with whisky,
dressed him. They fed him copious amounts of broth.
Above all, they congratulated him and wished him well in
his career. They said they'd never seen anything like it,
and wasn't it amazing how long that Sassenach stood up
to him at the end there, meaning *why did it take you so
long to kill him?* He hurt.

They left him sitting at a table in the mess hall with
Hamish. He was blurry and sleepy, dazed by all the
whisky he'd drunk, all the blows to the head, sheer
exhaustion, but he hurt too much to sleep. In any case,
the sun shone and the tide was full. Master Stringer

would be sending for him soon. The pain did not bother him; he deserved it for not winning faster.

Hamish was counting the collection, dividing out a share for Gavin and himself, as tradition demanded. He was also inspecting every coin carefully before placing it on its correct pile. Whatever he was looking for, he hadn't found it yet. Whatever he thought he was doing was beyond the understanding of a stupid punch-drunk pug like *Longdirk of the Hills*. Hamish wasn't talking about it. Either he wasn't sure, or he felt it wasn't a safe matter to discuss in Inverary Castle.

"How long does it take to sail to Dumbarton?"

Hamish glanced up from the groat he was examining. "Depends on the wind." He laid the coin on one of the heaps. "Day, at least, I'd think."

Toby was too restless to stay silent, although every word hurt. He seemed to have exchanged roles with Hamish, who was not saying much at all.

"When's the ebb?"

"Soon. Ah!" He had found it. No, he hadn't—he peered closely at the coin, then added it to a pile.

Toby mumbled, "Be going then, I expect. You coming with me? Coming to find Eric?" Even through the fog in his eyes, he saw the kid's face twist in indecision.

"The master says I can stay here for over the winter and catalogue the library. Says his father's been wanting it done—all the old written books, and all the new printed ones, too."

"Take it! You'll end up as the earl's private secretary."

Hamish nodded glumly. "Pa'll approve." He sighed and went back to his coin inspection. "Ma'll dance on Beinn Odhar." He said, "Ah!" again, louder than before, then again decided it wasn't what he wanted. "Toby?"

"Mmph?"

"Er . . . " The kid hesitated, as if his verbal horse had balked at a fence. "Does Master Stringer remind you of anyone?"

"A grass snake, lives near the hob's grotto. Has the same chin."

Hamish did not smile. "You're waiting for him to send for you?"

"He wants a prizefighter, I'm his man." Toby spoke with much satisfaction. Being Master Stringer's man would not be the same as being, say, the earl's man. He wouldn't be one of a warband, or a vassal sharecropper. He would just be a servant, earning his living by winning fights as he had today—and free to leave anytime.

"But does he?"

"Huh?"

"Toby, doesn't it seem odd to you that the master's houseguest should suddenly turn out to be exactly what you wanted, one of the Fancy, a sponsor of pugilists? Funny coincidence?"

A small person had come into the mess and was running their way.

Toby squirmed uneasily. "Wha'd'juh mean?"

Hamish stared at him, chewing his lip. "Randal was a sailor. Oh, I'm sure he'd boxed before, but I think Rory just went and found a man on one of the ships here who would fight for money. I don't think Stringer cares a spit about prizefighting."

A battered brain full of whisky didn't think very well. "Why? Why would they do that?"

"I think Stringer wanted to take you with him to Dumbarton—maybe even to England, although I doubt that. I think he and Rory dreamed this up as a plausible way of explaining why he might do that."

"Why not just offer me a job carrying sacks? Why would he want me anyway, if not to fight for him? Why be so devious?"

"Maybe so as not to let you know . . . I don't know."

"Then why are you staring at all those coins?"

Hamish looked down at the copper groat in his fingers. "I'm trying to find one minted just after Fergan came back from England and was crowned king—before his first rebellion. There aren't many of them around anymore. They get kept as mementoes."

The runner arrived, a puffing blur of carroty hair and

reckles and fishing-pole limbs protruding from a plaid.

In shrill soprano, the page said, "The master wants
o see you in the hall, Master Longdirk."

Toby rose carefully. "You can look for mementoes later.
This library of yours . . . is it near the minstrel gallery?"

Hamish looked up, startled. "No. Why?"

"It's time to get back to work." Toby turned to the
iny page. "Lead on, chief."

Hamish began madly scooping the coins back in the
bag.

3

The hall was brighter than it had been the one other
time Toby had seen it. Sunbeams angled down from the
slit windows in the south wall, full of dancing dust motes,
but the crackling fire in the great hearth still gave more
light. He tramped over the rushes, past the long table,
approaching the two men standing by the fireplace. They
were drinking. The pain in his back made him limp; his
face had been beaten to raw haggis; his arms and chest
were discolored and swollen. Rory must be watching his
approach with considerable satisfaction.

Toby bowed to Maxim Stringer first, then made a
lesser bow to the master. Bowing hurt, and he couldn't
straighten up properly.

The two men exchanged glances. Stringer produced
his piece of glass and inserted it in his eye to study the
champion.

"You don't look as bad as I feared, young man. Sit
down if you wish."

Toby shook his head, which made the hall spin
briefly.

"Well, Killer," Rory said. "Master Stringer agrees that
you have displayed considerable promise as a pugilist.
However, he has regretfully decided not to take you on.
Sorry."

Toby twitched in sudden dismay, sending a blade of fire into his back. "I'd do my best to win for you, sir! I'm sorry I killed your man today."

The gangling Sassenach took a drink. "That isn't the problem. Deaths in the ring don't happen very often, you know. It should never happen, and certainly should not have happened this time. I'll be honest. I'm not a patron of the Manly Art. He wasn't my man, just a sailor we hired to test you. He was supposed to try you out, let you show your paces, and then take a dive."

Hamish had been right, as usual.

"Then . . . Well, why didn't he? Why'd he make a real fight of it?"

Rory drained his goblet. "I suppose he couldn't bear to be beaten by a boy. Another dram for the road, Max?"

"No more, thank you." Stringer put the idiotic monocle away in a pocket and laid his goblet on the mantel. "I blame his handlers. They kept dragging him up to Scratch at the end there. I don't know how he survived that beating for so long. They ought to be hanged for murder."

Rory shrugged. "I expect they wagered too much money on their own man. It happens." He was watching Toby as he spoke, but if there was some sort of message in his gaze, Toby's vision was too blurred to detect it.

He didn't need it. He could knock the devious aristocratic prig into the fireplace with one good punch, but his fists were too swollen to clench. If someone had offered outrageous odds to Randal's seconds, he could guess who that someone was. Rory had re-rigged the rigged fight.

Toby turned back to the merchant. "So you have no use for a prizefighter, sir?" Dreams crashed like falling icicles.

"Not for a prizefighter." Stringer no longer spoke like an idiot. He even seemed to have acquired more chin. "But today I saw a remarkable display of courage—a beaten man refusing to give up, persevering no matter what the cost, and going on to victory. I can use a man like that."

Rory stiffened, as if surprised. "Before you go any farther, sir, I think we should tell the Tyndrum Terror the latest news."

Bad news, obviously.

"Yes, I was about to." The thin man took a couple of steps away from the fire, as if the heat had suddenly become unpleasant. He cleared his throat. "While you were winning your spurs in the ring, lad, a courier came in. He brought word from Edinburgh. A very strange law has just been rushed through Parliament and signed by the governor. I don't recall any precedents in Scotland. Do you, Master?"

Rory said, "No," watching Toby.

"It's an Act of Attainder. It names you, Tobias Strangerson of Tyndrum in Strath Fillan. It convicts you of being possessed by a demon. It offers a reward for your corpse with a blade through your heart." Stringer had switched to Gaelic. His English accent was not as marked as Rory's.

"This is some sort of a joke?" Toby stared from one to the other.

"No joke," the merchant said. "Upon my honor. I don't recall that ever being done before. And even stranger—the reward. Five thousand marks."

Toby walked over to a chair and sat down. If he were sober, and if his brains were not all jangled up, then perhaps he might be able to make sense of this. Or perhaps not. If Rory alone had told him, he would never have believed anything so outrageous. "Isn't that the same price they've put on Ferg—on His Majesty?"

"It is," Stringer said. "We find it as incredible as you do. I have the paper here, if you want to see it."

Toby shook his head, which was again a mistake. There was more to this merchant than he had realized, a lot more. "I don't understand, sir. Why?"

"We don't understand, either. It must involve Valda, somehow. We think Baron Oreste has a hand in it."

Rory said, "You're in good company, Slugger—or should I call you Susie? You're mixed up in deep demonic affairs. You can't trust anyone now, you know. Five thousand is a sizable bag of change. I'm almost tempted myself. I can't guarantee anyone."

He was hinting that there might be a freelance posse of Campbells strapping on swords in the armory right now. Plain enough—but he could not resist a chance to twist the knife. "I doubt I can keep the news quiet for more than a day or so. You'll be planning an early start, I expect. We'll have the cooks make up a jammy bap for you to take."

"Not so fast, Master," Stringer said sharply. "I am sorry to be the bearer of such terrible tidings, Longdirk."

"Not your fault, sir." Which way could he run? Who would aid an outlaw with a demon in his heart? Rory would give him a day's start and run him down with the deerhounds. It was small wonder Stringer had lost interest in him as a prizefighter.

Yet the thin man was regarding him very intently. "The government and the English are both against you—not that there is much difference between them. You have no liege lord, I understand. Is there any person or group to whom you can appeal for protection?"

Rory laughed. "I once asked Muscles which king he supported. He wouldn't answer. Are you any clearer now, boy?"

"I can have no loyalty to a government that condemns me without trial."

"A wise decision. Wisdom comes too late, though."

Stringer said, "He is a cautious man, and I approve of that. He still hasn't answered, notice?"

Toby heaved himself to his feet and straightened, so he could look down on Rory and take a better look at the other. Now he realized what Hamish had been looking for in the old coins. But five thousand crowns reward! He was a walking corpse. He spelled disaster to everyone who came near him.

"I can't think why anyone would want me now, my lord—even King Fergan himself."

He stared at the king with mute appeal. The king

smiled grimly, but then he gave the outlaw the answer he needed so desperately now.

"I already said I want you."

Toby sank to his knees and raised his hands, palms together. "Then, Your Majesty, I am your man, of life and limb, against all foes, until death."

4

King Fergan had gone off to make his farewells to Lady Lora. Toby sat down carefully in one of the thronelike chairs and surveyed the great hall, with its high banners and its festoons of weapons. He eyed the silent minstrel gallery and wondered. When he had suggested that Hamish eavesdrop up there, he had not realized what dangerous things he would learn. Most likely the door was kept locked, or even guarded, to prevent just that sort of spying. What would it be like to be heir to such power and wealth as all this? The master of Argyll was a more fortunate man than the hunted king of Scotland, who must slink about his realm in the guise of an English merchant.

But the king of Scotland was the better man. Already, he was sure of that.

Rory came wandering back to the fireplace and seemed displeased to discover he still had a guest there.

"Are you waiting for a stretcher? If you miss the boat, I wash my hands of you."

Toby was not going to let the spite rile him. It was too petty to bother with. "I have a couple of questions to ask, Master."

"Ask quickly. I don't promise to answer." Rory poured himself another drink from a dusty flagon, without offering to share.

"Are you a rebel or a traitor?"

The master smiled and took a sip from his goblet. "Both."

"A double traitor, you mean?"

"Ah! You must not confuse cynicism with realism, lad. I'm mostly rebel, my father mostly traitor, but we switch roles once in a while. We play the two sides off against each other. Whoever wins in the end, we shall be there. Both sides know what we're up to, but they both need us. The Campbells are the key to the west. This is called politics. You wouldn't understand."

Even a lifelong cynic could find such cynicism disgusting. Refusing to play the game, as Toby had done until a few minutes ago, was better than playing and cheating.

"Inverary is very strategic," Rory said, scowling. "But perhaps not as strategic as it was, thanks to you. Did you bury Valda's creatures under that slide?"

"Some of them, I think."

"Father Lachlan says the demons will work their way to the surface fairly soon. Glen Kinglas will not be a road to recommend to one's friends in the future. You washed away half a village, too. You really are incredible, Muscles! You find a girl in trouble and earn yourself a death sentence. You get yourself pursued by at least one notorious hexer, probably two. Acts of Parliament are passed to raise the entire population against you. You're given a chance to show how you can box, and you beat your opponent to death. Everything you touch just dies! You are a disaster, a walking hob. You seem to mean well, but that's the best anyone can say of you."

Looking satisfied, Rory took another drink.

It was all horribly true.

"So why should the king want me? That's my second question: What was the real reason for staging that fight?"

The master took the flagon and walked over to an oak chest to lock it away. "What do you think the real reason was?"

Toby rubbed his throbbing jaw. "I think the king has hexers after him. He needs gramarye on his side. I think you put on that fight to see if my guardian demon would come to my aid."

"Partly, perhaps."

"Not a very nice thing to do to an innocent sailor, who thought he was just going to earn a few marks at fisticuffs."

"Oh, spare me! He was a brainless buffoon. He had too much pride to let his shipmates see a kid beat him. He died of his own stupidity."

"And it didn't work, did it?"

Rory laughed scornfully. "Not that I noticed. It isn't much of a guardian if it lets you get smashed to pulp."

That was comforting. It was not good to have killed a man in what should have been a friendly bout of fisticuffs, but to know he had slain him with his bare hands felt better than to have cheated by using gramarye. "So why does King Fergan still want me?"

"I told you he's an idiot. He saw a man who wasn't smart enough to know when he was beaten, and his romantic soul was thrilled by this display of courage. Display of stupidity, I call it."

Toby sighed. It was what he had been afraid of. He had been taken on as royal hexer, and he had nothing to offer.

"And that wasn't the only reason for the fight," Rory said, leaning an elbow on the mantel.

"What else, then?"

The silver eyes shone in the firelight. "As I recall, you were very insistent on our travels together that Kenneth Campbell of Tyndrum had placed his daughter in your care."

Toby froze. Bugles sounded danger in the back of his mind.

"So?"

Rory showed most of his teeth. "You claimed to be her guardian—on an unofficial basis, of course."

The big bumpkin was being outsmarted here somewhere, somehow. He just knew it. And mocked, too. "What do you mean?"

The smile became a sneer of triumph. "I mean, Tobias Bastard, that I have the honor to ask you for your ward's hand in marriage."

Toby was too stunned to say more than, *"Marriage?"*

"Marriage. My request is purely a formality, of course. Her parents will be here by tomorrow for the ceremony. To my future happiness!" The master of Argyll drained his goblet and tossed it into the fire.

"Meg has agreed to this?"

"Oh, yes! Even if she didn't, I am sure her family would persuade . . . but she has agreed. She plighted me her troth, as they say. Right after the fight, it was."

The fight where Toby Strangerson had shown himself to be a brainless, murdering brute, not merely getting himself pounded to porridge, but going on to kill his opponent. That had been the real reason for the fight all along.

"If you feel so inclined, you may congratulate me on my engagement," Rory said generously. He examined his fingernails. "Your trouble, Longdirk, is that you are a cynic. You don't believe in love." The silver eyes looked up challengingly. "Do you?"

"Sometimes."

"But not this time? Or do you accept love in women but not in men? Well, this time you must believe. My intentions are perfectly honorable, for once. The problem you cannot avoid, Longdirk, is that I am rich, I am handsome, I am the most eligible bachelor in all Scotland. By your primitive standards, I am probably a thoroughgoing scoundrel, but I have fallen so much in love with a tanner's daughter that I am going to make her my wife instead of just bundling her in the hay. Your cynicism can't handle that, can it? My grandmother was rather shocked, too, I admit, until she got to know Meg. I think she fell for her about as fast as I had—ten minutes, twelve at the most."

Meg in Inverary Castle, dressed up in Lady Lora's castoffs . . .

"It was the lute," the master sighed, admiring the nails on his other hand. "She sat beside me on the rock in the moonlight. I played the lute and she sang."

"And she fell in love?"

"No, I did. I thought she was the most incredible girl I

had ever met. She was totally innocent, yet she had fire, and gaiety, humor . . . I suddenly imagined life with Meg for company all the time and I sank without trace! Of course I could hardly announce my feelings at that point, although I was sure of them. And she could talk of nothing except the big, handsome Tyndrum lad who had saved her from the Sassenach. Then you came shuffling out of the darkness with a broadsword on your back, trailing your knuckles . . . "

Toby leaned back in the chair. Now he understood what had happened between them that night. "That was when the trouble started!"

"Indeed it was! Love is not all that can happen at first sight." Rory chuckled. "But now the trouble is over. I have won."

A penniless vagrant against the heir to Scotland's premier earldom? Even when Toby had begun to realize what the contest was, the match had never been fair. "Does that really surprise you?"

"I suppose not. No, it doesn't surprise me. My father is going to burn me at the stake, of course. He expects me to marry a flat-faced, flat-chested, flat-footed MacDonald frump. But Grandmother will handle him."

Bitterness would be useless. "I want to speak with Meg."

"You have a boat to catch."

"I have time to say good-bye, haven't I?"

"You punched a man to death in front of her eyes. Why would she want to speak with you?"

"Which do you fear: that I will carry her off, or that she will run away with me?"

"Watch your tongue, boy!"

Toby rose. "I am the king's man now."

"That king is a throneless mirage!" Rory pouted. His gaze wandered to the minstrel gallery and then returned to Toby. "What exactly do you wish to discuss with my fiancée?"

"To tell her I am overjoyed at her good fortune. To wish her happiness."

Obviously Rory did not trust him, even now. "You do understand, don't you? She is a tanner's daughter. I shall inherit an earldom, a thousand armed clansmen, Argyll, seven or eight castles, estates in England, houses in Edinburgh and other cities. You are nothing, and will always be nothing. She had a juvenile crush on you, I admit. I can forgive that, because she is very young. But you are only beef, Longdirk. You are unlikely to live a week now, and even if you do, you have no future, nothing to offer a woman. You do understand that, in the real world, she had no choice?"

"I understand that very well, Master. I never told Meg I loved her. I won't now. I will say nothing to upset her."

Rory hesitated, then said, "Wait here, then." He strode off along the hall.

All his vicious jibes were true. No girl in her right mind could be expected to turn down a rich and powerful—and handsome—noble for the sake of an ignorant, musclebound, penniless outlaw. He liked Meg, enjoyed her company. No more than that. If he loved her, he would have told her so, wouldn't he? As a friend, he must rejoice in her good fortune.

Why did it hurt so much? Was he just sore at losing? He hadn't even been playing the game, had he? So why care if he had lost?

When he was sure Rory was out of earshot, he looked up at the minstrel gallery and said, "Scram! You'll have company in a minute." There was no answer.

He heaved himself stiffly out of the chair to stand and gaze at the fire.

5

He turned at the sound of her tread on the rushes. She seemed very much a lady in a dark gown trailing to the floor with a high neck and sleeves puffed like pillows. Her hair was back in the silver net again. The string of pearls around her throat would buy all Tyndrum. He thought her eyes looked pink, and she was certainly very pale, as if the castle had fallen on her.

She winced at the sight of his face. He made a courtly bow, as well as he knew how and as much as his bruises would let him. She curtseyed solemnly, to the manner born.

"Congratulations, my lady. I am very happy for you. I wish you well." His throat hurt even more than his jaw. Why?

"Thank you, Toby."

Silence. He wished he could read the expression in her eyes. Under the shock and fear, there was a glimmer of triumph, wasn't there? Well deserved, yes? He wished he could make speeches.

"Is there anything more to say?" Meg asked. "Except thank you, of course. None of this would have happened without your help. I am very, very grateful."

What did she mean by that? His hurtful efforts to advise her might have strengthened her resolve to resist Rory's blandishments and thus provoked him into proposing marriage. Meg could never say that openly. He hoped that he had not offended her to no purpose.

"I am very sorry I said those bad things to you. I didn't mean to. I felt real bad."

She tossed her head. "You could have sent me a note."

Ah! Dear Rory!

"Well, I'm not much for writing, or for giving advice. I'm not much of anything, except muscle. I never had a family, never had friends. I don't know how to be friends, so I don't suppose I'll ever know anything about love. Lord Gregor's a fine man, and I'm sure he'll make you very happy."

She turned to the fireplace, so he could not see her face.

"Rory says love is like a flash of lightning, but it isn't like that for most people. My ma told me she was almost sick every time Pa even looked at her—after what the Sassenachs did to her, you know—and she thought her pa had done a rotten job of finding a man for her anyway, she admits that, but eventually, she says, she managed . . . She says she grew to love him."

Meg must not be allowed to ramble on like that. She didn't know her fiancé was listening up there in the minstrel gallery.

"I think you fell in love with Rory that night in Glen Orchy. You just didn't realize it."

She spun around. "Really? You really think so?"

"Yes, I do. The way you looked at him, and the way you kept telling me how handsome he was, the way you laughed at his jokes. . . . "

She blushed and turned away again. "Thank you, Toby. I'll try to believe that. Is Hamish going with you? You need someone to . . . Well, Rory says I mustn't ask where you're off to."

"Ask all you want, I don't know." *Oh, Meg, Meg!* He couldn't keep this up much longer. "I'll always remember you . . . " *even if I live a whole week* ". . . and our escape together. One day I'll be able to brag that I know the countess of Argyll!"

"You can brag that you saved her from being raped or murdered."

"No, I won't mention that. People might think you'd been stupid."

"Toby!" she stormed, but then she laughed. "I've learned sense now, haven't I? No romantic foolishness now. Hard, cold—"

"I won't kiss your fingers, my lady. I might get blood on them." Or tears. Funny—he wasn't usually a sentimental person. "Be happy." He bowed, and turned, and started to walk away.

"Toby! Wait!"

He went back.

She gazed up at him, frowning. "Will you not give me a wedding present?"

"Everything I possess—which is still nothing." He had his prize money, of course, but Meg had no need of money now.

"A promise?"

"What promise?"

"That you won't be a prizefighter anymore? Please?"
Meg Tanner pleading was as dangerous and disconcerting as a wild cat rubbing against your leg.

"Why not?"

"Killing for money? Hurting people?"

"It's no worse than being a mercenary soldier."

"Yes, it is! A mercenary's only a hired killer, anyway.
But at least a soldier has a chance of winning. He may
not die, may not be wounded, may grow rich on his loot.
But a fighter always loses. Even if you win every match,
Toby dear, you'll finish up a slobbering wreck! You know
you will. Promise me?"

He shrugged. As a king's man he would not be prizefighting, even if he had no hint of a clue as to what he
would be doing. "That's not what Master Stringer wants
me for, so I'm not planning to fight in the immediate
future. And I promise I'll remember your words if I ever
have the opportunity again. All right?"

That was not enough for Meg Tanner. She shook her
head vigorously.

"Just say the words, Toby, even if you don't mean
them. Then I'll be happy and not worry about you."

"I don't say words I don't . . . " He sighed. "I give you
my promise."

He wasn't going to live long enough to break it.

"Good-bye, Meg."

"Good-bye, Toby."

6

He came to the castle entry and was stopped in his
tracks, because King Fergan and Father Lachlan were
there, being seen off by Lady Lora and Sir Malcolm. Sure
he must not intrude, he hung back in the shadows.
The only light came from the doorway, which was

smaller than the door on an average cottage, although
the door itself was as thick as his arm, studded and
banded with iron. In a minute or so, the king bowed gra-
ciously, Father Lachlan muttered a benediction, and the
two guests ducked out into the wintery sunshine.

He supposed he should follow his new master at a
respectful distance, but that would mean he must pass
by his hostess. He ought to thank her. He was no good at
speeches! Why hadn't he foreseen this and asked Hamish
to make up something for him to say? It was too late to
hide, because the castellan had noticed him. He hurried
forward.

Lady Lora was bundled in a dark fur robe and a
plumed hat. As he loomed out of the dark above her, she
smiled up at him, then frowned when she caught sight of
his face.

"Master Strangerson! I hope you are recovering from
your wounds?"

He opened his mouth and it ran away with him like a
startled horse. "My lady, it was very kind and very brave
and very generous of you to take in a wanted fugitive and
give him shelter and I hope my visit here will not bring
trouble on your house but I know that all my life I shall
remember what you did for me and I thank you from the
bottom of my heart." He bowed clumsily and turned to
Sir Malcolm. "Sir, you and your men were very kind to a
gawky lad, and I shall probably bless these days many,
many times in future. I thank you."

Then he bowed again and ran out the door, ducking
low under the lintel. Gibberish! With any luck they would
not have made out a word he had said. However he
might serve King Fergan in future, it would not be as a
diplomat.

He blinked in the sunlight. The tall king and short
acolyte were crossing the bailey, heading for the barbican. He followed, passing close to a cart of peat being
unloaded, dodging washing hung out after the long spell
of rain. Then he remembered that he had forgotten to
collect his things from the tower room. *Zits!* It was too

late to go back for them. Well, they weren't worth much. But his prize money . . . Hamish had the prize money. . . .

Out from behind the cart came Hamish, with his own bundle on one shoulder and Toby's on the other. He handed Toby's over without a word and fell into step at his side, straining mightily to take the necessary strides.

"No library?"

The kid looked up with his bony face twisted in abhorrence. "I wouldna' work for that man if you paid me a million marks! He was going to throw you out and hunt you down in the hills! Whatever happened to Highland hospitality?"

"Keep your mouth shut about that!"

"Think I'm crazy?"

"You'd best ask Father Lachlan if you can accompany him to Glasgow, and *don't* mention His Majesty."

Hamish grinned. "Wasn't that one straight out of the old ballads! He has a beard on the coins, but I was pretty much sure." He was understandably very pleased with his wee self, was Master Hamish.

"You were! Very smart thinking!"

"Thinking's what I'm good at. Did you hear Meg . . . Never mind."

"You mean, did I hear Meg say I needed looking after? No, I didn't hear Meg say that."

Hamish guffawed. "Just fancy Meg Tanner as countess of Argyll! They'll be lighting bonfires in the glen when the news gets out!"

The news would set the Sassenachs on Toby's trail, but Rory wouldn't care overmuch about that.

"She deserves better than yon cootie!" Hamish decided. "Does she really love him, Toby?" He gazed up anxiously, wanting an explanation from his chosen counselor in matters romantic.

"Maybe not today, but she will by tomorrow. Don't worry about Meg! She's quite capable of handling Rory." Struck by a sudden thought, Toby bellowed out one of his awful guffaws, earning a stab of protest from his ribs. As he was then passing through the arch of the barbican, the result sounded like an artillery barrage. King Fergan and Father Lachlan turned their heads to see what the noise was.

"What's so funny?" Hamish demanded.

"Nothing. Nothing at all."

Rory had won the battle for Meg—even if he had been the only contestant—but he had also won Fat Vik as a brother-in-law!

"Wait a minute!" Toby said, before he could be questioned further. "You overheard Meg? You were still in the minstrel gallery when she came?"

"No," Hamish said innocently. "I never was in the minstrel gallery. It's kept locked."

"Then how . . . ?"

"There's a spy hole from the servants' pantry—so they can keep an eye on the diners' progress, I suppose."

"And how did you find out about that?"

Hamish preened. "In the muniment chest in the library—I found a set of builders' plans for the castle. There's a secret passage from the earls' bedroom, too, but I didn't dare explore that."

After a moment he added, "Guests shouldn't pry, you know."

EIGHT

—

A Foggy Dawn

1

In the gathering gloom of a fall evening, the *Maid of Arran* lay against the pier of the royal burgh of Dumbarton. Geese were trailing overhead, a few lights glimmered amid the buildings, and sounds of wheels and horses and voices drifted through the dusk.

Toby leaned on the rail, having trouble finding unbruised forearm for the purpose. He brooded. He had spent most of two days in the hold, healing . . . being seasick . . . getting steadily more hungry, too, for he still had trouble eating. In all that time, he had spoken with his new liege lord only once. Fergan had come to see how he was faring, but he had not dallied long in that smelly hold. Toby had asked how he might serve his king, while feeling that he was incapable of cleaning out a fireplace at the moment.

"First, we must solve this mystery of your superhuman powers, lad. Father Lachlan is sorely perplexed by you. So you will go to the sanctuary, and there you should be safe from the vigilantes, too. After that, we shall see. Don't worry, I'll find a use for you!"

The sorry vassal was supposed to be comforted by that, but he was not deceived. Men who would scorn a reward to betray their king would jump at the same money for turning in the corpse of a demonic husk. Even the two or three men on board who were fully in Fergan's confidence had eyed him narrowly. There was one called Kenneth Kennedy, a wizened, scrawny man, who seemed to be the senior. He had asked many questions and answered none.

Hamish had spent the entire voyage pestering the sailors. Now he was advancing his friend's education by describing *The Maid of Arran* in great detail. "She's a cog of a hundred tuns! That means she can carry a hundred barrels of wine. Of course she's bearing hides, now, bound for Portugal. Hides are one of Scotland's biggest exports. Just think—there may even be some from Fillan on board!"

Toby's nose had told him what the cargo was even before he had boarded.

The king had already departed. His hired demon would disembark under cover of darkness. Toby was even more conspicuous than usual, with his bruises at their ripest. His arms and chest were swollen in yellow and purple. What his face must look like, he could not imagine. A layer of stubble would not be improving it. He did not even have proper town clothes to wear yet, only his plaid.

"There's more than four hundred houses in Dumbarton!" Hamish declaimed. "They all crowd into the middle to be as close to the sanctuary as possible. Biggest port on the west coast. Glasgow's even bigger, because its tutelary is . . . um, better known."

If he was wondering whether the Dumbarton tutelary could know what he was saying, out here at the end of the pier, then he was right to wonder. It probably could. Toby could detect it.

"Can't sail to Glasgow, of course, because the river's too shallow. Pa took me there in a coach! That's the castle."

Of course that was the castle. And the spire in the center of the burgh must be the sanctuary, because there was *something* there. It wasn't visible, unlike the Fillan hob, or the specter Toby had seen in the hills, but he could sense it somehow, even at this distance. He wondered if it knew of him already. It gave him goosebumps.

And there was another *something* off to the west, either just outside the burgh or just inside. Valda? Baron Oreste?

Thirdly, there was Toby himself, with his mysterious guardian. Superhuman powers were gathering in Dumbarton.

"Ah, there you are!" Father Lachlan arrived, a flustered little ghost in his white robe. Hamish's flood of statistics came to a merciful end. "Almost dark enough now."

"Father?" Toby said. "Have you any idea why Master Stringer wants me?" The only real orders he had been given so far had come from Kennedy: never, *ever,* mention Fergan by name, and speak only English to him. Yes, the sailors were trustworthy, but . . .

"He is a very shrewd judge of men, that's why!" The acolyte chuckled, tugging his robe tighter against the evening chill. "You are strong, hardy, courageous, and—I hope—loyal. I am sure you are loyal, because you are not the sort of man who breaks his word. You have no distracting ties to clan or family. I think Master Stringer is rightly congratulating himself on acquiring a most valuable follower!"

"But I am a danger to him!"

"Do you mean a demonic danger or a mortal danger?"

"Not demonic!" Hamish protested. "If Toby had wanted to kill him, he could have broken his neck easily by now. Couldn't you have, Toby?"

Toby growled. Hamish knew that Stringer was Fergan, but did anyone else on the ship know that he knew?

"Maybe I ought to break yours! No, Father, what I meant was that I may get mobbed, or betrayed. The trail could lead back to Inverary, to this ship—to all of you."

Father Lachlan believed in staying cheerful. He set off for the gangplank. "You needn't worry about the ship, at any rate. She's leaving on the dawn tide for Lisbon. The sailors haven't heard about your problems, and they won't. Captain MacLeod has forbidden shore leave, because he's been delayed by the long wait in Loch Fyne. Ah . . . here he is. We're going ashore now, Captain."

MacLeod was standing watch himself—undoubtedly to enforce his ban on leave. He was a thickset, weathered man, presently only a solid shape in the gloom. He wished them well in his Moray accent as they trooped down the plank.

"Where was I?" Father Lachlan asked, bustling along the pier. "Oh, yes, Master Stringer. You needn't worry about him. He is a highly respected burgher and merchant in Dumbarton. He is under the tutelary's protection, just as you will be, I trust."

Toby shivered. "Is there some doubt about that?"

"Doubt? Oh, no. Not at all. I have told you that I don't believe you are possessed. In fact, I'm sure of it now, because here we are in Dumbarton! The tutelary will not allow such creatures into its realm."

Toby was fighting a strong reluctance to proceed any farther into its realm. Was that the tutelary's doing, or plain fear, or the work of his guardian demon? If the demon did not want to be exorcised, it could take him over and turn him around. Perhaps it was as uncertain as he was.

They reached the land and a narrow street between houses and the seawall, cluttered with carts and fishing gear. Father Lachlan turned to the right. Toby felt a surge of relief, and his feet began to move more easily. The streets were very narrow, very confining, very dirty. They followed no pattern at all, but the acolyte seemed able to find his way in the dark like a bat. Most of the buildings had stores or warehouses at street level, with homes above. They were constructed almost entirely of wood, few having any more stonework than chimneys. Many of the upper stories protruded over the road, low enough to be a hazard for a very tall man.

"This isn't the way to the sanctuary," Toby said.

"No, it isn't. How do you . . . Oh, you saw the spire, of course. Well, you see, my son, it seems wiser for me to approach the tutelary first, on your behalf. Explain matters."

So dear Father Lachlan was not sure of the reception Toby would meet, or not as sure as he implied. A group of men rolled by in the darkness, singing tunelessly. They did not notice the oversized outlaw, whose death could make them all rich.

"Toby can get refuge at the sanctuary, can't he?" Hamish asked indignantly.

"I expect so. Normally, a tutelary will not harbor strangers, but when there is a manifest injustice, then it will often make an exception. The fact that he has been allowed into the burgh at all is very encouraging."

"You mean the tutelary can sense demons at a distance?"

"Incarnate demons, creatures. Not the bottled variety, usually, unless they are activated by gramarye. Turn here. I will leave you at Master Stringer's house and then go on to the sanctuary."

"I want to come!" Hamish said. "I can offer a silver penny!"

Toby wondered which of his bruises that penny represented.

2

"**And he was at liberty for about six months after Norford** Bridge," said Kenneth Kennedy, "but some MacKays up near Inverness betrayed him, and then the Sassenachs paraded him around in a cage all winter, from one town to the next, and finally dragged him away, off back to England. And everyone all thought the song was ended then, but a few of us kept the fire alight, and eventually he escaped and came back. The Lowland dogs weren't too keen, but the Highlands rallied again to the lion banner."

Master Kennedy was drunk.

"And then the Battle of Parline Field," Toby said. "I tried to enlist, but the laird wouldn't take me."

"Well, you didn't miss a great deal." Between swigs, Kennedy was stropping a dirk with long, delicate strokes along a leather belt. One end of the belt was in his left hand, the other tied to the table leg. He leaned back on his stool, with his back against the wall and his dirty bare feet on the table. The single candle lit angles and cast shadows on his gauntness; his eyes glittered. He spoke with the musical lilt of the Isles, but there was nothing soft about him. He was only bones. "But you're his man now."

At the other side of the table, Toby was soaking a bap in milk and sucking the mush, which was all his loose teeth would allow. Kennedy did not intimidate him. One threatening move with that dirk, and Toby would pick up the table and swat him.

"I am that."

They were in the kitchen of Stringer's house, at the back of the ground floor. The building held no warehouse or shops and was larger than most, but all the rooms he had seen so far were tiny and restrictive. Nobody else was home. The only sound was a dog barking a few houses away.

Kennedy paused in his sharpening to take a swig from his flagon, raising giant shadows on the smoke-stained plank walls. "He says you have superhuman powers."

"Odd things happen around me."

The Islander considered that for a moment. His voice came from the Hebrides, but he wore Lowlander breeches and a ragged shirt. "He could be finding a good hexer useful."

"Is there such a thing as a good hexer?"

"Only dead ones, I'm thinking." His skimpy beard had flecks of white in it. If that was straight whisky he was downing, he was taking on a fair measure for his size.

"Why does he need a hexer?"

"The Sassenachs send demons after him. The tutelary catches them when he's in Dumbarton. But ye canna' run a rebellion from a fireside."

"And if the tutelary removes my hex, or whatever it is, so I don't have superhuman powers? What then?"

Kennedy stropped the dirk a few more times. "You could stop musket balls for him."

"Bodyguard, you mean."

"Aye."

Toby gave up on the baps and drained the rest of the milk from the bowl. The prospect of being King Fergan's mastiff did not appeal to him very much. He was not at all sure his loyalty would impel him to jump in front of Maxim Stringer when an assassin cocked a pistol at him. Life would be a long boredom in Dumbarton.

On the other hand, if Kenneth Kennedy had been a rebel since Norford Bridge as he claimed, then he had been on the run for eight years. The lush was worn out. The king needed some new retainers, and perhaps there would be a place for a willing lad after all.

Kennedy burped. "Might involve some traveling."

That was more encouraging. Father Lachlan had dropped a few hints at the keeper's house in Glen Shira.

"Eastward?"

The king's man eyed him suspiciously. "Why do you say that?"

"To seek the help of the Khan. The Golden Horde itself is the only power capable of breaking King Nevil now, they say."

Kennedy took another gulp and wiped his mouth on his arm. "Aye. That's what they say. I don't have this from *him,* you understand. It's just chatter."

Toby nodded.

"When the Horde conquered England," the king's man explained, sounding like Hamish beginning a lecture, "it was one of those times when the Sassenachs had conquered Scotland, or thought they had. So the English king did homage to the Khan's man for Scotland, too. There's hardly ever been a Tartar set foot in Scotland. Set hoof, would you say?" He chuckled and took another swig.

He wasn't making history sound any more worthwhile than Neal Campbell had, back in Tyndrum, but now Toby was the king's man, it seemed as if it should.

"So, laddie, the English have taxed us men and gold for all these years to send tribute to the Horde. But, if the Khan was to recognize Scotland as an independent satrapy, why then we would be free of the Sassenach, wouldn't we?"

Toby wasn't very smart, but he was sober. He could see no great advantage in exchanging one overlord for another. From what he had heard, the English king had been thumping the Tartars' vassals all over Europe for years. If this was King Fergan's Grand Design, then its merits escaped him.

"You think *he* might be going to travel to Sarai?"

"Could be," Kennedy muttered, taking up his dirk and strop again. "As I said, it's just chatter. But it could be." He winked.

"Sarai? That's on a big river somewhere?"

"The Volga. Long way. Long, *long* way!"

"Weeks?"

"Och, laddie, it's months you're talking about!"

Definitely promising!

Toby pushed his stool back. "Then I think I'll rest up for the journey. If they want me tonight, they'll find me. Have you a spare candle?"

The older man scowled and swung his feet to the floor. He held out the flagon. "Here, boy, put some real hair on that big chest of yours. You'll not be going off to bed now and leaving me drinking by my lonesome?"

Toby had to take a gulp of the awful stuff before he was allowed to leave, with Kennedy muttering dire comments about his lack of manhood. Holding both his own bundle and Hamish's, he paused in the doorway. "Where do I sleep?"

"Straight up, as far as you can go. If you see the stars, you've gone too far." Cackling, Kennedy sucked on his bottle again.

Straight up was a fair description of the stairs. They ended in a narrow passage, flanked by doors. At the far end was a ladder, leading up to a trapdoor. When Toby raised one side of that and peered through, he saw straw. He blew out the candle, went down to the floor for the bundles, and then scrambled up into a low attic. He could barely sit upright in it, let alone stand. In a moment or two he identified a faint light from gaps under the eaves. The wind came from those, too. There was a musty odor of chicken coop, which meant birds' nests somewhere.

He was a long time going to sleep, mostly because his bruises forced him to lie on his back, not facedown as he preferred. Even in his plaid, he was barely warm enough. Later he registered someone lifting the trap, replacing it, rustling in the straw. Whoever it was did not summon him away to the sanctuary. In what seemed no time at all, although he had probably dozed off in the meantime, he heard Hamish's familiar snores.

Life in a king's palace was not quite what he had expected.

3

It was not like Glen Orchy—this time Valda had no doubt where he was. He stood and watched her walking toward him, but she was indistinct, mist-shrouded. She stopped a few paces away and raised both arms to him.

"Susie?" Her voice seemed farther off than her image, but it was clear and compelling. "Susie, answer me!"

He watched, knowing in the silent certainty of dreams that if he did not speak, she could have no power over him.

Her shape seemed to brighten, clarify, her body glowing through a gauzy veil. He wondered how he looked to her.

"Toby Strangerson!" she said, louder.

He thought, *I am Toby Strangerson.*

She smiled, and the veil faded from her. He felt his body respond with a savage surge of desire.

"Then come to me. You will come to me."

I will come to you.

She was gone, and he was awake, drenched in sweat. Not really awake, he thought. I was just dreaming. It's the middle of the night.

But he couldn't just lie there. The call was too

strong. He had to go. He sat up, wincing at the stiffness in his limbs. Straw rustled. A faint dawn glow showed in the air holes under the eaves.

Other straw rustled. "Wha's matter?" Hamish mumbled.

"I have to go."

"There's a bucket in the corner." Hamish rolled over and went back to sleep.

Already Toby's arms and legs were moving him to the trapdoor. *Wait! I can't go out like this!* Panic seized him. *I've got to dress first!* But his limbs refused to listen. One hand was already lifting the trap when he realized his left knee was resting on his belt. He snatched it up and grabbed a corner of his plaid also. He scrambled down the ladder, bringing a cloudburst of straw with him. Hastily bundling himself as he went, he headed for the stairs.

It was impossible to put on a plaid properly while walking, or with hands still swollen like mealy puddings, but he managed the best he could. Reeling along the dark corridor, he managed to buckle his belt. He found his pin still in one corner.

He was walking into a trap, of course. He was probably going to his death, but there was nothing he could do about it. The house must be full of people—he could hear snoring. If he could just call out, they would come and stop him, come and save him; but he was forbidden to call out. He was forbidden to raise the alarm in any way. He moved deliberately, making as little sound as he could, although he could not prevent boards from creaking under his weight. More snoring audible through doorways . . . he wanted to scream. They would waken in the morning and find him gone. Why didn't they keep a dog?

He stumbled down the precipitous stairs. The house had its own little creaks and tappings. Rats, perhaps. Once he thought he heard footsteps overhead, but it was probably just someone else looking for a bucket in a corner. Inching along another black passage, he smelled the stale odors of smoke and fat from the kitchen. Still fighting to arrange his plaid, he came to the front door.

The door would not move. Saved! He could not break it down without rousing half the city. He fumbled his swollen hands over it, trying to identify bolts or bars or locks, but the shapes made no sense. Saved! *I can't come!*

Compulsion: He must go and find a window. Or there might be a back door, leading to a yard or alley.

With two sharp metallic clicks, the bolts slid of their own accord—they were both set vertically, one into the floor and the other into the lintel, which was why he had not recognized them. Hearing his own low moan of despair, he pulled the door open.

Cold dawn air washed in on his bare skin, bringing the salty scent of the Clyde. His feet wanted to move. He resisted, peering out at a murky pale fog. He could *not* go wandering around the burgh in daylight! There would be people around by now, or very soon. The fog would lift when the sun rose—the far side of the street was already a vague solidity with hints of doors and windows. The sky was paler, a narrow strip, high overhead. He had never been in a town before; already he felt shut in.

The urge to move became irresistible. He stumbled out into the road, cold and grubby under his bare feet. A dark shape glided in from the murk—a man in a hooded gown. It went past him without a sign, but he turned and followed. This was how he had been summoned. This was how the bolts had been opened—she had sent one of her creatures to fetch him. It moved swiftly and silently and he hobbled after it, treading in icy muck.

Sea fog billowed around him, clammy and salty. He caught glimpses of doors and storefronts, but he could not stop his legs. He heard hooves and wheels on cobbles in the distance. The town was waking. His demonic guide might not attract attention in its robe, but Toby's Highland plaid would make him conspicuous, his size would make him conspicuous. So would his purple, swollen face. Any honest citizen who saw him would remember the reward and raise the alarm. He had as much to fear from the civil authorities as he had from Valda.

The creature turned down a dark alley. He followed, smelling filth and horses and stale, ancient cooking. He could have lifted his arms and touched an elbow to the wall on either side. He thought he could see nothing except a faint, vertical strip of light ahead, but when something moved near his feet he realized that there were people lying there. Towns were not as glamorous as he had been led to believe, but he had never believed they would be. He stepped around or over the sleepers. Even if he could have deliberately trodden on them to waken them, homeless beggars would not rescue him from a demon. It was ironic to think of these penniless wretches huddled there in their misery while a vast fortune stumbled by them and vanished forever.

The husk showed as a dark shape against the light, then disappeared around a corner, turning left. He followed. Here the light was brighter, the space wider. He had lost sight of his guide, but his feet knew where to go. He crunched dead leaves, passed under tree branches. A pedestal with a statue on it loomed out of the fog, floated by, vanished astern.

He could not detect the sanctuary, as he had before. Nor could he sense the demon ahead of him as other than human. His superhuman awareness seemed to have been turned off. Still gliding silently forward, the husk turned another corner. So did he.

The fog was fading, the sky growing brighter. The sun must be up by now, about to break through. A steady clatter dead ahead brought a tiny agony of hope. Someone was coming! The creature stepped to one side and halted.

So did Toby, shivering with mingled cold and fear.

A man solidified out of the fog, hauling a rattling barrow. Bent forward, anonymous in cloak and hat, he passed within easy reach of the creature and did not look at it. Then he went by Toby with the same eerie inattention, leaving a momentary odor of fresh, warm bread. Toby tried to cry out, tried to whimper or even cough, but nothing happened. His arms, which up until now had been under his control, were suddenly frozen.

Valda's creature moved on again and he followed. If it ordered him to march into the firth and drown, he would have to obey. Demons were driven by hate, Father Lachlan had said.

The street was barely wide enough for two wagons to pass; timber walls towering up on either hand. The light seemed brighter ahead—he was almost out of the burgh, heading for open country. At the very last building, the creature turned aside, stopped, opened a door, and entered. Close on its heels, Toby caught a glimpse of a window of many tiny panes of glass and then the lintel was coming straight for his eyes. He ducked hastily and stepped down to a flagstone floor. The husk stood just inside—he saw its eyes glitter as he walked past, and he caught a whiff of a nauseating stench of decay. It closed the door quietly behind him and slid bolts while he continued across the floor.

He was in a dim apothecary's shop, not unlike Derek Little's in Crianlarich, but much better supplied. Two chairs for customers stood before a massive counter of oak. The walls were lined with shelves bearing crucibles, sets of scales, mortar and pestles, innumerable mysterious jars and vials, tall bottles of colored liquors, an alembic, a skull, weighty leather-bound tomes. He smelled familiar minty odors of herbs. Shadow masked the high ceiling, but there was some sort of stuffed beast hanging up there, something with many legs.

He detoured around the end of the counter, walked through an open door into blackness beyond—and stopped.

He felt a thin rug under his feet, smelled stale human habitation. Darkness slowly brightened into gloom. Shapes began to appear. A dozen candlesticks had been set wherever there was space, all around, flames were twinkling like stars. A brighter glow came from the open door of an iron stove and some light came from the doorway behind him.

A woman sat at ease in the chair by the fire. Her

voice was low and tuneful and familiar. "I see you have embarked on your career in pugilism without my assistance. How is your opponent?"

"Dead, my lady."

"I should be much surprised to hear otherwise."

He began to make her out—a glitter in her dark hair, the pallor of her face and hands. The rest of her was still invisible. Blue fire . . . On her breast hung a jewel as large as the top joint of his thumb. He forgot the hexer herself, his whole attention aimed at the fires of that sapphire. Certainly she might have a demon bottled in such a gem, but it was not the thought of another demon that caused the uprush of despair in his heart.

Fool! Idiot! Hulking, musclebound imbecile!

How does the demon stay close to you? Father Lachlan had asked him, and he had never thought of the amethyst Granny Nan had given him when she said goodbye.

It had lain in his sporran when he broke free of Valda and escaped from the dungeon. It had been with him when he eluded the wisp in Glen Orchy, when he bested Crazy Colin at the grotto, when he tore down the hillside. It had been there for all the miracles. And now?

In his mad, driven rush to leave the attic, he had left his sporran behind.

The amethyst was the answer to the mystery. Whatever its powers—whether it had come with them from Granny Nan or had somehow collected them during Valda's gramarye—they were lost to him. He was no more than mortal now.

4

Like a very weary pillar, he stood in the center of a small room. He suspected that his feet were forbidden to move, so he did not even try to move them. Were he laden with chains from neck to ankles he could be no worse off, for he could not resist the will of the demon, which was Valda's will. The stench of decay told him that the creature had come to stand right at his back. His skin crawled at the thought that it might be about to touch him. He should be able to hear its breathing, but he could not.

Valda said, "Krygon, fetch more firewood." With a barely audible hint of movement, the husk went to obey.

But then the hexer just sat, regarding her captive with interest, not speaking, but calm and poised as a queen on a throne. She might be waiting for her creature to return; she might be politely allowing Toby's eyes time to adjust to the gloom; or she might be letting his innards melt away altogether from pure terror. If the latter was her aim, she was succeeding admirably.

As his eyes adjusted, she came into view like a landscape at dawn. Her weighty black tresses were piled on her head with the same glittering tiara she had worn to dine with the laird in Fillan. Her face was carved from pure alabaster, adorned with lips as red as fresh blood and lashes longer than seemed humanly possible. Her tiny, perfect feet were clad in silver sandals, her nails painted dark, the firelight on the foot closest to the stove showing that they were crimson. Yet, surprisingly, her gown was a simple, somber thing that swathed her in wool from chin to her wrists and ankles. It was the sort of garment that might have belonged to any respectable burgher's wife, and not at all what he expected of Lady Valda. If she hoped such modesty would let her pass as an honest town wife, she was doomed to disappointment. Even in such a sack, she was intoxicatingly, maddeningly beautiful, and the glint in her eyes was utterly evil.

Something hissed briefly. Toby tore his attention from the hexer and glanced around the stuffy little room, trying to locate the noise. The roof was very low, the beams barely clearing his head. A ladder in one corner led up to a hatch. The single chair, a table with a striped tablecloth on it, and the remains of a meal, shelves with dishes and pots, an empty coal scuttle, a basket of dirty washing, a desk heaped with papers, an untidy dresser—this kennel was the apothecary's home. The low ceiling had been put in to make a sleeping loft overhead. There was no other door and no window, which explained the stale stink of the place. The extravagance of candles must be Valda's doing. She had made free with her host's hospitality, placing them on table, desk, shelves, even on the floor. The leaden casket on the table was hers, familiar from the dungeon in Castle Lochy.

Hiss! again.

The noise had come from the stove. He looked up. A dark stain disfigured the planks above it. "Blood?"

"Blood," Valda agreed. "Krygon is a messy killer."

He fought down a heaving sensation in his belly. He must not let her see how much she frightened him. "Is that our host up there?"

"And hostess, too, I think. I don't know if there were children—go and look if you are interested."

He shook his head, then yelped in pain as something slammed against his hand. The creature had returned, bringing one of the chairs from the front shop, and had taken the opportunity to strike him with it in passing.

"Krygon, put the wood on the fire," Valda said wearily, "and do not harm the man again—unless I tell you to, or am in danger."

Without a word, the creature proceeded to rip the chair apart and stuff the fragments into the stove. Watching it snap the long members without even putting them over its knee, Toby was impressed, horribly impressed. He knew he could not do that. That was the legendary demonic strength he had seen kill Crazy Colin. Demolition complete, the husk took up a heavy metal poker to mix the new fuel with the hot embers. When it straightened, it turned in his direction. He saw the glitter of eyes within the hood and remembered what Father Lachlan had said about hatred. He would have no chance against that monster, no matter which of them held the poker.

Another drop of blood hit the stove and hissed.

"Now," Valda said, as if coming to business. "I underestimated you, Master Strangerson. I do not recall ever being so wrong about any man before. I thought you were an ox and you turned out to be a notable opponent. I shall take no chances with you in future."

Not an ox, a mule. "Call it a draw and let me go."

She smiled wistfully. "I would, if that were possible. You have certainly earned it. Alas, though, you have something of mine that I cannot give up. Will you please explain to me how you bested me so thoroughly?"

She had abandoned the mocking contempt he remembered. She lacked even the air of a lady addressing a peasant, although she was a very great lady and he an extremely low peasant. His liege lord, Fergan, could not defend him against dangers of her sort—nor against many others, truth be told. Toby had found himself a lord to follow—a good, honest lord, he thought—but one without any real power. This foul hag, on the other hand, could work miracles. She was addressing him as an equal, which felt immensely flattering and also extremely dangerous. He told himself to remember her creatures, the depths of her villainy. A man must never cooperate with such wickedness! The diamond tiara and the painted toenails were the real Valda, not the goodwife dress.

"All I know is that you tried to turn me into one of those." He gestured at the hooded creature that stood with folded arms, still holding the poker and staring at him malevolently.

"No!" she said sharply. "I may be evil by your ways, but I do have standards of my own. I appreciate beauty, for example, and the fitness of things. Even kings do not use gold for chamber pots. I expect you dislike being described as beautiful." She smiled and his heart turned over. Her attention was as potent as strong drink. "Rugged? Virile? At the moment, of course, you are a disaster, but you were an exciting and striking young man before and you will still be an imposing one when you have healed. I shall make sure you heal without too much disfigurement. I would not waste such quality manhood on demonic incarnation. Krygon, let him see."

Toby opened his mouth to protest that he did not want to see, then realized that he would be wasting his breath.

The creature clattered the poker down on the stove and stripped, dropping its robe to the floor. The husk was . . . had been . . . a man. Its age was no longer evident, and certainly did not matter now, but perhaps around forty. He had probably been a scrawny specimen, even in his prime. Now he . . . it . . . was a ruin. A few rags still hung on the wasted frame, but they did not hide the filth, dried blood, open sores, the infestation of vermin. The creature's face had been blackened with soot at some time—Toby had thought the four in the dungeon were masked—and it was bearded. There was something wrong with its jaw. One side of its chest was caved in, with jagged ends of ribs protruding from rotted flesh. It leered at him, showing broken fragments of teeth and more bone. The stench of death filled the room.

Toby gagged and edged backward. "How does it live?"

"It doesn't in any normal sense." Valda sounded bored. "It likes to roll in mire and torment itself, because its original owner feels the pain, while it does not. It was in better shape a week ago, but then you dropped a mountain on it. It can't eat; it is almost used up. I shall have to find another husk for it soon, or put it back in its bottle. Won't I, Krygon?"

The thing tried to speak, but the ravaged mouth produced only a slobbering mumble. It nodded its head eagerly.

"So there is a demon for you, Tobias. You see why I would not have wasted your splendid physique on one of those. Never mind . . . you are not cooperating. I realize you have no cause to cooperate with me, and I need your cooperation to discover what went wrong and correct it. Time is short. Dumbarton is under siege, so I must adjust your attitude without delay."

"Siege?" A moment ago he had moved. His feet had obeyed him. . . . No, it was still hopeless, because Krygon could control him at a distance. There was no way he could get out of range fast enough to escape.

Valda rose from her chair. "Siege in a manner of speaking. Normally I wouldn't dare bring an incarnate like Krygon into a warded town, but the tutelary is fully occupied at the moment." She stepped to the table and opened the metal casket. "Oreste is on his way here. He will be accompanied by a whole retinue of creatures, many of them far more steeped in evil than Krygon. Dumbarton has worse worries than me—or you."

Father Lachlan had gone to pray to the tutelary. No help there? The hexer might be lying, of course. She had made her headquarters just inside the burgh limits. Was that significant?

"Krygon, freeze this man."

Instantly, Toby felt a coldness, but even more he felt all his muscles go rigid. He could not even blink. He could breathe, but only with a huge conscious effort, as if his chest were bound with iron hoops.

"I need a lock of your hair," Valda murmured, rising and going to the table. "You will forgive me if I don't trust you just yet?"

At the edge of his field of view, he saw her produce the gold bowl he had seen her use before, and the dagger with the yellow stone. She began doing things, clinking bottles, but at that angle he could make out no details. One thing he could see clearly was the leer of satisfaction on the walking corpse. Its mistress had forbidden it to harm Toby, but it was enjoying his frantic struggle not to suffocate.

"Oreste is after you, of course," she said absently.

All his attention was concentrated on just breathing, and he could not move his lips or tongue to speak anyway.

"And for me also, but mostly you now. He picked up my track when I returned to this country, and he tracked me to Fillan, so he knows about you. You won't have heard of him. He is a cunning adept, very skilled and dangerous, but he is bound to serve Rhym. Rhym is the one you know as King Nevil. Now . . . "

She strode over to Toby with the dagger and cut a curl from his head. She took it back to the table. He thought she put it in the bowl and then cut a lock of her own to accompany it, but he could not be sure. She poured liquid from a vial. She said something in a guttural language, of which the only intelligible word was the first: "Krygon." Whenever she gave the creature orders, she began with its name.

"We must complete our business here," she said, "and speedily begone. Whether Oreste or Dumbarton itself is victorious, we must take to the sea before a decision is reached. Neither can track us over the sea—not that the tutelary would, of course. . . . "

She made passes with her hands, speaking more words of gramarye. She came back into view, moving to the stove and placing the bowl on it. Then she lifted the silver chain over her head and held the sapphire high, speaking again in the strange tongue, although this time the words were so soft that Toby could barely make them out. He was close to fainting from lack of air. The demon seemed able to judge his strength exactly, so that he was convinced every breath must be his last and yet he could always force one more. His head swam.

Bluish fire flickered in the golden bowl, sending up faint curls of smoke. The glow brightened as the hexer lowered the sapphire, spinning in small circles within the fumes. Hideous blue light surged to fill the room like a fog, drowning out the candlelight, making Krygon in its rotted rags look more than ever like a corpse. Even Valda lost her humanity for a moment and became a leaden mannequin. Then jewel clinked against metal and the room plummeted back into gloom.

"We'll give it a minute to cool," her voice said quietly. The chair creaked as she resumed her seat. "Fortunately, there are several ships in the harbor at the moment. I shall enjoy a voyage with you, Tobias, once

our face has lost its resemblance to an offal bucket.
Even if you are still you, I promise you some lessons in
he arts of joy. You will be a rewarding pupil."

He could see her again. He felt he was fighting for his
life, even though he knew the battle was a fake. The
demon had been forbidden to hurt him, but its orders
did not say it could not keep him on the very edge of suf-
focation indefinitely, gradually releasing the pressure as
his strength faded. He wondered if Valda had even
noticed. If nothing else, she ought to see the lake of
sweat around his feet.

He could sweat, but he could not weep, although he
knew he was lost. From now on, the hexer would do
whatever she wanted with him and he would be helpless
to resist. There would be no demonic strength this time,
no mystical *dum . . . dum . . .* He would no longer be King
Fergan's man; he would be hers. Whatever power had
been in the amethyst was lost to him.

He had been a fool! When he should have been fleeing the country, he had dallied in Inverary Castle until
the price on his head was raised so high that every eye
in Scotland was looking out for him. Right from the start,
he had been a fool to refuse Lady Valda. How could he
ever have hoped to evade so great an adept? When she
had offered to employ him, at his trial before the laird in
Fillan, he had spurned her, instead of falling on his knees
with tears of joy and gratitude. Even earlier—when he
had met her on the road to Bridge of Orchy and first
sensed her power, he should have knelt at her stirrup
and pledged his heart to her service, in the vain hope
such a worthless trifle could be of interest to her. When
she had sought him out in dreams, he should not have
resisted her call. She was a great lady, with wisdom and
power such as he could not even comprehend, and he
was a brainless serf, a worthless bastard, ignorant and
dimwitted . . .

"That should be long enough," Valda said. "Krygon,
release him."

The invisible bands vanished. He lunged forward and

snatched up the sapphire from the bowl even before he had finished drawing his first free breath. He stood there in bewilderment, gasping for air, the jewel clutched in his clumsy muffled fist, loops of chain hanging free. No, that wasn't right. . . .

Valda chuckled. "Hang it around your neck, boy! It has to be next to your skin."

Oh, of course! He looped the pendant over his head so the jewel was on his chest, dangling just above the fold of his plaid. Then he sank to his knees, very conscious of being a clumsy, stupid, sweaty oaf unworthy even to exist in the same room with so courtly a lady, consort of royalty.

"I have been very wicked to cause you so much trouble, ma'am. I beg you to forgive me, although I know I do not deserve forgiveness. Is there any penance I can do, anything to try and make amends?"

She smiled. "Do you know the Tartar ceremony of obeisance?"

"Not in detail, ma'am."

"Do what you know of it."

He scrabbled forward on hands and knees and began to humble himself before her . . . then stopped. The sapphire had swung away from his chest. He straightened again, turned the chain around so the gem lay against his back. Then he was free to crouch down and put his face on the floor.

"I lift your foot?" It would be sacrilege even to touch her.

"Correct."

He took her ankle carefully between his broken fists and laid her foot on his head. It weighed nothing.

"I don't know the words, ma'am!"

"Swear to be my man, in body and mind and soul, to serve me in all ways, to the death."

He swore willingly. She removed her foot.

"Good. Now stand up."

He rose and then, because he felt it was disrespectful to make her crane her neck to see him, he backed away, almost to the door. He would feel happier kneeling in her presence, but she had told him to stand.

Valda smiled. "From this day forward we are partners?"

"No, ma'am! I am your slave!" He had found a far worthier and more potent liege than the outlawed rebel king. She would protect him, and he would serve her to his final breath.

He was her man.

She shrugged, seeming satisfied, and settled back in the chair. "And now you will tell me how you upset my plans so drastically! Do you know what you cost me, Tobias? I have spent many years collecting my little pets, teaching them to hate, training them to serve me. You buried two of them when you pulled down the mountain."

"I am sorry!" he cried.

She chuckled. "You will not offend again. Now tell me—"

A bell tinkled in the apothecary's shop. Valda straightened.

"Krygon, who is that?"

The creature mumbled words that made no sense to Toby, but the lady seemed to understand. "You despicable trash!" she snapped. "I shall make you suffer. And what has he been doing since?"

More gibberish.

She bit her lip and looked at Toby. "Did you understand that?"

"No, ma'am." He had failed her already. How useless he was!

"It says a boy followed you here. He has been prowling around, trying to find another way in, or a window to spy through. There isn't one, of course. This useless near-dead thing did not tell me—demons will obey no farther than they must, whereas mortals like you are eager to please in any way they can. Krygon, go . . . No, Tobias, you go. If the boy knows you, your face will not alarm him. Bring him here."

Toby ran. The outer room seemed dazzlingly bright, and despite his eagerness to do what the lady wanted, he paused a moment at the window to let his eyes adjust again. The street outside was just as foggy as before. A man plodded by in the center of the street, leading a horse and cart, and they were gray wraiths.

As soon as they had gone, he unbolted the door and opened it a crack. He peered out at the salty mist. There was no one there.

He could guess who the boy was. He was a devious brat, that one! He would have rung the bell and then retreated to a safe distance until he saw who or what came to answer.

Toby warily put his head out, reluctant to be seen. A few ghostly pedestrians were visible through the fog, but if he could not make them out, they could not see him clearly either.

"Hamish?" he called. "Hamish!"

A face appeared out of a doorway two stores along.

Toby waved. "Come on! It's me!"

Hamish came, but slowly, one step at a time. He looked ready to bolt at any second, and the sickly pallor of his face exactly matched the fog.

"You all right, Toby?"

"I'm fine! Come on in."

Hamish shook his head violently. "Who else is in there?"

Toby laughed as convincingly as he could. He certainly must not let Hamish Campbell go racing back to the others to raise the alarm. "Friends, believe it or not! We were just about to have breakfast. Come and join us."

Hamish stopped just out of reach and regarded Toby with extreme suspicion. "What friends?"

A couple of women carrying bundles on their heads were emerging from the fog, progressing from pale gray clouds to solid shapes. Time was running out by the second.

Toby glanced around and lowered his voice to a conspiratorial whisper. "Friends of Master Stringer's."

"Oh. Well, I won't come in, thank you." Hamish stretched out a hand, palm up, offering Granny Nan's amethyst without coming an inch nearer to Toby than he had to. "I just thought you might need this. Er . . . what's that chain around your neck?"

5

Toby shouldered the door closed behind him and marched across the shop to the back room, clutching Hamish to his chest with one brawny arm and keeping his other hand over the boy's mouth. The boy kicked and squirmed helplessly, feet well off the floor.

"Smoothly done, Tobias," Valda said, sounding amused. "What have you brought me?"

The praise sent a rush of pleasure through him. "A whelp named Hamish Campbell, ma'am. But he's got a demon in his hand."

The hexer jumped to her feet. "Does he know its conjuration?"

"No, ma'am. I'm not sure it has one. It's the hob from Fillan, bottled in an amethyst."

"Well, put it in there, just in case." She gestured to the metal casket.

Toby set Hamish down in front of the table and transferred his grip to the boy's arms. "You heard the lady!"

Hamish wriggled like a landed fish, vainly kicking and butting. "No! No! Toby, she's hexed you! This isn't you, Toby!"

"It is now." He banged the kid's wrist on the edge of the casket. "Drop it!" He banged again, harder. "I'll break it!"

Hamish released the amethyst and it fell inside. Valda slammed the lid down.

"Over there!" Toby said and shoved his prisoner away, sending him staggering into the corner by the stove. "You said you needed a new husk for Krygon, ma'am. He would do, wouldn't he?"

Valda smiled with secret amusement. "He would, indeed! I see you will be a loyal and helpful assistant."

Toby gulped with joy. "I shall always try my best!" He pulled the sapphire around to hang on his chest again, where he could glance down and admire it. It was a badge of his service, a sign of his loyalty to his mistress, like a medal, or an officer's sash. Men did not normally wear jewelry, of course, but he would be wearing Lowlander garb from now on, likely, and a shirt would hide it. He had been very lucky that it had been out of sight when he went to get Hamish, who would certainly have guessed what it was if he had noticed it.

A choking wail from the corner indicated that Hamish's eyes had adjusted well enough for him to make out Krygon.

Valda resumed her seat. "Now tell me the story. How did you gain possession of the hob?"

Toby had barely had a chance to work it out himself. "The witchwife was my foster mother, my lady, but she was very old. I think she knew she was about to die and then I would leave the glen. The hob was puzzled that all the young men were going away and not coming back. I think this is what happened: She persuaded the hob to move into the jewel so it could find out for itself where we were going; and then she gave it to me to take with me, thinking that it would protect me, so she had helped both of us." He stared in dismay at the lady's disbelieving frown. "The hob isn't very smart, ma'am! And Granny Nan was pretty much crazy, too."

"So you think the hob . . ." Valda shook her head. "How did you use it, then? By what commands did you conjure it?"

"None, ma'am! Whenever I was in trouble, it came to my aid. I could see what it was doing, but I never told it what to do."

She frowned. "This is no gramarye known to me! You think the witchwife *persuaded* an immortal into a jewel? I can't believe it! An adept must use another demon to harvest an elemental. They don't just come for the asking!" The lady drummed scarlet nails on the arm of her chair. "And even if I could believe that, then I certainly can't believe that it worked for you as you say."

Appalled, he sank to his knees. "My lady! I would not lie to you!"

"I'm sure you wouldn't, Tobias, but your explanation is not credible. An incarnate demon, like Krygon there, does have a small amount of initiative. It can follow orders, although you've seen that it does so reluctantly—it did not tell me you had been followed here, for instance. But I can give it general instructions: 'Protect me,' or, 'Go and bring Toby Strangerson back here without harming him or alerting anyone.' It has a human brain to think with, so it can do what is required to carry out orders. A bottled demon, though, must be directed specifically. Like Oswood." She smiled.

He wanted to hug himself when she smiled at him, it felt so good. "Oswood, my lady?"

"That jewel that so enhances your manly chest. I harvested that elemental at a place called Oswood. Just now I gave it two very specific instructions. I told it to keep you loyal to me always, and I told it to prevent you from removing the jewel. That way you can never move out of its range, you see. That is how Rhym controls his mortal creatures like Oreste. Oreste commands a dozen demons of his own, but he cannot remove the beryl on his finger, which binds him, nor order them to remove it for him."

"I would not want to move out of its range, my lady! I enjoy serving—"

"Yes, I know you do. How long have you had that amethyst?"

"Since the day we met, ma'am. And that was when the miracles began!"

Lady Valda pondered for a moment, staring at the fire. Toby remained on his knees. Hamish cowered against the wall by the stove, paralyzed by horror, while Krygon watched them all with undisguised hatred, unobtrusively scratching skin off its thigh. The fire crackled. A drop of blood fell from the ceiling and hissed on the stove.

That continual dripping of blood was worrisome. Dead bodies did not bleed. It would be in character for Krygon to have left someone alive and suffering up there in the loft. Still, if Lady Valda was not worried, then it was not up to Toby to raise the matter. She might send

him to finish the job, and he would rather not do tha
sort of dirty work. He would do it if she told him to, o
course, but he would prefer not to volunteer for it.

"'Tis strange!" the lady said at last. "But I suppose i
an elemental entered a jewel voluntarily, it might retair
the free will it had in its own habitat. An unrestrained hol
would be a dangerous companion, Tobias! Totally unpre
dictable! Still, it can do us no harm inside that casket."

She sighed. "Time passes! Oreste approaches, and
still have not solved the problem I started with." Sh
turned a dark and frightening gaze on him. "Many years
ago, a friend of mine obtained a most potent demon
known as Rhym. It was ancient, powerful, cunning, and
for centuries had been bottled in a yellow diamond. My
friend and I attempted to utilize this immortal in a conju
ration. We knew the ritual to command it, but that nigh
we were not specific enough in our instructions."

"King Nevil?"

She raised an eyebrow. "Indeed! So you have hearc
the tale? Well, it is true. Under certain circumstances, at
critical moments in rituals, an exchange is not only pos
sible, but actually quite easy. Rhym managed that
exchange. The demon infested the king's body, and the
king's soul was immured in the jewel that I later put or
this dagger."

Toby nodded. Even a muscle-bound bareknuckle
yokel could work it out now. "So you fled with the soul o
the king, and Rhym set out to conquer all Europe?"

"That is what I was about to explain, yes. It has taken
me many years to acquire the support I knew I woulc
need to restore my beloved. Rhym hunted me tire
lessly—it fears the king, because he knows the true name
of Rhym. Many times I have escaped its clutches by
inches! When at last I felt ready to proceed, having
acquired and trained new pets to replace those I hac
lost, I returned to Britain and sought out a fitting vesse
to hold the soul of my love. He was about your age wher
it happened, you see."

Toby shuddered. "I will do as you command, my lady."

"Indeed you will. Get up!" She rose from her chair.

He rose also, and walked forward to stand before her. He could not hide his shivers, but he must be brave in her service.

"I know that Nevil is no longer in the jewel on the dagger," she said. "So he passed into you as I planned. Something went wrong."

"The hob interfered?"

"I don't think so. I did not know you had a demon of your own, of course, but I don't think it interfered. It is you who are the problem. My creatures assure me they can see signs of possession on you, but you are not Nevil, are you?"

"No, my lady."

"Yet he is in there inside you. Somehow he is suppressed. We must release him."

Toby worked his injured tongue around until he could find enough spit to speak. "How?"

She smiled sadly. "You are a resolute young man, Toby Strangerson! I think where I erred was in underestimating your strength of will. Had I seen you smothered in bruises as you are now, then I might have realized what a doughty soul you are—any man who submits to such a beating voluntarily is a man of unusual courage and determination, whatever one may think of his judgment. Somehow you suppress my beloved. You have him locked away in a corner of your heart."

"Not . . . not knowingly, my lady!"

She stepped very close, gazing up at him with eyes of black fire. "Knowingly or not, you have. Now you have promised to cooperate. I have made quite certain that you will cooperate! So reach into the depths of your soul, Toby Strangerson, and seek out my missing lord, my lost love. He is in there. Call him forth!"

He stared into those black pools. He was conscious of her musky, floral perfume. Sweat trickled down his bruises. He tried. He tried desperately to do what she wanted of him. The stove hissed once . . .

"Let him *be,* Toby Strangerson! Let him live again. In

your heart, kneel to Nevil, the king, your lawful liege. Call him forth to the light."

The stove hissed twice . . .

Valda sighed and stepped away. "It isn't working! Your grip on life is too strong. We must try the other way."

He did not ask. Whatever she wanted of him, of course. . . .

She stalked over to the table and scratched at the cloth with her nails. "I dislike this! If there were any other choice . . . It seems such a shame to waste you."

Death! "However I may serve you, ma'am," he said sadly.

"Yes. Worse, it is dangerous for Nevil." She paced back to face him again. "I must have Krygon diminish you. I will let it have your soul, nibbling it away little by little, until my lord can emerge from your shadow. I do not know how much of you will remain by then, Tobias—probably almost nothing, and of course you will be no more able to act then than Nevil can act now. Know that I have enjoyed our little tussle. In an odd way, I admire you."

She leaned up and touched her lips to his.

He closed his eyes, shuddering with an unholy mingling of terror and desire.

The lady stepped back. "Now, Krygon—"

Hamish grabbed up the poker and swung it with all his strength, clubbing Toby in the middle of his chest. There was a sharp cracking sound and a bright blue flash that momentarily lit the room like a noonday sun.

Lady Valda screamed piercingly.

Dazzled, stunned by the pain, taken by surprise, Toby staggered back into Krygon and was hurled bodily aside by one sweep of the thing's weedy arm. He stumbled over the table, collapsing it under his weight with all its miscellaneous contents of vials, casket, dagger, dishes, and candlesticks. He landed on his broken ribs and two or three hundred bruises. Through all the racket, he heard Hamish whoop in shrill triumph and throw down the poker.

Lady Valda screamed again, even louder. Bewildered, blinking, Toby tried to make sense of what his eyes were telling him. A turquoise blaze enveloped her. Then the harsh light changed shape and he made out a thing of fire—a jagged, glittering being that flickered back and forth between near-human form one instant to a whirl of claws or sharp faceted edges the next.

Oh, merciful spirits! It was Oswood! By smashing the jewel on Toby's chest, Hamish had released the demon, and now it had backed the screaming hexer into a corner and was ripping her face off.

Toby was about to be scorched—the cloth on the table had caught fire, setting the contents of the vials to blaze in billows of red flame. He sat up and located the door. Now was a good time to leave.

The collapsing table had dropped the metal casket right at Hamish's feet. He had snatched it up, but Krygon reached him before he could open the lid. The husk grasped the box and slammed it back against the wall like a hammer on an anvil, with Hamish himself being the work between them. He cried out, then slithered limply down the wall, gasping for air.

Toby was on his feet. The creature turned and hurled the casket at his head. He ducked, hearing it crack into the dresser behind him and dislodge a shower of crockery.

Lady Valda writhed on the floor, her screams taking on a hideous choking quality. The flashing, glittering demon on top of her was still tearing at her, showering the room with fragments of blood-soaked cloth and quivering lumps of flesh.

"Hamish, come on!" Toby staggered toward the door. He was alone. Turning, he saw that the Krygon creature had Hamish by the neck and was shaking him, probably about to strangle him. Whatever else Toby did, he must help the boy escape to make amends for having dragged him into this. His fists were broken, but his feet still worked. He took a stride and kicked as hard as he could, slamming a heel into the thing's kidneys. The husk cannoned into the wall. Unfortunately Hamish cushioned the impact.

The Krygon thing spun around and came at Toby, rags flapping, hands outstretched like claws, aiming for his eyes. He jabbed a left at its broken jaw, but the creature was ready for him this time, as unyielding as rock. An explosion of agony in his fist almost stunned him, then he was struck by a runaway wagon—an impossible bodily impact sent him sprawling, measuring his length with the rotting husk on top of him. Joy and hate glowed in its eyes as it lowered its jagged mouth to tear out his throat. He braced his hands against its face and tried to push it away, but all his strength was useless against its demonic power. Only a blade through the heart . . . Nauseated by its stench, Toby yelled to Hamish to find Valda's dagger. Hamish must have reacted, because Krygon released Toby and sprang free. He swung a leg wildly . . . struck one of its ankles, tripped it, sent it headlong into the stove with a sickening boom that would have certainly brained a mortal.

Oswood was still tearing at Lady Valda, spraying blood. From the noises she was making, she had little left to scream with. Although the demon was only a flickering, shifting fire with no discernible face, somehow Toby was certain it was already looking around for another victim.

Both the rug and the basket of laundry blazed now, filling the room with flames and smoke. The Krygon creature lurched to its feet and at the same time hurled the chair at Hamish, bowling him into a corner.

As Toby struggled to rise, he registered the metal casket within reach. He sprawled back and grabbed it, pulled it to him. The hob was inside there! He sat up, wrapping an arm around the box and gripping the lid with a half-useless hand. If he could just release the hob, it would come to the rescue.

Krygon caught him by the left ankle and jerked him flat on his back again. Then it hauled him across the floor toward the stove, leering grotesquely as it prepared